"*A Place at our Table* is a moving story of forgiveness and the healing power of love. Amy Clipston weaves beautiful tales of Amish life, family ties, and heartwarming romance. She has always been one of my favorite Amish authors."

—JENNIFER BECKSTRAND, AUTHOR OF
RETURN TO HUCKLEBERRY HILL

"Themes of family, forgiveness, love, and strength are woven throughout the story . . . a great choice for all readers of Amish fiction."

—*CBA MARKET MAGAZINE* ON *A PLACE AT OUR TABLE*

"This debut title in a new series offers an emotionally charged and engaging read headed by sympathetically drawn and believable protagonists. The meaty issues of trust and faith make this a solid book group choice."

—*LIBRARY JOURNAL* ON *A PLACE AT OUR TABLE*

"A tender story about heartache, healing, and hope. This is a story Amy Clipston fans will absolutely love."

—KATHLEEN FULLER, AUTHOR OF THE AMISH
LETTERS SERIES, ON *A PLACE AT OUR TABLE*

"Warm and homespun as kitten tangled yarn, Amy treats the reader to hearth and table, flame and love. The invitation is open for a soul satisfying read. Come in and be blessed!"

—KELLY LONG, BESTSELLING AUTHOR
ON *A PLACE AT OUR TABLE*

"Clipston (*The Cherished Quilt*) fills these four cheerful Amish romance novellas with uplifting, simple love . . . Fans of Clipston's wholesome stories will relish these novellas."

—PUBLISHERS WEEKLY

"These sweet, tender novellas from one of the genre's best make the perfect sampler for new readers curious about Amish romances."

—LIBRARY JOURNAL ON *AMISH SWEETHEARTS*

"Clipston is as reliable as her character, giving Emily a difficult and intense romance worthy of Emily's ability to shine the light of Christ into the hearts of those she loves."

—RT BOOK REVIEWS, 4 1/2 STARS, TOP
PICK! ON *THE CHERISHED QUILT*

"Clipston's heartfelt writing and engaging characters make her a fan favorite. Her latest Amish tale combines a spiritual message of accepting God's blessings as they are given with a sweet romance."

—LIBRARY JOURNAL ON *THE CHERISHED QUILT*

"Clipston delivers another enchanting series starter with a tasty premise, family secrets, and sweet-as-pie romance, offering assurance that true love can happen more than once and second chances are worth fighting for."

—RT BOOK REVIEWS, 4 1/2 STARS, TOP
PICK! ON *THE FORGOTTEN RECIPE*

AMISH SWEETHEARTS

Other Books by Amy Clipston

The Amish Homestead Series

A Place at Our Table

Room on the Porch Swing

A Seat by the Hearth

A Welcome at Our Door (available May 2019)

The Amish Heirloom Series

The Forgotten Recipe

The Courtship Basket

The Cherished Quilt

The Beloved Hope Chest

The Hearts of the Lancaster Grand Hotel Series

A Hopeful Heart

A Mother's Secret

A Dream of Home

A Simple Prayer

The Kauffman Amish Bakery Series

A Gift of Grace

A Promise of Hope

A Place of Peace

A Life of Joy

A Season of Love

AMISH SWEETHEARTS

Four Amish Stories

Amy Clipston

ZONDERVAN

Amish Sweethearts

Copyright © 2017 by Amy Clipston

This title is also available as a Zondervan e-book. Visit www.zondervan.com.

Requests for information should be addressed to: Zondervan, *3900 Sparks Dr. SE, Grand Rapids, Michigan 49546*

ISBN: 978-0-310-35429-1 (mass market)

Library of Congress Cataloging-in-Publication
Names: Clipston, Amy, author.
Title: Amish sweethearts : four Amish novellas / Amy Clipston, Amy Clipston.
Description: Nashville : Zondervan, 2018.
Identifiers: LCCN 2017039623 | ISBN 9780718091156 (softcover)
Subjects: LCSH: Amish--Fiction. | GSAFD: Christian fiction. | Love stories.
Classification: LCC PS3603.L58 A6 2018 | DDC 813/.6--dc23 LC record available at https://lccn.loc.gov/2017039623

All Scripture quotations, unless otherwise indicated, are taken from the Holy Bible, *New International Version*®, *NIV*®. Copyright © 1973, 1978, 1984, 2011 by Biblica, Inc.™ Used by permission. All rights reserved worldwide. www.zondervan.com.

Any Internet addresses (websites, blogs, etc.) and telephone numbers in this book are offered as a resource. They are not intended in any way to be or imply an endorsement by Zondervan, nor does Zondervan vouch for the content of these sites and numbers for the life of this book.

Printed in the United States of America

19 20 21 22 23 / QG / 5 4 3 2 1

CONTENTS

A Home for Lindsay

For Becky Biddy, with love and appreciation

Glossary

ach—oh
aenti—aunt
appeditlich—delicious
boppli—baby
bruderskinner—nieces/nephews
danki—thank you
dat—dad
Dummle!—Hurry!
fraa—wife
freind/freinden—friend/friends
froh—happy
gegisch—silly
gern gschehne—you're welcome
gude mariye—good morning
gut—good
gut nacht—good night
haus—house
Ich liebe dich: I love you
kaffi—coffee
kapp—prayer covering or cap
kichli/kichlin—cookie/cookies
kinner—children
kumm—come
liewe—love, a term of endearment

maed/maedel—young women, girls/young woman

mamm—mom

mei—my

naerfich—nervous

narrisch—crazy

onkel—uncle

schee—pretty

schtupp—family room

schweschder/schweschdere—sister/sisters

sohn—son

Was iss letz?: What's wrong?

Wie geht's—How do you do? or Good day!

wunderbaar—wonderful

ya—yes

*The German dialect spoken by the Amish is not a written language and varies depending on the location and origin of the settlement. These spellings are approximations. Most Amish children learn English after they start school. They also learn High German, which is used in their Sunday services.

Kauffman Amish Bakery
Family Trees

Eli m. Elizabeth Kauffman

Robert m. to Sadie	Daniel m. to Rebecca	Kathryn m. to David Beiler	Timothy m. Miriam Lapp	Elizabeth "Beth" Anne m. to Paul Bontrager	Sarah Rose m. to Peter Troyer (deceased), then Luke Troyer

Robert m. Sadie Kauffman

Samuel	Katie	Nancy	Raymond	Jane	Linda	Aaron

Daniel m. Rebecca Kauffman

Jessica Bedford: niece	Lindsay Bedford: niece	Daniel Jr. ("Junior")	Emma	Grace

David m. Kathryn Beiler

Amanda	Lizzie	Ruthie	David Jr.	Manny

Timothy m. Miriam Lapp
|
Nellie

Beth Anne m. Paul Bontrager

| Lydia | Titus | Irma | Ruth |

Sarah Rose m. Peter Troyer (deceased), then Luke Troyer

| Twins: Seth and Rachel | Twins: Benjamin and Peter |
| (fathered by Peter) | (fathered by Luke) |

Elmer m. Sally Yoder
|
Jake Miller: grandson

Clyde m. Anna Mary Miller

| Jake | Jeremy (deceased twin) |

Titus m. Irma King

| Naomi m. Caleb Schmucker | Elam | Lizzie | Anne | Amos | Willie | Levina | Sylvia | Leroy | Joseph |

Caleb m. Naomi Schmucker

| Susie (from Caleb's deceased wife) | Millie |

Jesse (deceased) m. Nellie Glick (deceased)

| Betsy m. Earl Lantz | Matthew |

Earl m. Betsy Lantz

| Suzanne | Ella |

CHAPTER ONE

The rocks under Matthew Glick's boots crunched as he walked up the driveway that led to his sister's small farmhouse. At the back of the modest clapboard two-story white structure, he could see lights burning in the kitchen. He imagined Betsy, Earl, and their daughters, Suzanne and Ella, sharing supper around their table earlier, but it was late now. Perhaps Betsy and Earl were having a snack.

As his driver backed down the driveway, the headlights from his car cast ghostlike shadows on the skeleton of the house Matthew was building for Lindsay Bedford, his fiancée, at the back of the property. A smile turned up the corners of his mouth. In only five months he and Lindsay would be married and start a new life in that house.

He started for the back-porch steps of his sister's home but then halted. Instead he stepped into his workshop off Earl's barn. He lifted a Coleman lantern from his workbench, clicked it on, and walked toward his unfinished house. The only sounds came from the singing cicadas and a distant car.

As he stood in front of the work he'd accomplished so far, an image of Lindsay filled his mind. When he first met her, he was awestruck by her red hair and emerald eyes, but her beauty wasn't all that drew him to her. Her sweet and thoughtful personality quickly won him over. He'd been shy and taciturn when he arrived in Bird-in-Hand, but Lindsay had been determined to be his friend.

The move to Bird-in-Hand hadn't been under the best of circumstances. He'd brought his mother there so Betsy could help nurse her in her last days. He'd needed Lindsay more than he wanted to admit. She was a bright light during that dark time in his life, and he'd quickly fallen in love with her easy sense of humor and giving heart.

With no front steps for a porch yet, Matthew had to set down his lantern and haul himself up into the framework of his house. As he walked around the first floor, he thought about when he had proposed to Lindsay, he had promised to build her a home on Betsy's farm. Keeping his promise to her, the house would have five bedrooms, a good-size kitchen, and a spacious family room. It certainly would be all they'd need.

He walked to the far side and shone his light where the kitchen would be. An image came into clear focus in his mind—oak cabinets with a tan granite counter, a window above the sink, a long oak kitchen table with six chairs. He imagined Lindsay standing at the counter, preparing supper. She would smile over her shoulder when he came home after a long day working at the Kauffman & Yoder Amish Furniture store. He would kiss her cheek before they sat down to eat together, and they'd discuss their days and then spend the evening in each other's company. Their relationship would grow over time, and hopefully, with God's blessing, they would raise a few children in this house.

Lindsay was the love of his life, his future, his everything. He could hardly wait to start a new life as her husband.

Matthew turned and stared out a window frame toward the trees that separated this property from Robert Kauffman's pasture next door. Tomorrow night he would join the Kauffmans for their weekly Saturday-night gathering. He'd been blessed beyond measure when Eli Kauffman, the family patriarch, hired him to work at his store. Not only had he met Lindsay, Eli's great-niece, but he'd also been accepted into that warm and loving extended family.

Because his father abandoned his family when he was ten years old, Matthew hadn't known what it was like to have a consistent father figure in his life. Daniel Kauffman, Lindsay's uncle and guardian, however, quickly became like a father to him, offering advice and encouraging his work. He was grateful he'd be part of the Kauffman family, and he prayed he was worthy of Lindsay's hand in marriage.

He was looking forward to spending time with her at the gathering. They hadn't seen each other since yesterday.

A sudden yawn overtook him. He'd worked hard today at the furniture store, staying late to finish a project, and he was ready to eat the supper Betsy saved for him and go to bed. He jumped down from the house and headed for his sister's back porch.

Matthew climbed the steps and quietly entered the house through the mudroom. He didn't want to wake up his nieces if they were already asleep. He removed his straw hat and boots.

When he stepped into the kitchen, he saw Earl at the table, staring dejectedly at a pile of papers. Betsy leaned with her back against the counter, wiping red and puffy eyes. Matthew froze as alarm swept through him. Should he leave and give them privacy? Or should he ask them if they were all right?

"Matt. You're home. How was work today?" Betsy's voice sounded thin as she gave him a watery smile.

"It was *gut*." Matthew remained in the doorway as a thick fog of anxiety hung over the kitchen. Maybe he should go back outside. But this was his home, too, and he was tired. Maybe he should go straight up to his room. When his stomach growled in protest, he shifted his weight on his feet.

"You worked late." Betsy sniffed again as her body shuddered, the apparent remnant of a sob. "Did you finish that dresser that's been giving you a fit?"

Matthew nodded. "*Ya*. The customer picked it up today. Daniel told me the customer was very *froh* with it."

"I'm not surprised. You do *gut* work." She nodded toward refrigerator jars sitting on the counter. "The *maed* are already upstairs for the night. I saved some food for you. Would you like some?"

"*Ya. Danki.*" Matthew crossed the kitchen and washed his hands at the sink while Betsy put meat loaf, mashed potatoes, and green beans on a plate. "That smells *appeditlich*."

"It's still warm." Betsy placed the plate on the table and smiled, but the smile didn't reach her golden-brown eyes. At thirty, she was ten years older than Matthew, but she shared the same eye color and curly hair he'd inherited from their mother.

Matthew gathered utensils, poured himself a glass of water, and sat down across from Earl. After a silent prayer, he began to eat. Now Earl was scowling at the stack of papers as he flipped through them. Betsy put clean dishes into a cabinet, and the rustling of papers, clinking of dishes, and scraping of utensils were the only sounds. The tension in the kitchen nearly choked Matthew as he ate.

"Everything is delicious," he finally said.

Betsy didn't reply. Her shoulders were stiff as she kept her back to Matthew and her husband.

Matthew took a long drink from his glass and then divided a look between Earl and Betsy. "Is everything all right?"

Betsy let out a strangled noise from deep in her throat as she sagged against the counter.

Matthew's heartbeat seemed to gallop. "What's going on?"

Betsy spun around. Her face was crumpled and tears ran down her face.

Matthew jumped up from his chair and went to her. "Did someone die?"

"No." She shook her head and looked at Earl as her bottom lip trembled. "We have to tell him."

Earl nodded, his expression solemn. "*Ya*, you're right."

"Tell me what?" Matthew looked back and forth between them. When they remained silent, he blew out a frustrated sigh. "Please tell me what's going on."

Betsy pointed to his chair across from Earl. "Please sit down."

Dread wafted over him, and as he sat back down, Betsy dropped into the chair next to Earl. She wiped her nose with a napkin and then cleared her throat.

"*Was iss letz?*" Matthew asked.

"We're broke." Her voice shook.

"Broke?" Matthew blinked, trying to comprehend her words. "What do you mean?"

"I mean we're broke." She grabbed another paper napkin from the holder and began to shred it. "As you know, Earl hasn't been able to find a steady job. The bills have been piling up."

She pointed to the top paper on the pile in front of Earl. "We owe an exorbitant amount of back taxes. Plus, our taxes have gone up this year since the *haus* you're building has added to our property value." She cleared her throat again. "We've been trying to figure out how to get caught up, but it's impossible. The money *Mamm* left me isn't enough to cover our debt." She looked down at the napkin she'd ripped, and her next words came out in a rush.

"So we have to declare bankruptcy. We're going to lose the farm, and then—"

"Whoa!" Matthew held up his hands in confusion. "What did you say?"

"You heard me." Her voice shook again as she looked up at him, tears streaming down her face.

"We're buried in debt, and we've been refused for every loan we applied for to try to consolidate it. Earl has been to more than one bank, each one more than once. But they turned him down because he hasn't been able to secure a permanent job. His parents don't have any money to loan us, but they said we can move in with them until we're back on our feet. So that's what we're going to do."

"You're moving to Western Pennsylvania?" Matthew ran his hands down his face as the situation came into clear focus in his mind. "You're declaring bankruptcy, and you're going to lose the farm."

"We don't have a choice," Earl chimed in. "It's the best option for our *maed*."

Betsy nodded, wiping her eyes again. "We're going to lose everything. We have no choice but to let the farm go and move in with Earl's parents."

"How long have you known, Betsy?"

"I . . . well, I mean, we've known we were in trouble . . . and then today we realized—"

"How long?" It was all he could do to keep his voice down, but he didn't want his nieces to hear.

She swallowed. "About two months." Her voice was barely above a whisper.

White-hot fury burned through him as he glared at his sister. "You've known you might have to declare bankruptcy and lose the farm for two whole months?"

She nodded.

Matthew's mind filled with an image of his house, abandoned. The house into which he'd poured his money, his time, and his dreams. He was about to lose everything too—maybe even his whole future with Lindsay if he broke the promises he made to her when he asked her to marry him.

"Why didn't you tell me?" Losing the battle to keep quiet, Matthew pushed his chair back with such force that it fell onto the floor with a clatter. Betsy startled, and Earl half rose from his chair.

Betsy held up her hand as if to calm him. "I'm so sorry. I know this means you're going to lose your *haus* too."

"We didn't want to tell you until we knew for sure," Earl said as he sat back down.

Fury clouded Matthew's vision as his mouth worked and no words came out. The walls began to close in on him, and he couldn't breathe.

"I need to get out of here." He turned and stomped out of the kitchen. After pushing his feet into his boots, he headed out the back door and down the driveway.

Anger and despair warred in his gut as he stalked down the street. His world was shattered. And to make matters worse, Betsy and Earl had known for *two months* they were probably going to lose their farm and leave him with a house he couldn't finish, let alone live in. His sister hadn't given him any indication she and Earl were in financial trouble. Why didn't Earl tell Matthew the truth, man-to-man?

He felt betrayed.

What was he going to do now? His heart squeezed as angry tears formed in his eyes. Maybe the bank would divide up the land so he could buy the acreage where the house sat.

The idea took shape in his mind as he turned back.

Emotional turmoil still surged through his veins as he went into the house and entered the kitchen. Earl and Betsy had remained at the table, looking miserable.

"Matthew." Earl stood and held out his hand. "I'm so sorry I—"

"Why didn't you tell me sooner?" Matthew stood in front of him and jammed a finger in his brother-in-law's chest. "Why would you keep me in the dark when this affects me too?"

"I was wrong to keep it from you." Earl looked at his wife and she looked down at her hands. "I asked Betsy not to tell you because I was hoping we could work it out. But there's nothing we can do. We're going to let the farm go."

"You've watched me work on *mei haus* for months now." Matthew pointed toward the back of the property. "Were you going to clue me in on the day you packed up and left me here?"

"No, no, no." Betsy leapt to her feet and rushed over to Matthew. "We were never going to leave you here. You can come with us."

"*Ya, ya.*" Earl nodded. "*Mei dat* has a dairy farm. We can all live and work there. He has three extra bedrooms in the *haus*—one for the *maed*, one for you, and one for us."

"You can bring Lindsay too." Betsy forced a smile. "We'll make room for all for us."

Matthew snorted. "So I should tell Lindsay we're moving in with Earl's parents?"

"Right," Betsy said, confirming that plan.

Matthew pressed his lips together. "I could never take her away from here."

"Why?"

"She deserves stability after losing her parents, separating from her *schweschder*, and then dealing with the back and forth between Rebecca's *haus* and her parents' *freind* Trisha's *haus*." He shook his head. "She's finally found a home after all the turmoil of her childhood, and I have no right to ask her to leave Bird-in-Hand."

"But she'd still have you."

"It will never work." He started to back away from them. "You had no right to keep this from me for so long."

"We didn't mean to hurt you." Betsy stepped closer. "This has been painful for us, and we hoped we could find a solution before we shared it with you."

"What exactly do you owe on taxes and your other bills?" Matthew asked.

Earl pointed to the pile of papers. "Let me show you."

Matthew sat down beside him and sifted through the documents, taking in the overwhelming numbers. He ran his hand down his face as dread mixed with worry choked back words.

"I was hoping we could still dig out of it," Earl said with a solemn expression. "But today I realized it's time to face the facts. We need to just stay positive and move on. God will provide for us."

"That's right." Betsy stood next to Earl and threaded her fingers with his. "We'll get through this. We just have to have faith. You're part of our family, Matt, and we weren't planning on leaving you behind. You're welcome to come with us."

Earl nodded. "That's right."

"How soon are you leaving?" Matthew held his breath.

Betsy and Earl looked at each other, and Matthew's stomach constricted with apprehension.

"We have to be out by June first," Earl said.

"In three weeks?" This time his voice rose.

"Matt, please listen." Earl held up his hands. "That deadline was finalized only today. We didn't know—"

"I'm going to go to the bank on Monday and see if they'll divide up the land." The idea Matthew had considered while he was out walking had crystallized in his mind.

"What do you mean?" Earl asked, his dark eyebrows drawing together.

"I wonder if I can get a mortgage for the few acres around the *haus*. That way I can finish it, and Lindsay and I will have a place to live."

"That's a *gut* idea." Betsy nodded.

"*Ya,*" Earl said, agreeing.

Betsy pointed to Matthew's plate. "Finish your supper. I can warm it up in the oven if you'd like."

"No, *danki*." Matthew's appetite had dissolved as soon as he learned what was about to happen. "I'm going to bed. *Gut nacht.*"

He scraped the remaining food into the trash and then carried his plate to the counter.

"I'll wash it," Betsy offered as she met him by the sink. "*Gut nacht.*"

He climbed the stairs and hurried past his nieces' bedroom to his own at the end of the hallway. As he changed his clothes for bed, his jumbled thoughts spun like a tornado. He'd started the evening dreaming of his finished house and ended it in a suffocating nightmare.

CHAPTER TWO

W hat's on your mind?" Jake Miller asked as he sat next to Matthew on Robert Kauffman's back porch the following evening.

Shrieks and giggles sounded from the Kauffman grandchildren as they ran around the yard playing tag. A group of the Kauffman men stood by the driveway talking while the women gathered inside the house.

Sometimes Betsy and her family came to the Kauffman gathering when it was here next door to them, and Matthew was grateful they hadn't come tonight. Jake was sensing something was going on anyway, and they'd all agreed not to talk about the turn of events until Betsy and Earl told their girls.

"Not much." Matthew lifted his glass of iced tea and shrugged. "I was just thinking about the new project I have at work. I need to get started on that bed frame since it's due next week."

Jake lifted an eyebrow. "I've known you for how many years now?"

"Almost four."

"Right. And you've always been intense, but you've been a little more intense than usual today. Are you going to tell me what's going on? Or do I need to start guessing?"

Matthew gazed out toward the road and swallowed a deep sigh. Lindsay would arrive with Daniel and his family any minute. If he wanted to share his stress with his best friend, now was the time to do it.

After asking Jake to promise not to tell anyone, Matthew relayed the conversation he'd had with Earl and Betsy the night before, being careful to keep his voice low.

When he finished with the worst of the news, the timing, Jake gasped. "You have to be out in three weeks?"

"Right."

"All because they're losing the farm?"

"*Ya.* Earl showed me how much they owe."

"How much?"

"A lot." The knots in Matthew's shoulders tensed.

Jake paused. "What are you going to do? You're not going to Western Pennsylvania, are you?"

"No. I'm going to see if I can get the bank to divide up the property. Then maybe I can get a loan to buy the acreage with the *haus* and finish it for Lindsay. I want to be positive, so I even worked on the *haus* today."

Matthew settled back in the rocker and rested his forearms on the arms of the chair as he tried to ignore the muscles tightening in his back. But he couldn't help but notice Jake's blue eyes studying him.

"I think that's a great plan," Jake finally said. When Matthew didn't respond, he added, "Is something else bothering you?"

"*Ya.* I have to be able to provide for Lindsay, but how

can I if so much of my money goes to buying land as well as finishing the *haus*?"

"It might take time for you to get on your feet, but you will. You're a talented carpenter, and you have a great future at the store. I'm in the same position you are. I'm living with my grandparents while I save up money to buy a place for Katie and me. There's nothing wrong with changing your original plan. You'll still have a *haus*, and that's more than I have."

Matthew nodded and took a drink of his iced tea. But he couldn't quell the voice in his head.

I'll never be enough for her.

. . .

"Lindsay!" Katie Kauffman yelled as she rushed over to the buggy to greet them. "Hi, *Aenti* Rebecca and *Onkel* Daniel."

"Hi, Katie." Lindsay climbed out of the back of the buggy and then helped her much younger cousins, Emma and Junior. "How are you?"

"I'm *gut*." Katie took Emma by her hand. "I've been waiting for you to get here."

"We had a bit of a late start." Lindsay grabbed Junior's hand as he tried to run off. "Slow down. You'll see your cousins in a minute." Then she turned to Katie. "Is Matthew here?"

"*Ya*." Katie gestured toward the back of the house. "He's sitting on the porch with Jake."

"Oh, *gut*." Lindsay couldn't wait to see him. He'd filled her thoughts as she worked at the bakery this morning and then helped *Aenti* Rebecca with chores all afternoon.

"Hi, *Aenti* Rebecca!" Katie's younger sister, Nancy, rushed over and held out her arms. "Would you like me to take Gracie?"

"*Danki.*" *Aenti* Rebecca handed the baby to Nancy and then turned to Lindsay and Katie. "I'll take the *kinner* so you can go visit with Matthew and Jake."

Lindsay hesitated. *Aenti* Rebecca looked tired. She had dark circles under her eyes. "It's all right. I can take care of them."

Aenti Rebecca smiled. "I don't mind. Go have fun." She stretched out her arms toward her older children. "Emma and Junior. *Kumm.*" The children took her hands, and then she walked beside Nancy as they headed toward the front porch.

Lindsay and Katie hurried up the rock driveway. Lindsay's happy mood deflated when she spotted Matthew talking with Jake on the back porch. His expression was serious and his forehead furrowed as he spoke. Something was definitely bothering him. Maybe something was wrong.

His gaze collided with hers as she climbed the back steps, and he gave her a tentative smile.

"Hi, Lindsay." He tapped the arm of the rocker next to his. "How was your day?"

"*Gut, gut.*" She sank into the chair. "How was yours?"

"*Gut.*" Matthew offered her his glass of iced tea. "Do you want a sip?"

"No, *danki.*" She glanced toward the children playing in the yard and then looked back at him. "I'm sorry we didn't get here earlier. Gracie was fussy, so I had to feed her before we left. I'm wondering if she's coming down with a cold. She's been fussy since last night."

"I hope she feels better." Matthew settled his glass on the arm of the rocker as he gently moved the chair back and forth.

Beside him, Katie and Jake fell into a conversation. For a few minutes Matthew and Lindsay listened in as Katie talked about working in the bakery and Jake told her about his latest project at the furniture store.

"Did you work on the *haus* today?" Lindsay finally asked Matthew.

"*Ya*, I did." He stared out toward the pasture.

"Did you start on the sheetrock?"

He nodded, his eyes still focused in front of him. Was he avoiding looking at her, the question, or both?

"Could we go see it?" She kept her voice gentle in hopes that the house wasn't the source of his reticence.

To her surprise, Matthew smiled at her. "Sure." He stood and held out his hand. She threaded her fingers with his, enjoying the strength and warmth of his touch.

"Where are you going?" Katie asked.

"We're going to see our *haus*." Lindsay nodded toward Betsy's farm. "Would you like to come with us?"

"*Ya*." Katie turned toward Jake, who nodded in agreement. "Let's go."

After Katie let her mother know where they'd be, they cut through the tall trees that separated the two properties. As the framework of the little house came into view, Lindsay's pulse picked up. She squeezed Matthew's hand and quickened her steps.

"Slow down." He chuckled. "There's no need to run."

"*Ya*, there is." She began to jog. "I can't wait to see our *haus*."

"You should've been on my softball team," Katie called after her with a laugh. "We could've won more games if only you'd gone to school with me!"

Lindsay stopped at the front of the house and grinned. She turned to Matthew and threw her arms around his neck. "It's so *schee*."

At first he stiffened, but then he encircled her waist with his arms.

She looked up at him as her worry returned. "What's wrong?"

Frowning, he hesitated. Then he said, "I haven't made much progress on the *haus* this week. I've been working late at the furniture store."

"But what you've done looks fantastic. It's going to be perfect—and so close to both our families."

Something in his eyes flickered. Was it chagrin? Or maybe concern? But why wouldn't he be happy about their house? Something else was bothering him, but she couldn't prod him with Katie and Jake there. She needed to get him alone so they could talk without an audience.

Katie stood beside Lindsay and took in the structure. "It looks great."

"I can't believe I'm going to have a *haus* that's finally mine," Lindsay gushed. *Aenti* Rebecca and *Onkel* Daniel had always made her feel welcome in their home, but she still considered it *their* home. She couldn't wait to make this house her own.

"Can we go inside?"

"Of course." Matthew and Jake climbed onto the first floor where the front door was planned. Then they each held out their hands to help up Lindsay and Katie.

Once inside, Lindsay gestured around the house. "Give me a tour."

For the next thirty minutes, the four of them walked around the first floor as Matthew described the rooms and Lindsay and Katie discussed how to furnish each one. Lindsay's soul swelled with excitement as she imagined living in the house with Matthew as they started their new life as a married couple. She could hardly wait to bake in her own kitchen and sew in her own sewing room.

Soon the sun began to set, staining the sky in vivid streaks of yellow, purple, red, and orange. A cool breeze filtered through the house, and Lindsay shivered, rubbing her bare arms.

"It's getting late." Jake started toward where the front door would be. "We should head back to your *dat's haus*. He might be looking for you."

"*Ya*, you're right." Katie followed him, and after Jake climbed down, he helped her to the ground.

"Could we visit your *schweschder*?" Lindsay asked as Matthew helped her down.

Lindsay was surprised when he hesitated for a moment. Maybe what he was worried about had something to do with his sister. But then he said, "*Ya*, I think she'd like that."

"Would you like to visit Betsy with us?" Lindsay asked Jake and Katie.

Katie frowned. "I'd better get home. You know how strict *mei dat* is. Would you tell her Jake and I said hello?"

"*Ya*, of course." Lindsay recalled how Katie's father had punished her when she first became friends with Jake because he wasn't Amish. Now that he had decided to join the faith, her father had loosened up on his rules slightly. But he didn't allow her to be away from the house for long. "Would you please tell *Aenti* Rebecca I'll be back soon, after a quick visit with Betsy?"

"*Ya*, I will." Katie waved before she and Jake disappeared through the trees.

Now that they were alone, Lindsay stopped and faced Matthew at the bottom of Betsy's back-porch steps. "What's really bothering you?"

He paused and then rubbed his clean-shaven chin. "I'm just tired."

"Are you sure?" She worried her lower lip as she silently willed him to confide in her.

"*Ya.*" He touched her cheek. "Everything's fine. Let's go see Betsy before your *onkel* comes looking for you."

"Okay." She let him take her hand, steer her up the steps and into the house and through the mudroom.

They found Betsy sitting at the kitchen table, writing in what looked like an accounting journal.

"Hi, Lindsay." Betsy closed the journal and stood. "How are you doing?"

"I'm well. How are you?" Lindsay hugged her.

"All right," Betsy said after quickly glancing at her brother. Then she crossed to the kitchen counter and picked up a container. "Would you like some *kichlin*? I can put on *kaffi*."

"Oh, no. Please don't go to any trouble." Lindsay went to her side.

"It's no trouble." Betsy filled the percolator and set it on the stove. "How is your family?"

"They're *gut*. We missed you at the gathering tonight. You should visit us at *Onkel* Daniel's *haus* sometime soon." Lindsay glanced toward the table. Matthew was staring at the journal. "Gracie is getting so big."

"Oh, I bet she is." Betsy carried the container to the table. "Let's share these *kichlin*. I made oatmeal raisin and chocolate chip earlier today."

"*Danki.*" Lindsay sat down at the table and Matthew sank onto the chair beside her. "Where are the *maed*?"

"They're out in the barn with their *dat*. They like to help with chores at night." Betsy opened the container and they each took a cookie. "How is the bakery doing?"

As Lindsay talked about her work, she took in the dark circles under Betsy's eyes. Somehow, they looked different from the dark circles under her *Aenti* Rebecca's eyes, as though they were the result of something more than what can make a mother so tired. And although Matthew's sister was being pleasant, Lindsay thought she detected sadness in her demeanor.

She wondered again if something happening with Betsy was the source of Matthew's blue mood.

Soon the coffee was ready, and Lindsay helped Betsy gather mugs, sugar, and milk. As they enjoyed the refreshments, they talked about family and friends, and Lindsay was careful not to ask any questions that might seem like prying.

She glanced at the clock above the stove and realized it was after seven.

"We better get going, Matthew. We have church in

the morning." The next day was an off Sunday for her family's church district, but not for Matthew's, so she was going to accompany him.

Lindsay stood and carried two of the mugs to the counter. "*Danki* so much for the *kichlin* and *kaffi*."

"*Gern gschehne.*" Betsy stood and hugged her, lingering a little longer than she normally did. What was going on?

When they broke apart, Lindsay swiveled toward Matthew. "Would you please walk me back to Katie's?"

"*Ya.*" He took her hand and they went outside.

Worry gnawed at Lindsay's insides as she and Matthew walked to Katie's. When they reached the end of the tree line, Lindsay spun toward him. This was their last chance to be alone before she joined her family.

"If something is troubling you, you can tell me. It doesn't matter what it is. I'll listen without judgment. You can trust me." She searched his eyes. "You know that, right?"

But his expression didn't seem to relax. "Of course I know that. I'm just tired after working on the *haus* most of the day. I promise you everything will be okay." He touched her shoulder. "*Ich liebe dich.*"

"I love you too." She smiled. But she was still concerned—about Matthew and his sister.

Leaning down, he brushed his lips over hers, sending warmth through her veins and making her knees wobble.

"I'll see you in the morning, Lindsay."

"I'll be waiting for you." She squeezed his hand as they stepped through the trees.

CHAPTER THREE

*G*ude mariye!" Lindsay sang as she climbed into Matthew's buggy the following morning, hoping he'd be in a better mood. *"Wie geht's?"*

"I'm fine. How are you?" He gave her a slight nod before turning toward the horse and directing it down the driveway to the road.

"I'm *gut*." Apprehension nipped at her as she studied his handsome profile. "Did you sleep well last night?"

"Ya." He kept his eyes trained straight ahead while guiding the horse. "Did you?"

Her smiled faded. The deep purple circles under his eyes told her he hadn't slept much at all, and the strong set of his jaw revealed something was bothering him—no matter what he'd said the night before.

"Ya, I did. *Danki."*

They rode in silence for several minutes. He hadn't seemed like it last evening, but was he angry with her for some reason?

Lindsay fingered the wooden heart in her apron pocket. Matthew gave it to her the day she was baptized, and she often put it there when she was with him. She was glad to find it as the anxiety that had haunted her last night came over her once again.

She couldn't stand the silence any longer.

"Are you upset with me?" The question leapt from her lips as Matthew halted the horse at a red light.

"What?" He turned toward her, his dark eyebrows drawn together. "Why would I be upset with you?"

"I don't know." She turned her hands palms up. "You've been acting distracted and upset since last night. You said you slept well, but the dark circles under your eyes seem to tell a different story."

A muscle in his jaw twitched as he looked at her. "You're right. I didn't sleep well last night."

"Why?" A new thought gripped her emotions. "Have you changed your mind about marrying me?" Her voice wobbled as tears threatened to fall.

"No!" He touched her hand. "I would never change my mind about you or about us."

"Okay." She sniffed, but her stomach still felt tied in worried knots.

He glanced toward the traffic light and then guided the horse through the intersection.

"If it's not me, then what is it? *Was iss letz?*" She bit back the urge to beg him to tell her what was troubling him.

He blew out a deep sigh and something flashed in his eyes, but she wasn't sure what it was. Maybe apprehension? He was silent for a few more beats, and she held her breath.

Please tell me the truth, Matthew.

"I've just been concerned about the *haus*," he finally said.

"What do you mean?"

"I want to finish it on time." He gave her a quick,

sideways glance. "I don't want to disappoint you by not having it done in time for our wedding."

She raised her eyebrows and waited for him to elaborate. When he remained silent, she blew out a sigh of relief.

"Is that all that's bothering you?" He nodded while focusing on the road ahead. "It's only May. You have six months to finish our *haus*. And if it's not done in time we can always live with your *schweschder* or *mei aenti* until the *haus* is done. There's no rush to finish it."

He gave her a curt nod, but something unspoken remained in his rigid posture and steely gaze. He wasn't revealing everything troubling his heart, and the revelation cut her to the quick.

He glanced at her and she saw warmth in his eyes. "Is that a new dress?"

She glanced down at the emerald-colored dress she'd made earlier in the week. "*Ya*, it is."

He steered the horse into the Ebersol family's driveway, already lined with buggies. "You look *schee* today. That green is fantastic. It really brings out your red hair and green eyes."

"*Danki.*"

"*Gern gschehne.*"

She smoothed her hands over her apron as confusion settled over her. Maybe he wasn't upset with her and he really was concerned only about the house. But if that was true, then why did tension still radiate off him?

"I'll see you after the service," he said as he halted the horse.

"*Ya.*" She touched his hand, and he met her gaze. "Remember I love you. You can tell me anything."

"I know." His voice was soft.

"If there's something else on your mind, you don't need to be afraid to share it with me." She squeezed his hand and then climbed from the buggy.

. . .

"What's bothering you?" Katie leaned in close as she sat beside Lindsay on the backless bench in the unmarried women's section of the barn. The service had yet to begin.

Lindsay glanced across the barn to where Matthew sat with Jake and then crossed her arms over her apron. "Matthew seemed preoccupied and upset about something last night, and this morning too. I tried to get him to talk to me about it, but all he would say is he's worried about finishing the *haus* in time for our wedding."

"Oh." Katie nodded slowly. "But you think it's more than that?"

"*Ya.*" Lindsay angled her body toward Katie. "I know it sounds *narrisch*, but I just have this feeling he's not telling me something. Do you ever have that feeling with Jake?"

"I don't know." Katie glanced across the barn toward where the young men sat. "We haven't been together as long as you and Matthew have, but we seem to talk about everything."

"We do too. At least I thought we did." She looked

over at Matthew, who was staring at his lap. "Maybe I'm overreacting. Maybe he's only concerned about finishing the *haus* on time."

"What did you say when he told you he was worried about the *haus*?"

"I told him there isn't any rush to finish it." She met Katie's concerned gaze. "I said we could live with his *schweschder* or *mei aenti*. I just want to be with him."

Katie touched her arm. "Just keep telling him that, and he'll calm down. You know how serious he can be. Keep showing him how much you'll love and support him no matter what, and everything will be fine."

"I hope so." Lindsay looked again at Matthew. Maybe he would open up to her soon.

. . .

"You look like you're about to come out of your skin," a voice said.

Matthew glanced over at Jake, who seemed to be studying him again. "What do you mean?"

Jake glanced around and then leaned closer, lowering his voice. "You seem even more stressed out than you were last night."

Matthew shrugged. "I didn't sleep well. I'm just *naerfich* about going to the bank tomorrow."

"What did Lindsay say when you told her what's happening? I assume you two talked after you visited your *schweschder* last night."

"No, I haven't told her." Matthew folded his arms over his chest.

"You haven't told her?" Jake gave Matthew a light punch on his shoulder. "When are you going to?"

"I don't know." Matthew looked over at Jake's stunned expression. "First I need to have a concrete plan for what I'm going to do."

"Have you considered asking Daniel for help? He's not just one of your bosses. He's your *freind*."

Matthew shook his head.

"Why not? Daniel has a lot of respect for you. He would help you. You should ask him for advice."

"I have a plan for now. If it doesn't work out, then I'll talk to Daniel."

Jake opened his mouth to respond just as the service began with a hymn. He closed his mouth and picked up the songbook.

"Jake." Matthew leaned over and spoke into his ear. "Please keep this to yourself. Not only are Earl and Betsy not ready to tell everyone what's going on, but I'm not ready to let Lindsay or the Kauffman family know either. Promise me again you won't tell anyone what I told you."

"I promise."

"*Danki.*" Matthew swallowed his frustration and joined in as the congregation slowly sang the opening hymn. A young man sitting behind them served as the song leader, singing the first syllable of each line. Then the rest of the congregation joined in to finish the verse.

As Matthew tried to redirect his thoughts toward the service, he silently prayed God would send him a solution so he wouldn't lose Lindsay and the future he'd planned for them.

• • •

"*Danki* for taking me to church with you," Lindsay said as Matthew halted the horse by her back porch. "The luncheon was *gut*, as usual."

"*Gern gschehne.*"

He gripped the reins and she once again took in his rigid posture and the hard line of his jaw. "Would you like to come in and visit for a while? I brought home some goodies from the bakery yesterday."

"No, *danki*." He shook his head. "I'm going to go home and take a nap."

"Are you sure? The *kinner* would love to see you. They ask about you constantly."

"I appreciate the invitation, but I'm really tired after not sleeping much last night. I promise I'll come visit soon."

"Okay." Her shoulders fell as her hope deflated. "Matthew, please. If you need to talk to me, I'll listen."

He swallowed, and he seemed tenser than ever. "*Danki*. But I'm fine."

Was he holding back emotion? Alarm surged through her. She opened her mouth to beg him to tell her what was wrong, but he cut her off.

"I should go. Please tell Rebecca and Daniel I said hello." He reached out and touched her hand. "Have a *gut* day."

"You too." Lindsay pushed open the door and climbed out. She waved as his horse and buggy started down the driveway toward the road.

Foreboding, heavy and suffocating, pressed down

on her shoulders as she climbed the porch steps and entered the house. She walked into the family room, where *Aenti* Rebecca sat in the rocking chair with Gracie against her chest. Lindsay crossed the room and touched Gracie's back.

Aenti Rebecca smiled up at her. "How was church?"

"It was *gut*." Lindsay sank into the high-backed chair beside her. "Where are the other *kinner*?"

"They're taking a nap. Daniel is too." She tilted her head. "*Was iss letz?*"

Lindsay's lower lip quivered.

"*Ach, mei liewe.*" *Aenti* Rebecca leaned over and touched her arm. "Did you have a disagreement with Matthew?"

"It's worse than that." Lindsay dabbed her tears with her fingers. "Something's wrong, and he won't tell me what it is. I've tried more than once to get him to talk to me, but I feel as though he's not telling me everything." She explained their conversation about the house and how she told him she didn't care where they live after they were married. "He refused to come in and visit today because he said he was tired after not sleeping well last night, worrying over it."

She ran her fingers over the chair arms. "But I know that's not what's wrong. I can't help him if he won't talk to me. I asked him if I'd done something, and he said it wasn't me, and that he hasn't changed his mind about us. But I can't help feeling as though I'm going to lose him." She sniffed as tears leaked down her cheeks, splattering her arm.

"*Ach*, no. Don't cry." *Aenti* Rebecca set a sleeping

Gracie in the nearby swing and then moved the rocking chair closer to Lindsay before sitting back down. She handed Lindsay a handful of tissues. Lindsay wiped her nose and leaned her head against the back of her chair.

"Look at me," *Aenti* Rebecca instructed, and Lindsay turned her head. "Matthew loves you, and he's devoted to you. I could tell when you first started dating each other." She paused as if gathering her thoughts. "Matthew reminds me a lot of Daniel. He's quiet and intense, but he's also devoted and loyal. You remember how tough things were between Daniel and me when you and Jessica came to live with us, right?"

"*Ya*, of course I do." Lindsay sniffed.

"He and I had some rough times, but we made it through. When he gets upset about something he shuts down, and it takes him a while to open up. I think Matthew is the same way. Something is bothering him now, and he's still processing it. He'll open up to you when he's ready to share it." She rubbed Lindsay's arm.

Lindsay gasped. "You're right. He *is* a lot like *Onkel* Daniel. I never made the connection before."

Aenti Rebecca smiled. "Daniel has shut me out many times. It's frustrating, but I've had to learn to live with it. I try to get him to talk to me, but sometimes it doesn't work. I just have to wait it out."

"It just hurts so much." Lindsay hugged her arms to her chest. "I feel like my heart is going to shatter."

"*Ya*, that's exactly how it feels for me too. Of course, after we work things out, I remind Daniel how much it hurt me. He understands, but it's his personality to get quiet while he works things out on his own."

Aenti Rebecca sighed. "I know this is difficult, and I would take away your pain if I could. But you need to be strong, Lindsay. You need to have faith in your relationship with Matthew and give him time to work through whatever is bothering him. Let him come to you when he's ready, and then listen to him and offer your support. After the smoke clears, tell him how much it hurt you when he shut you out. If you tell him how you feel, your relationship will get stronger."

"Okay." Leaning forward, she hugged her aunt. *"Danki."*

Aenti Rebecca patted her back. *"Gern gschehne.* You're a strong *maedel.* You'll get through this and come out stronger as a couple. Be sure to pray for Matthew, and everything will be just fine."

"Ya, I will." Lindsay sat up straighter as confidence surged through her. She would give Matthew the time he needed. In her heart, she believed their relationship was strong enough to make it through the hard times, and she prayed he believed it too.

CHAPTER FOUR

"How did it go at the bank?" Jake asked the follow-ing afternoon as he leaned on the workbench in Matthew's work stall.

"Not well." Matthew shook his head and sat down on a stool beside the headboard he'd been sanding.

Jake's smile faded. "Oh no. What happened?"

"The bank refused to break up the land. I explained I'm building a *haus* there, but they said it's impossible." He looked across the shop where carpenters worked on various furniture pieces. Hammers banged, saw blades whirled, and air compressors hummed. The sweet scent of wood and stain filled his nostrils.

"I don't have enough savings to pay the back taxes and take over the mortgage for the whole farm, so I'm stuck." Matthew ran his hand down his face. "I feel like a buffoon for building a *haus* on a piece of land I can't live on. I don't know what to do now."

"That's terrible." Jake looked about as somber as Matthew had ever seen him.

When a yawn overtook him, Matthew covered his mouth.

Jake raised an eyebrow. "Did you sleep at all last night?"

"Not really."

"You can't keep this up. You should just talk to Daniel." Jake gestured toward the office where Daniel stood in the doorway, talking to his father, Eli. "Tell him what's going on and ask for help. He can give you *gut* advice."

Matthew crossed his arms over his chest and considered the suggestion. Then Jake stood up straight as Daniel stepped out of the office doorway and started for the center of the shop.

"Here he comes. Now's your chance." Jake headed to his stall on the other side of the shop. As Daniel approached Matthew's stall, Jake turned and mouthed the words, "Do it!"

Matthew swallowed a groan.

"How's your project going?"

Matthew looked up as Daniel stood over him. "Oh, it's going well." He gestured toward the king-size headboard. "I'm almost done sanding it."

Daniel stepped into the stall and ran his fingers over the headboard. "You do great work."

"*Danki*." Matthew paused. "I need to ask you something."

When Daniel faced him, the words stalled in Matthew's throat.

Daniel tilted his head and raised his blond eyebrows. "What do you want to ask me?"

Matthew's thoughts spun and anxiety flooded his soul. He needed Daniel's help, but how would it look if he admitted he wasn't sure he had a place to live anymore? As Lindsay's guardian, Daniel could break their engagement, and Matthew couldn't take that risk. Without Lindsay, he truly would have nothing.

"Are you all right?" Daniel's forehead furrowed.

"*Ya.*" Matthew forced a smile. "Do you have any other projects ready for me since I'm almost done with this headboard?"

Daniel paused for a moment and glanced toward the front. "Check with Elmer and see if he's taken any other orders." Then he nodded toward his younger brother's stall, across the shop. "But I think Timothy will get the next order since he's finished with the curio cabinet he was building."

"Okay." Matthew tapped his finger on the workbench. "I'll check with Elmer when I finish this project." He grabbed the sandpaper and leaned over the headboard. He felt the weight of Daniel's stare as he began sanding, but he kept working, hoping Daniel would walk away.

"Matthew," Daniel said. "Is everything okay?"

Matthew froze and then cringed. He glanced over his shoulder at Daniel and nodded. "*Ya*, everything's fine."

Daniel pursed his lips and then nodded. "All right. Keep up the *gut* work."

When Daniel walked away, the muscles in Matthew's shoulders loosened slightly. He looked over at Jake, who gave him a questioning look. Matthew shook his head and Jake frowned before returning to the end table he'd been staining.

As Matthew went back to work, he considered all his options. He could look for a small piece of land to buy, but then he wouldn't have enough money to build a house. Still, having a piece of land was better than nothing. He would go back to the bank tomorrow morning and apply for another loan. Maybe he could afford to buy land and build a smaller house. He just didn't know where he would stay until it was ready.

. . .

On Friday night Matthew circled his unfinished house, and disappointment and frustration settled over him as he kicked a stone with his shoe. After applying for a loan at two different banks so he could purchase some land, he'd been turned down flat. They said his credit history wasn't long enough and his income wasn't high enough. They didn't seem to care that he had some money in the bank.

He turned toward his sister's home as guilt wafted over him. He did have money in the bank, but Betsy and her family were floundering. He should give them those funds to help them get back on their feet. Their children, his sweet nieces, deserved a better life. Helping them was the Christian thing to do.

After all, when a loan became impossible, he'd started to come to terms with the idea of starting a new life somewhere else. His cousin Sherm had once offered to get him a job working with him in the RV factory in Sugarcreek, Ohio. That seemed the only logical solution to his predicament.

But how can I leave Lindsay?

His heart squeezed at the idea of leaving her, but he wasn't worthy of her love if he couldn't give her a home. She'd be better off with someone else.

Matthew climbed his sister's back steps and walked into the house. He left his boots and hat in the mudroom before going into the family room. Betsy sat on the sofa reading a Christian novel. Earl was in his favorite chair, reading *The Budget*. Having come to a decision about their own future, they seemed calm. He needed to settle on a plan too. Jake was right. He couldn't go on this way.

"Matt." Betsy looked up at him, and her forehead furrowed. *"Was iss letz?"*

"I've made a decision. I couldn't get the bank to divide up the land, and I can't get a loan to buy land anywhere else. So I want to give you what I have in savings. You can use the money for moving expenses and to start your new life." He shared the balance he had in his account.

Betsy and Earl looked confused.

"That's awfully generous of you." Betsy sounded doubtful. "But aren't you and Lindsay going to move with us? You'll need that money."

Matthew shook his head. "No."

"Are you going to move in with Lindsay's family, then?" Earl asked.

"No." Matthew sank into the wing chair across from them. "I'm going to check into a few other options."

"Why would you give us your money?" Betsy wiped away a tear.

"I want to help you and *mei bruderskinner* start a new life. I'll make out a check and leave it on the kitchen table. Tomorrow I'll go by the bank and transfer the money into my checking account to cover it." Matthew stood. "I need to make a phone call." He started toward the stairs.

"Matt!" Betsy called after him.

He glanced over his shoulder at her.

"*Danki*," she said.

"*Gern gschehne*," he said before jogging up the steps to his room. After he wrote out the check, he left it on the kitchen table and headed outside.

Despondent, he walked to the phone shanty and dialed Sherm's number. While the phone rang, he imagined his cousin's house with the phone shanty out by the barn. He hoped he would answer before voice mail kicked on.

After several rings, Sherm picked up. "Hello?"

"Hi, Sherm. It's Matthew."

"Matt! How are you?" Sherm sounded happy to hear from him.

"I'm—uh, well, I've been better."

"Oh? What's going on?"

"I need your help." Matthew wrapped his fingers around the phone cord as he told him what was happening with Betsy's farm. Sherm gasped when Matthew explained he had only two weeks to find a place to live.

"So I need a . . . a new start. You once told me you could get me a job at the factory where you work. Do you still think so?"

"I do. But why do you want to move out here?" Matthew sensed Sherm wanted to ask about Lindsay, but he hoped he wouldn't. Not now.

"Like I said, for a new start. You also told me if I got that job I could stay with you until I found a place of my own," Matthew said. "I don't want to impose, but if that offer is still open, I'd like to discuss it."

"You're always welcome here. Let me talk to my supervisor and see if he has a job open. I can let you know tomorrow night. Does that work?"

"*Ya*, that would be perfect. *Danki*."

"*Gern gschehne*. Please tell Betsy, Earl, and the *maed* I said hello."

"I will. *Gut nacht*."

After hanging up, Matthew leaned back against the wall and covered his face with his hands. He was going to do it; he was going to move to Ohio. Going to a new place to start over seemed like the best solution. Better to end his relationship with Lindsay now than not be able to provide for her and their family if they married.

He took a deep, shuddering breath and then stepped out onto the rock driveway. Lifting his lantern, he walked toward the house.

"Matt?"

He spun and spotted Jake cutting through the trees.

"What are you doing here?"

"I was just heading home after visiting with Katie. I thought I'd walk over to check on you since you hardly spoke to me at work today." Jake frowned. "How are you?"

"I've made a decision." Matthew told him he couldn't get a loan, so he'd given his money to Betsy and was going to release Lindsay from their engagement. "I'm going to go to Ohio and start a new life."

Jake gasped. "What? You're going to leave Bird-in-Hand?"

"*Ya*, I am." Matthew nodded toward the phone shanty. "My cousin in Sugarcreek thinks he can get me a job at the RV factory where he works. I just called him, and he said he'll talk to his supervisor and call me back tomorrow night."

"You can't be serious." Jake shook his head.

"I am."

"Why would you want to leave here? You have a great job, where you're thriving. Just the other day I heard Daniel singing your praises to Eli and *mei daadi.*"

Matthew pursed his lips. "I can still make furniture as a hobby."

"But what about Lindsay? How will she take the news that you're leaving her?"

"It's better this way." Matthew turned and headed toward the house. *"Gut nacht."*

"Matt, wait!" Jake followed him. "Don't walk away from me. I want to know how you're going to tell Lindsay you're running away from her. You're going to break her heart."

Matthew kept walking as his body trembled.

"You know you're a coward, right?"

"I'm not a coward." Matthew had spun and spat the words at Jake. "I'm a realist. And I'm not running away—I'm doing this for her."

"How do you figure that?" Jake stood inches from his nose.

"If I leave, Lindsay can find someone worthy of her, someone who can provide for her."

Jake raised an eyebrow. "Why would she want someone else when she's in love with you?"

Matthew raked a hand through his thick, curly hair. "She'll get over me and find someone who can give her everything she needs."

"That's really what you want?" Jake asked, and Matthew nodded. "You want to imagine your Lindsay married to someone else?"

Matthew's mouth dried. "You don't understand."

"You're exactly right. I don't understand how you can give up so easily."

Matthew started up the back steps.

"Tell me one thing," Jake called after him. "Did you ever talk to Daniel?"

Matthew stopped and faced him. "No, I didn't."

Jake shook his head. "Why not?"

"Why would he help me?"

"Why *wouldn't* he help you?" Jake pointed at him as his eyes narrowed. "Even though the Kauffmans gave you a chance when you moved here, your whole problem is you still can't imagine anyone else giving you a chance. You still think because your *dat* left you and your *mamm* and *schweschder* penniless, no one would want to help you."

"That's not true." Fury simmered through him. "My problem is I don't want to be like him. I want to support my family. If I can't support Lindsay, then I shouldn't be with her."

Jake held up his hand as if to reason with his friend. "Look, Matt, I'm just trying to help."

"I don't need your help." Matthew jammed a thumb toward the house. "I'm going to bed. I'll see you tomorrow."

Jake hesitated and then nodded. *"Gut nacht."*

As Matthew stepped into the house, he imagined Lindsay's beautiful face as he told her he was going to break their engagement and leave. She would be crushed, but he hoped he could make her understand why he had to do this.

He wished he could wait for the perfect time and

place to tell her, but he knew he'd have to tell her tomorrow night, after the gathering at her house.

. . .

As she and Katie sat with their friends and cousins on her back porch, Lindsay laughed at a story about how tourists who visited the bakery had asked silly questions about the Amish.

The older women were visiting inside the house and the older men were talking out by the barn. As she took a sip of root beer, she glanced to where Matthew stood talking with Jake and her cousin Samuel. The sky above her was cloudy, and the scent of rain filled the air as thunder rumbled in the distance.

Noticing the tray on the table beside her was empty, Lindsay picked it up and stood. "I'll get more cookies," she announced.

"I'll come with you," Katie said. "Let me get the door." She held it open, and Lindsay stepped through into the mudroom and kitchen. A murmur of conversations sounded from the family room.

Lindsay set the tray on the counter and opened a container of cookies she'd brought home from the bakery. "I think there's another container of cookies in that cabinet above you. Would you please grab it?"

"Sure." Katie retrieved the container and handed it to her.

"*Danki.*" Lindsay opened both containers and set the cookies on the platter. When she felt Katie staring at her, she turned. "Is something on your mind?"

Katie bit her lip and hesitated.

"What is it? You've been quiet all evening." Lindsay leaned against the counter. "Did you and Jake have an argument?"

"No." Katie shook her head. "I'm just worried about you."

"What do you mean?" Lindsay asked. "I'm okay. I talked to *Aenti* Rebecca about Matthew, and I've decided to let him come to me when he's ready to talk. Everything's going to be fine because we love each other. We're going to get through this."

"Oh. Well, then I guess so." Katie seemed unconvinced as she reached for the tray.

"Wait a minute." Lindsay held up her hand. "What do you mean by that?"

"I'm just surprised you can be that patient. If I knew my fiancé's *schweschder* and her family were losing their farm and had to move away—"

Lindsay gasped. "What?"

Katie's eyes widened. "You didn't know?"

Air rushed from Lindsay's lungs, and she grabbed the counter to steady herself. "Who told you that?"

"Jake told me. He heard it from Matthew and was upset, partly because of what it means for your *haus*. I assumed you knew all about it." Katie touched Lindsay's arm, but Lindsay swatted it away.

"What else did he tell you?" Lindsay asked.

"All I know is they owe a huge amount of back taxes and can't pay it. They have to let the farm go."

"*Ach*, no. This can't be true. It can't be." Lindsay cupped her hand to her mouth as the reality crashed over her. Betsy was going to lose her farm, which meant she and Matthew wouldn't be able to live in the house he'd been building for them. No wonder he'd been so distant. But why didn't he tell her?

"Lindsay, I'm so sorry," Katie repeated. "I didn't realize he hadn't told you."

"I need to go." Lindsay rushed out of the house, down the porch steps, and over to where Matthew leaned against the pasture fence talking to Jake and Samuel. She was wringing her hands as she approached them.

When Matthew saw her, he stood up straight. "Hi, Lindsay."

"Could I speak to you alone, please?" she asked, her voice shaking.

"*Ya*, of course." He nodded toward the far end of the fence. "Let's go over there."

She followed him down the fence line, away from everyone else.

"What do you want to talk about?" he asked once they were alone. "You seem upset."

"Katie just told me your *schweschder* is losing her farm. Is that true?"

He blew out a puff of air as he scrubbed his hand over his face.

"It's true?" she demanded.

"I didn't want you to find out this way. I was going to tell you later—"

"How long have you known?"

"For a week." His voice was shaky too. "I found out last week." He explained how he'd walked in when his sister and Earl had just faced the reality that they couldn't avoid bankruptcy and would lose the farm. His golden-brown eyes filled with tears. "They have to be out of their *haus* at the end of the month, and they're going to move to Western Pennsylvania to live with Earl's parents. They asked me if I wanted to go, but I turned them down. I've been trying to figure out what to do."

"That's why you've been so distant." Her own eyes stung with threatening tears, but she tried to keep them from multiplying. "I can't believe you didn't tell me."

"I didn't know how to tell you, and anyway, I wanted to make a plan before I did." He'd been holding out his arms as he talked, as if to plead for her understanding. But now he dropped them at his sides and stared at the ground.

Thunder rumbled closer, and his voice grew thick as he continued. "I tried to get the bank to divide up the land and let me buy the parcel our *haus* is on, but they won't. Then I tried to apply for a loan to buy another piece of land, but two banks turned me down."

"It's okay. We'll get through this." She wiped away a tear trickling down her hot cheek.

"How?" His gaze collided with hers, and his eyes challenged her. "There's no way to get through this. I have nowhere to live and nothing to offer you."

"What are you saying?" A cool mist wafted over her cheeks as lightning lit up the sky.

"I'm saying I can't provide for you." His voice rose and his face twisted into a pained scowl. "I called my cousin in Sugarcreek, Ohio, and asked him to see if he can get me a job in the factory where he works." His lips formed a thin line. "I think this is the best solution."

"Okay." She sniffed. "We can make a life in Ohio."

He shook his head. "That's not what I mean."

"I don't understand." Thunder sounded, and she jumped.

"I don't think you should go with me." He was saying the words slowly, enunciating each word as if she were a child. "You deserve stability, and I can't give that to you. You'd be miserable without your family in Ohio. You lost your home and your parents and were thrown into this strange community where you had to learn how to be Amish. Then you spent a summer in Virginia Beach helping your parents' *freinden*. It's not fair of me to ask you to move again. I'm going to Ohio alone."

"You want to leave me here?" The rain beat a steady cadence now, soaking her apron and her prayer covering. "Why would you want to do that? I'm your fiancée. We're going to get married."

"I think we need to go our separate ways. I've already given Betsy and Earl most of my money to help them. I want *mei bruderskinner* to start a new life." He shook his head as his voice faltered. "If I take you to Ohio, you'll resent me. You belong here with Rebecca, Daniel, and their *kinner*."

"How can you say that?" Her voice pitched as tears streamed down her face. "You said you loved me. How can you walk away from me and everything we're building together?"

"It's better this way. You'll find someone who can give you everything you need." He gestured widely with his arms. "I can't afford to buy any land, and I can't give you a *haus*."

"So you're going to give up, just like that?" She pointed toward her aunt's house. "We can live with *mei aenti* for a while until we can afford our own place. Maybe we can add on a couple of rooms and stay there. Isn't that better than just giving up?" Her voice squeaked as if she were six years old, not nineteen.

"I think it's better if we break up. You should move on without me." His eyes glistened with unshed tears.

She shook her head. She had to be dreaming! Her body began to shake as if she were standing outside in February without a coat. This couldn't be real.

"You can give up on me that easily?" Her voice shook as her tears continued to flow.

"I'm not giving up on you. I'm thinking about what makes sense in the long run. *Mei dat* couldn't handle the responsibilities of a family, and I thought I was different. But it turns out I'm not. Better to cut things off now instead of our lives falling apart down the road when we have *kinner*. I'm going to move to Ohio. You should find someone else. You deserve better than what I can offer you."

Lightning split the sky, followed by a loud crash of thunder.

He pointed toward the house. "Go inside. You're getting soaked."

"So that's it?" She shivered as she hugged her arms to her waist. "You're just going to send me on my way?"

He lowered his head. "I'm sorry, Lindsay."

"I'm sorry too." She turned and raced toward the house as her heart shattered into a million pieces.

CHAPTER FIVE

Tears continued to flow down Lindsay's cheeks as she rushed past her friends and cousins. They called her name, but she kept going. She wrenched open the back door and ran through the mudroom and kitchen and up the stairs to her bedroom. She slammed the door behind her before flopping onto her bed and sobbing into her pillow.

In less than thirty minutes, her fiancé had broken up with her, and it all seemed like some terrible nightmare. But it was real, so very real. Her chest ached, and she could hardly breathe.

"Lindsay? Lindsay?" Katie's voice was close. "I'm so sorry. I thought you knew. I didn't mean to upset you."

"Please go away." Lindsay's words were muffled by her pillow.

"Talk to me." Katie rubbed her back. "Tell me what happened."

Rolling to her side, Lindsay looked up at Katie, who had sat down on the edge of her bed. Nancy lingered in the doorway, obviously concerned.

"How long have you known?" Lindsay asked.

Katie hesitated.

"Tell me. How long?" Lindsay demanded.

"Jake told me last night," Katie said, holding up her hands. "I would never keep anything from you intentionally. I thought you knew, and I was hoping you would tell me how you felt about it." She touched her arm. "What did Matthew tell you? Please share it with me."

Lindsay's tears began to flow again as she recalled her conversation with Matthew. "He broke up with me. He's moving to Ohio and leaving me here. He says I'm better off without him because he can't offer me a home." Covering her face with her hands, she began to sob again.

"What? Jake only told me about the Lantz's losing their farm and that Matthew was trying to figure out what to do. He didn't tell me—Nancy, please go get *Aenti* Rebecca. *Dummle!*"

She patted Lindsay's back. "Please calm down. We'll get through this. Matthew will change his mind. I promise it will be okay."

After a few moments, *Aenti* Rebecca appeared in the doorway. "*Ach*, no. What happened?" She made her way over to the bed.

Katie stood, and *Aenti* Rebecca took her place. Katie left the room as Lindsay sat up and began to tell her aunt everything.

"I don't understand how he can just break up with me and leave me." Lindsay shivered with emotion. "How can he do that?"

"I don't know." *Aenti* Rebecca shook her head. "I think he's desperate and confused."

"But he seemed so determined. I could see in his eyes that his mind was already made up. Nothing I could say was going to make a difference." Lindsay wiped her face with a tissue as she leaned back against the headboard. "I just don't understand it. How could he just give up on us?"

Aenti Rebecca put her arm around her niece's shoulders. "Why don't you give him a day or two to think about it and then try talking to him again?"

Lindsay fingered her quilt as questions flowed through her mind. "Is there anything you can do?"

"What do you mean?" *Aenti* Rebecca tilted her head.

"Can you help us?" Lindsay pleaded. "Can you and *Onkel* Daniel convince him to stay?"

Aenti Rebecca clicked her tongue. "*Ach, mei liewe.* I don't know, but I'll talk to Daniel."

"Please. Maybe *Onkel* Daniel can make him realize we don't need a *haus* right away. We can live here with you until we're on our feet. Other couples do it all the time, right?"

Aenti Rebecca smiled. "That's a *gut* solution. I'll ask Daniel what he thinks." She squeezed Lindsay's hand. "Why don't you take a shower? Everyone is leaving because of the storm. I'll make you some tea, and we can talk some more. Everything will be okay. Just have faith."

"Okay."

As her aunt walked out of the room, Lindsay prayed she was right.

. . .

The rain completely soaked through Matthew's shirt as he stepped out of the barn after stowing his horse. But his guilt and frustration were so great they seemed to drown him as he made his way down the rock driveway to the phone shanty. Inside, he shook water off his hands and arms and dialed to retrieve their voice mail messages. His pulse pounded when Sherm's voice echoed through the phone.

"Hi, Matt. I talked to my supervisor today, and he said he'd love to have you join the company. One of my coworkers just gave notice, and his last day is next Friday. You can start anytime. Just give me a call and let me know what you think." He hesitated. "But I'll understand if you've changed your mind. Talk to you soon."

When Sherm's message clicked off, Matthew stared down at the phone as doubt nearly overtook him. Was he making a mistake?

An image of Lindsay's face filled his mind, and his hands shook. She was heartbroken. How could he leave her?

She's better off without me!

But if that were true, why did the idea of leaving her affect him so deeply? Why would God lead him to this decision if both he and Lindsay would be crushed?

Shoving the thought away, Matthew dialed his cousin's number and waited for either Sherm to pick up or for voice mail to kick on. After he heard a recorded message and a beep, he began to speak. "Hi, Sherm. This is Matthew. *Danki* for talking to your supervisor for me. I'd like to accept the job and start right away. I plan to come to Sugarcreek next Saturday. Let me know if that works for you. *Danki* again for everything. Talk to you soon."

After he hung up, Matthew stepped out into the pouring rain and ran for the house. In the mudroom he removed his boots and hat before going into the kitchen. His sister and Earl were sitting at the table.

"Hi, Matt." Betsy smiled. "You're home early tonight."

"I have something to tell you. I've made another decision. I'm going to move to Ohio and work in an RV factory with Sherm. He already has a job lined up for me. I'm going to pack up my things, sell my horse and buggy, finish up work at the furniture store, and take a bus to Ohio next Saturday."

Betsy looked shocked.

"Is Lindsay going with you?" Earl asked.

Matthew shook his head. "No. We broke up tonight."

Betsy gasped. "*Ach*, no. Why?"

"It's for the best." Matthew started to leave before she could ask more questions. "*Gut nacht.*"

"Wait!" she called.

He swiveled toward her.

"Did you decide to break up with her and go to Ohio because you gave us your money?"

"No. It's just for the best." Matthew walked toward the stairs.

"Just a minute." She raced after him. "I'll give you back the money if it will make things right between you and Lindsay. I don't feel right taking it."

He sighed as he looked into his sister's glistening eyes. "Most of that money was from *Mamm* when she sold our farm, and she would want to help you, Earl, and the *maed*. Consider it a gift from her."

A noise that sounded like a choked sob came from

her throat and tears streamed down her face. "*Danki*," she whispered before sitting back down at the table.

Matthew made his way up to his room and knelt on the floor, searching under his bed for a duffel bag to start packing his belongings. When he spotted a small box, he lowered himself to a sitting position and began to sift through its contents. He found letters Lindsay wrote to him while she was in Virginia Beach last summer, and when he pulled them out and read them, his eyes filled with tears.

Digging deeper in the box, he found cards and notes she'd written him while they were dating. He took in her beautiful handwriting and sweet words of love and devotion.

Memories drenched him as raindrops tapped against his window. She was the most important person in his life, the one person with whom he wanted to have a family. But he wasn't worthy of her love. He had to leave and start a new life somewhere else. The pain would get easier, wouldn't it?

When a single tear traced down his cheek, he brushed it away. He had to be strong. After all, this was God's will, and he had to follow the right path—even though he felt as though his soul had been shredded.

· · ·

"Lindsay?"

Lindsay rolled onto her side and faced the doorway, where *Aenti* Rebecca stood with her dark eyebrows cinched together. She rubbed her eyes and swallowed a yawn. She'd spent all night alternating between sobbing, praying, and staring at the ceiling as she replayed her conversation with Matthew over and over.

She kept hoping he would appear outside, toss a pebble at her windowpane, and talk to her on the porch for hours, telling her he'd made a mistake and wanted to marry her. But no pebble hit her windowpane. Pain and sorrow were her only companions during a sleepless night.

"It's past time to get up and get ready for church." *Aenti* Rebecca's voice was gentle. "Are you going to come with us?"

Lindsay shook her head. "I don't think I'm in any shape to go. I didn't sleep last night, and I don't think I could make it through the service without crying. I'm also not ready to tell everyone Matthew and I broke up." Her lips trembled and she covered her face with her hands as a groan seeped out of her. "I hope Katie and Nancy didn't tell everyone last night before they left."

"Don't even worry about that right now." *Aenti* Rebecca sat down on the edge of her bed. "You should try to get some sleep, and then you'll feel better. Everything will work out. Just have faith."

Lindsay sniffed as she looked up at her aunt. "Did you tell *Onkel* Daniel?"

"*Ya*, and he said he'll talk to Matthew." *Aenti* Rebecca rubbed Lindsay's arm. "Right now you should concentrate on getting some rest."

"All right."

Leaning down, *Aenti* Rebecca hugged her. "I'll see you later. I love you."

"I love you too."

As tired as she was, Lindsay knew she wouldn't be able to sleep. She waited until after her family left for church before she got dressed. As she started to walk out of her bedroom, her gaze landed on the beautiful cedar hope chest Matthew gave her when he proposed.

She ran her fingers over the smooth wood, breathing in the sweet cedar. It had belonged to Matthew's mother and he refurbished it before giving it to her. This gorgeous piece of furniture had always represented Matthew's love, but now he'd decided to throw away all the promises they'd made to each other. How could their relationship have fallen apart so quickly, with hardly any warning?

Lindsay swallowed back a sob as she went downstairs. With the weight of her disappointment and heartache pressing down on her shoulders, she tried to eat a piece of toast, but it tasted like sawdust. After tossing it, she peered out the kitchen window and stared at the phone shanty. She longed to call Matthew to try to talk some sense into him, but her pride held her back.

A sudden and overwhelming need to speak to her sister grabbed her. She glanced at the clock. It was only eight thirty. Jessica would probably still be sleeping, but this was urgent. She needed her sister now. Surely Jessica would understand.

After slipping on a pair of shoes, she rushed out the back door to the phone shanty and dialed Jessica's cell phone. Her older sister picked up on the third ring.

"Lindsay?" Jessica's voice was gravelly.

Lindsay's felt tears coming at the sound of her sister's voice. "Hey, Jess."

"What's up?"

Lindsay could hear her yawning, and she took a deep breath. "Can you talk?"

"Yeah. What's wrong?"

Lindsay heard rustling and she imagined Jessica sitting up in bed.

"Matthew and I broke up last night." Lindsay fought the urge to start crying again. It was a wonder she had any tears left to shed.

Jessica gasped. "Oh, no. What happened?"

She somehow managed to tell Jessica all about it while keeping her tears at bay.

"Oh, Lindsay," Jessica said when she finished her story. "I don't even know what to say. I'm in shock."

"I know. I am too." She sniffed. "I don't know what to do. I just needed to hear your voice."

"What if I come to see you? I could be there in a few hours."

"Really?" Lindsay shook her head. "Wait. What about school?"

"I have one more final later this week, but it's going to be an easy one. I have a few free days before the test."

"You really wouldn't mind coming?"

"Are you kidding? I was hoping to visit next weekend anyway. So do you want me to come or not?"

"*Ya*, I do want you to come. I need you right now."

"Good. I'm glad to be needed. I'll pack a few things and get on the road."

"Thank you, Jess."

"That's what sisters are for," Jessica insisted. "Hold tight. I'll be there soon."

As Lindsay hung up, she wondered if by the time Jessica arrived she'd have any more insight into Matthew's decision—and whether it was possible for anyone to convince him to change his mind.

. . .

Later that night Lindsay climbed into bed next to Jessica and snuggled into her pillow. They had spent the day visiting with the family and talking. It felt like old times, just like when they'd first moved in with *Aenti* Rebecca and *Onkel* Daniel nearly five years earlier.

"I'm so glad you're here." Lindsay rolled over to face her sister in the dark.

"I am too. I just wish I could be more help to you."

"Just being here is helping me. May I ask you something?"

"You can ask me anything."

"Do you think Matthew will change his mind?"

Jessica blew out a deep sigh, and Lindsay braced herself for her sister's honest—and perhaps harsh—words.

"When you first told me you were going to become Amish, I was against it because I thought you were just doing it to try to impress Aunt Rebecca. I was wrong. You're happy, and you belong here." She paused for a moment. "And when you told me you were engaged to Matthew, I was worried you were too young. But again, you were so happy with him."

"So you thought all along it wasn't going to work?" Lindsay squeezed her eyes shut, regretting the question.

"No, that's not it at all. As I said, I was worried you were too young, but I also realized you and Matthew complemented each other well. He's a really good man, and I believe he would be good for you." Jessica sighed. "I think he's confused and overwhelmed right now, but I also think he's going to realize he made a mistake and come back to you."

"Do you think he's really going to move to Ohio?"

"Yes, I do, but I think he'll come back. He loves you, Linds. I don't think he'll stay gone for long."

"I hope not," Lindsay whispered.

"Why don't you get some sleep, and we'll talk more in the morning. Okay?"

"I'd like that."

"Just do me one favor."

"What?"

"Don't snore like you did when we were kids."

Lindsay laughed despite her anguish.

"It's good to hear you laugh." Jessica rolled over, putting her back toward Lindsay. "Good night."

"Good night." Lindsay smiled, and a tiny glimmer of hope ignited deep inside. Maybe, just maybe, everything would eventually be okay.

CHAPTER SIX

Matthew's heart felt heavy as he climbed the steps to the furniture store at six thirty Monday morning. He wanted the place to himself for a while so he could work without any interruptions.

He'd spent most of Sunday morning holed up in his room alone, making a list of everything he had to do before he left for Ohio on Saturday. Questions and doubts haunted him throughout the rest of the day, but he held fast to his belief that this was the path God had chosen for him. Despite the heartache his decision was causing both him and Lindsay, he could see no other way.

Matthew unlocked the store with his key and moved through the showroom as the smell of wood and stain filled his senses. When he entered the work area, he was surprised to see a light burning in the office at the far end of the shop. He didn't expect anyone else to be here before seven thirty. He set his lunch box on his work-bench and crossed the floor.

Standing in the doorway of the office, Matthew saw Daniel sitting at the desk, reviewing a furniture cata-log. His boss and friend looked up at him and smiled.

"*Gude mariye.* You're here early." He pointed to the chair on the other side the desk. "Have a seat."

Matthew's mouth dried as he sat down. This was the moment he'd been dreading—he had to tell Daniel he was going to Ohio and explain why he had to leave Lindsay behind.

"How are you doing?" Daniel's blue eyes seemed to assess him, as if he already knew the answer to the question. Of course Daniel knew the answer! After all, Lindsay was his niece and lived in his house.

"I need to give you notice. My last day here will be Friday." Matthew's voice sounded strange to him—unsure and weak. He sat up straighter. He was a man, and he had to stand behind his decisions. "I'm moving to Sugarcreek, Ohio. I'm going to work in a factory with my cousin." Then he explained how Betsy and Earl were going to lose their farm and planned to move in with Earl's parents.

Daniel nodded slowly as he fingered his blond beard. "So you've decided to break your promise to Lindsay instead of trying to find another way." His words were gentle, but their meaning punched Matthew in the stomach. What Daniel cared about most was his niece. But Matthew didn't want to talk about Lindsay. It was too painful.

"I looked into different options, and nothing has panned out." He leaned back in the chair, looked out into the shop and then back at Daniel. "Even with this job, I can't afford to buy land and build another *haus*. I was turned down for a loan at two banks. I don't want to go to Western Pennsylvania with Earl and

Betsy. Besides, it's time for me to be on my own. I'm almost twenty-one. I gave most of my money to *mei schweschder* to help her and her family start a new life. This seems to be the best option for me."

"The best option for *you*." Daniel pursed his lips, studied Matthew for a few moments, and then leaned forward on the desk. "Tell me why you didn't ask me for help."

Matthew paused and stared down at the floor, feeling both regret and discomfort. "I didn't feel right asking you for help."

"Why?"

He met Daniel's curious stare. "Because you're Lindsay's guardian. I was embarrassed for you to know I can't take care of her like a husband should."

"We've all had hard times. This doesn't make you any less of a man." Daniel's expression was warm. "Do you really think you're the first young man who has had to change his plans? Rebecca and I were fortunate when we married because she had inherited her family's *haus*. We didn't have to build a home or struggle to buy land, but not everyone is that fortunate." He's expression grew grim. "Lindsay is devastated."

A lump swelled in Matthew's throat, and he fought to keep his emotions in check.

"Do you truly believe going to Ohio is the right choice?"

Matthew nodded. "*Ya*, I do. And I told Lindsay it's best if we break up since she'd be miserable there without her family. I don't want her to regret leaving here and then wind up resenting me."

"Would you stay if I offered you a loan?"

Matthew shook his head. "I can't take money from you."

"Why?" Daniel's eyebrows drew together. "You were considering taking a loan from a bank. I would be much more understanding than a bank if you fell on hard times and had to skip a payment."

"No, I couldn't. You're one of my bosses, and you're Lindsay's guardian. It's not right."

"So you think it's better to run away instead of staying and finding a solution to your problem?"

"I'm not running away. I'm obviously not prepared for the responsibilities of a family, and it's not fair for Lindsay to have to wait around until I make something of myself."

"You've already made something of yourself." Daniel gestured around the shop. "You have a *gut* job here, and you're a talented carpenter."

"It's more than that." Matthew took a deep breath. "I feel it's God's will. When I called my cousin and asked him if there was a job available at the factory, he told me there was. Everything is falling into place, so I believe it's meant to be. I need to move on. It's going to be difficult to build a life without Lindsay, and I know she's hurting too. But she'll find someone else who can take care of her and give her what she needs. I'm not that man."

Daniel leaned back in the chair as he again studied Matthew. "I think we sometimes misunderstand God's will. Rebecca and I waited many years for a *boppli*. I was certain it was God's will that we would never have *kinner*. It was tough for me to accept, but I was convinced there was a higher purpose. And then Rebecca had Daniel Junior. Soon after that, we had Emma and then Gracie. I had convinced myself it was God's will for us to be without *kinner*, but I was wrong."

He pointed at Matthew. "You've convinced yourself it's God's will to leave Lindsay, your *freinden*, your job, and your community to start a new life in Ohio. What if that's not God's will? What if it's God's will for you to find a way to stay and build a life and a family with Lindsay?"

Matthew swallowed, but then shook his head. Daniel was wrong. He had to be wrong. "I disagree."

"You should reconsider before you make a mistake that will haunt you the rest of your life. You're a *gut* man. As I told you when you asked for my permission to marry Lindsay, Rebecca and I think the world of you. We'd be devastated to see you go." He paused. "And Lindsay is beside herself. She's completely heartbroken. I imagine you are, too, but you're not going to admit it to me."

Matthew stood and moved to the doorway. "My mind is made up. Friday will be my last day."

"I hope you'll change your mind."

"*Danki* for this talk." Matthew rested his hand on the doorway. "I appreciate all you've done for me since I came to work here. You've been like a *dat* to me. I'll have all my projects done and my workstation cleaned up by the end of day on Friday." He turned to head into the shop.

"Matthew!" Daniel called after him. "Sometimes God's will isn't as clear to us as you think!"

Matthew balled his hands into tight fists as he walked to his workstation. Swallowing back overwhelming guilt and frustration, he set to work.

· · ·

Jake approached him later that morning. "Matt, I'm really sorry about Saturday night. I shouldn't have told Katie anything, but I was so upset . . . She noticed and I have a hard time keeping things from her. But it wasn't my place to share anything about what was going on with your *schweschder*'s family, especially after I promised you I wouldn't. I hope you can forgive me."

"It's fine." Matthew picked up a bottle of water from his workbench. "I should have told Lindsay sooner. And I had to tell her what I've decided to do."

"Have you changed your mind about going to Ohio?" Jake looked hopeful.

Matthew shook his head. "No. It's all set. My last day here will be Friday." He pointed to the nightstand he'd been sanding. "I should have this done, but if not, you can finish it and keep the money."

Jake's expression darkened. "I don't want your money. I want you to stay. You have to know you're making a huge mistake."

"My mind is made up." Matthew took a long drink from the bottle. "I need to get back to work." Then he returned to his sanding, trying to convince himself there was no doubt about his making the right decision. When no one else seemed to think he had, it was difficult to stand his ground. Perhaps they just didn't understand what God had been trying to tell him—the truth that went beyond current circumstances.

He loved Lindsay with all his heart, but he'd had no business asking her to marry him.

. . .

"I have an interview with an accounting firm in Philadelphia." Jessica smiled and cradled her cup of tea in her hands.

Lindsay gasped as she grabbed her sister's arm. "Really? You might move to Pennsylvania? You'd be so close to us!"

Jessica nodded. "I'd be only about ninety minutes away."

"Oh, Jessica! This is so exciting!" *Aenti* Rebecca clapped her hands. "You've decided against going back to New York City, then?"

"Yeah." Jessica shrugged as if it weren't a big deal, but her smile told them otherwise. "I realized I want to be closer to my family." She nodded toward Gracie, who gazed around the room while sitting in her swing. "How could I not be close to my adorable cousins?" Then she looked at Lindsay. "And my sister, of course."

Lindsay grinned. "Oh, this is the best news. When were you going to tell me?"

"Like I told you, I was hoping to come next weekend, and I was going to tell you then. I've just been working out the details." Jessica's smile faded. "But how are you doing this morning?"

Lindsay stared down at her cup. "I don't know. I

keep hoping Matthew will show up and tell me he's changed his mind. I can't believe it's Monday morning and I haven't heard from him. I still don't understand how he could just give up on us so easily." She looked across the table at her aunt. "Should I go see him?"

Aenti Rebecca tapped the table. "No, let him come to you."

"But what if he doesn't?" Lindsay could hear her own voice shaking. "What if he really does leave for Ohio without another word?"

"Give him time to think things through. Remember what I told you about how Daniel and Matthew are similar. They have to process concerns on their own." *Aenti* Rebecca reached across the table and squeezed her hand. "Daniel is going to talk to him today. He went to work early to try to catch him alone. Matthew has a lot of respect for Daniel, so maybe Daniel can get through to him."

"She's right, Linds," Jessica chimed in. "Give Uncle Daniel a chance to talk to him, man-to-man."

Lindsay nodded, but an overwhelming sense of trepidation gripped her.

"I'm so glad you were able to take today and tomorrow off from the bakery," Jessica said. "That means we have two days together before I have to go back to school for that one last final. So what are we going to do today?" Jessica's excitement sounded forced, as if she were trying to redirect Lindsay's mood. "Why don't we go shopping?"

"That's a *gut* idea," *Aenti* Rebecca said. "I need to get some fabric to make a couple of new dresses for Emma."

As her aunt and sister planned the day, Lindsay sent up a silent prayer to God, begging him to bring Matthew back to her. She didn't know where she truly belonged without him.

. . .

Lindsay was setting a pot roast on the table when *Onkel* Daniel entered the kitchen that evening. Anticipating news of how his conversation went with Matthew, she held her breath as he greeted her, Jessica, and his children. Then he kissed *Aenti* Rebecca's cheek.

"How was your day?" her aunt asked him as he washed his hands at the sink.

"It was *gut*." He turned, leaned back against the counter, and dried his hands with a paper towel. "How was yours?"

"*Gut*." *Aenti* Rebecca strapped Emma into her booster seat while Jessica settled Junior in his chair. "We went shopping, and I bought some groceries and fabric for sewing."

"That's great." *Onkel* Daniel took his seat at the head of the table, taking a moment to smile at Gracie who was cradled in a high chair.

Lindsay set a bowl of mashed potatoes on the table as Jessica filled their glasses with water. Then they all sat down for the silent prayer. When *Onkel* Daniel shifted in his seat and they knew the prayer time was over, the adults helped the children with their food and then filled their own plates.

Lindsay cut up her pot roast and worried her lower

lip as questions surged through her mind. When was *Onkel* Daniel going to share the results of his conversation with Matthew? Perhaps the conversation didn't go well and he wanted to wait until they were alone before he told her. But she was certain the anticipation was going to be the death of her if he didn't tell her soon!

After several minutes, she couldn't wait any longer. She had to know, whether it was good news or not.

"*Onkel* Daniel," she began, her nerves almost getting the best of her, "did you talk to Matthew today?"

"*Ya*, I did." His expression grew grim as he set his fork down on his plate.

Lindsay swallowed a ragged breath as tears began to form.

"I tried to reason with him, but his mind is already made up. He says his last day of work is Friday and he's going to Ohio on Saturday." He shook his head. "I'm sorry. But it's only Monday. At least I have the rest of the week to try to change his mind."

"*Danki.*" Lindsay sat back in her chair as disappointment and sorrow clamped around her chest like a vise. She stared down at her plate and fought back the tears that threatened to fall.

"Don't give up hope," Jessica whispered as their aunt and uncle turned their attention to the children. "Uncle Daniel will get through to him, but it might take him a few days."

Lindsay crumpled her napkin. "I hope you're right."

. . .

"I wish you didn't have to go." Lindsay hugged Jessica Wednesday morning as they stood in the kitchen at the bakery. "This visit was too short."

"I know." Jessica held her tight. "But I promise I'll be back after graduation."

"I wish you'd let me come to the ceremony." Lindsay released her from the hug.

"Oh, don't worry about it." Jessica waved off the suggestion. "I don't need a big celebration. I just want to get my diploma and get on with my life."

"I'm proud of you." Lindsay touched her shoulder. "You went after your degree and got it."

"Thanks." Jessica shrugged. "Now I just need to get that accounting job in Philadelphia so we can see each other often."

Elizabeth Kauffman pulled Jessica in for a hug. "It was so *gut* seeing you, Jessica!"

The rest of their aunts and cousins also gathered around Jessica and gave her hugs before Lindsay walked her outside. After one last hug, Lindsay waved as her sister drove away from the bakery.

"I'm sorry about Saturday night."

Lindsay spun toward Katie. "I didn't know you were standing there."

"I didn't mean to cause problems. I hope you'll forgive me." Katie's lower lip trembled. "I honestly thought you knew, and I—"

"It's okay." Lindsay touched her arm. "You're *mei* best *freind,* and I could never be angry with you for long. I was just upset."

"Have you talked to Matthew since Saturday night?"

Lindsay shook her head. "*Onkel* Daniel tried to talk to him on Monday, but Matthew still insists he's leaving this Friday. *Onkel* Daniel is going to try again, but it sounds like his mind is made up."

"Jake has tried too." Katie frowned. "I don't understand why he won't stay and try to work it out, but Jake said he was serious."

"I know." Lindsay pointed toward the bakery. "We should go back inside and get to work." As she walked past her cousin, Katie grabbed her arm.

"Don't give up on him." The conviction in Katie's blue eyes seemed fierce. "He loves you, and he's going to realize leaving you would be the worst mistake he could make. You have to believe he won't get on that bus."

"I'm trying." Lindsay forced a smile, but the ache in her heart only worsened.

CHAPTER SEVEN

"Sherm, this is Matt again," Matthew said in his voice mail Friday night. "I just want to confirm plans. I bought my bus ticket today, and I'm leaving in the morning." He recited his itinerary. "I sold my horse and buggy to one of my *freinden*, so I'll have money to give you for rent." He paused. "I'll see you tomorrow evening. *Danki* again for the job. Good-bye."

After hanging up, Matthew stepped out of the phone shanty and looked toward the far end of the pasture. His half-built house stood staring at him like a cruel, painful reminder of all the broken dreams he would leave behind in Bird-in-Hand.

This afternoon Daniel and Jake each begged him to stay, reminding him of how much Lindsay loved him and how much the community needed him. Daniel again offered him a loan, but Matthew refused it, insisting it was God's will for him to go to Sugarcreek.

He felt as if he had a hole in his heart as he again remembered the hurt in Lindsay's eyes when he broke up with her last week. He longed to go see her and say good-bye, but he knew he would never leave if he saw her one more time. Pushing the painful thoughts away, he headed into the house.

When he reached the kitchen, he found his sister and nieces already packing some of their dishes. He gave them a curt nod before rushing up to his room and closing the door. He surveyed the space, which looked bare now that the tops of his dresser and nightstand had been swept clean. Next to his bed sat two boxes of books he planned to leave behind for Suzanne and Ella.

He opened his dresser, pulled out socks, and dropped them into his duffel bag. Next he opened the drawer with his shirts and set them in the bag. When he removed the last shirt, he found an envelope and opened it. Inside was the card Lindsay gave him on Valentine's Day. He opened it and read her pretty handwriting.

Dear Matthew,

Happy Valentine's Day! While this day is special because we have each other, it's also special because it's our last Valentine's Day as boyfriend and girlfriend. Just think—next Valentine's Day we'll be married, and we'll be living in our very own *haus*.

I'm so very thankful God brought you into my life. You're the kindest and most generous man I know. I'm so grateful you picked me to be your girlfriend and next your *fraa*! In only nine months we'll be married, and we'll start a new life together. We have so much to look forward to.

Danki for believing in me and for loving me. I'll love you forever!

Always,
Lindsay

Tears burned as he read her note over and over. He stepped to his bed and sank down onto a corner as memories stormed his mind: The first time he met Lindsay, at a Kauffman family gathering. The time they sat together at a youth gathering and he made her a dandelion necklace. Their late-night talks on her uncle's porch. The letters they wrote to each other when she was in Virginia Beach helping her parents' friends. A tear trickled down his cheek.

How could he possibly walk away from Lindsay and allow someone else to snatch her up and marry her? She was the love of his life. She was his future.

"I can't do this, God," he whispered as he wiped the tear away. "I can't leave Lindsay. And I don't believe now you want me to, not with so much love in my heart for her. Have I misunderstood your will, just as Daniel thought? Please forgive me for stubbornly refusing to listen to those you've placed in my life to counsel me. But I'm still not sure what to do. You know my heart, God. Help me, please."

After a few more minutes in prayer, Matthew set the card on his dresser and jolted down the stairs to find his sister. When he almost ran into the kitchen, Betsy spun from the sink and faced him, startled.

"*Was iss letz?*" She took a step toward him. "Have you been crying?"

"*Ya.*" He cupped his hand to the back of his neck, his breath coming in spurts. "I've been so confused."

Betsy turned to his nieces, who stared up at him with confused expressions. "I'll finish the dishes, *maed.* Would you please go get your baths?"

They nodded and then slipped past Matthew and up the stairs.

Betsy pointed to a kitchen chair. "Sit down and talk to me."

Matthew slumped into the chair and placed both hands on top of his head.

"What's going on?"

"I thought I could leave Lindsay, but I can't do it. It rips me to shreds to think of her with someone else as her husband. God just showed me I love her too much to just walk away." He stared down at the table-top and ran his fingers over the wood grain. "I can't leave Lindsay, but I can't provide for her the way she deserves." He paused. "The truth is I'm afraid I'm too much like *Dat*."

"Oh, Matthew, you're nothing like *Dat*. You just gave us all your money to help with our new start. *Dat* walked away and left us nothing. We survived only because our *onkels* helped pay the bills until you and *Mamm* moved here."

He shook his head while keeping his gaze focused on the table. "It's my responsibility to care for my family. I can't promise to support Lindsay if we have an uncertain future, can I? I don't know what to do."

"Did you ever think that by walking away from Lindsay you're following in *Dat*'s footsteps?"

His gaze snapped to hers. "What did you say?"

She sighed. "Matt, you're so worried about the future that you're ignoring the present. You don't see what's in front of you. You and Lindsay love each other and you have your whole life ahead of you. You don't need to know all the answers right now. What you need is a solid foundation of love, trust, and honesty on which to build your marriage. You have that. Everything else will fall into place because the Lord will provide for you."

He stared at Betsy as her words sank in.

She gestured around the kitchen. "Earl and I weren't expecting to lose our farm, but we're going to get through this together because we love each other and believe in our marriage. We know God will take care of us. You should rely on God and have faith in Lindsay. That's all you really need."

Matthew nodded as the answer came through loud and clear. With God's help, he and Lindsay could make their life and their marriage work—if she still believed in him and would forgive him.

"I need to go talk to her." He stood. *"Danki."*

Betsy smiled. *"Gern gschehne."*

Matthew rushed outside just as Earl was stepping out of the barn.

"Earl! Could I please borrow your horse and buggy?"

Earl blinked and then nodded. *"Ya,* of course."

"Danki!" Matthew rushed into the barn, praying he wasn't too late.

. . .

Lindsay was setting a clean dish in the cabinet when she heard a knock on the back door. She was afraid to hope it could be Matthew. "Who could that be?"

Aenti Rebecca nodded toward the door. "Go and see."

Lindsay dropped her dish towel on the counter and

hurried through the mudroom. When she pulled open the back door, she gasped. Matthew stood on the porch with his hat in his hand.

"Lindsay." He twirled the hat, looking uncertain. "Could I please talk to you?"

"*Ya*, of course." She slipped her hand into her apron pocket to run her fingers over the wooden heart he'd given her. She'd kept it in her pocket all week, hoping it would give her strength as she faced losing him, perhaps forever.

He pointed toward the glider on the porch. "Would you sit with me?"

She stepped outside, sat down, and held her breath while fighting back tears. *Please don't tell me good-bye! Please stay!*

"I was packing my things and came across the card you gave me for Valentine's Day." His eyes seemed to plead with her as he sat down beside her. "Do you remember what you wrote in that card?"

"*Ya*. I said something about how it was our last Valentine's Day as boyfriend and girlfriend and next Valentine's Day we would be married."

"Right." He took her hands in his as his face clouded with what looked like despair. "I have a bus ticket for Sugarcreek tomorrow, and I sold my horse and buggy. My things are almost all packed, but I have a problem."

"What's that?" She blinked back tears.

"I don't know how to leave you, but I also don't know how to stay." His voice trembled.

"I don't understand."

"I love you, Lindsay." His eyes searched hers as if

they held all the answers he needed. "Before I came over, God helped me see how my love for you means everything and I might have been misunderstanding what his will is for my life and yours. And then I talked to *mei schweschder*. I told her I don't see how I can stay and take care of you the way a man should take care of his *fraa*. But she believes with God's help we can have a future even if it's uncertain. Do you think that's true? Tell me how I can make this work."

"I don't know what you want me to say," she whispered. "I don't want to lose you. I don't care where we live as long as we have each other, and I do believe God will provide."

She pulled the wooden heart out of her pocket and handed it to him. "You once told me to take care of your heart for you, and that's what I want to do—if you'll let me."

He held up the heart as a soft noise escaped his throat. He shook his head. "I can't believe you still carry this. Not after—"

"Excuse me."

Lindsay's head spun toward *Onkel* Daniel's voice. He was standing at the bottom of the porch steps.

"Daniel." Matthew popped up from the glider and slipped the heart into his pocket. "I didn't see you there."

"I wasn't trying to eavesdrop, but I overheard your conversation." He climbed the steps. "I have a proposition for you. Would you like to talk now?"

"*Ya*, of course." Matthew nodded at *Onkel* Daniel, and his expression brightened slightly. "What do you want to discuss?"

Onkel Daniel came to stand beside Matthew. "You're like a *sohn* to me. You know that, right?"

Matthew nodded. "*Ya.* You've always been like a *dat* to me, the *dat* I never had."

"Well, we don't abandon our families, do we?"

Matthew shook his head.

"Isn't that why you gave Betsy and her family your money?"

"*Ya*, it is." Matthew cleared his throat. "I wanted to help them."

Onkel Daniel leaned back against the porch railing and crossed his arms over his chest. "Exactly, and I'd like to help you. I want you to stay with us." He pointed toward the house. "We have an extra bedroom Rebecca uses as a sewing room. We can make that into your bedroom and move the sewing supplies into a corner of our *schtupp*. What do you say?"

Lindsay cupped her hand over her mouth and swallowed a gasp as she experienced a flood of appreciation.

Matthew stared at her uncle.

"Well, Matthew? What do you think?" *Onkel* Daniel asked. "You and Lindsay can still get married." He pointed to the floor of the porch. "You can save money and build a life right here. Does that sound *gut*?"

"*Ya, ya*, of course," Matthew finally said, his head bobbing up and down.

"*Gut*." *Onkel* Daniel shook his head. "It's settled, then. You'll stay here in Bird-in-Hand with us."

"Wait." Matthew held up his hands. "I want to pay you rent while I live here."

Onkel Daniel frowned. "We can talk about that

later." He turned toward Lindsay. "I'll let you two visit." Then he winked at her before heading into the house.

As soon as the door clicked shut, Lindsay jumped up from the glider. "So you'll stay?"

"*Ya*." Matthew's smile was wide. "I will."

"And you'll let *Onkel* Daniel make a room for you here?" She stood in front of him, sure he could see new hope in her eyes.

"*Ya*, I will." He rested his hand on her shoulder. "Will you forgive me and still marry me?"

"Of course I will." She gazed up at him and happiness warmed her soul. "I never stopped loving you."

He leaned down, and her breath hitched. He brushed his lips across hers, sending her stomach into a wild swirl. She closed her eyes, savoring the sweet taste of his mouth against hers.

When they parted, Matthew's look was intense. "You're my first and only love, Lindsay. I'm sorry for hurting you, and I'll do my best to never hurt you again."

As he pulled her close, Lindsay silently thanked God for sending Matthew back to her. Only in his arms did she feel truly at home.

EPILOGUE

Lindsay was filled with happiness as she stood beside Matthew outside *Onkel* Daniel's barn. She shivered in the November air as she threaded the fingers of one hand with her husband's. The day had finally come—they were married! She was now Lindsay Glick, and her life couldn't be more perfect.

The past six months had flown by at lightning speed. When Earl and Betsy left with their daughters for Western Pennsylvania at the end of May, Matthew moved in with Lindsay and her family. *Onkel* Daniel had kept his promise and turned the sewing room into a bedroom for him. She and Matthew had been saving their money and hoped to someday soon either start building a house of their own or add on to *Onkel* Daniel's house.

Lindsay glanced toward the back porch and smiled when she spotted Jessica talking with their cousins and Jessica's boyfriend, Kevin. Jessica won the job at the accounting firm in Philadelphia and soon after had met and started dating Kevin. Lindsay was thrilled to have her sister living close by so they could visit on weekends.

"Congratulations," *Onkel* Daniel said as he and *Aenti* Rebecca sidled up to them.

"*Danki*," Lindsay said as she squeezed Matthew's hand.

Matthew nodded. "*Ya, danki.*"

"We haven't had a chance to give you our wedding gift yet." *Aenti* Rebecca smiled at *Onkel* Daniel.

"You're right." *Onkel* Daniel grinned back at her. "I think now is the perfect time." He turned to Lindsay and Matthew again. "Becky and I would like to give you ten acres." He nodded toward the pasture behind them. "And we'd like to help you build a *haus.*"

Lindsay gasped, and she couldn't stop the tears as she looked at her new husband. He seemed stunned.

"Are you sure?" Matthew looked at *Aenti* Rebecca, then again at *Onkel* Daniel.

"Of course we are." Daniel shook Matthew's hand. "We're family, and we want to help you."

"*Danki.*" Matthew's voice shook with emotion.

"*Gern gschehne.*"

Lindsay hugged her aunt. "*Danki* for everything."

"I'm so *froh* for you," *Aenti* Rebecca whispered in her ear. Then she turned to *Onkel* Daniel. "We should check on the *kinner.*" She took hold of his hand and they walked toward the house.

"We're going to have a *haus!*" Lindsay exclaimed as the couple walked away. "What a *wunderbaar* gift."

"I know." Matthew took a deep breath as his golden-brown eyes glistened in the light of a nearby lantern. "I'm so sorry I almost left you. All that matters is we have each other and our family. Building a *haus* may take time, but that's okay. This is the path God wanted for me all along, and I'm so very grateful—to him and for you."

"I'm grateful too. Everything is working out the way God intended. We have each other and our family, and everything else will fall into place." Her pulse sped up as she looked up into his eyes. "I knew it was all going to be okay after you agreed to live with us."

He raised an eyebrow. "You never had any doubts?"

"No, none at all." She touched his elbow. "That's because I never lost faith in you or in us. *Mei aenti*, Jessica, and Katie told me not to lose faith, and I held their words close to my heart."

"Hold out your hand." He pulled something out of his pocket.

She turned her hand palm up, and when he dropped the wooden heart into it, she said, "I gave this to you the night you decided to stay."

"I kept it because I wanted to give it back to you on our wedding day. Will you still take care of my heart?"

"I'll guard it with my life." She ran her fingers over the smooth wood and then dropped it into the pocket of her apron.

Matthew ran his finger down her cheek. "*Danki*. I will do my best to take *gut* care of you."

"I know you will." She squeezed his hand.

As Matthew leaned down to kiss her cheek, Lindsay closed her eyes and silently thanked God for her husband—and for giving her a home of her own.

Discussion Questions

1. Matthew is devastated when he learns his sister and her husband are going to lose their farm and he'll lose his house. Think of a time when you felt lost and alone. Where did you find your strength? What Bible verses helped you? Share this with the group.

2. Daniel helps Matthew decide to stay by offering to give him a room in his house. Why do you think Daniel felt compelled to open his house up to Matthew?

3. Lindsay feels God is giving her a second chance when Matthew decides to stay. Have you ever experienced a second chance? What was it?

4. Which character can you identify with the most? Which character seemed to carry the most emotional stake in the story? Was it Lindsay, Matthew, or someone else?

5. Betsy and Earl believed they were shielding Matthew from hurt when they kept the truth about their financial problems from him, but it's still painful when Matthew finds out. Do you think Betsy and Earl's decision to withhold that information was

justified? Have you ever found yourself in a similar situation? If so, how did it turn out? Share this with the group.

6.   When Lindsay and Matthew break up, she turns to her older sister for solace. Does someone in your life help you through difficult times? How does this person help you?

7.   By the end of the story, Matthew realizes he can't leave Lindsay or Bird-in-Hand. What do you believe made Matthew change his mind? Share this with the group.

Acknowledgments

As always, I'm grateful for my loving family, including my mother, Lola Goebelbecker; my husband, Joe; and my sons, Zac and Matt. I'm blessed to have such an awesome and amazing family that tolerates my moods when I'm stressed out on a book deadline.

Special thanks to my mother and my dear friend Becky Biddy, who graciously proofread the draft and corrected my hilarious typos. Becky—thank you also for your daily notes of encouragement. Your friendship is a blessing!

I'm also grateful for my special Amish friend who patiently answers my endless stream of questions. You're a blessing in my life.

Thank you to my wonderful church family at Morning Star Lutheran in Matthews, North Carolina, for your encouragement, prayers, love, and friendship. You all mean so much to my family and me.

Thank you to Zac Weikal and the fabulous members of my Bakery Bunch! I'm so grateful for your friendship and your excitement about my books. You all are amazing!

To my agent, Natasha Kern—I can't thank you enough for your guidance, advice, and friendship. You are a tremendous blessing in my life.

Thank you to my amazing editor, Becky Monds, for your friendship and guidance. I'm grateful to each and every person at HarperCollins Christian Publishing who helped make this book a reality. I'm grateful to editor Jean Bloom, who helped me polish and refine the story. Jean, you are a master at connecting the dots and filling in the gaps. I'm so happy we can continue to work together!

Thank you most of all to God—for giving me the inspiration and the words to glorify You. I'm grateful and humbled You've chosen this path for me.

LOVE AND BUGGY RIDES

*For Eric Goebelbecker, the coolest
big brother on the planet.*

GLOSSARY

ach—oh
aenti—aunt
appeditlich—delicious
bedauerlich—sad
boppli—baby
bruder—brother
bu / buwe—boy / boys
daadi—granddad
daadihaus—grandparents' house
daed—dad
danki—thank you
dat—dad
dochder—daughter
Englisher—a non-Amish person
fraa—wife
freind / freinden—friend(s)
froh—happy
gern gschehne—you're welcome
gude mariye—good morning
gut—good
gut nacht—good night
haus—house
Ich liebe dich—I love you
kaffi—coffee

kapp—prayer covering or cap
kichli / kichlin—cookie(s)
kind—child
kinner—children
liewe—love, a term of endearment
maed—young women, girls
maedel—young woman, girl
mamm—mom
mammi—grandma
mei—my
naerfich—nervous
onkel—uncle
schee—pretty
schweschder—sister
Was iss letz?—What's wrong?
Wie geht's—How do you do? or Good day!
wunderbaar—wonderful
ya—yes

Amish Heirloom Family Trees

Timothy m. Sylvia Lantz

Samuel (m. Mandy)   Marie   Janie

Samuel m. Mandy Lantz

Becky

Martha "Mattie" m. Leroy Fisher

Veronica   Rachel   Emily

Vera (deceased) m. Raymond Lantz (deceased)

Michael ("Mike") (mother—Esther—deceased)   John

CHAPTER ONE

Janie Lantz sank down onto a wooden picnic table bench at the far end of the parking lot, next to Old Philadelphia Pike. The fresh, cool September breeze held a hint of the autumn weather on its way to Lancaster County as she opened her lunch bag and unwrapped her turkey sandwich. Before taking a bite, she glanced back at the Lancaster Buggy Rides and Souvenirs shop. Rows of pumpkins lined up in front of the store, and orange-and-brown wreaths hung on the door and windows.

So far her first day as a cashier at the shop had gone well. But though she enjoyed talking with the tourists, her aching feet made her thankful for the opportunity to sit down while she enjoyed her lunch.

The *clip-clop* of hooves drew her attention to the highway. She recognized the long gray buggy full of tourists as one of the buggies her boss owned. Throughout the day, the buggies took tourists on rides around the Bird-in-Hand area. She hadn't met the three buggy drivers yet, but she'd seen the Amish men from a distance earlier in the day when they were standing by the stable next to the store.

Janie took a bite of her sandwich and watched the driver start to guide the buggy into the driveway leading to the parking lot.

Suddenly a silver sedan sped up behind the buggy. The car's driver appeared to be looking down at something in his hand—just before he looked up and hit his brakes.

Then, almost as if in slow motion, the car slammed into the back side of the buggy, shattering the right rear wheel and causing the buggy to teeter. The buggy shifted awkwardly and then fell on the right rear corner, sending the driver and a few passengers on that side tumbling onto the ground. The car behind the buggy had come to a stop.

Janie gasped in horror as she jumped up from the bench, dropping her sandwich and knocking over her bottle of water. She rushed across the parking lot to the store's main entrance, reaching the door just as two customers were coming out.

"Excuse me!" Janie yelled. "Do you have a cell phone?"

One of the women nodded as she stared at Janie with confusion on her face.

"Would you please call nine-one-one? There's been an accident." Janie pointed toward the driveway, and both women turned, taking in the scene.

The woman who had nodded pulled out her phone and started punching in the numbers.

Janie burst through the front door and spotted her boss, Craig Warner, talking to her coworker, Eva, near the cash register in the center of the large store.

Janie ran to them, beckoning for Craig to follow her.

"Craig! Craig! You need to come quickly! A car hit one of our buggies while it was turning into the driveway. It just happened. I'm sure people are hurt."

"Eva, call nine-one-one," Craig instructed as he started walking. "Tell Bianca to find the first-aid kit and get the ice packs from the freezer."

"Okay." Eva's brown eyes widened as she nodded and grabbed the store phone to make the call.

Craig hustled toward the door and Janie trailed behind him. "I asked a customer to call nine-one-one too."

"That was a good idea."

In his midforties, Craig was tall and fit. Janie was nearly jogging to keep up with his long strides. She knew his brown eyes, which matched his hair and goatee, had to be filled with worry for his driver and customers.

Once outside, Craig groaned as the accident came into view. "Oh no. This is much worse than I hoped."

A shiver raced up Janie's spine as she took in the scene playing out in the driveway and parking lot. A crowd had gathered around the broken buggy and car, which had a smashed front bumper and headlights. Sirens already blared in the distance, announcing the approach of first responders.

Craig rushed over to the buggy and joined someone helping an older woman sitting on the ground with a bloody gash on her forehead. A middle-aged man and woman sat on the ground as well, looking bewildered as the customer who had called nine-one-one for Janie knelt beside them. One young man was already helping

some of the passengers to nearby benches. The horse
looked spooked, but not injured, and two men were
doing their best to soothe it.

The driver of the car still sat behind the wheel,
looking stunned as a man leaned in, no doubt asking
if he was all right. She guessed the driver was around
nineteen.

At first glance, Janie thought most of the passengers' injuries seemed to be minor, but no one could be
sure until EMTs arrived. As Janie wrung her hands,
wondering what else she could do to help until then,
she turned and nearly walked right into a man who
towered over her by several inches. She immediately
recognized him as one of the buggy drivers she'd seen
that morning.

He was helping the remaining two passengers climb
out of the buggy, but Janie could see he was favoring his
left arm. Blood seeped from a cut on his head as well,
streaming down the side of his face, a stark contrast to
his paled face and dark brown hair.

"Take your time," he told a woman as she climbed
down to the ground. He grasped her arm with his right
hand and grimaced as she leaned on him.

Once the woman was safely out, he swayed slightly,
closing his eyes for a moment as if trying to regain his
balance.

Janie came closer. "Are you all right?"

He gave her a brief sideways glance. "*Ya*, I'll be fine."

"Your head is really bleeding," Janie warned. "I think
you need to sit down."

"I'm okay," he insisted before turning toward the

last passenger. "Give me your hand, and I'll help you down."

When the woman hesitated, he offered her a shaky smile. He was clearly trying to ignore his injuries. He swayed again, and Janie held up her hand to grab him. But then she stopped, not wanting to appear forward.

"I won't let you fall," he promised his passenger. "We need to get you out of this buggy before the other back wheel collapses."

The woman took his hand, and again he grimaced as he helped her down. He let a young man who had been leading the passengers to the benches take over, then placed a shaky hand on the side of the buggy for support as the blood continued to trickle down his cheek and drip onto his gray shirt.

"Please listen to me," Janie pleaded, her voice thick with worry. "You need medical attention. Look." She pointed at the red spots dotting his shirt.

He glanced down at his chest and then met her gaze. His eyes were honey brown. "I'll be okay. I need to take care of my passengers."

"I don't think you should—" Before Janie could finish, the man took a step and then staggered. Janie grabbed his arm, steadying him. "Lean on me, and I'll get you to that picnic table over there," she instructed, nodding toward the table where she'd been eating lunch. "I'm Janie Lantz. This is my first day working here."

"Jonathan Stoltzfus."

The man followed her instructions, and she slowly led him to the picnic table. He sank down onto the bench and slouched back against the table.

"*Danki*," he muttered, squeezing the bridge of his nose. "I don't know what happened."

"You need medical attention," she repeated, taking a clean handkerchief from her apron pocket. "Now, sit here before you fall and hurt yourself worse, and press this against that cut to stop the bleeding."

Before Jonathan could take the handkerchief, Craig rushed over. "Jonathan! What happened?"

"I'm not sure." Jonathan shook his head and rubbed his left arm. "I thought I signaled before I turned into the driveway, but the driver hit us out of nowhere."

"Janie, Jonathan needs a bandage for his head," Craig said. "Would you please go find Bianca?"

"*Ya.*" Janie turned to Jonathan and handed him the handkerchief. "Wait for me here, okay?"

"I can't just sit here." Jonathan shook his head. "I need to take care of my passengers."

"I'll check on everyone," Craig promised. "And the EMTs should be here any minute. Let Janie take care of you."

Jonathan hesitated, then blew out a deep sigh. "All right."

Janie touched Jonathan's shoulder. "I'll be right back."

The sirens became deafeningly loud as two ambulances, a state police cruiser, and a fire engine steered into the parking lot. The firemen and EMTs began assisting the injured passengers, and the two state policemen approached the driver of the car.

Janie saw Bianca rushing toward the chaos, her auburn ponytail bouncing behind her. Janie raced over to her.

"Bianca, Jonathan fell out of the buggy and has a gash on his head. We need some supplies for him."

"Sure. Take what you need while I distribute these ice packs. Just leave my kit on that bench there."

Janie gathered an alcohol wipe, antibiotic ointment, gauze pads, and a large bandage. When she returned to the picnic table, Jonathan looked up at her. His bright brown eyes stunned her. She'd never before seen eyes that resembled the honey she purchased at the Bird-in-Hand Farmers' Market.

"Let me look at that wound," she said, taking away the bloodied handkerchief and examining Jonathan's forehead. "I'm going to clean it with alcohol and then put on some ointment and a bandage. Are you allergic to antibiotic ointment?"

Jonathan gave her a blank look. "I don't think so. Are you a nurse or something?"

She looked incredulous. "No, of course I'm not a nurse, but I helped take care of *mei onkel* Raymond until he passed away in the spring. He was weak from dialysis, and I took care of his wounds a few times when he fell." She cleaned the gash with the alcohol wipe, and he sucked in a breath. "I'm sorry."

"It's all right," he said softly, his eyes squeezed shut.

She cleaned the blood off his face, applied ointment to the wound, and covered it with the bandage.

"I did the best I could, and it doesn't look too bad despite so much blood. But you should still have a doctor look at it in case you need stitches," Janie said.

"Danki," he said, again softly, absently rubbing his left arm.

"Do you think your arm is broken?" she asked as she slipped the wrappers from the bandage, alcohol wipe, and ointment into her apron pocket.

Jonathan glanced down at his arm. "The impact threw me out of the buggy, and I landed on it. I don't think it's broken, but it hurts. It might be sprained."

"I saw you fall." She pointed at her abandoned lunch bag behind him. "I was sitting here eating lunch when it happened."

"You saw it?"

"*Ya.*"

"I thought I signaled before I started guiding the horse into the driveway. Did you happen to notice if I did?"

"You did." She nodded. "I saw your blinker." She started to tell him the driver wasn't paying attention when his face contorted with anguish.

"I can't believe it. I was so careful." He seemed to be talking to himself instead of to her.

Maybe she should wait to tell him the rest until after he had calmed down a little. Besides, she'd already confirmed he signaled his turn, and that alone made him completely innocent.

"Can I get you anything else?" Janie asked, stepping closer to him. "Do you want me to see if I can find some ice for your arm?"

"No, *danki.* I'll be fine." Jonathan glanced around the parking lot. "I hope everyone is all right. I thought it was safe when I slowed to turn. I never expected that car behind us to hit the buggy."

Janie sank down onto the bench beside him,

determined to ease his obvious distress. The man was shaking. "From what I saw, it wasn't your fault. You did signal before you turned." She pointed at his arm. "I really think you need to get your arm examined before you think much more about this." She spotted an EMT talking to one of the passengers nearby. "Do you want me to get an EMT to look at it?"

Jonathan shook his head again. "No, there are people who need help more than I do."

"Jonathan." Craig appeared in front of them. "One of the police officers would like to get your perspective on what happened. He's on his way over."

"Sure." Jonathan cleared his throat.

Janie stood. "I'll see if I can help anyone else." She stepped away and headed toward Bianca. She hoped she'd have a better opportunity to tell Jonathan and Craig what else she saw later.

. . .

Jonathan tried in vain to will his body to stop shaking, but he continued to tremble like a leaf caught in a windstorm. His arm throbbed, and the wound on his forehead stung. He took in the tumultuous scene around him and it all felt surreal. His passengers were receiving medical attention from a group of firefighters and EMTs. One of the passengers was lying on a stretcher, and others had bandages on their heads or arms.

His stomach pitched as trepidation seized him. How could he have allowed this to happen? How could he put his passengers' lives at risk?

Less than thirty minutes ago, he was enjoying giving another tour around the Bird-in-Hand area. For nearly a month, he'd been working as a buggy tour driver and relishing every minute of it.

He'd originally come to Bird-in-Hand for a short visit with his grandparents, but when Craig Warner, his grandparents' next-door neighbor, had offered him the job, Jonathan decided to stay through the end of November. He was not only making money to help his grandparents, but avoiding going home to Mechanicsville, Maryland, for a while longer.

"Jonathan?" A police officer—a balding, portly, middle-aged man with graying brown hair and dark eyes—broke through his thoughts. "Would you please state your full name?" Pen poised, he was ready to take notes.

"It's Jonathan Omar Stoltzfus," he said, then spelled his last name.

"What do you remember from before the crash?" the officer asked.

Jonathan ran his hand down his face. It was all a blur. Why couldn't he think straight?

"Just take your time," Craig said as he sat down next to Jonathan on the bench.

"We were coming back from the tour," Jonathan began, his voice shaky. "I thought I had signaled to turn into the parking lot. As I started to turn, I felt the jolt of the car hitting the right rear wheel, and then the back of the buggy collapsed and I was thrown to the ground. As soon as I got my bearings, I jumped up and started helping the passengers."

The officer was silent as he wrote frantically in his notebook, then asked his next question. "What is the route you take for the tour?"

Jonathan explained the route and the officer wrote that all down too.

"How long have you worked here?"

"Almost a month."

"Had you ever given buggy tours before you started working here?"

"No, but I'm a cautious driver. I always put my passengers' safety first."

The officer nodded and then fired off a few more questions.

"I'll be in touch," he said when he was finished. "I'm going to talk to a few of the passengers and find out what they saw." He pointed toward Jonathan's arm, the one he hadn't realized he was still rubbing. "You should get that looked at."

"He's right," Craig said as the officer left. "I want you to go to the hospital and get an X-ray. I'll get someone to drive you."

"Thanks." Jonathan glanced around the parking lot, and his eyes found Janie.

Jonathan studied her as she leaned down and said something to a man before placing an ice pack on his knee. Jonathan had never met an Amish girl with red hair before. Janie had been so attentive when she'd tended to his head wound. Craig mentioned last week that he had a new employee starting today, but Jonathan hadn't seen Janie until she approached him after the accident. Something about her intrigued him, but he pushed those thoughts away as Bianca came up to him and Craig.

"Jonathan, Janie told me you took a hard fall from the buggy. How are you?"

"I'm fine." Jonathan tried to shrug off his injuries even as his arm continued to throb.

"I think he should go to the hospital for an X-ray," Craig said. "I need to stay here. Would you take him?"

"Of course I will." Bianca's brow furrowed with concern. "You look like you're in a lot of pain, Jonathan. We should get going."

Jonathan followed Bianca to her SUV. As he walked past Janie, she gave him a concerned smile, and he nodded before climbing into the car.

. . .

Jonathan couldn't get the picture of the damaged buggy and injured passengers out of his mind. Later that evening, as he sat at the small kitchen table in his grandparents' modest two-bedroom cottage on his uncle's farm, the feeling of dread that had taken hold of him earlier that day continued to consume him. He kept wondering what he could've done to prevent the accident.

His tour had seemed so typical, but then it turned into a horrible nightmare. What had he done wrong? Janie said he signaled, but was she right? Witnessing the accident must have been upsetting for her, maybe enough to think she saw him signal when he hadn't.

He stared down at his plate filled with food, but his

stomach remained tied in knots. The thought of eating made him feel nauseated.

"You need to eat," *Mammi* said from the other side of the table. "You're much too skinny, Jonathan. Isn't your *mamm* feeding you enough?"

Jonathan shook his head. "I usually make my own meals now that I have my own *haus*."

Mammi blotted her mouth with a napkin. "Your *mamm* should cook for you since you don't have a *fraa*. I'll have to discuss that with her the next time I speak with her."

"*Mammi*, I'm going to be thirty in February," Jonathan gently reminded her. "I'm capable of cooking my meals."

"You're obviously not cooking enough," she grumbled as she scooped more mashed potatoes onto her own fork.

"Now, Mary," *Daadi* chimed in, "how is Jonathan going to find a *fraa* if he's fat?"

Jonathan nearly choked on his water. "I'm not planning on getting fat, and I've all but given up on finding a *fraa* to marry. At this point, I think I'm too old to date."

"If you're not dead yet, then you're not too old," *Daadi* said with a wink.

Jonathan smiled a little despite the guilt that had settled on his shoulders, tightening his already-sore muscles. He'd always enjoyed visiting his father's parents. It was a shame they lived nearly 160 miles away from his home in Maryland. Jonathan's parents met while his mother was in Pennsylvania visiting her cousins one summer, when they were both in their early twenties. After Jonathan's father married his mother, they moved to Maryland to live near her family. From the time he was a young child, Jonathan always looked forward to visiting his grandparents.

A knock on the back door startled him. Before either of his grandparents could stand, he jumped up and hustled to open the door. Craig was standing on the back porch.

"I'm sorry to bother you at suppertime. But I wanted to check on you."

"Come in." Jonathan opened the door wide and led him into the kitchen.

Craig greeted the older couple and then turned to Jonathan. "How are you feeling?"

"Sore, but I'm okay. I didn't need any stitches in my forehead, and I just have to ice my arm later. The doctor said it's a sprain, but it's really nothing." He wasn't exactly truthful. His arm hurt, but he was more worried about the tour group that had been in his buggy.

"Jonathan, could I talk to you outside for a minute?" Craig asked.

"Of course."

Craig said good-bye to Jonathan's grandparents, then stepped out onto the small porch as Jonathan followed him.

"How are all the passengers doing?" Jonathan held his breath, afraid of what Craig might say.

"They're doing all right." Craig nodded and rested his hand on one of the pillars that held up the porch roof. "One man suffered a minor concussion after hitting his head on one of the posts in the buggy. Another woman broke her arm, but the rest only have minor bumps, bruises, and cuts."

Jonathan nodded as more remorse plagued him. He should have prevented the accident . . . somehow.

"It could have been much worse." Craig sighed, and his look of concern for the passengers turned to . . . was it regret?

"Jonathan, I spoke to my lawyer, and he thinks it would be a good idea if we took you off driving duty for a while. Things may get messy if anyone in the tour group decides to sue us. The driver of the car insists you didn't signal. He will only admit to possibly following too closely, but he says he didn't have time to brake fast enough to avoid hitting the buggy."

He shook his head. "I have a difficult time believing you were careless, but when I spoke to the passengers, they all said they weren't paying attention to you. They were just enjoying the end of the ride." Craig sighed again. "Jonathan, I still want you to work for me, but I'd like you to work in the stable for a while until we get this cleared up. How do you feel about that?"

Jonathan rubbed his chin as disappointment mixed with guilt. He didn't want to give up his job as a buggy tour guide, but he understood Craig's reasons. "That's fine. I enjoy working with the horses."

"Great." Craig shook Jonathan's hand. "I'll see you tomorrow then?"

"*Ya*, I'll be there."

"Good night." Craig descended the porch steps and headed toward his large farmhouse next door.

Jonathan suddenly remembered something he'd wanted to ask his boss. "Craig!" he called, causing the man to turn and face him. "Did you pick up my straw hat by any chance? I lost it when I fell out of the buggy."

Craig shook his head. "I'm sorry, but I didn't see it."

"Well, maybe someone else picked it up, but I have a spare. Thanks." Jonathan stepped back into the kitchen and sat down at the table.

"What did Craig have to say?" *Daadi* asked as he cut up a piece of chicken on his plate.

"Did he have any more news about the tourists who were in the accident?" *Mammi* chimed in.

Jonathan shared what Craig had reported about the passengers.

"Thank the Lord their injuries weren't worse." *Mammi*'s eyes were sympathetic.

Jonathan ran his fingers over his glass of water. "Craig said he needs me to stop driving the buggies for a while. His lawyer thinks it would be a *gut* idea in case any of the passengers sue. He wants me to work in the stables."

"Oh." *Daadi* leaned back in his seat. "Did he say how long he needs you to work in the stables?"

Jonathan shook his head and his throat dried. "I just feel so terrible about the accident. I never meant to put those people in harm's way." He cleared his throat, fighting back his raw emotion. "Craig said the driver of the car insists I didn't signal before I started to turn into the driveway, but I thought I did. One of the store's employees told me she saw me signal. I'm always cautious."

"We know you are." *Mammi* rested her hand on his. "It was an accident."

"You've never been reckless." *Daadi* spooned peas from his plate. "I have a difficult time believing you didn't signal."

"Everyone who was in the accident is going to be okay." *Mammi* pointed to his plate, still filled with chicken, potatoes, and peas. "You need to eat. Your food is getting cold."

Jonathan glanced down and tried to will his stomach to relax, but all he could think about was the sound of the buggy wheel shattering and the passengers' screams when the car struck.

CHAPTER TWO

It's a miracle no one was killed," *Dat* said before sipping his coffee.

Janie had spent most of supper telling her parents and her older sister, Marie, about the accident and the events that took place afterward when the emergency responders arrived to help. Her family had listened with interest as she described the scene in detail.

"*Ya*, I agree," Marie said as she cut a slice of their mother's homemade apple pie. She placed it on a plate and handed it to *Dat* before tucking a strand of her brown hair behind her ear. "It sounds like it was bad." Janie could see the concern in her sister's brown eyes, the ones that matched *Dat*'s. Janie, two years younger than Marie's twenty-two years, had inherited their mother's blue eyes. But *Mamm*'s hair was light brown and Janie was the only person in the family with red hair.

"You must have been so scared," *Mamm* chimed in as she stirred her coffee. "I can't believe it happened right in front of your eyes."

"It was scary," Janie insisted as Marie handed her pie. "I was just sitting there eating my lunch when it all happened." She lifted her fork and frowned. "I overheard one of the police officers tell Craig that the driver said the accident was Jonathan's fault. He said Jonathan didn't signal, but he did. I saw it."

Marie handed *Mamm* pie and then cut a piece for herself. "It sounds like the driver lied. That's a sin."

"That's not the worst of it." Janie took a deep breath. She'd had to hold the secret in all day. "The driver was texting on his phone."

Marie's eyes widened. "Are you sure?"

Janie nodded with emphasis. "I saw him looking down at something in his hand, and I'm sure it had to be a cell phone. He definitely was not watching the road. I was going to tell that police officer, but I never had the opportunity. Bianca ended up really needing my help, and before I knew it, the officers and medical personnel were leaving.

"Then as soon as all the passengers were on their way and Craig had talked to his lawyer on the phone, he had Eva and me call our drivers, closed the shop early, and drove off to join Bianca at the hospital. I'm going to tell him tomorrow what I saw."

Dat frowned and pushed his fork through the flaky piecrust. "No, Janie. Don't get involved. Let the authorities handle the case."

"But it's not fair that Jonathan is being blamed for something that's not his fault. I heard Craig talking on the phone to his lawyer." Janie set her fork next to her plate. "What if Jonathan gets fired over this? I can't let that happen when I know the truth."

"You need to stay out of it, Janie," *Dat* warned again.

"You just need to worry about your job. Let Craig handle the accident."

Janie nodded, then looked down at her uneaten piece of apple pie.

"My day at the schoolhouse wasn't nearly as exciting," Marie said. "In fact, the *kinner* all behaved quite well."

While Marie talked on about her job working as a teacher's assistant at the nearby schoolhouse, Janie pushed her fork through the pie. She couldn't stop herself from recalling the anguish in Jonathan's brown eyes as she took care of the gash on his head. She was certain Jonathan blamed himself for the accident even though he had signaled, but if no one else saw what really happened, only she knew the truth. How could she allow Jonathan to be charged with an accident that was not his fault?

The question continued to swirl through her mind after her father went out to the barn to care for the animals. As Janie cleared and wiped down the table, her mother started washing the dishes.

"I really like teaching," Marie said as she dried a pot. "I'm so thankful the assistant position opened up this fall. Maybe I can become a full-time teacher next year."

"That would be really nice," *Mamm* said, smiling at Marie. "You'd make a very *gut* teacher."

Janie's focus moved to the end of the counter where Jonathan's straw hat sat. She'd picked it up at the scene of the accident after he and Bianca left, and she planned to give it back to him tomorrow. She gnawed her lower lip as she listened to her mother and Marie talk. She wanted to discuss the accident and the information she had about the driver, but she didn't want to go against her father's instructions.

"*Mamm*, do you think *Dat* is right about the accident?" The question burst from Janie's lips before she could stop it.

Mamm spun to face her. "What do you mean?"

"Do you think I should keep the information about the driver to myself?" Janie fingered the washrag she still held in her hands. "I feel as if I need to share what I saw so Jonathan can clear his name."

Mamm frowned as she turned toward Janie, wiping her hands on a dish towel. "I know you want to help Jonathan, but you need to listen to your *dat*. Besides, you know it's not our way to get involved in legal issues. Leave that to the *Englishers*." She gave Janie a little smile and turned back to the sink.

Janie finished cleaning the table and then swept the kitchen floor as Marie talked on about her students. Janie tried to concentrate on her sister's words, but her thoughts were still stuck on the accident and Jonathan's innocence.

After her chores were done, Janie headed upstairs to her room. She chose a book off her shelf, sat on her bed, and began to read, hoping to take her mind off the day's events. She had just started the second chapter when a knock sounded on her doorframe. She looked up and found Marie watching her with concern in her milk-chocolate brown eyes.

"Are you all right?" Marie asked, stepping into the room.

"*Ya*, I'm fine. Why?" Janie closed the book and set it on the bed beside her.

"You seemed so concerned at supper." Marie crossed the room and sat down on the corner of the bed. "I'm worried about you."

Janie fingered her dress. "I can't stop thinking about the accident."

"Do you want to talk about it?"

"*Ya*, I do." Janie shared how she'd taken care of Jonathan's wound. "I can't stop thinking about how upset Jonathan was. He blames himself for the accident, even though I told him I saw him signal. I know it wasn't his fault. And I want to help him with the rest of the information I have."

Marie ran her fingers over Janie's maple-leaf-pattern quilt. "You know it's not a *gut* idea to go against *Dat*, so why are you even still thinking about this?"

"If you had only seen Jonathan's eyes, Marie, then you would understand." Janie sighed, removed her prayer covering, and started to pull the bobby pins out of her hair. "I just can't stop thinking about him and the accident. It was all so . . ."

"Traumatic?" her sister finished her thought.

"*Ya*." Janie released her bun, and her red hair fell in waves past her shoulders. "All those people were hurt. And I didn't mean to eavesdrop, but Craig had his door open when he was talking on the phone to his lawyer. I heard Craig say he didn't want to fire Jonathan, but he understood what the lawyer was saying about liability.

He said he and Bianca have put all their savings into the business, and they could lose everything they've worked for.

"The driver should be the one taking the blame, Marie. How can I stand by and let Jonathan take the blame?"

Marie gave her a sad smile. "I know you want to help. It's your nature to step in and take care of everyone, but *Dat* doesn't want you to get involved. You told Jonathan you saw him signal, and now you need to leave everything to him and Craig. It will be fine."

Janie nodded, but she wasn't convinced keeping quiet was the best way to handle this situation.

Marie stood. "I'm going to take a shower. I'll let you know when I'm out so you can take yours."

"All right." Janie placed the handful of bobby pins on her nightstand.

As Marie walked to the door, she looked back over her shoulder. "You have that look in your eye like you're planning something. Promise me you won't do anything that will get you in trouble with *Dat*."

Janie sighed. "I promise."

"Danki." Marie hurried out the door and disappeared into the hallway.

Janie stared down at the book beside her on the bed as she contemplated her sister's words. Marie was right. Janie needed to be an obedient daughter. Yet she still couldn't stop the feeling that she needed to tell Jonathan and Craig what else she'd witnessed.

. . .

After thanking her driver the following morning, Janie hefted her tote bag onto her shoulder, gripped Jonathan's straw hat in her hand, and climbed out of the van.

As she walked past the stables, Janie spotted Jonathan standing by one of the stalls. He must have worn his spare hat today. Since her driver had dropped her off fifteen minutes early, she had time to talk to him for a moment. She'd spent most of last night worrying about him, and she longed to check on him as well as return his hat.

The scent of animals and wet hay filled her senses as she stood by the entrance to the stable. She watched Jonathan gently rubbing a horse's forehead and muzzle as he quietly talked to the animal. She recognized the chestnut-colored Belgian from the accident. She was drawn to Jonathan's concern for the horse as she took in the sight of the man in front of her. Jonathan was tall and slender, but muscular. He was handsome with chiseled cheekbones and a perfectly proportioned nose. He looked older than she was.

Janie had never seen him before yesterday, and she wondered where he lived. Jonathan's strong jaw was clean-shaven, so he wasn't married.

Janie stepped into the stable. Her shoes crunched on the hay, causing Jonathan to turn toward her. Her cheeks burned with embarrassment, and she hoped her thoughts weren't written all over her face.

"*Gude mariye*," she said as she walked over to him. "How are you feeling today?"

"I'm fine. *Danki*." He smiled, but the happiness didn't reach his eyes. He still seemed upset.

"How's your arm?"

Jonathan glanced down and rubbed it. "It's sore, but the doctor said it's only a sprain. He gave me a sling, but I don't need it. I iced my arm for a while last night, and it seemed to help." His attention moved to the straw hat in her hand. "Is that mine?"

"*Ya*, it is." She'd been so busy admiring Jonathan that she almost forgot she was holding his hat. "I picked it up yesterday."

"*Danki.*" He took the hat from her hand and examined it. "I was wondering if it had been damaged in the accident."

"No, it seems like it's still perfect." She smiled up at him.

"I appreciate that you picked it up for me. I asked Craig about it last night when he stopped by my grandparents' *haus* to see me, and he said he hadn't seen it." He gave her another tentative smile and then hung the hat on a hook beside the stall door. He pointed to his forehead, where a fresh bandage covered his wound. "Thanks also for taking care of me yesterday. You'd make a *wunderbaar* nurse."

Janie chuckled and fingered the strap of her tote bag. "No, I don't think so. I just know how to apply ointment and bandages."

"You do a *gut* job." Jonathan leaned against the stall, and the horse sniffed his hat and then his shoulder.

"How is he?" she asked, pointing to the horse.

"Bucky is fine." Jonathan turned toward the horse and rubbed his chin. "He was a little spooked but he's okay."

Janie's thoughts turned to the accident, and her father's words of warning echoed through her mind.

"I'm going to be working in the stables now," Jonathan said while keeping his eyes focused on the horse.

"What do you mean?" She stepped closer to him and inhaled his scent of earth mixed with sunshine.

"Craig doesn't want me doing the buggy tours anymore. Well, at least for now." He shrugged, but she found disappointment in his eyes. "He asked me to work in the stables instead."

"Why doesn't he want you to give tours?" Janie knew the answer, but she wanted to hear what Craig had told Jonathan.

"He said his lawyer felt I should step down from giving the tours in case anyone in the tour group sues." He faced her and gestured around the stable. "I enjoy taking care of the horses, and mucking stalls isn't so bad."

"But the accident wasn't your fault." The words slipped from her lips before she could stop them. "I saw you signal before you guided the horse into the parking lot. And the driver was—"

"I appreciate your concern, but it doesn't matter." Something flickered in his brown eyes, but he shook off her words. "I'm *froh* to have the job. I'm just trying to help out my grandparents while I visit them for the fall. And we don't have much interaction with tourists in Maryland, so this is like a treat for me."

Janie let his words soak through her. Jonathan was only visiting his grandparents for the fall, and then he'd return to Maryland. Why did this information bother her so much? She didn't even know him.

And maybe she should stay out of this, just as her father asked, and not even tell Jonathan she saw the driver distracted. Surely she wasn't the only one who saw him signal, so just as Marie said, he would be okay. She'd have to keep that information to herself to obey her father.

"Thanks again for retrieving my hat. It's my favorite one," Jonathan said, changing the subject. He nodded toward the hat, still hanging on the hook beside the stall despite Bucky's interest.

"Gern gschehne." She pointed toward the building that housed the souvenir shop and the offices. "I'd better get to work. I'm going to eat at the picnic table where we sat yesterday if you'd like to join me for lunch." She wasn't planning on asking him to eat lunch with her, but again, the words seemed to escape her lips without forethought. She held her breath, hoping he wouldn't reject her.

"I'd love to." His smile was genuine this time, lighting up his handsome face.

"Great," she said. "I'll see you around noon."

"I look forward to it."

Janie hurried toward the main building as excitement rushed through her. She couldn't wait to see Jonathan again at lunchtime. Not only was he handsome, but he was nice and easy to talk to. She felt as if she'd made a new friend, and she couldn't wait to get to know him better.

• • •

Jonathan watched Janie head toward the souvenir shop. She was several inches shorter than his six-foot stature and stunningly beautiful. Her green dress complemented the red hair peeking out from under her prayer covering. Her hair resembled the deep orange hues of the summer sunset. Her eyes were bright blue, like the cloudless summer sky, and her skin was pale, reminding him of the porcelain dolls he'd once seen in a gift shop in Baltimore.

Jonathan surmised Janie was in her early twenties, which was much too young for him, but there was something about her that captivated him. Was it her sweet spirit? He shook the thoughts away, reminding himself that he was going to return to Maryland in a couple of months. It was silly to think about a *maedel* he'd never see again.

Jonathan grabbed a shovel as he contemplated his conversation with Janie. She seemed determined to defend his innocence in the accident even though he told her he was fine with working in the stable. It warmed his heart that she would insist on supporting him even though she barely knew him.

As Jonathan mucked out a stall, he realized how much he was looking forward to eating lunch with Janie and learning more about her. All he knew was that she used to take care of her sick uncle until he passed away. He wondered where she lived. Did she have a boyfriend?

Jonathan stopped shoveling and grimaced. Why was he torturing himself by thinking about Janie that way? He was leaving soon, and he didn't know when he'd be back to Pennsylvania. Besides, relationships never turned out the way he planned. After having his heart broken twice, he'd given up on love. He was better off alone.

Jonathan swiped the back of his hand across his brow and returned to the task at hand. He would put Janie out of his mind for now and not think about her until lunchtime.

. . .

Janie retrieved her lunch bag from the refrigerator in the break room, plucked her sweater from a closet, and hurried out through the front of the store, waving to Eva as she headed outside. She'd spent all morning thinking about Jonathan. She found herself watching the clock, impatiently awaiting noon. She couldn't wait to find out more about his life in Maryland.

Her excitement dissipated when she found the picnic table empty. Where was Jonathan? Maybe he had gotten too busy in the stables to break for lunch, or even forgotten about their plan to eat together.

Janie sat facing Old Philadelphia Pike and opened her lunch bag. She pulled out her chicken breast sandwich and bottle of water and then bowed her head in silent prayer. When she opened her eyes, she turned around and saw Jonathan crossing the parking lot, holding a brown paper bag in one hand and waving to her with the other. She smiled and waved back as happiness rang anew inside her.

"Sorry I'm late," he said as he sat down across from her. "I lost track of time."

"It's fine," she said. "I'm glad you could make it."

After a prayer, Jonathan pulled a sandwich and bottle of water out of his bag. "How was your morning?"

"*Gut.*" She opened her bottle of water. "The store has been busy today."

"I noticed," he said, glancing around the parking lot. "The horses and buggies have been going all morning too." He seemed to be in a much better mood.

"*Ya*, they have." She took a sip of water as she considered her curiosity. Would she seem too forward if she began firing off questions about his life?

"Do you live far from here?" Jonathan asked before biting into his sandwich.

"No, not very far at all," Janie said with a smile, relieved that he started the conversation. "I live in Ronks."

"Oh," he said with recognition twinkling in his eyes. "I know where that is. My grandparents live close by. They're near the bakery. Do you know where the bakery is in Bird-in-Hand?"

Janie nodded while chewing.

"They're only a few blocks from here, and they're right next door to Craig and Bianca. My grandparents live in a *daadihaus* on *mei onkel*'s farm." He took another bite of his sandwich.

"How long are you going to visit them?" she asked, hoping she didn't sound as eager as she felt.

Jonathan shrugged. "I'll probably be here through November."

"Oh." She pulled a plastic zippered bag of peanut butter cookies from her lunch bag and held it out to him. "Do you like peanut butter *kichlin*?"

He grinned. "Are you kidding? I love them."

Janie laughed. "Take a few. *Mei schweschder* makes the best *kichlin*."

"*Danki.*" Jonathan bit into one and nodded. "They are fantastic."

"I'll tell her you said that."

"Is your *schweschder* older or younger than you?" he asked before taking another bite of the cookie.

"She's two years older. She's twenty-two." Janie took a sip of her water.

"Do you have any brothers?"

"*Ya, mei bruder*, Samuel, is married. He and his *fraa*, Mandy, have a *boppli* named Becky." She smiled. "Becky is the sweetest little *boppli*. How about you?"

"Two *bruders*. I'm the middle *kind*." Jonathan broke another cookie in half. "*Mei bruder* Daniel is thirty-two, and *mei bruder* Peter is twenty-seven. I'm the middle one and the shortest."

Her eyes widened. "You're the shortest?"

Jonathan chuckled, and she enjoyed the rich warmth of his laugh. "That's the truth. Daniel is six-foot-two, and my baby brother, Peter, is six-foot-four."

"Oh goodness." Janie gasped. "They're very tall."

"*Ya*, they are, and they like to remind me I'm shorter than they are." He opened his bottle of water and fingered the cap. "They're both married and have *kinner*. I'm the outcast who isn't married and doesn't have a family. *Mei mamm* keeps telling me she's worried about me because I'll be thirty in four months and I haven't found a *fraa*." He shrugged as if it didn't bother him, but she saw vulnerability in his eyes.

"Oh." Janie studied his face. "What kind of business do your *bruders* run?"

"Peter is a dairy farmer, and Daniel is a carpenter.

Daniel went into business with *mei dat*." He spun the cap with his fingers and watched it turn. "I work with *mei dat* and Daniel, but I came up here to get away for a little while. I wanted to visit my grandparents and help them out. *Mei onkel* takes care of them, but he's so busy during harvest time." He looked sheepish. "I'm sure you're bored with hearing about my life. Tell me about yours."

"Well, there's not much to tell." Janie placed her sandwich on her napkin. "I live with my parents and *schweschder*, Marie. *Mei dat* and *bruder* work at Bird-in-Hand Builders, the shop *Dat* and *mei onkel* Raymond owned together, but they don't need *mei schweschder* and me to work there. *Mei bruder* and cousin help *Dat* run things just fine.

"Marie and I used to take care of our *onkel* Raymond. He was on dialysis, and our *aenti* had died several years ago. Marie and I took turns caring for him while our cousin Mike worked. After *Onkel* Raymond passed away, I babysat for my neighbor for a few months. *Mei freind* Eva also works here. We grew up together, and we're in the same youth group. When she told me Craig had an opening, I jumped at the chance to work here."

"And you had an exciting first day." Jonathan held up his bottle of water toward her as if to toast her.

"That is true." She took another bite of her sandwich. Again, she was amazed at how Jonathan's outlook had improved since just that morning. Maybe he had begun to really believe the accident wasn't his fault.

They were both silent for a few moments as they chewed. The *clip-clop* of hooves filled the air as a horse and buggy returned to the parking lot after a tour. They both looked over toward the buggy, and Jonathan's smile faded.

"Craig told me the passengers who were in the crash are going to be okay," Jonathan said. "The worst injuries were a broken arm and a mild concussion."

"I'm *froh* to hear they will all be okay." She studied his handsome face and once again saw guilt there. "I'm glad you're okay too. When I saw you fall, I was afraid you were badly hurt."

"You were worried about me?" He looked stunned.

"Of course I was. Why wouldn't I be?" Janie handed him another cookie, and his hand brushed hers. Her skin tingled at the contact. Had he felt that too?

"*Danki,*" Jonathan said, his intense eyes studying hers. "I always loved coming to see my grandparents when I was little. Bird-in-Hand is one of my favorite places."

"What sort of things did you do when you visited?"

"*Mei daadi* always took *mei bruders* and me fishing," Jonathan said with a smile. "One time, *mei bruders* and I all wound up in the water."

Soon they were both laughing at his funny fishing stories, and when they finished eating, they walked across the parking lot, side by side.

"I enjoyed lunch," Jonathan said as they approached the stables. "May I join you again tomorrow?"

"Absolutely," Janie said, thrilled that he would ask.

Jonathan grinned and tipped his hat to her, and Janie's heart fluttered as she smiled. She watched him amble into the stable, and she knew she was already falling for Jonathan Stoltzfus.

CHAPTER THREE

Janie hummed to herself while organizing the post-
cards for sale in the souvenir shop. The store had
opened thirty minutes earlier, and a group had already
come in and bought tickets for the first round of buggy
rides. After the group left, Janie and Eva busied themselves with straightening the displays and preparing
for the next rush of customers.

She'd thought about Jonathan all weekend and couldn't
wait to see him again. She hoped he'd thought of her during the weekend too. And, most of all, she hoped he would
eat lunch with her again this week as he had every day last
week. She looked forward to the one hour each day they
spent talking and laughing together.

After the postcard display was straightened, she
moved to the T-shirts on display and began folding and
organizing them by size.

"*Gude mariye*, Janie."

Startled, Janie spun and saw Jonathan grinning at
her. "Jonathan," she said with surprise. "Hi. *Wie geht's?*"

"How was your weekend?" he asked, crossing his
arms over his wide chest. His blue shirt complemented
his tan skin and dark hair.

"It was *gut*," she said, trying her best not to stare at him. "How was yours?"

"*Gut.*" He paused for a moment. "Lunch today?"

"*Ya,*" she said, hoping she didn't sound too eager. "Of course."

"Great." Jonathan held up a paper sack. "I brought some of *mei mammi*'s *kichlin* to share with you. You can tell me if they are as *gut* as Marie's *kichlin*."

"I can't wait." And she couldn't.

"I have to get out to the stable, but I'll see you later." He gave her another electric smile and headed toward the back of the store.

"Janie," Eva gushed, sidling up to her. "Jonathan likes you!"

"Shh," Janie hissed. "Keep your voice down or he'll hear you."

"He's in the break room," Eva said, waving off Janie's worry. "So what's going on with you two?" Her grin was wide.

"Nothing. We're just *freinden*." Janie picked up another stack of T-shirts and began absently folding them to avoid her friend's questioning stare. "We ate lunch together last week."

"Every day?" Eva asked.

"Every day except for Monday. It's not a big deal, Eva. We only talk about our families and share funny stories." Janie saw Jonathan walking back through the store, and she gave Eva a warning look.

"See you later," Jonathan said as he moved past them. "Have a *gut* morning."

"You too," Janie and Eva sang in unison.

"That's so sweet that you ate together," Eva commented once Jonathan was gone. "I'm sure he's grateful for your friendship."

"What do you mean?" Janie asked.

"His *mammi* told Bianca that Jonathan had his heart broken twice. He dated two *maed*, each for a long time, and they both broke up with him. His last girlfriend is going to marry one of his *freinden*." Eva shook her head. "He was so heartbroken he decided to come up here and spend the fall with his grandparents. He didn't want to be in town for their wedding."

"That's so *bedauerlich*." Janie clicked her tongue. Now she understood the vulnerability she'd seen in his eyes when he said he was the only son in his family who wasn't yet married.

Eva suddenly smiled. "You're just what he needs."

"Don't be ridiculous," Janie said. "I'm sure he's not interested in me." *But I wish he was.*

"Why wouldn't he be interested?" Eva pointed toward Janie's hair. "You're so *schee*. All of our *freinden* are envious of your hair."

"*Danki.*" Janie frowned, not convinced. She considered herself ordinary, which was why she'd never had a boyfriend. What was she thinking? "He's so handsome, and I can't see why he would be interested in me. Besides, he's going back to Maryland before Christmas."

Eva touched Janie's arm and looked hopeful. "Maybe he'll stay."

"I doubt it," Janie said.

The bell above the door rang, and a group of tourists entered.

"We'd better get back to work," Janie said.

"We'll talk more later. I'll help the customers so you can finish what you're doing." Eva headed toward the tourists. "May I help you?"

While Janie finished folding the last stack of shirts, her thoughts were stuck on Jonathan and his heartaches. Would Jonathan ever share that story with her? She hoped someday he would tell her the truth about what happened to bring him to Bird-in-Hand for the harvest season.

. . .

Janie stood in her sister's bedroom doorway that evening and found Marie sitting on the edge of her bed, brushing her waist-length brown hair.

"Hi, Janie." Marie looked up at her. "Did you need something?"

"*Ya*, I was wondering if you had a minute to talk." Janie fingered the long braid dangling over her shoulder.

"Of course I do." Marie gestured for Janie to enter the room.

"*Danki.*" Janie stepped into her room and sat on the cedar chest at the foot of Marie's double bed. She took a deep breath and looked up into Marie's concerned eyes. "I think I'm falling in love with Jonathan."

Marie gaped. "Jonathan? The man who had the buggy accident?"

"*Ya.*" Janie crossed her arms over the front of her pink nightgown. "We've had lunch together every day since last Tuesday. We enjoy talking to each other. And he's so handsome, Marie. He's tall and has *schee* brown eyes. He's so sweet and charming." She sighed. "I don't know what to do."

"Janie." Marie leaned forward and touched her arm. "I don't understand what the problem is."

"He's going to be thirty in three months. Do you think *Dat* would approve?"

Marie frowned, and Janie dropped her hands into her lap.

"I'm sorry, but I'm not sure if *Dat* would approve," Marie said gently. "You might want to discuss it with *Mamm* first and get her thoughts. Do you want me to go with you?"

"No, I'm not ready to tell them yet." Janie touched the hem of her nightgown. "He's from Maryland. He's only here to visit his grandparents for a few months before he goes back home."

Marie looked concerned. "If you were to marry him, would you move to Maryland with him?"

"I don't know." The question had occurred to Janie earlier today as she'd eaten the cookies Jonathan had brought to share during lunch. If she were to marry Jonathan, would he expect her to move to Maryland? Janie shoved away the question. She was getting ahead of herself by already thinking about marriage.

Marie's face brightened. "I have an idea! Why don't you invite Jonathan over for supper one night? That would be the best way for *Mamm* and *Dat* to meet him. You've already mentioned Jonathan is charming, so I'm certain *Mamm* and *Dat* would like him too."

"That's a great idea!" Janie popped up from the

cedar chest and hugged Marie. "*Danki.* I knew you could help me." She started for the door, her long braid bouncing off her back.

"Janie, wait."

Janie looked over her shoulder at Marie. "What?"

"Just be careful, okay?" Marie's face was full of caution. "I don't want to see you get hurt. Don't forget he's leaving in a few months, and things might not work out."

"Okay." Janie's smile faded. Her sister was right. Janie was risking her heart, but somewhere deep in her soul she had a feeling Jonathan cared for her as much as she cared for him.

. . .

Jonathan hummed to himself as he finished caring for the horses in his grandfather's barn Wednesday evening. The week had gone well so far. He'd cherished the one hour each day he and Janie spent together, sharing stories along with their lunches. She was sweet, funny, and beautiful. He thought about her constantly, and he couldn't wait to see her tomorrow.

Once he finished caring for the animals, Jonathan stepped outside and closed the barn door. When he turned, he found his grandfather smiling at him.

"Were you just humming?" *Daadi* asked with a sly grin.

Jonathan shrugged. "*Ya,* I guess I was."

"What's gotten into you?" *Daadi* raised an eyebrow. "Have you met a *maedel*?"

Jonathan shoved his hands in his pockets. "*Ya*, I suppose I have."

"Let's go sit on the porch and talk. I want to hear all about this *maedel* who has stolen my grandson's heart." *Daadi* climbed the back steps, sank into the swing, and grinned with enthusiasm. "Well?"

Jonathan chuckled to himself as he climbed the steps and then leaned back against the railing across from *Daadi*. "Her name is Janie Lantz, and she works in the souvenir shop."

"What does she look like?" *Daadi* asked, resting his hands on his rotund middle.

"She's beautiful." Jonathan smiled. "She has red hair and blue eyes. She's very sweet." He shook his head. "It will never work out though."

Daadi squinted at him through his glasses. "Why not?"

"She's only twenty. I'm a decade older than she is."

"So?" *Daadi* shrugged. "Your *mammi* is nine years younger than I am."

"She is?" Jonathan was stunned to hear this fact.

"*Ya*, she is." *Daadi* shrugged. "When I met her, I was thirty, and she was twenty-one. What matters is how you feel about this young woman and how she feels about you, Jonathan."

Jonathan nodded. "*Danki, Daadi.*"

"Are you going to tell her how you feel?" *Daadi* asked with a hopeful look on his wrinkly face.

"I will eventually," Jonathan said as he sat on the railing.

"Eventually?" *Daadi* scrunched his nose. "What are you waiting for?"

"The right time." Jonathan frowned. "I have a history of sharing my feelings too soon and winding up alone after the *maedel* changes her mind. I don't need to go through that again. Twice was already too many times."

"I can understand that, but don't wait too long either." *Daadi* shivered as a cold breeze wafted over them. "Fall is here." He stood. "Let's go inside before it gets any colder."

As Jonathan followed *Daadi* into the house, he wondered if his grandfather was right. Could a relationship work out between Janie and him despite their age difference? But more important could Janie be the *maedel* who would truly love him and not break his heart? The thought took hold of him and a renewed hope settled deep in his soul. Before he shared his feelings, Jonathan had to make sure Janie felt the same way about him that he felt about her.

· · ·

Janie smiled at Jonathan as they sat at the picnic table and shared a bag filled with the chocolate chip cookies she and Marie had made the night before.

"I can't believe tomorrow is Friday already," she quipped, snatching another cookie from the bag. "The week has flown by."

"It has gone by quickly." He took a cookie and then met her eyes. "Janie, I want to ask you something."

Janie's stomach tightened at the seriousness in his eyes. "Okay."

"Do you have a boyfriend?" He looked worried.

Janie had to bite her lip to stop a laugh from escaping her mouth. "No, I don't."

"Oh." Relief relaxed his features.

"Do you have a girlfriend?" Even though Eva had told her the answer, she wanted to hear Jonathan confirm it.

"No." Jonathan looked down at his napkin covered with cookie crumbs. "I haven't told you the real reason I came to visit my grandparents."

Janie's stomach clenched again, this time with anticipation. Was he finally going to share his story of heartaches?

"I was dating someone," he began with a melancholy look in his eyes. "I was so sure she was the one for me. In fact, I was trying to work up the courage to ask her to marry me, but I never got the chance to ask. She broke up with me, and she's marrying one of *mei freinden* in November."

"I'm so sorry," Janie whispered, her voice thin with sympathy.

"Thanks." He gave her a bleak smile. "I couldn't stand the idea of being there for their wedding. I would be expected to go since it's in my church district. I came up with the idea of spending the fall with my grandparents to get away from the situation." He grimaced. "I'm a coward."

"No, you're not." Janie resisted the urge to reach across the table and touch his hand. "I can understand why you wanted to get away. My cousin's girlfriend, Rachel, went through the same thing. Her ex-boyfriend is dating her former best friend. She told me it was difficult to see them at every youth gathering and every church service. You can only take so much."

"*Danki* for understanding. *Mei bruders* think I overreacted by leaving the way I did, but I don't regret my decision. I'm helping my grandparents too." A smile found his lips. "And I met you."

Butterflies danced in Janie's stomach. She suddenly remembered her sister's advice. "Would you like to come to supper one night to meet my family?"

He smiled. "I'd love to."

"*Wunderbaar.*"

He looked hesitant. "Do you think your family will like me?"

"Absolutely." Janie started a mental list of what she and Marie could make for supper the night he came.

She also said a silent prayer, asking God to help her parents approve of her friendship with Jonathan.

CHAPTER FOUR

Jonathan guided the last horse toward the stable the following evening. A brisk breeze whipped over him as he glanced up at the fluffy clouds dotting the late-afternoon sky. He halted the horse and climbed down from the buggy. As he started to unhitch the horse, he saw movement in his peripheral vision. Looking up, he found Janie standing in front of him, hugging a black sweater over her blue dress and black apron. Her tote bag was slung over her shoulder.

"Jonathan." She smiled. "I'm glad you're still here. My driver is running a little late, so I thought I'd stop by to say hi."

"How long is your driver going to be?"

"He said he had to make a run to Philadelphia and is stuck in traffic. It's going to be at least another forty-five minutes." She shook her head. "Craig and Bianca had to leave; they usually visit some relatives on Friday evenings. Since I don't have anyone else to call for a ride, I told my driver I would wait. I hope you don't mind if I wait out here."

An idea flashed in Jonathan's mind. He pointed toward the buggy. "Would you like to go for a ride? I can take you on the route I normally take the tourists."

She hesitated. "How long is the ride?"

"It's about thirty minutes, but I can shorten it."

"I don't know." She shivered and hugged her sweater closer to her body.

"I'll grab a quilt," he offered.

"Okay," Janie said, finally agreeing. But then she held up her hand to stop him. "Wait. Are you allowed to take the buggy out? I don't want to get you in trouble."

"I can still drive a buggy," he explained, "but I can't take any tourists out. You're *mei freind*, not a paying passenger."

"Okay."

Jonathan got a quilt from the stable and then took Janie's hand and helped her climb up into the buggy. He enjoyed the warm, soft feel of her skin and resisted the urge not to release her hand. Once she was settled in the seat, he walked around the buggy, climbed up on the seat beside her, and took the reins.

"Are you cold?" she asked, moving closer to him. "Would you like to share the quilt?"

Jonathan nodded. "Sure." How could he say no to her request? He savored the thought of sitting close to her.

Janie tossed the blanket over his lap and slid closer to him. He breathed in the scent of her shampoo—apple.

"When is your driver coming to get you?" she asked.

"I walk to work since it's only a few blocks," he explained, guiding the horse toward the road. "Sometimes I get a ride from Craig and Bianca, but I don't mind the walk. It gives me time to think and enjoy the fresh air. I love being outdoors."

"Oh." Janie's lips turned up in a sweet smile, and his pulse galloped.

Janie was so pretty with her warm smile and bright blue eyes. The sun was starting to set, and the deep orange hues in the sky nearly matched her hair. She scooted closer to him, and his leg brushed hers under the blanket.

"I'm *froh* my driver was late so I can spend more time with you today," she said, breaking through his thoughts.

"I'm enjoying it too," he said as he slowed the horse at a red light.

"I love autumn," Janie continued with her eyes fixed on the road ahead. "I enjoy seeing the leaves change and the cooler nights." She looked over at him. "What's your favorite season?"

Jonathan looked over at her face and all his worries melted away. *Any season with you is my favorite.* "I think it's autumn."

"You think it's autumn?" She laughed, and he relished the sweet sound. "Don't you have a favorite season?"

"I'm not fussy." He guided the buggy down a quiet residential street, and the aroma of the smoke from a fireplace permeated the air.

"October will be here soon," she said. "It will be much colder then." Her smile faded. "But I don't want October to come."

"Why not?" he asked.

"October is closer to November, and you're leaving in November." Janie's big blue eyes misted over. Was she going to cry?

Jonathan halted the horse at a stop sign and angled his body toward Janie. He cupped her cheek with his hand, and she turned her face toward it. The air around them sparked with electricity. He felt the overwhelming urge to kiss her, but he knew it would be inappropriate.

"I really like you, Janie," he said, his voice husky with emotion.

"I like you too," she whispered in response, her voice sounding equally sentimental.

Jonathan moved his thumb over her cheek, and she closed her eyes. A horn blasted behind him, and he quickly grabbed the reins and guided the horse down the road. The scent of rain saturated the air as their trip wore on.

"Do you think it's going to rain?" Janie asked.

"It might," Jonathan said. He looked up at the sky.

"Do you like the rain?" she asked, scooting even closer to him.

"I do when I'm not working outside."

"I love falling asleep to the sound of rain tapping on the roof."

For the remainder of the ride, they sat in contented silence, peppered with moments of conversation about the sights they passed. When they returned to the parking lot, she helped him stow the buggy and horse.

As they walked out of the stable, Janie took Jonathan's hand in hers. He glanced down at her, and she smiled up at him.

"I had a *wunderbaar* time tonight," she said. *"Danki."*

"Gern gschehne." Jonathan squeezed her hand. "I hope you have a nice weekend." He couldn't stand the

thought of saying good-bye to her and not seeing her for two whole days.

"I hope you do too." Janie opened her mouth to say something but stopped when headlights gleamed in their faces. She released his hand and hefted her tote bag farther up on her shoulder. "That's my ride. I'll see you Monday."

"Take care," he said as she hurried toward the van and climbed into the front passenger seat.

Jonathan waved as the white van steered through the parking lot, then started his journey on foot to his grandparents' house. His mind swirled with thoughts of Janie and their buggy ride. He had enjoyed every moment he'd spent with her, snuggled close under the blanket as they rode under the beautiful sky. Janie had worked her way into his heart, and he wanted to spend as much time with her as possible. He dreaded the thought of going back to Maryland and not seeing her again.

A cool mist of rain sprayed over him, and he shivered. He crossed his arms over his middle and picked up speed. He hurried down the street and smiled despite the damp weather. For the first time in nearly a year, he felt himself falling in love, and he prayed somehow he and Janie could find a way to make their relationship work.

• • •

"You went on a buggy ride with him after work?" Marie asked with a gasp as she washed the dishes later that evening.

"*Ya*, I did," Janie said, smiling so widely her cheeks hurt. She lifted a dish from the drain board and began to dry it. "It was really romantic. We went on the route he takes passengers, and it was nice and cold. He gave me a quilt to stay warm. He's so sweet." She sighed as sadness threatened to squelch her euphoria. "I just can't stand the thought that he's going to go back to Maryland."

"Who's going back to Maryland?"

Janie glanced over her shoulder to where her mother stood watching as she leaned on a broom. Janie hadn't heard her mother come in after sweeping the porch.

"Jonathan," Janie explained, her cheeks burning. "He's the one who was in the buggy accident."

"He's still working at the buggy rides?" *Mamm* tilted her head with surprise.

"He's working in the stable." Janie frowned. "It's not fair. The accident wasn't his fault at all, but he said he's *froh* to have the job. His *onkel* cares for his grandparents, but this is a chance for Jonathan to help them too."

"He's supporting his grandparents?" *Mamm* asked, and Janie nodded. "But you said he's from Maryland? He's only visiting them?"

"*Ya*, that's right. He said his *daed* is from here, but his *mamm* is from Maryland. After his parents married, they moved to Maryland to be by her family." Janie began drying another dish. "He came to spend some time with his grandparents. He said he loves coming here and working since they don't have much contact with tourists in Maryland." She considered sharing the story about his ex-girlfriend, but she felt it wasn't her place to share something so personal.

Mamm studied her for a moment. "Did I hear you say you took a romantic buggy ride with him?"

The tips of Janie's ears blazed with embarrassment. "We did. He took me on the route where he used to take the tourists. He's very respectful and friendly. I want you to meet him."

"When is he going back to Maryland?" *Mamm* frowned.

"In late November." Janie placed the dish on the counter and grabbed a handful of utensils to dry.

"You know you shouldn't get attached to him, Janie." *Mamm*'s voice held a hint of warning. "He's already planning to go back to Maryland, and you don't know when you'll see him again."

"But what if he decides to stay?" Marie suddenly chimed in. "He may fall in love with Janie and decide to stay here. He could build a *haus* near his grandparents and ask Janie to marry him."

Janie's pulse fluttered at the thought, but her mother's skeptical look brought her back to reality.

"I think you should take it one step at a time," *Mamm* said gently. "Jonathan might decide to stay, but you should prepare yourself in case he doesn't. Just enjoy being his *freind* for now and see what the future brings."

"*Ya.*" Janie nodded. "I'd like to have him over for supper one night so you all can meet him. He already said he'd like to come sometime."

Mamm began to sweep the kitchen floor. "*Ya,* we'll

see. Maybe when things slow down some at the shop. You know orders at the shop pick up again during the harvest season. Between that and the farm, your *dat* is very busy right now. Maybe in a couple of weeks we can have him over."

"All right." Janie couldn't wait for her family to meet Jonathan, but her mother's warning echoed in the back of her mind. Would Jonathan return to Maryland and forget all about her?

. . .

The next two weeks flew by as quickly as the autumn leaves blew from the trees. Janie and Jonathan ate lunch together every day and discussed everything from the cooler temperatures to their favorite foods. When Janie finally invited him over for supper, he accepted her invitation, and she almost jumped with joy.

Janie rushed home from work on Wednesday evening during the last week in September. The day had finally come for Jonathan to come over, and excitement skittered through her as she fluttered around the kitchen.

Marie appeared in the doorway. "Need some help?"

"*Ya*," Janie said as she mixed the meat loaf. "Would you please set the table and then mix up the brownies?"

"*Ya*," Marie said with a grin. "You're awfully *naerfich*. You really like him, don't you?"

"You already know the answer to that question." Janie frowned. "I just hope *Dat* likes him."

"What are you worried about? The age difference?"

Janie nodded and looked down at the meat-loaf mix.

"I'm worried he won't approve and won't let me date Jonathan. He's the first man who has ever shown an interest in me, and I'll just be devastated if *Dat* doesn't approve."

Marie placed her hand on Janie's shoulder. "Have faith that it will work out well tonight."

"*Danki.*" Janie prayed Marie was right.

. . .

At six o'clock, the warm aromas of meat loaf and brownies permeated the kitchen and the table was set. Janie smoothed her hands down her favorite green dress and black apron and touched her prayer covering, hoping it was straight.

"You look *schee*," Marie whispered. "Everything will be fine."

"*Danki,*" Janie whispered in return as she stared out the window above the kitchen sink and watched for Jonathan's driver.

When the crunch of tires sounded on the rock driveway, Janie's stomach lurched. A combination of joy and anxiety rioted inside of her.

"I think he's here," *Mamm* said, entering the kitchen from the family room. "What can I do to help?"

"We're all set," Marie announced. "Janie is very *naerfich.*"

"No, I'm not," Janie said, clearly fibbing. "I'm fine. Where's *Dat*?"

"He's in the barn. Do you want me to go get him?" Marie offered.

"He'll come in when he hears the car," *Mamm* said, patting Janie's shoulder. "Relax, *mei liewe*. Dinner will be *appeditlich*. Your meat loaf is always *wunderbaar*."

"That's not what I'm worried about." Janie turned to face her mother. "What if you and *Dat* don't like Jonathan?"

Mamm touched Janie's cheek. "If you like him, then we will like him too."

Janie turned her attention back to the window and saw Jonathan climbing from the burgundy van. He looked handsome clad in clean black trousers, a tan shirt, and black suspenders. He said something to his driver and then waved as the van drove away.

Janie held her breath as her father appeared from the barn and walked over to Jonathan. When they both smiled, Janie's shoulders relaxed and a smile spread across her face. Mamm *and Marie are right; everything is going to be fine.*

After talking for a few minutes, Jonathan and *Dat* walked up the short path toward the house. Janie crossed the kitchen to the doorway leading to the mudroom. The back door opened, and *Dat* stepped into the mudroom with Jonathan close behind him.

"Hi, Jonathan," Janie said, her voice a little higher and more excited than she'd hoped.

Jonathan gave her a breathtaking smile, and her heart raced. "Hi, Janie."

Her father washed his hands at the sink as Jonathan stepped into the kitchen.

"*Mamm*, Marie, this is Jonathan." Janie gestured between Jonathan and her sister and mother.

"It's nice to meet you," *Mamm* said. "I'm Sylvia, and I see you've met Timothy. Please have a seat."

"We're so *froh* you could come today," Marie said. "We've heard a lot about you."

Janie swallowed a gasp.

"Danki." Jonathan met Janie's stare. "I'm glad to meet you all too. Where would you like me to sit?"

"Sit here," Marie said, putting her hand on the back of a chair. "You'll be next to Janie."

Jonathan sat down on the chair, and *Dat* sat to his right at the head of the table.

"So," *Dat* began, "what kind of business do you have in Maryland?"

"I'm a carpenter," Jonathan said. "I work with *mei dat* and *bruder* making furniture. We fill a lot of custom orders for bedroom suites and dining room sets."

"Oh." *Dat* nodded and fingered his beard. "So you're only here to visit your grandparents?"

"That's right," Jonathan said, running his finger over the gray tablecloth.

"How long are you planning to stay?" *Dat* asked.

While *Dat* and Jonathan got acquainted, Janie, Marie, and *Mamm* began placing the platters and bowls of food on the table. Once the meal was delivered, they took their seats and bowed their heads in silent prayer.

After the prayer the sound of utensils scraping the dishes overtook the kitchen. They filled their plates with meat loaf, mashed potatoes, and green beans.

"Everything smells *appeditlich*," Jonathan said, dropping a spoonful of mashed potatoes onto his plate.

"Janie did the cooking," Marie announced. "I helped a little."

Janie gave Jonathan a shy smile. "It wasn't difficult. Meat loaf is easy to make."

"How do you like working at Lancaster Buggy Rides and Souvenirs?" Marie asked.

"I like it," Jonathan said. "I miss giving the buggy rides, but I enjoy working in the stables. I love visiting Lancaster." Then he took a bite of meat loaf.

"Is it much different from where you live in Maryland?" *Mamm* asked.

Jonathan nodded and swallowed. "We're more conservative in Maryland and don't have much contact with *Englishers*."

All through supper, Janie's parents and sister peppered Jonathan with questions, continuing as they ate brownies and drank coffee. But Jonathan didn't seem to mind sharing stories about his life in Maryland.

Once they finished dessert, Janie carried mugs to the sink and Marie collected the rest of the dishes. Now *Dat* was talking to Jonathan about his work at Bird-in-Hand Builders too.

Mamm stepped over to the counter and touched Janie's arm. "Marie and I will clean up. Why don't you go sit on the porch with Jonathan?"

Janie glanced over her shoulder to where *Dat* was telling Jonathan about his business. Jonathan nodded politely as if he was hanging on his every word.

"Save him," *Mamm* said with a smile. "I'm sure he'd rather talk to you than hear your *dat* talk about our store."

"Go on," Marie chimed in as she filled the sink with frothy water. "We'll handle this. Go enjoy your guest until his driver comes to pick him up."

Janie smiled. *"Danki."* She stepped over toward Jonathan and he gave her a sideways glance as her father continued talking about the items they created and sold at the store. He was detailing the wishing wells, planters, swings, lighthouses, and other lawn ornaments. When *Dat* paused to take a breath, she grabbed the opportunity to jump in.

"Jonathan," she began, "would you like to sit on the porch and talk while you wait for your driver to come for you?"

"That would be nice." Jonathan looked at her father as if awaiting his permission.

Dat nodded. "That's a *gut* idea. Go and enjoy the night. I don't think it's too cold out there yet, but the cold weather is coming soon."

Jonathan stood. *"Danki* for supper. I had a great time."

After saying good-bye, Jonathan followed Janie into the mudroom, where he retrieved his hat and jacket, and she grabbed her wrap.

"Do you need to call your driver?" Janie asked as they stepped onto the back porch. She hugged her wrap around her.

"Ya, I do." Jonathan jammed his thumb toward the small shed next to the barn. "Is that your phone shanty?"

"Ya," Janie said. "Go right ahead and use it."

As Jonathan hustled down the porch steps, Janie sank onto the porch swing and glanced up at the sunset, which sent streaks of yellow, orange, purple, and pink across the sky. She hugged her wrap closer and smiled, recalling how Jonathan had fit in with her family during supper. Her parents and sister seemed to like him, and her heart warmed at the thought.

Jonathan's footsteps startled Janie back to the present.

"I didn't mean to scare you," he said as he crossed the porch. "You looked as if you were lost in thought."

"It's fine." She scooted to the other side of the swing and patted the bench beside her. "Have a seat." Looking up at his face, she saw the gash on his forehead was healing and barely noticeable.

"Thanks." He sank down beside her, his long legs stretched out in front of him. "Your family is great."

"*Danki.*" She gave the swing a little push, and it gently moved them back and forth. "I think they liked you."

"I hope so." He turned toward her. "I just have a question for you."

"What's that?"

"Your *mamm*'s hair is light brown, and your *dat* and *schweschder* are brunettes." A smile played at the corners of his mouth. "Where did you get that *schee* hair of yours?"

Janie's cheeks heated as his warm eyes remained focused on her. "*Mei mamm* told me her *mammi* had red hair. She thinks I inherited it from her."

He looked up at the sky. "Your hair reminds me of the sunset." He pointed. "See that orange there? That's almost the same color."

Janie gaped. No one had ever described her hair that

way. *"Danki,"* she said softly, marveling inside at the unexpected compliment.

"That was what I thought the first time I saw you." His fingers brushed her shoulders, sending chills dancing up her spine as he rested his arm on the back of the swing. "I immediately thought your hair was the color of a sunset. I'd never seen a *maedel* with hair like yours. It's unique and *schee.*"

"Danki," she repeated, not knowing what else to say.

"September is flying by quickly." Jonathan turned his attention back to the sky. "I can't believe it will be October next week."

"I know." Janie wanted to ask him to stay in Pennsylvania, but she didn't want to be too forward.

"We'll have to make the most of the next two months." He turned back toward her. "It's nice to spend time together."

"I agree."

"Great," he said.

It seemed as though the rest of their conversation had barely begun when the hum of an engine and the reflection of headlights on the side of her father's large barn drew Janie's focus to the driveway. Her smile faded. She dreaded the idea of saying good night to Jonathan.

"I guess it's time for me to go." Jonathan's frown mirrored her mood. "But I'll see you tomorrow."

They both stood and he held out his hand. She took it, and warmth zipped through her body. As they walked toward the waiting van, Janie relished the feeling of walking by his side. She felt as if she belonged there. Did he feel it too?

"Thank you for supper," Jonathan said when they reached the passenger side door. "I had a great time."

"I did too." Janie smiled up at him. "I'm glad you came."

Jonathan was silent as he gazed down into her face. She longed to know what he was thinking. He brushed his fingers over her cheek, and she sucked in a breath.

"*Gut nacht,*" he finally said.

"*Gut nacht.*"

He climbed into the passenger seat, and Janie waved as the van backed down the driveway. As it disappeared down the road, Janie closed her eyes and silently asked God to help Jonathan decide to stay in Pennsylvania.

CHAPTER FIVE

Jonathan paid the driver and then walked past his uncle's house and down the path to his grandparents' cottage. His gait was as light as if he were walking on clouds after spending the evening with Janie and her family. Her father had asked a lot of questions, but it didn't bother Jonathan. Her mother and sister had made him feel welcome.

The best part of the evening, however, had been sitting on the porch with Janie. Jonathan was so comfortable with her. It was as if he could tell her anything. She was attentive, much more attentive than his ex-girlfriend Grace had ever been. Janie was the *maedel* he'd waited for his whole life.

But this is wrong! I have to go back to Maryland in November!

The warning rang out from deep in his soul, and it choked the happiness that had been brewing inside of him all evening.

With a sigh, Jonathan climbed the front steps and entered the cottage, stepping into the small family room. As he hung up his coat, he saw his grandmother sitting in her favorite chair, reading a devotional by the light of the propane lamp. His grandfather snored quietly in his wing chair on the other side of the room.

"How was your supper?" *Mammi* asked softly.

"It was *gut*." Jonathan smiled over at his grandfather, shaking his head.

Mammi stood and took Jonathan's hand in hers. "Let's go talk in the other room." She steered him into the kitchen.

"Sit," she instructed, then brought a plate of oatmeal raisin cookies to the table. "I made your favorite this afternoon."

"*Danki.*" He didn't have the heart to tell her he was full. Instead, he swiped a cookie from the plate.

"Tell me all about your evening." *Mammi*'s brown eyes sparkled with curiosity. "How was her family?"

"They were great. I had a *gut* time." Jonathan bit into the cookie as his worries continued to nip at him.

"*Was iss letz?*" *Mammi* seemed to sense his hesitation.

"I really care about her," Jonathan admitted. "I just don't see how it can work."

"Why not?" *Mammi* picked up a cookie. "You both seem to like each other and that's probably the most important part of a relationship. If you don't like each other, you won't make it through the tough times." She bit into the cookie while seeming to ponder something. "Is it the distance? You know you're always welcome here. You don't have to rush back home unless your *dat* is tired of taking care of your *haus* and animals."

Jonathan couldn't lie. The distance was part of his hesitation. "It's not only that." He took another cookie from the plate. "I just don't see how it can work with our age difference."

"Why not?" *Mammi* lifted her eyebrows. "Your *daadi* and I have made it work." She grinned. "In fact, we still like each other after all these years."

Jonathan chuckled. "That is fantastic, *Mammi*, but I'm not sure her *dat* will give me his permission to date her. He seemed to be grilling me from the moment I stepped out of the van."

Mammi waved off his comment. "*Mei dat* did the same thing to Omar, but he came around. They got along wonderfully. It's a *dat*'s job to make sure his *boppli* marries a *gut* man. If you ever have a *dochder*, you'll do the same thing to her boyfriends."

Jonathan nodded and took another bite of the cookie. He wanted to believe his grandmother's encouraging words, but he knew in the back of his mind—in his heart—he was afraid to trust another woman after the way Grace had hurt him. Janie was too sweet to mean to hurt him, but maybe she wouldn't care about him enough to look past their age difference, even if he could.

"Are you worried she'll break your heart the way Grace did?" *Mammi* asked gently.

Had she been reading his mind?

"Janie is a different *maedel*."

"I know." Jonathan stared down at the table. "But I'm just not sure."

"It's late," *Mammi* said after a few moments of silence between them. "I need to get your *daadi* out of his chair and into his bed. I go through this every night."

"I'll help you." Jonathan popped the last of his cookie into his mouth and headed into the family room. As he tried to coax his snoring grandfather awake, he wondered if his grandmother was right. Maybe he and Janie could somehow make their relationship work.

. . .

Janie's smile was wide as she climbed the porch steps after saying good-bye to Jonathan. The dinner had gone better than she'd ever imagined it would. Her parents were welcoming, and Jonathan seemed comfortable getting to know them and Marie.

She stopped walking when she reached the porch swing. Their visit on the porch had been even more romantic than the buggy ride. She was still stunned by the way he'd described her hair. No one had ever said her hair was as beautiful as the sunset. When she was in school, the boys used to make fun of her, saying her hair was the color of orange crayons. She always felt different and strange because she was the only redhead in the school.

When she was with Jonathan, however, she felt beautiful and special. He wasn't like any other man she'd met. None of the boys in her youth group were interested in her, but Marie never had any trouble getting the boys' attention. Janie always assumed it was due to her strange hair, but Jonathan told her he noticed her hair when they first met. He felt like a gift sent to her by God, and she was so very thankful!

Her feelings for him were growing deeper and

deeper with each passing day. She wondered if this was how true love felt. If Jonathan felt the same way about her, he could possibly be the man who would love her for the rest of her life. Her spirit soared at the thought of settling down and raising a family together.

Janie stepped into the house and hung up her wrap. Then she found her parents sitting at the kitchen table. She smiled as she greeted them. Her cheeks ached from smiling so much.

"*Danki* for allowing me to invite Jonathan over tonight. He said he had a very nice time." She started toward the stairs. "I'm going to go get ready for bed."

"Janie, wait," her mother said. "Please sit down for a moment. We'd like to talk to you."

Janie spun, and their dismal expressions sent dread pooling in her belly. "Is something wrong?"

"No, but we'd like to speak with you." *Dat* cleared his throat and rested his elbows on the table.

"Did I do something wrong?" Janie asked, her voice squeaking like a young child's. She sat down across from her parents and felt as if she were facing the congregation after she'd been caught committing a sin. But she hadn't deliberately done anything sinful.

"No, of course not. We'd just like to discuss Jonathan with you." Her mother glanced at her father, and he nodded. "He's a very nice young man, but we have some concerns."

"Concerns? I don't understand." Janie's throat suddenly became dry, and she tried in vain to swallow.

"I spoke to him outside when he arrived," *Dat* began, his eyes somber. "I asked him what his intentions are with you, and he said he would like to get to know you better. He said he cares about you."

A glimmer of hope ignited inside of Janie, but her father's serious face quickly extinguished it.

"He's planning to go back to Maryland in early December," *Dat* said. "Your *mamm* and I don't want you to get involved with him and then decide to move away. We'd like all three of our *kinner* to stay in our community."

"He could decide to stay here," Janie offered. "He hasn't left yet." Janie looked at her mother, hoping for her support, but instead, her mother continued to frown.

"Your *dat* is right," *Mamm* said. "We don't want you to move away, but we also don't want to see you hurt when he leaves. You need to keep going to youth group, and you'll find the right *bu* for you in our community."

"No," Janie said, her voice now trembling with emotion. "I'm not interested in the *buwe* in my youth group. I want to get to know Jonathan better. Why can't you give him a chance? You'll see why I like him."

Her parents exchanged bleak looks.

"Do you realize he'll be thirty in a few months?" *Dat* asked her.

Janie nodded. "*Ya*, he told me, and I'll be twenty-one in June."

Dat shook his head. "I'm not comfortable with you dating a man who is nearly a decade older than you. It's not right."

Mamm nodded. "I agree."

Janie gasped and tears stung her eyes as she looked

back and forth between her parents. "But, *Mamm*, you said he's a nice man. Why does his age matter if he's a *gut* Christian man?"

"I would like you to find someone your age or at least closer to your age," *Mamm* said. "You have shared life experiences with your *freinden* from your youth group."

"Shared life experiences?" Janie wiped away an errant tear with the back of her hand. "What does that even mean? Jonathan and I are both Amish and we have a special connection I've never felt with any other *bu*. We enjoy each other's company. What more do we need?"

"I don't want to see you get hurt, Janie." *Mamm*'s eyes were sympathetic as she leaned forward to hold Janie's hand, but Janie moved her hands out of her mother's reach. "As your *dat* said, Jonathan is going to go back to Maryland and will leave you here with a broken heart."

"You don't know that," Janie retorted with more resentment than she'd meant to share. She turned her focus to her father. "You said he told you he cared about me. Please give him a chance."

Dat shook his head, looking unconvinced. "I don't think he's right for you. If he asks for permission to date you, I'm going to tell him no."

Speechless, Janie turned to her mother again, but her mother only shook her head.

"I don't understand you," Janie said, her voice radiating with anguish. "You want me to get married and have a family like Sam, but you won't approve of the man I want to see. It doesn't make sense."

"There will be other *buwe*," *Mamm* said, her eyes warming. "I promise you, Janie." She glanced at *Dat*. "I had my heart broken before I met your *dat*. Jonathan won't be the last man you care about."

"Your *mamm* is right," *Dat* said. "We're only doing this for your own *gut*. We know what's best for our *kinner*."

"You can be his *freind*, but we can't allow you to date him," *Mamm* clarified. "I know you enjoy talking to him at work, and there's nothing wrong with that, right, Timothy?"

Dat gave a quick nod. "There's nothing wrong with being his *freind*, but that's all."

Janie bit back angry words as she wiped away more tears. She would never speak belligerently to her parents, but she was crushed by their decision. She'd never known her parents to be so unreasonable. Why couldn't they see how special Jonathan was? Why couldn't they support Janie's choice in a suitor?

"I'm going to bed," Janie finally said, softly. *"Gut nacht."* She stood and rushed up the stairs, throwing herself onto her bed and letting her tears flow into her pillow.

Janie heard her door click shut, followed by light footsteps crossing her room. She squeezed her eyes shut and hoped it wasn't her mother who had come to see her. She couldn't stand the idea of hearing more negative words about Jonathan.

The bed shifted and a gentle hand touched her shoulder.

"Janie?" Marie's sweet voice asked. "Are you all right?"

Janie shook her head, still facing the wall. "No, I'm not."

"I heard everything," Marie admitted as she rubbed Janie's back. "I'm sorry for eavesdropping, but I couldn't help it. I'm so sorry *Mamm* and *Dat* don't approve of Jonathan. I think he's perfect for you." She sighed. "I was hoping *Dat* and *Mamm* would see past his age."

Janie rolled over and sniffed as she looked up at her sister. "I was hoping too." She hugged her arms around her middle as if to stop her heart from breaking. "They said I can be his *freind*, but *Dat* will never permit him to date me. I just don't understand. I thought they would see how wonderful Jonathan is and be *froh* that I found him. You've never had a problem finding *buwe* who like you, but they never like me. What if I never find anyone else who likes me?"

Marie clicked her tongue. "You can't possibly believe that, Janie. You'll find someone. For now, you can enjoy being Jonathan's *freind*. At least *Dat* will allow you to do that."

Janie nodded. "You're right." The tiny flicker of hope took root inside of Janie. She would cherish Jonathan's friendship for as long as she could.

· · ·

Janie lifted a tray of peanut butter spread and stepped out from the Riehls' kitchen the following Sunday. This week's church service was hosted by the Riehl family on their farm only a mile away from where her family lived, and now the noon meal was being served in their barn.

She shivered as the October breeze caused her black sweater and purple dress to flutter in the wind. Her thoughts had been stuck on her conversation with her parents Wednesday night. She hadn't told Jonathan what her parents had said about him, and she tried to hide her disappointment from him. Janie was grateful she could still enjoy lunch with him every weekday, but she longed for their relationship to progress.

"Janie!" Marie called behind her. "Janie, wait!"

Janie turned as her sister hurried toward her, carrying a coffeepot. *"Was iss letz?"*

"Nothing is wrong." Marie grinned. "You'll never guess who is here."

Janie shrugged. "I have no idea."

"Jonathan!" Marie pointed toward the barn. "I saw him sitting near Samuel and Mike."

"He is?" Janie asked with surprise. "I didn't see him during the service."

"I didn't either, but we were sitting all the way in the back." Marie held out the coffeepot. "You take this and go fill his mug. I'll handle the peanut butter spread."

"Danki." Janie took the pot and headed into the barn. She found the table where Jonathan sat next to a man, who must be his grandfather, and was surprised to see her brother sitting across from them. Excitement overtook her at the prospect of introducing Jonathan to Samuel. Perhaps Samuel could help convince her parents that Jonathan was an acceptable choice for a boyfriend.

She began filling coffee mugs and worked her way down the table toward Jonathan. When she reached him, her smile broadened and happiness surged through her.

"*Kaffi?*" she asked.

Jonathan looked up and his eyes widened in surprise. "Janie. I saw your *dat* earlier, but I didn't see you." He touched the arm of the elderly man beside him. "*Daadi*, this is *mei freind* Janie. Janie, this is Omar."

"It's nice to meet you." Janie shook Omar's hand and then looked at her brother and cousin, who were sitting across from Jonathan. "Have you met *mei bruder*, Samuel, and my cousin Mike? Sam and Mike, this is Jonathan and his grandfather, Omar."

Samuel leaned over the table and shook Jonathan's hand. "We were talking earlier, but I didn't realize you were *freinden* with *mei schweschder*."

"Hi, Jonathan," Mike said.

"It's great to meet you," Jonathan said, shaking Mike's hand. Then he looked up at Janie. "I didn't realize we were visiting your district, but I should have known since we're not far from your *haus*."

"I'm glad you could come today." She pointed toward the end of the table. "I need to go now."

"Maybe we can talk later?" he asked, his brown eyes hopeful.

"*Ya,*" she said with a nod. "I'd like that."

. . .

After lunch, Jonathan smiled and nodded as his grandparents introduced him to a few of their friends. While he tried his best to be friendly with their acquaintances, he couldn't stop scanning the knot of people for Janie. His grandparents had suggested they visit another church district since it was an off Sunday in their home district, but Jonathan hadn't realized he was going to Janie's district.

He was surprised when she appeared at his table with the coffeepot. He was thankful to see her beautiful smile this morning. She'd been on his mind nonstop since he'd had supper at her parents' house. The hour they spent together at lunch every day at work was never enough to satisfy his growing desire to be with her.

As he glanced around, he saw Janie's parents standing on the other side of the barn, talking to another couple. Her mother met his gaze and raised her hand in greeting, and he returned the gesture. He'd seen Janie's father earlier, and Timothy had been pleasant as well. He hoped that meant they approved of him. Janie hadn't indicated they didn't like him, but he still worried.

Jonathan looked through the barn door and spotted Janie standing near the pasture fence, talking with a petite and pretty woman with light brown hair. The young woman was holding a baby, and he assumed she was Janie's sister-in-law. He excused himself from his grandparents' conversation and made his way toward the two women.

When Janie saw him, her pretty face lit up with a warm smile. "Jonathan, this is my sister-in-law, Mandy, and my niece, Becky."

"Hi, Jonathan," Mandy said with a nod. "I've heard a lot about you."

Janie's cheeks turned pink, and she was even more adorable.

Samuel and Mike sidled up to them, along with a little blond boy, who resembled Mike, and a pretty brunette, who was holding Mike's hand.

"Are you ready to go?" Samuel asked Mandy, and she nodded.

"Jonathan," Janie said, "you met Mike earlier. This is Mike's girlfriend, Rachel, and his younger *bruder*, John. This is *mei freind* Jonathan. We work together."

Jonathan greeted them, and then they said good-bye before heading to the buggies, leaving Jonathan and Janie standing by the fence alone.

"I'm so glad I got to meet more members of your family today," he said, silently admiring how the sunlight made her hair resemble fire. She was so beautiful he couldn't take his eyes off her.

"I am too." She watched her family walk toward a buggy. "Marie and I used to take care of Mike and John's *dat*. He was our *onkel* Raymond."

"He was the one on dialysis?"

"That's right. We miss him." As she turned toward him, he saw her face brighten. "I talked to your *mammi* in the kitchen earlier. She's very nice." She peered up at him, and her eyes somehow seemed a deeper shade of blue. "Did you have a *gut* day yesterday?"

"*Ya*, I did." He leaned against the split rail fence. "I helped *mei daadi* and *onkel* with a few projects around the farm. I always have a *gut* time when I'm with them. How about you?"

"I had a *gut* day too. I did some baking and cleaning."

She rested her hand on the rail beside him. "The weekends go by too fast."

"They do, but I look forward to our time together at work during the week."

"I do too." Janie looked pensive, as if she was mentally debating. She opened her mouth to speak but was interrupted by someone calling her name.

"Janie!" Marie called from across the driveway. "It's time to go."

Janie stepped away from the fence. "I'm so sorry. My family is ready to go. It was *gut* seeing you."

"*Ya*, it was." Jonathan smiled. "I'll see you tomorrow."

"Good-bye," she said, then rushed off to meet her family.

Jonathan's smile faded. He wondered what she was going to say before her sister interrupted their conversation.

CHAPTER SIX

Janie handed the *Englisher* her change and bag of souvenirs with a smile. "Thank you for shopping here. Please come back soon."

"Thank you, sweetie," the woman said, then turned for the door.

Eva rushed over, looked around the room, and leaned in close to Janie. "I've been waiting until we had a lull in the store. It's finally empty," she said softly. "I need to tell you a secret."

"What secret?" Janie asked, bewildered.

"I heard Bianca and Craig talking in the office this morning when I put my lunch in the refrigerator." Eva craned her neck to look toward the back of the store where the staff offices were. "Bianca said the driver of the car and some of the passengers in the buggy accident are blaming Jonathan and they're going to sue the store."

Janie gasped. "No!"

"Shh," Eva said, hissing her warning with a frown. "Keep your voice down. I don't want Bianca or Craig to hear me. Craig said if the passengers sue them, they could lose everything. Bianca said their lawyer told them they have to fire Jonathan now so they eliminate the liability or something."

Janie's stomach plummeted. "They're going to fire Jonathan?"

Eva nodded solemnly. "That's what Bianca said."

"*Ach,* no." Janie gnawed her bottom lip as an urgency to tell Craig or Bianca what she'd witnessed the day of the accident took hold of her. Her father's warning for Janie to steer clear of any of the business associated with the accident echoed through her mind. She had to obey her father, but how could she not tell Craig and Bianca what she saw when Jonathan was not only wrongfully accused but would now lose his job?

Worst of all, if they fire him, I'll never see him again.

That was the final straw. Janie couldn't stand by and watch Jonathan get fired when she held the key to his exoneration.

"Eva, I need to go talk to Craig. I have to tell him I know the accident wasn't Jonathan's fault."

"You know for certain?" Eva asked, raising her eyebrows.

Janie nodded. "I witnessed it."

"Go," Eva said as a line of customers filed into the store. "I can handle things up here."

"*Danki,*" Janie said.

She wove past the displays of wooden signs, magnets, and cloth dolls as she made her way to the back of the store. When she reached a door with a sign that read Employees Only, she pushed it open and entered the hallway leading to the storeroom, offices, and break room.

She approached Craig's office and found him working

on his computer. She knocked on the doorframe, and he looked up at her and smiled.

"Hi, Janie," he said. "Is everything all right in the store?"

"Everything is fine." She folded her hands over her apron. "May I speak with you for a moment?"

"Of course. Come in." Craig gestured toward a chair in front of his desk. "Have a seat."

"Thank you." Janie sank into the chair.

"Well, what's on your mind this fine Monday afternoon?" Craig leaned forward on his large wooden desk and steepled his fingers.

"I want to tell you something about the accident." Although her father's warning not to get involved still echoed through her mind, she pushed on. "I was eating lunch at a picnic table near the entrance to the parking lot, so I saw everything. That's when I ran into the store to get you."

Craig gasped, his eyes widening. "The police asked me for possible witnesses, and I completely forgot you were outside and might have seen the whole thing. Please tell me what you remember."

Janie paused and breathed in a deep, shuddering breath.

"Take your time," Craig said.

"The accident wasn't Jonathan's fault," she said, her heart pounding with anxiety. "Not only did Jonathan signal before he turned into the parking lot, but the driver of the car was distracted."

"What do you mean?" Craig asked.

"He was looking down at something in his hand

instead of watching the road. I think he was texting on his cell phone." An invisible load lifted from Janie's shoulders as she said the words aloud.

"He was texting?" Craig asked, and she nodded. "Are you sure?"

"It looked like a cell phone. But the point is, he was looking down, not at the road to see Jonathan's signal. He didn't brake until he looked up to see he was about to crash into the buggy." Her words came in a rush now. "Craig, it has bothered me that Jonathan was blamed when the accident wasn't his fault. Jonathan wasn't reckless. He did nothing to endanger those passengers. I'm so sorry I didn't tell you before. I was hoping someone else saw Jonathan signal too."

Craig blew out a puff of air. "I'm glad you told me now." He raked his hands through his dark hair. "You have no idea what a relief this is. Would you be willing to talk to a police officer if he needs more information?"

Janie nodded, but her father's instructions to stay out of the investigation reverberated through her mind once again. She hoped she wouldn't have to recount the story numerous times.

"Thank you, Janie," Craig said. "I appreciate your help."

"You're welcome." As Janie walked back into the store, she hoped she'd helped save Jonathan's job.

. . .

Jonathan's boots crunched on dry leaves as he led Bucky toward the stable. He hummed to himself as he contemplated the conversation he'd shared with Janie at lunch. He cherished every moment he spent with her and tried not to think about how November was just around the corner.

"Jonathan!" Craig called as he ambled from the store toward the stable. "I need to talk with you for a moment."

"Okay." Jonathan stopped the horse and began rubbing his neck while waiting for Craig. "You're a *gut bu*, Bucky," he murmured to the horse. "*Ya*, you are."

"I'm glad I caught you before you left for the day," Craig said as he walked over to him.

"Is everything all right?"

"Yes." Craig smiled. "In fact, I have fantastic news. The driver of the car admitted fault."

"What?" Jonathan tried to process what Craig had said. "He admitted he caused the accident?"

"That's right." Craig folded his arms across his chest. "I just spoke to my lawyer, and the driver admitted he was distracted because he was texting his girlfriend. You're off the hook, and you can return to giving buggy rides tomorrow if you want. You're completely cleared of any wrongdoing."

Craig held out his hand, and Jonathan shook it as questions swirled through his mind.

"I'm still a little confused," Jonathan said. "Why did he suddenly admit guilt? I thought he blamed me for the accident."

"Janie came to see me on Monday. She not only saw you signal, but she insisted she witnessed the driver looking down at what seemed to be a cell phone, probably texting. I called my lawyer right away, and he contacted the driver's lawyer. Apparently the driver was caught in a lie. He said he wasn't texting, but the police looked into his cell phone records and found the evidence. He sent a text just as the car hit the buggy, and his lawyer told him he had to admit fault. You can thank Janie. She got the process started."

"Janie did that for me?" Jonathan asked with surprise.

"That's right. I'm not sure what made her tell me now, but it's a good thing. Our lawyer said the driver and some passengers were going to sue, and he was pressuring us to fire you, Jonathan. And that's the last thing we wanted to do.

"So do you want to go back to giving tours tomorrow?" Craig asked, rubbing his hands together.

"I'd love to," Jonathan said. "Thank you."

"You're welcome." Craig patted Jonathan's back. "I'll see you tomorrow."

Jonathan silently marveled at the great news as he led Bucky into the stable. He was astonished Janie had gone out on a limb to make things right for him, and he hoped she wasn't in any trouble for it. The Amish didn't like to get involved in legal matters. Had she suspected he really might lose his job if she didn't step forward? She was a truly special *maedel*. He had to thank her. But a question lingered in his mind—why hadn't she told him she'd spoken to Craig on Monday?

Jonathan finished his chores in the stable and then stepped out into the parking lot. When he spotted Janie walking toward the white van idling nearby, he took off running.

"Janie!" he called. "Janie, wait!"

Janie spun toward him, her eyes wide with question. "Jonathan?"

"Janie," he said, trying to catch his breath. "I need to talk to you."

"What's wrong?" Her eyes searched his.

"Nothing is wrong. In fact, everything is right."

"I don't understand." Janie tipped her head in question, and she looked even more adorable than usual.

"I need to thank you," he said, taking a step closer to her and breathing in the sweet apple scent of her shampoo. "I know you said you saw me signal, but *danki* for telling Craig not only that, but that the driver wasn't paying attention."

"Oh." She waved off the words. "It wasn't anything."

"It was something," he insisted. "Because of you, the driver admitted he caused the accident, and I'm cleared of any wrongdoing. And I got my driving job back."

"Oh, that's fantastic!" Janie gasped. "I'm so *froh* for you!" She dropped her tote bag and threw her arms around him, pulling him into a warm hug.

Stunned, Jonathan held her in his arms, and he felt something spark between them. A small flame ignited inside of him and then settled deep in his soul.

I love her.

The feeling was so intense that his pulse accelerated. Janie had somehow broken through the wall he'd built around his heart after Grace left him. He closed his eyes and longed to freeze this moment in time. He wanted to hold her close to him forever.

"Oh." Janie suddenly stepped away from him. She

smoothed her hands down her sweater, and her cheeks were the color of a Red Delicious apple. "I'm so sorry. I didn't mean to be so—"

"It's fine." Jonathan touched her cheek. "And *danki* again."

Janie nodded, her cheeks still flaming. *"Gern gschehne."* She glanced back at the van and then turned toward him again. "I need to go, but I will see you tomorrow."

"Gut nacht," he said.

"Gut nacht," she repeated before climbing into the van.

As the van drove away, Jonathan said a silent prayer, thanking God for sending him to Bird-in-Hand to meet Janie.

• • •

"Jonathan was cleared of all wrongdoing today," Janie finally blurted as she cut up her piece of pork later that evening. "The driver of the car admitted he was distracted and was texting when he hit the buggy."

"Really?" Marie asked, her brown eyes wide with interest. "That's *wunderbaar.*"

"Ya, I'm so *froh* for him," Janie said, hoping her cheeks wouldn't burn with embarrassment as she remembered how she'd hugged Jonathan earlier. What had possessed her to be so forward? She had never done anything that forward or impulsive before. Why did she feel so comfortable with him? It felt natural to hug him.

Janie suddenly realized her family was studying her. Had she missed part of the conversation?

"I asked you a question," *Dat* said.

"Oh, I'm sorry." Janie did her best not to look guilty even though she knew her parents would have been furious if they'd seen her behavior earlier. "What did you say, *Dat*?"

"I asked you why the driver suddenly confessed," *Dat* said, placing his glass of water on the table. "Did you hear what made him change his mind and tell the truth?"

With her father's brown eyes watching her, Janie realized she'd shared too much. Now she had to admit she went against her parents' wishes. But maybe her father would go easy on her when he realized she helped Jonathan keep his job.

"Janie?" *Dat*'s voice was laced with irritation. "Why are you acting so strangely tonight? Are you not feeling well?"

"I'm fine," Janie said softly, placing her fork and knife on her plate.

"Then what is it?" *Dat* demanded. "You've been distracted all evening."

Janie took a deep breath. It was time for her to tell the truth. "I'm the reason the driver admitted the truth. I told Craig I saw the driver texting. Craig spoke to his lawyer, and then—"

"You disobeyed me?" *Dat*'s voice boomed throughout the kitchen.

Janie nodded as tears stung her eyes. "I did, but I only wanted to help Jonathan. I found out he was going to be fired because some of the passengers in the buggy and the driver were going to sue Craig—"

Dat's face turned bright red as he wagged a finger at her. "I told you to stay out of it, Janie Lynn. The last thing I want is for you to be dragged into court as a witness. The *Englishers* love to sue each other, and it's against our beliefs to get involved in that." He fisted his hands. "You are not to see Jonathan any longer. I don't want you to have any contact with him."

"Why?" Janie asked. "This isn't Jonathan's fault. It was my choice to talk to Craig. Jonathan didn't know anything about it."

"I don't care," *Dat* continued, his voice full of anger. "You are not to see him at all. I don't want you to eat lunch with him or talk to him. You don't make logical decisions when he's around. Steer clear of him. He'll be back in Maryland in a month, and then we can forget all about this mess."

"But, *Dat*," Janie began, her voice trembling with both grief and regret. "I care about him. I can't pretend I don't know him."

"You can and you will," *Dat* ordered. He turned his attention to his plate and speared a piece of his pork.

Janie looked at her mother for help, but *Mamm* merely shook her head and frowned. Janie knew her mother would never go against her father, but she'd hoped somehow her mother could help. Janie looked at Marie, who seemed nearly as upset as she was.

Janie trained her eyes on her plate and willed herself not to cry. She'd prayed she and Jonathan could make their relationship work, but in a matter of a few minutes, all her hopes and dreams had dissolved. All she had left was a hole in her heart.

• • •

Jonathan sipped his cup of coffee and looked across the table at his grandmother. "I still can't believe Janie came forward for me," he said after explaining what had happened that afternoon. "I've never known a *maedel* like her."

Mammi gave him a knowing smile. "She's special to you."

"She is." Jonathan took a deep breath. "I think I'm in love with her."

Mammi patted his hand. "Oh, Jonathan, I'm so *froh* to hear you say that. I know Grace hurt you deeply."

"Grace did," Jonathan admitted as he cradled the warm cup in his hands. "But I don't think I felt this way about Grace. It's different this time. I've been thinking all evening that I want to stay here in Lancaster. I think I want to sell *mei haus* back in Maryland and move here. I'll find a job and—"

"Oh, that's *wunderbaar!*" *Mammi* clapped her hands. "We'd love to have you, right, Omar?"

"Absolutely," *Daadi* said. "You can stay with us until you build a *haus*. You can get a job working for your *onkel* or one of your cousins."

"That would be great." Jonathan's heart raced with the possibility of starting a new life in Pennsylvania, a new life with the beautiful Janie Lantz. He couldn't wait to tell her.

CHAPTER SEVEN

Jonathan hurried into the souvenir shop the following morning. He was bursting with excitement. He couldn't wait to see Janie and tell her he loved her. He couldn't wait to start their future together.

He entered the store, and when he saw her standing in front of the cash register, he stopped in his tracks. Janie was ringing up T-shirts for a customer, but Jonathan could tell her smile wasn't genuine. Her eyes were dull, and he could see purple circles under them. Alarm surged through him. Where was the happy *maedel* who had hugged him last night?

He padded up toward the counter and stood close by until she handed the customer her change and told her to have a nice day.

"Janie?" he asked. "How are you?"

"Jonathan," she said, her smile gone, her voice flat and devoid of emotion. *"Wie geht's?"*

Jonathan's heart splintered over the sadness in her eyes. What had happened to her? He glanced around the store and saw only a few customers. He reached for her arm and then stopped himself.

"May I speak with you for a moment?" he asked.

She hesitated, but then gave a curt nod. "Let me go find Eva."

Worry washed over him as she hustled to the back of the store. She whispered something to Eva, who looked over at Jonathan and smiled. Then Janie gestured for Jonathan to follow her into the Employees Only area. They entered the break room, and Janie closed the door behind them.

She fingered the hem on her black apron and studied her shoes, seeming to avert her eyes on purpose. Anticipation and worry were eating away at his soul.

"*Was iss letz?*" he finally asked. "Janie, I can't take this silence between us."

When Janie looked up, her eyes glistened with tears. "I can't be your *freind* anymore." Her voice trembled with raw emotion as tears trickled down her pink cheeks.

"What?" He took a step toward her, the grief on her face stabbing at his heart. "I don't understand. Is it your parents?"

"It's *mei dat.*" She wiped her tears with the back of her hand. "He instructed me not to get involved with the accident, but then I admitted to telling Craig what I saw. He was furious I disobeyed him. I tried to explain I only did it so you wouldn't get fired, but he still wouldn't listen to me."

"You thought I was going to get fired?"

Janie nodded. "Eva overheard Bianca and Craig talking. Some of the passengers and the other driver were going to sue, so they were going to have to fire you to help save their business. I couldn't let that happen."

Jonathan was speechless.

"So now I have to steer clear of you, and I can't even have lunch with you anymore." She sniffed as more tears escaped her eyes. "I'm sorry."

"No, Janie," he said. "I'm sorry this happened to you." He longed to touch her arm and hug her the way she'd hugged him last night, but he couldn't disobey her father. He didn't want to make things more difficult for her, but the thought of not having her in his life was so painful it stole his breath.

"I have to go," she said, her voice hitching on the last word.

Before he could respond, Janie rushed out of the break room and into the staff restroom, the door lock clicking behind her.

Jonathan leaned his back against the wall and squeezed his eyes shut. His life had changed dramatically within the past twelve hours. He'd gone from realizing he was in love and wanting to start a new life in Pennsylvania to losing that love before he even had a chance to share his feelings with her. Disappointment, anger, and guilt warred within him. If only he could convince her father that he loved her.

Pushing off the wall, he ambled through the store and tried to think of a way to convince Janie's father his feelings for her were pure and that he would love Janie and take care of her for the rest of his life.

• • •

Janie sat alone in the break room and tried to eat her lunch. Her turkey sandwich tasted like sand as she slowly chewed it. She wasn't hungry even though she couldn't stomach her breakfast either. Last night, she'd tossed and turned all night long and cried until she was convinced she had no tears left to shed. The thought of losing Jonathan's friendship had cut her to the core, and the anguish on his face when she told him the news had jammed the knife even further into her heart.

Janie had tried to talk to her mother last night, begging her to convince *Dat* to change his mind about Jonathan. Despite Janie's best efforts, *Mamm* had refused, explaining she couldn't go against his decisions. Janie knew she was out of options. There was nothing she could do except try to avoid Jonathan and pray her heart would someday heal.

The door opened, and Eva entered the break room. She tilted her head in question.

"What are you doing in here?" Eva asked as she crossed the room and opened the refrigerator. "Is it too cold to eat outside?"

"I decided to eat in here."

"Where's Jonathan?" Eva retrieved her lunch bag and sat down across from Janie. "Don't you two eat together every day? Is he out on a buggy run?"

"No." Janie studied her half-eaten sandwich. "I can't eat with him anymore."

"You can't eat with him?" Eva pulled out her sandwich. "I don't understand."

Janie met her friend's curious eyes and shared her father's reaction to the news that she had told Craig the truth about the other driver.

"So now I can't see him." Janie cleared her throat in hopes of dissolving the lump that swelled there.

Eva gave a sympathetic frown. "Janie, I am so sorry. Just give your *dat* time to calm down and maybe he'll change his mind."

"He won't." Janie heaved a deep sigh. "I don't regret helping Jonathan. I couldn't keep the truth to myself, but I couldn't lie to *mei dat* either. I thought Jonathan and I might someday be more than *freinden*, but now I just have to find a way to get over my broken heart." Tears flooded her eyes, but she willed them not to fall. She'd already cried too much since last night.

"Don't give up hope, Janie." Eva leaned across the table and touched Janie's hand. "Jonathan obviously cares about you, and I have a feeling he won't let you go so easily. Maybe he can find a way to show your *dat* you belong together."

"I doubt it," Janie muttered as more heartache drowned her.

. . .

Craig came out of his office one afternoon in late October as Janie straightened the T-shirt display and Eva arranged the shelves of cloth dolls.

"Could one of you possibly lock up tonight?" Craig asked. "I meant to ask you earlier in the week, but I forgot. Bianca and I are having a Halloween party tonight, and she needs me to run a few errands." He rested his elbow on the counter. "I'm sorry this is last minute, but the party is a big deal to Bianca. She loves Halloween and invites all her friends."

Eva grimaced. "I'm sorry, but I can't stay. I promised *mei mamm* and *dat* we'd go see *mei* cousin Esther's new *boppli* tonight."

Janie shrugged and looked at Eva. "I can stay."

"Are you sure?" Craig asked with concern. "Are you comfortable locking up alone?"

"*Ya.*" Janie nodded with emphasis. "I helped Eva lock up last week, and she showed me what to do. I have my own set of keys. I'll just call my parents and my driver. It's no problem."

"And you remember how to make the deposit?" Eva asked. "Can your driver take you by the bank?"

"Oh *ya.*" Janie waved off the question. "It's not a problem at all."

"Thank you so much, Janie." Craig smiled with relief. "You just saved me from getting in trouble with Bianca. I'll see you both tomorrow."

The remainder of the afternoon flew by as Janie and Eva helped customers and restocked shelves.

After Eva left for the day, Janie vacuumed, dusted a few shelves, and closed out the register, pushing the stacks of bills into the zippered bank bag for the nightly deposit. She slipped the bank bag into her tote bag, put on her sweater, and then gathered her purse, tote bag, and lunch bag before turning off the lights and walking to the front door. The keys jingled as she pulled them out of her apron pocket. She flipped the electronic Open sign to Closed, made sure the front door was still locked, and then stood there, listening.

An eerie feeling prickled Janie's spine as she looked out at the deserted parking lot. Only a little moonlight and a couple of lampposts from neighboring businesses illuminated the grounds outside the shop. She couldn't stop the feeling that someone was watching her. She tried to push the ridiculous thought away. *Of course there's no one there.*

Janie moved to the side door to wait for her driver. She looked toward the stable and saw a light burning inside. She wondered if one of the buggy drivers had forgotten to turn off the lights before leaving. Had Jonathan been the last one to close up tonight? Her heart kicked at the thought of his handsome face. Oh, how she'd missed him the past two weeks.

Janie had tried her best to avoid him, but he seemed to appear when she least expected it. She ran into him in the break room one afternoon last week, and although he offered her a kind greeting and smile, she quickly excused herself. The following morning he arrived at the store at the same moment she did, and they shared an awkward greeting before parting ways like two mere acquaintances.

When Janie walked past the stable a few days later, she saw him talking to two pretty *Englisher* girls, who giggled and smiled at him. She gritted her teeth at the sight, and something that felt a whole lot like jealousy bubbled up inside of her. Jonathan looked over at her and gave her a cordial smile and wave, and she hurried past the stable toward the store. She'd tried to put on a brave face, but every time she saw Jonathan, her heart seemed to shatter a little more.

Now as Janie stood gazing out over the dark parking lot at the side of the building, she longed for the warmth of Jonathan's protective hand to calm her nerves. She'd never been afraid of the dark, but something felt wrong tonight—she just couldn't put her finger on what was amiss. When she saw headlights reflecting off the side of the stable, she looked up at a clock over the door that read seven fifteen. Frank, her driver, was early, but Frank was often early.

Janie stepped outside, and the cold October air seeped in through her dress, sending goose bumps up her arms. She longed for a warmer sweater. The door clicked shut behind her.

As Janie pushed the key into the lock and turned it, she thought she heard footsteps. The hair on the back of her neck stood as she turned around. She had to be hearing things. The headlights were gone and there was no van in sight. The driver of the vehicle must have been turning around in the parking lot. Frank wasn't there.

Janie heard the sound again. Her hands shook and her mouth dried. Perhaps it was an animal, maybe a stray cat. She'd seen a mother cat and kittens near the stable the other day.

"Hello?" Janie's voice shook. "Is someone there?" she tried to shout, but her voice was thin, and her hands trembled as she gripped the strap of her bag. "Hello?"

Suddenly, out of the darkness, a man rounded the corner of the building and came at her. Janie's heart hammered as her eyes focused. Under the dim light mounted over the door, she could see he was dressed in black from head to toe, with a black knit cap over his dark hair. His face and lips were covered with sores and blemishes, and when he flashed a menacing smile, he was missing a few teeth. He pointed something metal at her, and it gleamed in the light above her.

Janie gasped as her eyes focused on the metal object. *A gun.*

Icy fear slithered up her back, and panic tightened her throat.

"Give me the money," he said, stepping closer to her. He smelled like sweat and onions, and she willed herself not to gag.

Her mind raced with confusion and terror. Was she dreaming?

"Don't play dumb with me! I saw you put the money bag in there through the window," the man bellowed, training the gun on her tote bag. "You have two choices. You either give it to me willingly or I will take it by force. What's it gonna be?"

The gun clicked, and Janie stood frozen with fear. She opened her mouth to scream, but no sound came. A tear trickled down her cheek.

This is it. I'm going to die.

· · ·

Jonathan rubbed Bucky's neck. "Want some fresh water, *bu*?"

Bucky nodded his head in response.

"All right, then." He walked toward the back of the stable to get a bucket of water.

Jonathan had told Craig he was going to stay late

tonight to fix the stall doors, but the truth was he had to stay busy in a lame attempt to keep his mind off Janie. He'd nearly gone crazy with regret and heartache since she'd stopped talking to him. Seeing her at work every day was sweet torture. Staying busy was the only thing that kept him sane.

As Jonathan approached the sink near the stable door, he thought he heard a voice outside. He cracked the door open and listened. It sounded as if he'd heard a man's voice, but it was after seven o'clock. Everyone should've gone home by now. He stepped into the doorway, looked toward the store, and was surprised to find two figures standing by the side entrance to the store.

Suddenly the scene came into focus. A tall man was standing in front of Janie and had a gun pointed at her face.

Jonathan's stomach plummeted, and adrenaline surged through him. He spun, grabbed a two-by-four piece of wood, and dashed toward the store.

As Jonathan approached, the man spun and trained the gun on him. Jonathan swung the piece of wood, knocking the gun from the man's hand. The gun flew through the air and skidded across the parking lot. The thief's eyes widened and he lunged for Jonathan as Janie screamed. Jonathan held the piece of wood up, preparing to hit the man with it.

Bright beams of light danced around the parking lot and blinded Jonathan for a split second. When his eyes focused again, he saw a white van speeding toward them.

The man swiveled to face the van and then sprinted

across the parking lot toward the road. Jonathan blew out a puff of air and dropped the piece of wood with a clatter, his hands shaking.

"Jonathan!" Janie cried before rushing over and throwing herself into his arms. *"Danki."* Her voice was shaking. "I thought he was going to kill me. Thank you so much." She wrapped her arms around his waist and held on to him.

He rubbed her back and tried to will himself to stop shaking. "I'm just glad I was here," he whispered.

"What happened?" Frank, Janie's driver, had rushed from his van.

Without letting go of Janie, Jonathan explained.

"We need to call the police and give them a description," Frank said. "We can use my phone."

Janie looked up at Jonathan. "Will you stay with me?" Her eyes pleaded with him to say yes.

He stared into her blue eyes and found fear mixed with relief. "Of course I will."

. . .

Nearly two hours later, Janie sat in the backseat and held Jonathan's hand as Frank's van steered down her street. Her mind kept replaying the scene at the store, and she shuddered at the memory of the man's face. She'd never been so terrified in her life. She couldn't stop wondering what would've happened if Jonathan hadn't been working late in the stable. Would the man have shot her just to get the money?

She squeezed Jonathan's hand and looked up into

his brown eyes. He gave her an encouraging smile, and her eyes misted over again. She loved him deeply.

"I've missed you," she whispered.

"I've missed you too," he echoed, his finger gently pushing an errant lock of her hair back from her face.

"Thank you so much for saving me."

Jonathan smiled. "I think that's the hundredth time you've thanked me. You don't have to keep saying that."

Janie leaned her head against his shoulder and closed her eyes while still holding his hand. Warmth and security replaced her earlier panic and fear. She didn't want to ever let go of Jonathan.

The van came to a stop at the back door of her house, and her parents rushed out, followed by Marie.

"Janie!" *Mamm* hollered as Janie climbed out of the van. "We got Frank's message that a man tried to rob you. Are you hurt?" Her eyes were wild with worry.

"Are you all right?" *Dat* asked, looking equally concerned.

Marie's eyes were red as if she'd been crying. "What happened?"

Janie took a shaky breath and then felt Jonathan's calming hand on her shoulder. She glanced up at him.

"Do you want me to tell them?" he asked.

Janie nodded, knowing she'd start to cry if she spoke.

Jonathan slowly explained what happened while her family gaped as they listened. "The man ran when Frank drove up. It was perfect timing."

Frank shook his head and scowled. "I'm just so sorry I didn't come early tonight." He turned to Janie. "I'm so sorry."

Janie opened her mouth to say it wasn't his fault when her mother interrupted.

"*Ach!* Jonathan," *Mamm* said, tears glistening in her eyes, "you saved *mei dochder*." She hugged him. "*Danki.* That man could have killed her."

"I'm so *froh* you were there," Marie said, her voice thick. "I don't want to think about what could have happened."

Dat approached Jonathan and shook his hand, then gently slapped his shoulder. "*Danki*, Jonathan. I can't thank you enough."

A tear trickled down Janie's cheek. She sniffed and tried to hold back her emotions.

"Timothy," Jonathan began, his voice trembling, "I love your *dochder*. I've decided to sell *mei haus* in Maryland and move here. I'm going to talk to *mei onkel* and cousin about going into business with them. I want to make a life here, and I would be honored if I could date Janie." He turned toward her. "I would do anything in my power to take care of her and keep her safe."

Janie's eyes widened. For the second time tonight, she was speechless.

Jonathan looked back at her father. "I know I'm quite a bit older than Janie, but age doesn't mean anything to me. My grandparents are nine years apart, and they've built a wonderful life together. They both told me their ages never mattered. What mattered to them was how they felt about each other." He paused as if to gather his thoughts. "All I know is I care about Janie, and I would be honored to have your blessing."

To Janie's surprise, her father smiled. He turned

toward her mother, and she nodded. Janie gasped with surprise.

"Jonathan, you have our blessing," *Dat* said. "Come back tomorrow for supper and we'll talk more. I think we all need some sleep after this stressful night."

For the second time tonight, Janie wondered if she were dreaming. Renewed hope and happiness blossomed inside of her.

Jonathan nodded. "*Danki* so much, Timothy."

Dat's smile suddenly faded as he looked back and forth between Janie and Jonathan, and worry shoved away Janie's happiness. She held her breath in anticipation of what her father was going to say.

"I owe you both an apology," he began. "I never should have told Janie to keep the truth about the accident from Craig. Telling the truth is always the right thing to do, and I was completely wrong. I'm sorry it took something like this for me to realize my mistake." His focus settled on Jonathan. "I also was wrong to instruct her to stay away from you, Jonathan. I'm grateful you've come into Janie's life. You're a blessing."

"*Danki, Dat*." Tears clouded Janie's vision as she gave her father a quick hug.

"Let's go inside," *Dat* said to Janie.

"Would you give me just a minute?" she asked.

"Five minutes."

Her parents and Marie said good night to Jonathan and Frank and then headed into the house. Frank climbed into the van and left Janie and Jonathan standing together on the rock driveway.

Jonathan cupped Janie's cheek with his hand and

smiled down at her. "I meant what I said to your father. I love you and I want to build a life with you."

Janie's heart thudded as warmth flooded her body. "*Ich liebe dich*, Jonathan."

He leaned down and his lips brushed hers, sending electric pulses singing through her veins. She closed her eyes, savoring the feel of his lips against hers.

"I'll see you tomorrow," Jonathan whispered, his breath warm against her cheek.

Janie opened her eyes and nodded. "*Danki* again for saving me."

Jonathan shook his head and smiled. "Janie, you've saved me, so we're even. When I came here, I'd given up on love. You showed me I could love again."

As he kissed her again, Janie silently thanked God for sending Jonathan to her.

DISCUSSION QUESTIONS

1. Janie is determined to clear Jonathan's name despite her father's warning to stay out of the legal issues surrounding the buggy accident. She feels torn between her yearning for justice for Jonathan and her obedience to her father. Have you ever felt compelled to go against your family in order to do something you believed was important?

2. At the beginning of the story, Jonathan is convinced he's too old for Janie; however, his feelings about that change throughout the story. What do you think causes his feelings to change?

3. Jonathan came to Pennsylvania for a long visit with his grandparents after his girlfriend betrayed him. Were you ever betrayed by a close friend or loved one? How did you come to grips with that betrayal? Were you able to forgive that person and move on? If so, where did you find the strength to forgive?

4. Timothy, Janie's father, does not approve of Janie and Jonathan's friendship becoming something deeper. He's concerned Jonathan will return to Maryland and break Janie's heart, and he is convinced Jonathan is too old for her. He changes his opinion, however, near the end of the story.

What do you think is the catalyst for Timothy's change of heart?

5. Which character can you identify with the most? Which character seemed to carry the most emotional stake in the story? Was it Janie, Jonathan, Timothy, or someone else?

6. Janie's heart is broken when her father forbids her from spending any time with Jonathan. She was certain she'd finally found her soul mate, and then she lost him. Think of a time when you felt lost and alone. Where did you find your strength? What Bible verses would help with this?

7. Jonathan realizes that he longs to move to Pennsylvania and start a new life with Janie. Have you ever longed to make a huge change in your life? If so, did you follow through with that change? How did your family and friends react? What Bible verses helped you with your choice?

8. What did you know about the Amish before reading this book? What did you learn?

ACKNOWLEDGMENTS

As always, I'm thankful for my loving family. Special thanks to my Amish friends, who patiently answer my endless stream of questions. You're a blessing in my life.

To my agent, Natasha Kern, I can't thank you enough for your guidance, advice, and friendship. You are a tremendous blessing in my life.

Thank you to my amazing editor, Becky Monds, for your friendship and guidance. I'm grateful to editor Jean Bloom, who helped me polish and refine the story. Thank you also for connecting the dots between my books. I'm grateful to each and every person at HarperCollins Christian Publishing who helped make this book a reality.

Thank you most of all to God—for giving me the inspiration and the words to glorify You. I'm grateful and humbled You've chosen this path for me.

WHERE THE HEART IS

For Joe, Zac, and Matt, with love

GLOSSARY

ach—oh
aenti—aunt
appeditlich—delicious
bedauerlich—sad
boppli—baby
bruder/bruder— brother/brothers
bu/buwe—boy/boys
daadi—grandfather
danki—thank you
dat—dad
Dummle!—Hurry!
fraa—wife
friend/freinden—friend
froh—happy
gegisch: silly
gern gschehne—you're welcome
grandkinner—grandchildren
gude mariye—good morning
gut—good
gut nacht—good night
haus—house
Ich liebe dich—I love you
kaffi—coffee
kapp—prayer covering or cap

kichli/kichlin—cookie/cookies
kinner—children
kumm—come
liewe—love, a term of endearment
maed/maedel—young women, girls/young woman
mamm—mom
mammi—grandmother
mei—my
naerfich—nervous
narrisch—crazy
onkel—uncle
sche— pretty
schmaert—smart
schtupp—family room
schweschder/schweschdere—sister/sisters
sohn—son
Was iss letz?—What's wrong?
Wie geht's—How do you do? or Good day!
wunderbaar—wonderful
ya—yes

Family Tree

Featuring *Summer Storms* novella characters from the *Amish Summer* Collection

Marvin m. Roseanne Smucker

Tobias Ariana

Ira m. Florence Zook

Nathaniel Jesse Caleb

Ammon m. Edna Ebersol

Mariella Susannah Barbara

CHAPTER ONE

Despite the November chill, Tobias Smucker's hands were clammy as he stood staring at the two-story brick farmhouse owned by his bishop, Ammon Ebersol.

"Hey, buddy!" the cab driver bellowed from the yellow Prius taxi. "The meter is running. Do you want me to wait or what?"

Tobias swiveled toward the taxi, where the man had both his palms face up.

"Are you going to pay me now or do you want me to wait? It's your choice." He pointed to the meter. "It's your money."

Tobias bit his lower lip as doubt rooted him in the rock driveway. If Ammon agreed to speak with him, their meeting could take more than an hour. But if he told the driver to leave and then Ammon refused to talk to him, he'd face a three-mile walk in the cold. At least the trek would help him clear his head before facing his parents.

His parents.

Dat. He hadn't seen or talked to his father in five months.

Will Dat *allow me back in the house after I snuck out in the middle of the night? Will he even acknowledge me after I admitted needing help for alcoholism?*

Even though he'd apologized for his behavior in a letter to his family three weeks after he left, neither his sister's nor his mother's return letters had given any real indication of how his father would receive him when he returned someday.

"Hey, kid!" The tax driver's gruff voice slammed him back to reality.

Tobias swallowed against his dry throat. "Would you please give me just a minute to see if the owner of the house will speak with me?"

The man shrugged. "Yeah, sure, but it'll cost you. I'm going to charge you for every minute I have to wait."

"That's fine." Tobias adjusted his duffel bag on his shoulder before walking up the driveway and climbing the steps to the house. When he reached the front door, he dropped his bag on the porch with a thud, knocked, and took a deep breath to calm his spiking pulse.

This was a bad idea. I never should've come back to Pennsylvania. I should've stayed in Florida.

The door opened, and Mariella Ebersol, his sister's best friend, gasped as she stared at him with surprise. He noticed what a deep brown her eyes were. Like chocolate.

"Tobias! You're back!"

"Hi, Mariella." She seemed friendly. Perhaps she didn't know anything other than that he'd been away. He forced a smile.

She opened the screen door wide, and the aroma of what he thought was pot roast wafted over him, causing his stomach to gurgle. "Ariana didn't tell me you were back." She stood on her tiptoes and craned her neck as she looked past him. "Is she with you?"

He shook his head. "No. She doesn't know I'm back."

"She doesn't?" She tilted her head, and the ties from her prayer covering bounced off her shoulders.

"No one knows I'm back. I took a cab directly here from the bus station." His hands were shaking and he jammed his fists into the pockets of his jacket. "I was hoping to speak to your *dat*. Is he home?"

"*Ya*." She looked past him once again. "What's the cab driver doing in the driveway?"

"He's waiting to see if I need him to take me to my parents' *haus*."

"Why don't you tell him to go? *Mei dat* can take you, or we can call our driver."

Tobias made a quick decision. If Ammon rejected him, it was true he could just hire another driver.

"All right." Tobias jogged down the steps, paid the fare, and then returned to the porch.

"Come inside." Mariella motioned for him to enter the house. "We just finished eating. Are you hungry?"

His stomach growled again and he nodded. "*Ya*. I haven't eaten since lunchtime." He picked up his duffel bag and stepped into the family room, where he set his bag by the front door.

"Oh my goodness. It's almost six. You must be starved. I'll make you a plate."

She took his jacket, hung it on a peg, and then led

him through the large family room to the kitchen at the back of the house.

Mariella stepped into the kitchen, but Tobias halted in the doorway. Mariella's mother, Edna, was washing dishes, and her younger sister, Susannah, was drying them. Her youngest sister, Barbara, was wiping down the long kitchen table. For some reason, he noted all four women shared the same deep-brown eyes and golden hair Mariella had.

He lingered in the doorway as doubt again washed over him. Did he have any right to be in the bishop's home after the way he'd run away from his community? He should leave right now, call a cab, and go back to the bus station. He didn't belong here.

Barbara turned, met his gaze, and gasped. Edna and Susannah spun toward him, and all three women began speaking at once.

"Tobias! It's so *gut* to see you!"

"When did you get back?"

"How was Florida?"

Mariella touched his arm. "I'll go get *mei dat*. He's out in the barn."

"Danki," Tobias told her, surprised again by a friendly greeting.

"Susannah," Mariella said, "please make Tobias a plate of food. He just got into town, and he hasn't eaten since lunchtime." Then she disappeared through the mudroom.

"I'll be *froh* to make you a plate." Susannah began to flitter around the kitchen. "Barbara, would you please get a plate?"

While the sisters gathered food, Edna smiled at Tobias.

"You just got into town?"

Tobias nodded. "*Ya*. A taxi brought me here from the bus station."

"I'm surprised you came here first. Your parents must be eager to see you."

"They didn't know I was coming."

Edna's blonde eyebrows lifted. "Oh?"

"It's sort of a surprise." He rubbed his clean-shaven chin. Lying was a sin, but he wasn't exactly telling a fib since his family *would* be surprised when they saw him.

"Why would you—?"

"Tobias!" Ammon entered the kitchen, interrupting Edna's question. "*Wie geht's?*" He held out his hand, and Tobias shook it.

"I'm doing pretty well. How are you?"

"*Gut, gut.*" Ammon smiled, another friendly greeting. Tobias thought the bishop was, like his own father, in his midfifties, making his graying brown hair and matching beard no surprise. "Mari told me you wanted to talk." He motioned toward the family room. "Why don't we go sit in the *schtupp*?"

"Okay." Tobias's stomach constricted as he stepped toward the family room.

"Wait," Barbara said. "What about the food I'm warming up for you in the oven? We have pot roast, broccoli, mashed potatoes, and rolls, and I know you're hungry."

"*Danki*, but if it's okay, I'd like to talk to your *dat* before I eat."

"Of course. It won't be ready for a while."

Tobias followed Ammon into the family room and sat down on the sofa as the bishop sank into a wing chair across from him. Where should he start with his confession? It seemed obvious his family hadn't confided in the bishop, but he had to. He had to tell the truth. All of it. Did he have the right words to apologize for leaving the way he had? To admit his problem with alcohol?

Memories of the night before he left came back to him in an instant. He'd spent the day at the lake with his youth group. When they arrived back at Mariella's house, Tobias had started drinking, a decision he'd regretted for the past five months. He crashed his buggy on the way home that night and then argued with his *dat*. The angry and disrespectful words he'd aimed at his father echoed through his mind.

"How do you expect to get married and raise a family if you can't take care of yourself?" *Dat* had growled. "You need to learn to take responsibility for your actions. Racing buggies in the rain won't earn my praise. It's time you started acting like a man instead of an overgrown *kind*."

"I'm going to live my life the way I want to, and I don't need your permission."

"Is that so?" *Dat* had folded his arms over his rotund middle. "As long as you live in *mei haus*, you will follow my rules and ask for my permission."

"You've made that abundantly clear," Tobias had snapped. "Maybe it's time that changed."

Dat had stood nose to nose with him, fury radiating

off him. "I don't see you moving out anytime soon since you don't have any means to live on your own."

Tobias took a deep, shuddering breath as the recollection dissolved from his mind. He had been a terrible son. He didn't deserve to be welcomed home. What if Ammon threw him out of his house and told him to never return to the community he'd grown up in?

"What do you want to talk to me about, Tobias?"

Please, God, give me the right words to explain why I left.

"The reason I left the community in June was to get some help," he said. "I sneaked out of the house in the middle of the night, but I sent a letter to my family in July, explaining where I'd gone and why."

Ammon folded his arms over his chest. "I heard you'd gone to Florida, but I didn't know you needed help. What sort of help?"

"Rehabilitation for alcoholism. I'd been hiding a drinking problem, and I recalled *mei mamm* telling us about her younger *bruder*, Earl. He left the community and went to Florida years ago. I found his address and took a chance that he would allow me to stay with him. I discovered he also struggled with alcoholism, and he helped me get into a treatment program. I'm clean and sober now." Tobias held his breath while awaiting Ammon's reaction to his confession.

Ammon pursed his lips. "Was alcoholism the only reason you left?"

Tobias shook his head and frowned. "No."

"What were your other reasons?"

"*Mei dat* and I have a complicated relationship."

"What do you mean by 'complicated'?"

Tobias ran his sweaty palms down his pant legs, carefully choosing his words. "We argued often, and at the time, I was sure leaving was the best solution. But I know now it was the coward's way out."

"What prompted you to come back?"

"*Mei schweschder* wrote and asked me to come back for her wedding next month." Tobias looked at his duffel bag on the floor. The letters from both Ariana and his mother were tucked in its pocket. He'd reread them over and over when he couldn't sleep. They'd kept him going.

"So you're only here for the wedding?"

Tobias shook his head. "No. I want to work things out with *mei dat*."

"Why?"

"I want my family back. I want my community back." He hated the tremor in his voice.

Ammon blew out a deep breath as he stroked his long beard. "You're aware that alcoholism is a sin."

Tobias nodded. "*Ya*, I know. I knew it when I was drinking, and I knew it when I left the community and asked for help."

"Because you're a baptized member of the congregation, you'll have to publicly confess to make yourself right with the church again. Are you willing to do that? Are you truly repentant?"

"*Ya*, I am."

"Tomorrow's a church Sunday. I can call a meeting for baptized members following our service. If they agree you're ready to come back to the church, the church members will vote on your reinstatement, and then you can confess."

Tomorrow. Tobias's throat went bone dry in an instant. Was he ready to confess his sins in front of his congregation? But wasn't that what he wanted? A chance to reenter the fold?

"Is it too soon?" Ammon asked.

"No. I'll do it tomorrow."

"Gut." Ammon gave him a nod. "How is your *onkel* Earl? I went to school with him and your *mamm.*"

"He's doing well. He owns an auto repair shop in Sarasota. I worked there after I finished rehab."

"Really? So Earl is a mechanic."

Tobias nodded.

"Did he teach you how to work on cars while you were there?"

Tobias shrugged. "Not really. I mostly answered the phone and took customer orders. He taught me more about the cash register than cars."

Ammon's loud, boisterous laugh filled the family room. Just as Tobias began to tell him more, Barbara came into the room to say his food was ready.

Around their kitchen table and between bites, he told the whole family what it was like to live in Florida. The bishop didn't mention he'd been in a treatment center, and neither did he. His alcoholism would come up tomorrow, and that was soon enough.

When his plate was empty, Tobias stood. "I should get going. *Danki* for talking with me."

"I'm glad you're back." Ammon shook his hand. "We all missed you."

"*Danki.*"

Tobias carried his dishes to the counter by the sink and then turned to Edna and her daughters. "*Danki* for supper. May I use your phone to call for a ride?"

"I'll take you home." Mariella popped up from her seat.

"That's not necessary." Ammon started toward the back door. "I'll just get my hat and hitch the buggy to my horse."

Mariella faced her father. "I was thinking of going over there anyway. I can deliver a quilt I finished to Ariana and her *mamm*. They've been waiting for it so they can fulfill an order from one of their customers." She looked at her mother. "Remember, *Mamm*? The order was promised for tomorrow, but I only finished it this afternoon because of the difficult stitching." Her mother nodded.

"And if I deliver it to them this evening, they'll be certain they can keep their promise. Besides, they need me to give them some information about the quilt for the customer."

Ammon shrugged. "That's fine. You can go." Then his expression turned serious. "Just don't be too late since we have church in the morning. I'll go hitch up the horse, and you get the quilt."

"All right. I'll take a pie too." She turned toward Tobias. "I'll just be a minute." Then she rushed out of the kitchen.

"I'll help you, Ammon," Tobias said. "Let me get my jacket and duffel bag." He retrieved his bag, thanked

Edna, Susannah, and Barbara again, and walked out to the barn with his bishop.

. . .

Mariella clutched a queen-size quilt against her chest with one hand and balanced a pie in the other as she made her way toward the horse and buggy.

Tobias rushed over to her. "Let me help you with those."

"*Danki.*" As she handed him the quilt, their fingers brushed, and heat rushed to her cheeks. She pushed away her embarrassment and looked up at her father as Tobias loaded the quilt and his duffel bag into the back of the buggy. "I won't be long, *Dat.*"

He lowered his voice. "Don't forget, his family hasn't seen him yet. They may need some time alone to talk."

She nodded. "I understand."

"Are we ready?" Tobias stood by the buggy and motioned toward the horse.

"*Ya.*" She smiled. "Do you want to guide the horse?"

"Ah, well . . ." He rubbed his chin. He was adorable.

"Do you remember *how* to guide a horse?" she asked, and her father chuckled.

"I think I do." Tobias grinned, and her heartbeat fluttered.

"Why don't you give it a try?" She climbed into the passenger side and rested the pie plate on her lap.

"Be safe," *Dat* called before heading back into the house.

Tobias took his spot in the driver's seat, flipped on a Coleman lantern, and took the reins.

"Do you need me to explain how to guide the horse?" she offered.

He turned toward her and raised one of his dark eyebrows. "Are you enjoying teasing me?"

"*Ya.*" She laughed.

"Before you ask, I do remember how to get to my parents' *haus.*"

"Oh *gut.* That was my next question," she said, joking again as she settled back in the seat. "I guess that means I can relax now."

Tobias was the man she remembered, but at the same time something about his appearance was different. He still had the same gorgeous dark-brown hair and deep-brown eyes, but as she'd studied him at their kitchen table, she realized he looked even more handsome than she remembered. Perhaps it was because he looked healthier than she recalled. His skin was pink, and his eyes were bright and intelligent.

As she grinned at him, a bright smile overtook his face. The look in his eyes made her pulse start to pound. Did he already know she'd loved him from afar since she was ten years old? Oh no. Ariana would be furious if she found out Mariella had a crush on her brother! When they were younger, and Mariella had been tempted to tell her friend the truth, Ariana said she was tired of girls in their youth group feigning friendship with her just to get close to Tobias. She never wanted Ariana to doubt her loyalty, so she'd kept her feelings for Tobias a secret for years.

"It's really *gut* to see you." He turned toward the windshield and flipped the reins as he guided the horse toward the street.

She silently blew out a sigh of relief as Tobias kept his attention to the road. How ridiculous of her to be worried he could tell how she felt about him. Even if he could, he wouldn't be interested. He'd never paid much attention to her. She was never more than his sister's best friend, and that's all she'd ever be to him.

"That pie smells heavenly." He gave her a sideways glance. "Is it lemon meringue?"

"*Ya*, it is. I thought your *mamm* and *dat* might enjoy it."

"That's very thoughtful of you. *Danki.*"

She adjusted the pie plate on her lap and then took in his profile. Despite his smiles, tension seemed to be coming from him in waves. Even by the light of a lantern, she could tell his knuckles were white as he gripped the reins.

"Are you all right?" she asked.

"*Ya.*" He halted the horse at a red light and then turned to her. "Why?"

"You seem *naerfich.*"

He snorted. "You could say that."

"About going home? Why?"

"Let's just say I don't expect *mei dat* to welcome me back with open arms."

"Why wouldn't he?"

"I didn't exactly leave on good terms." The light turned green and he guided the horse through the intersection. "If he kicks me out, could you take me to

Jesse's *haus* before you go home?" Jesse was not only his sister's fiancé, but his best friend.

He cringed as if remembering something. "Wait. Jesse wouldn't want me either. I left on a bad note with him too. I suppose I might have to find a hotel room." He sighed. "I made a lot of mistakes before I left, but I'm ready to apologize and make things right. If *Dat* doesn't forgive me, though, I guess I'll have to go back to Florida and try to make a life there."

She leaned toward him. "He'll not only forgive you but he'll be *froh* to see you. Everyone missed you, and they're going to celebrate you being home." She held up the pie. "That's the real reason I brought this."

He gave her a small smile. "I appreciate your encouragement, but I don't think you know how badly I hurt my family and Jesse. *Mamm* and Ariana seemed to forgive me right away. They wrote me letters once I let them know where I was. But *Dat*? I never heard from him."

"I do know what happened. Ariana told me you checked yourself into a treatment facility for alcoholism, but I never shared that information with anyone. Not even *mei dat*. Your *schweschder* and parents were so worried about you."

They rode in silence for a few minutes as he kept his eyes focused on the road ahead.

"How are you doing now?" she finally asked.

"I'm doing well." He gave her a quick glance before looking back toward the road. "I feel better than I have in a long time."

"That's *wunderbaar*. How was Florida?"

"It was *gut*. I lived with *mei onkel* and worked in his auto repair shop."

"You have an *onkel* who fixes cars?"

"*Ya*. Imagine that." His smile was back, and it warmed her heart. "He left the community when he was eighteen and went to Florida. He took me in and helped me find a rehabilitation place. Once I got out of the program, he let me live with him and work in his shop to earn some money. I sent *mei dat* a check to replace the buggy I wrecked before I left, and then I saved most of the rest. *Onkel* Earl wouldn't take any money for rent."

"That was generous of him. What are your plans now?"

"My plans? I suppose that depends on what *mei dat* says when he sees me."

"Oh."

They fell silent as he halted the horse at another red light. When the light turned green, he flipped the reins and glanced toward her. "Are you getting married this wedding season too?"

Mariella gave a bark of laughter and then clapped her hand over her mouth.

"Why is that funny?" His dark eyes sparkled with mirth.

"It's funny because I would need a fiancé to get married."

"Oh. Do you have anyone special in your life?"

"No." She shook her head as embarrassment again heated her cheeks. "I don't have a boyfriend or a fiancé." She stared out the windshield to avoid what she imagined would be a curious stare. Or maybe her romantic status didn't surprise him at all.

"Ariana told me her wedding is the first weekend in December."

"*Ya*, it's coming quickly. I'm helping her and your *mamm* with the preparations. We're working on the dresses between our quilt orders." She looked at him again. "Did Ariana tell you we're making quilts to sell now?"

"*Ya*, she did. I think that's great. Do you get a lot of orders?"

"Oh, *ya*. We've been busy. We supply some of the local stores and we have private customers too."

"What's been your most popular order?"

"Oh, it's definitely been for queen- and king-size quilts. Most of our customers like the log cabin design." He asked her a few more questions about their business until his parents' farmhouse came into view.

As he guided the horse up the long, rock driveway, his expression hardened. She wasn't sure how, but maybe she could be an encouragement to him as he faced his father for the first time in five months.

CHAPTER TWO

As his heart hammered with apprehension, Tobias stared at the back of the whitewashed two-story farmhouse where he'd been born and raised. He gripped the strap on his duffel bag with one hand and held Mariella's quilt over his other arm as more of the disrespectful conversation he'd had with his father before he left filtered through his mind.

"Why were you racing? What were you thinking?" *Dat* had shaken a finger inches from Tobias's nose. "What do you have to say for yourself, Tobias John?"

"Nothing," Tobias snapped.

"Nothing?" *Dat*'s bushy eyebrows had shot up toward his receding hairline. "Why not?"

"Because I don't have to say anything," Tobias had said, seething. "You'll say it for me."

Tobias cringed as the memory faded. Coming home was a colossal mistake. He should have remained in Florida and continued working for his uncle. Maybe he could have become his partner and learned how to repair cars. Then he wouldn't have to face his father and confess his sin to the church. The congregation might not believe his heart was pure enough to return to the church. They could reject him before he even had a chance to make his confession.

Worse, his father might never forgive him.

"Don't stand out here in the cold. Come inside." Mariella's voice broke through his mental tirade as she stood on the rock path leading to the back of the house, beckoning him. The warmth in her eyes gave him enough confidence to propel him forward. He followed her to the porch.

She climbed two steps, but then swiveled toward him, her face crumpled into a scowl.

"Was iss letz?" he asked.

"I'm so sorry. I don't mean to barge in on your reunion with your family, to intrude." She descended the steps. "You should go first."

His anxiety dissolved as he dropped his bag and touched her arm. "You're not intruding. In fact, you're the reason I'm still here."

"What do you mean?"

"You just gave me the confidence to walk up these steps. I was considering just going back to Florida until you told me to get out of the cold. You calmed me, and I'm grateful you're here."

"Oh." Her cheeks flushed pink as she looked up at him and smiled. "I'm glad I can help you."

Suddenly he realized—for the first time—just how attractive she was with her golden-blonde hair peeking out from beneath her prayer covering and her astute, dark-chocolate eyes. She was stunning. Had he been blind all these years? Or had she transformed while he was gone? Why hadn't one of the young men in their community already snatched her up?

"Tobias?" She tilted her head. "Are you okay?"

"*Ya*." He hauled his heavy bag onto his shoulder and climbed the porch steps. When he reached the door, he knocked.

She appeared beside him and rolled her eyes before turning the doorknob. "You grew up here, remember?"

"Right." He pushed open the door and stepped into the mudroom. Instantly, the smells of home—his home—filled his nostrils. They were familiar and comforting.

"Hello?" *Mamm's* voice called from the kitchen.

He hesitated.

Mariella nudged him forward. "Go."

He stepped into the kitchen. His parents, Ariana, and Jesse sat at the table, drinking coffee.

Mamm and Ariana gasped and jumped to their feet.

"Tobias!" Ariana called.

Mamm made a strangled sound in her throat, and her brown eyes filled with tears as she came near. When Tobias set his bag on the floor and draped the quilt on the back of her empty chair, *Mamm* pulled him into her arms. He closed his eyes and breathed in her familiar scent as his heart swelled with happiness—and regret. Oh, how he'd missed her!

When she released him, she cupped her hand to his face and looked up at him. Tears trickled down her cheeks. "You're home," she whispered, her voice wobbly.

"*Ya*, I am." His voice shook too.

"Tobias." Ariana touched his arm and then pulled him into a hug. "It's so *gut* to see you. You got my letters?"

"I did." He released her from the hug. *"Danki."*

Jesse appeared beside him. Ariana seemed to think all was forgiven in her letters, but now that he was here, would his best friend reject him?

"I'm glad you're back."

Tobias hesitated, but then stepped forward to shake Jesse's hand. Instead, Jesse gave him a quick hug, tapping his shoulder.

"It's *gut* to see you," Jesse said when he released him.

The anxiety that had been clamping down on Tobias's shoulders loosened slightly at Jesse's words. Then he turned toward his father, who now stood beside him.

"Dat," Tobias said, holding out his hand. He held his breath.

Dat gave him a curt nod as he shook his hand. He remained silent, but his hazel eyes were glassy as if he were holding back tears. Was he as happy to see him as *Mamm* was? Was all forgiven with his father as well?

"Did you just get back to town?" *Mamm* asked.

"I did, and Mariella brought me here from her *haus.*" Tobias had almost forgotten Mariella had come inside with him. He turned toward the doorway where she stood with a sheepish smile, holding the pie plate. She'd already shed her coat in the mudroom, no doubt to give him a few minutes alone with his family.

"Mariella. Come in." Tobias beckoned her, just as she'd done in the driveway.

"I brought that quilt I needed to finish," she said as

she waved a hand toward where Tobias left it. "And a lemon meringue pie." She held up the plate.

As a brief silence followed, Tobias averted his eyes to avoid his family's questioning looks. They were no doubt wondering why he hadn't come directly home. But he wasn't ready to explain.

"*Danki* for bringing the pie," Ariana finally said as she moved to the counter. "I'll make more *kaffi*."

Mamm took his coat and then instructed, "Tobias, sit."

Tobias sank into the seat he'd always taken for meals. To be back in the kitchen where he'd eaten nearly all his meals from birth felt surreal, almost like a dream.

"Have you eaten supper?" *Mamm* gestured toward their gas-powered refrigerator.

"*Ya*, I ate at Mariella's *haus*." Tobias fingered the blue tablecloth, still feeling uncomfortable.

Mariella placed the pie on the table. "Do you want me to get plates and forks?" she asked his mother.

"I'll get them." Ariana began pulling dishes out of the cabinets.

Mariella joined her at the counter. "I'll get a knife to cut the pie."

Jesse sat down across from Tobias. "How was Florida?"

"It was *gut*," Tobias said as Ariana set a mug in front of him.

"And how are you doing?" *Mamm* asked, her brown eyes showing concern.

"I'm doing well," Tobias said. "Really. I completed my rehabilitation and I feel better than ever."

"*Gut*." *Mamm*'s expression relaxed. "How is *mei bruder*?"

"He's great."

Tobias told them about his work in *Onkel* Earl's shop and, over pie and coffee, what it had been like to live in Florida. His father remained silent the whole time.

When they reached a lull in the conversation, *Mamm* glanced at his duffel bag. "Are . . . are you staying?" Her expression was hopeful.

Tobias glanced at his father. "I planned to, if I'm welcome here."

"For how long?" *Dat* lifted his mug of coffee as the question hung in the air like a thick fog covering the kitchen.

"I'd like to stay for *gut*, if you'll allow me to move back." Tobias gripped his empty mug, trying to stop his hands from quaking. It was time to face the gravity of what he'd done, not just by leaving his family, but by leaving his community. "When I arrived at the bus station, I took a taxi to Mariella's *haus* so I could speak to her *dat* before coming here."

"What did you discuss with him?" *Dat*'s eyes were trained on him.

Tobias opened his mouth, but the words stuck in his throat. He looked at Mariella sitting beside him, and when she gave him a shy smile, he found the courage to continue.

"I told him why I left the community and that I want to come back. If the congregation will allow me, I'm going to confess at church tomorrow." Tobias bit his lower lip as silence filled the kitchen.

Mamm took a shuddering breath as tears began to fall.

Dat remained silent, his dry eyes still assessing his son.

"Am I welcome to stay here?" Tobias asked.

"*Ya, ya*, of course!" *Mamm* reached over and squeezed his hand. "You're our *sohn*, and this will always be your home."

"*Danki*." Tobias looked at *Dat*, but his father said nothing, his eyes turned down. Why would *Dat* tear up upon his arrival, yet behave as though the deepest chasm remained between father and son? Perhaps Tobias had hurt him more than he imagined. How was he ever going to make it up to him?

"So you'll be at our wedding, right?" Ariana chimed in.

"Of course I will," Tobias said, forcing a smile. He didn't want his troubles to dim his sister's happiness.

She grinned as she took Jesse's hand. "Great!"

. . .

"I should get on the road." Mariella carried some of the dishes and utensils to the counter. "I promised *mei dat* I wouldn't be too late."

Tobias looked at the clock on the wall and cringed. Where had the time gone? "I didn't realize it was nearly eight thirty. I'm sorry for keeping you here so late."

"It's okay." Mariella shrugged. "I had a *gut* time."

Tobias gathered the empty pie plate and knife and carried them to the counter. Mariella started filling one side of the sink with hot water.

"I'll take care of the dishes, Mariella." Ariana set three mugs on the counter. "You just go."

"Are you sure?" Mariella glanced at Ariana over her shoulder. "I hate leaving you with a mess."

"I'll help too," *Mamm* offered as she moved to the sink. "*Danki* for the *appeditlich* pie. I'll call Mrs. Wilson to come and get the quilt after I finish the dishes. The quilt is *schee*. She will love it. It's the perfect wedding gift for her niece."

"Oh, I'm thrilled you like it." Mariella washed the pie plate and then dried it with a dish towel.

"I'll walk you out," Tobias offered.

"I should go too." Jesse placed his mug on the counter. "*Danki* for supper, Roseanne."

"*Gern gschehne,*" *Mamm* tossed over her shoulder as she scraped crumbs into a trash can. "Be careful going home. We'll see you both at church tomorrow."

Mariella and Jesse said good night to Tobias's parents, and along with Ariana and Tobias they retrieved their coats from the mudroom. Tobias grabbed a Coleman lamp and then suggested to Mariella that she stay inside where it was warm while he checked her horse and buggy.

As the men brought the horses from the barn, Jesse gave Tobias a sideways glance. "I can't believe you're back."

"You didn't think I'd come back?"

Jesse shrugged as he led his mare to the buggy. "I supposed you'd return at some point, but I didn't think it would be this soon. Did Arie's letters inspire you to come home?"

"*Ya*, that was part of it."

They worked in silence for a few moments, but Tobias knew it was time to apologize. He struggled to find the right words. When the buggy was ready, he faced Jesse and took a deep breath.

"I'm sorry for all the awful things I said to you before I left," Tobias began. "I realized through counseling that I blamed everyone else for my problems with *mei dat*. I used drinking to try to escape them, and it did nothing but destroy my relationships with the most important people in my life. I hope you can forgive me."

"I do forgive you." Jesse rested his hand on Tobias's shoulder. "In fact, I should thank you for opening my eyes to my own shortcomings."

"What do you mean?"

"You said I was privileged, and I never had to work for the things I have. You were right. I took everything for granted, including Arie. You may have been drunk when you said all those things, but you were right." Jesse leaned against the buggy. "After you left, your *dat* broke my engagement to Arie, and I had to prove to him that I was worthy of her hand in marriage. I worked harder than I ever have in my life, and I proved to your *dat* and Arie how much I care about her. I've promised her I will never take her for granted again, and I intend to keep that promise. I realized I had a lot to prove to her, and I'm glad you helped me realize that."

Stunned, Tobias blinked.

"I'm grateful for everything you said," Jesse continued. "I'm not angry with you at all. I'm really glad you got the help you needed and you're back. We've all missed you."

"*Danki.*" Tobias silently thanked God for his best friend. For so long he'd been focusing on the blessings he thought he'd thrown away, and now God was showing him the blessings he still had. He was grateful.

But had he damaged his relationship with his father beyond repair?

. . .

"Tobias looks great," Ariana said. She and Mariella had decided the brisk air might be good for them, and now they stood by the porch steps. "Our prayers have been answered. God sent him back to us."

"*Ya*, he did." As Mariella hugged her pie plate to her chest, she took in Tobias's relaxed stance by the light of his lantern. With the lantern hanging on the buggy, he'd folded his arms over his wide chest and was talking to Jesse. "He was really *naerfich* during the ride over here, but I told him you and your parents would be *froh* to see him."

Ariana's dark eyes widened as she turned toward Mariella. "Did he think we wouldn't welcome him home?"

"Well, not you, and not so much your *mamm*. But he was worried your *dat* would reject him. He wasn't sure Jesse would want to see him, either. He asked me if I could take him to a hotel if it didn't work out here."

Ariana clicked her tongue. "No matter what, we're family."

"That's true. I told him you would all be *froh* to see him and would welcome him back. I assured him everyone missed him."

They stood in silence for a few moments as they watched the men talk. Mariella's emotions spun at Tobias's handsome profile. Would he ever think of her as more than just Ariana's best friend? Would he be happy in the community after experiencing the *Englisher* way of life?

"Did his talk go well with your *dat*?" Ariana asked.

Mariella nodded. "*Ya*, it must have. *Mei dat* seemed very supportive. I think everything will go well tomorrow at church."

"I hope so." Ariana sighed. "I don't want to lose *mei bruder* a second time. It would be too painful for my parents and me to bear again."

Mariella squeezed her hand. "I don't think you will."

"Arie," Jesse called. "I need to get going." He waved at Mariella. "*Gut nacht*, Mariella."

"*Gut nacht*," she echoed with a wave.

Ariana hugged her. "*Danki* for bringing *mei bruder* home. I'll see you tomorrow."

"*Gut nacht*," Mariella said before Ariana jogged over to Jesse's buggy.

Mariella went to her own buggy, where Tobias held the lantern as he checked out the horse. "I think the buggy must be hitched correctly to the horse," she said. "After all, you helped *Dat* hitch it, and you do still remember how to properly hitch a buggy to a horse, right?"

She couldn't stop a smile when he grinned at her. "How long are you going to accuse me of not remembering how to be Amish?"

"I don't know." She tapped her chin with her finger as she pretended to contemplate the question. "You were gone for five months, so should I tease you for five months?"

"You can tease me for as long as you'd like, Mari."

She froze, stunned by what he'd said. He'd never called her by the nickname her family gave her.

"I think things went well tonight." He rested his hand on the buggy door as his smile faded. "I mean, they went as well as they could."

"They went really well." She set the pie plate inside the buggy and looked up at him. "You seem disappointed. What's bothering you?"

He pressed his lips together in a thin line and then said, "I guess I had hoped *mei dat* would talk to me more."

"He will." Mariella stepped closer to him. "Just give him time. I'm sure he was overwhelmed when he saw you and he needs time to process that you're back. You know how strict and tough your *dat* is."

He snorted. "*Ya*, I know that very well."

"I think emotions are tough for him, so it's not as easy for him to react to things. Especially when they're a surprise."

He raised an eyebrow. "When did you get so *schmaert*?"

She lifted her chin. "I'm only two years younger than you."

"You may be twenty-two, but I think you're decades smarter than I am."

"I'm twenty-three, actually. My birthday was last month."

"I'm sorry. Twenty-three. And happy belated birthday." He smiled, sending warmth curling through her body despite the cold evening. "*Danki* for bringing me over here tonight and for encouraging me to face my family. I couldn't have done this without you."

"I didn't do much at all."

"*Ya*, you did." He touched her hand, and the warmth she'd felt turned to heat, rushing to the spot where his skin brushed hers. "*Danki*, Mari."

"*Gern gschehne.*"

He tapped the buggy. "Will you be okay going home alone in the dark?"

Her eyes narrowed. "I know how to guide a horse in the dark."

"I know that, but I worry about the drivers on the road who don't respect buggies. Do you want me to ride with you?"

Her tendency toward resentment dissolved as his care and concern replaced it. "I promise I'll be careful."

"All right." His shoulders visibly relaxed. He paused and then lowered his voice. "Do you think the congregation will welcome me back into the fold?"

"I'm certain they'll be just as thankful as I am that you've come back." She swallowed a gasp when she realized how much of her heart she'd just revealed to him.

"I hope so." He tapped the buggy. "You should get home. I don't want your *dat* upset that you stayed out too late."

"Gut nacht," she said as she climbed into the driver's side.

"Gut nacht. I'll see you tomorrow."

As she guided the horse down the driveway, she sent up a prayer asking God to give Tobias the confidence and strength he needed to face the congregation and confess his sins.

CHAPTER THREE

Tobias thought Jesse must be able to hear his heart thudding in his chest as they sat beside each other on one of the backless benches in the Allgyer family's barn. Singing along during the final hymn, he gripped his hymnal so hard his fingers hurt.

As he glanced around at familiar faces, his gaze moved to his father sitting in the section for married men. *Dat* stared down at the hymnal in his hands as his mouth moved in sync with the rest of the congregation. He looked anything but content.

The events of the night before swirled through Tobias's mind, sweeping disappointment over the tension he felt. After Mariella and Jesse left, he went back into the house with the intention of speaking to *Dat*, but he had already gone to bed. Tobias had hoped to spend an hour or two working out their differences.

Mariella's words, however, had echoed in his mind. He did need to give *Dat* time. After all, he'd been disrespectful and argumentative before he left. Perhaps *Dat* was giving him what he deserved—silence.

After saying good night to his mother and Ariana, he unpacked his duffel bag in the bedroom that had been his since childhood. He'd hoped to fall asleep, but instead he stared at the ceiling most of the night, worrying about today's vote and, if he were allowed to make it, his confession.

This morning the family had come to the service in his parents' buggy, and he was grateful Ariana and *Mamm* kept conversation going by discussing wedding plans. When they arrived at the Allgyer family's farm, Tobias spoke to Ammon to confirm the special meeting would indeed take place after the service.

And now he sat rigidly on the bench as the last hymn came to a close. Anxiety coursed through him. If his congregation refused to accept him back into the church, he'd lose his place in the community forever. Would that loss send him spiraling back to drink? He slammed his eyes shut.

Please, God. Keep me strong. Guide my words as I confess to my congregation. Keep leading me back to you.

When the hymn ended, Ammon stood and faced everyone. "And now I invite all the nonmembers of the congregation to please exit and the baptized members to stay for a special meeting."

Tobias's mouth ran dry. This was it. This was when the baptized members of the church would decide if he would be allowed to confess and be reinstated.

He looked across the barn to where Mariella and Ariana sat together in the unmarried women's section. Ariana met his gaze, and she looked just as nervous as he was. Mariella, however, gave him her beautiful, encouraging smile. How did she know just what he needed?

"It's going to be fine." Jesse's voice was low in his ear. "Go outside. We'll be certain to support you during the meeting."

"Danki." Tobias stood and looked at his father as he made his way toward the end of the row. *Dat* frowned, but he also nodded. *Mamm*, her eyes glimmering, watched him from her seat with the other married women.

As Tobias stepped out into the cold noon air, he glanced up at the sky. The next hour would determine his place in the community. His path was God's plan, but was he strong enough to accept whatever the congregation decided?

. . .

Mariella discerned the fear and worry in Tobias's eyes when he looked at her after her father's announcement. She fought the urge to pop up from her seat, rush across the barn, and hug him. She longed to console him and convince him everything would be okay. But not only would a hug be disruptive during the hymn; it would also be inappropriate and forward. She had no right to hug him when they were only friends. It was presumptuous for her to even consider it. Still, she longed to help him, and a smile seemed to be the only way for her to offer encouragement to him.

When she smiled at him, his stoic expression had relaxed a fraction, and the hard line of his jaw had loosened. She hoped she had somehow given him confidence with her small gesture of comfort.

When Mariella had gone to bed last night, Tobias had been in the forefront of her thoughts as she kept replaying their conversation in his driveway. He'd teased her, called her by her nickname, thanked her for encouraging him, and offered to take her home to be sure she had a safe journey back to her parents' house. He was definitely different from how she'd remembered him. While he'd always been pleasant to her in the past, he'd rarely had a private conversation with her, let alone poured his heart out to her. What had caused him to finally see her as a friend?

"We're having a members-only meeting because one of our *bruders* has fallen into sin," her father announced to open the meeting. "Tobias Smucker left the community in June to go to Florida, where he had treatment for alcoholism. He wrote a letter to his family explaining why he left, and he's now back and ready to return to the church. He told me he's ready to confess. The ministers and I agree if you vote to accept Tobias today, we're going to immediately welcome him back into the fold instead of first excommunicating him for six weeks.

"Now, I need to know if each of you agrees he's repentant and ready to be received back into the church." *Dat* pointed to the side of the barn where the men sat. "I will ask the men, and Mel will ask the women."

Mariella sat up taller as Mel Allgyer, one of the ministers, walked over to her section of the barn. On the opposite side of the barn, her father asked the men. She overhead each man take turns saying, "*Ya*," and she silently asked God to encourage every member to echo that response.

Ariana grabbed Mariella's hand and squeezed, her brown eyes expressing concern. She leaned in close and lowered her voice. "Do you think everyone will forgive him?"

"*Ya*, I do. Have faith."

"Do you believe Tobias Smucker is repentant and ready to be received back into the church?" Mel asked the unmarried women.

"*Ya*," Mariella said when it was her turn.

"*Ya*," Ariana echoed.

Each woman after Ariana gave the same response, and the muscles in Mariella's back eased.

When Mel moved to the married women section, he again asked if they agreed. Each of the women responded with, "*Ya*."

"Everyone has said *ya*. I'm so thankful." Ariana sniffed as tears trickled down her face.

Mariella pulled a tissue from her pocket and gave it to her.

"*Danki*," Ariana whispered, wiping her cheeks.

Her father moved to the center of the barn. "We will invite our *bruder* back in to confess now."

Ariana sucked in a breath as she turned toward Mariella.

"Tobias will do fine. I can feel it in my heart," Mariella whispered as her father walked toward the barn doors.

· · ·

Tobias stood at one corner of the barn and watched the children play on Mel Allgyer's elaborate wooden swing set. Teenaged girls talked as they leaned on the fence near the children.

It seemed like only yesterday he and Jesse were teenagers too. They got into a fair amount of trouble with their antics, but life was still simpler back then. He and Jesse attended youth gatherings together, he didn't drink alcohol, and his relationship with his father wasn't as contentious as it became when he turned twenty-one.

Now he stood at a crossroads between his Amish life and his brief *Englisher* life. Soon he would learn if his Amish community would allow him back into the fold. Although he'd needed to get away five months ago, he now felt the call of the community of his birth. He prayed he could make amends and start a new life.

"Tobias."

He jumped with a start. Ammon had come around the corner. He looked serious.

"We're ready for you. You can confess now."

Although he was relieved to have come this far, Tobias still tried in vain to swallow against a swelling lump of emotion in his throat.

"Tobias. Are you ready?"

"I think so." Tobias heard the thread of fear in his voice.

Ammon gestured toward the barn doors. "Let's go. The congregation is waiting."

Tobias took a deep breath and followed the bishop, his heavy steps bogged with the weight of the apprehension pressing down on his shoulders.

When he reached the barn's entrance, his breath seized in his lungs. Would the congregation accept his confession as he knelt before them? Would they believe his intentions were sincere?

Ammon stood inside the barn and swiveled toward him. "Are you going to come in?"

Unable to speak, Tobias nodded. He followed Ammon up the center aisle, between the sections with unmarried men and unmarried women. Mariella met his gaze and the brightness in her eyes ignited something deep in his soul. Suddenly he recalled her comforting response when he asked if she thought the congregation would allow him back into the church:

I'm certain our congregation will be just as thankful as I am that you've come back.

He looked toward his father, and when he met his impassive expression, unease hit him once again. No, this wouldn't be as simple as confessing. The congregation wouldn't be satisfied with his honesty. They would never forgive him for his transgressions.

"Our *bruder* Tobias is going to confess his sins." Ammon's words slammed Tobias back to reality as they stood in front of the congregation. Then the bishop turned to Tobias. "Go ahead."

Tobias cleared his throat and searched for the right words. He folded his hands in front of his body as his pulse pounded in his ears. "I left the community five months ago and went to Florida to stay with *mei onkel* Earl." He scanned the congregation, taking in their somber expressions.

When he found his mother's face, he paused as she

wiped away the tears streaming down her face. He focused on her as he continued to speak. "I knew I had a problem with alcohol, and *mei onkel* helped me find a rehabilitation center. I got help, and I'm doing better now. I'm sober, and I don't plan to touch alcohol again. I'm ready to make my heart right with God and the church. I want to be part of this community and live a life that is *gut* in God's eyes."

Silence hung over the barn like a suffocating cloud, the only sound the echoes of children's voices outside. He glanced around the knot of people staring at him, and his eyes stopped on Ariana and Mariella. While Ariana swiped the back of one hand over her eyes, Mariella simply nodded and smiled at him. Did she believe Tobias had said enough to prove his intensions were pure?

"Are you done?" Ammon asked.

"*Ya.*" Tobias nodded as doubt nearly choked him. Had he said enough? Did the congregation expect him to say more to convince them to allow him back into the church?

"Go down on your knees now," Ammon instructed.

Tobias's legs wavered as he knelt in front of the congregation. He bowed his head and closed his eyes as tears threatened to fall. "I can confess that I have failed God and the church, and I want to be more careful and watchful."

Silence fell over the barn once again as Tobias held his breath. Would Ammon say he was forgiven or tell him he was shunned? His life was going to change in a matter of moments.

Ammon touched his shoulder. "Tobias, stand up."

Opening his eyes, Tobias took Ammon's hand and stood.

"We welcome you back into the fold," Ammon said.

Tobias blew out the breath he'd been holding, and his knees wobbled. Had he heard the bishop correctly?

"Did you hear me?" Ammon asked. "You are forgiven."

Tobias shook Ammon's hand. *"Danki. Danki."*

"The meeting is over," Ammon announced.

A murmur of conversation started in the congregation as the men quickly began converting the benches into tables for the noon meal.

"Tobias." *Mamm* came up behind him. "I'm so *froh.*" She sniffed as she reached for him.

"Danki, Mamm," he said as he hugged her. "I am too."

Ariana and Jesse came.

"You looked so *naerfich* and terrified you made me cry." Ariana smacked his shoulder and gave him a watery smile. "It's so *gut* to have you back."

"Danki." He blew out a nervous laugh. "I'm sorry for making you cry."

"Just don't leave us again," Jesse added.

"I don't plan to." Tobias looked across the barn to where Mariella stood with her sisters. She gave him a little wave before they all left the barn. He hoped he could talk to her later and thank her once again for giving him the courage to face his fears.

"Let's help set up for the meal," Jesse said. "I'm starved."

"I am too." Ariana touched *Mamm*'s arm. "We can help serve."

"*Ya*, of course." *Mamm* looked at Tobias again. "I'll see you after lunch."

Jesse pointed to the benches at the far corner of the barn. "We can help get the tables set up over there."

Tobias looked to where his father was talking to Ammon and Mel, and a sudden determination overwhelmed him. He needed to speak to *Dat*. He needed to know if he shared his mother's happiness about his return to the church. Surely he did.

"I'll help in a minute. I need to take care of something first."

Tobias crossed the barn and came to a stop beside *Dat*. He crossed his arms over his chest and waited while the three men discussed the possibility of snow coming early to Lancaster County.

After glancing at Tobias, Mel pointed across the barn. "Well, it looks like they could use our help preparing tables, Ammon. Why don't we offer a hand?"

"*Ya*, we should." Ammon shook *Dat*'s hand and nodded at Tobias. "We'll see you both at lunch."

When the men had gone, Tobias dropped his arms and faced his father, waiting—hoping—for him to say something. A flurry of activity had exploded throughout the barn, but Tobias remained focused only on his father, as if they were the only two people in the room.

His father chose instead to look at the activity, but at least he didn't just nod and walk away.

"I'm a member of the church again," Tobias finally said. "My sin has been forgiven."

Dat turned to look at him. "*Ya*. That's *gut*." Tobias

had hoped for a glimmer of joy, but his father's hazel eyes remained serious.

"I guess this means I need to buy a new buggy."

Dat crossed his arms over his white shirt and black vest. "I didn't cash the check you sent me. I sold the other buggy for parts, and I have that money too. You can have it all to purchase a new buggy."

"You don't need to give me that money. Keep it. I owe you a lot more than that for the pain and heartache I caused you and *Mamm*." Tobias longed for his father to say something positive about his return, but did he deserve any kind words from him? "Are you glad I'm back?" He heard the plea in his voice.

Dat's expression suddenly warmed. "Of course I am."

"Marvin! Tobias!" Mel called from a nearby table. "Come and join us for lunch."

The moment was over. *Dat* didn't seem angry or unforgiving. Just distant. As Tobias walked beside him toward their friends, he wondered if he and his father would ever have the close relationship he craved. If not, he had himself to blame.

. . .

After lunch, Tobias hitched his father's buggy to his horse. Then he leaned against the buggy and waited for his parents to finish talking with another couple in the driveway. His mind swirled with a mixture of well-being and anxiety as he considered all that had happened today. He'd been welcomed back into the church, and then he ate lunch with his congregation members, who treated him as if he'd never left. He should be elated. God had showed him yet another blessing. But instead he felt as if something was missing in his life.

He yanked himself from his thoughts as Ariana and Jesse approached.

"I'm going to go home with Jesse to visit with his family this afternoon," Ariana said. "Would you let *Mamm* and *Dat* know I'll be home for supper?"

"*Ya*, of course." Tobias shook Jesse's hand. "Please tell your parents and *bruders* I said hello."

"I will. Do you need me to come over and help with chores tomorrow?" Jesse offered.

"No, *danki*. I can handle them now. But I can't tell you how grateful I am for your help while I was gone, Jesse." He extended his hand, and his friend shook it with a nod.

Ariana and Jesse started down the driveway, and then Ariana spun to face Tobias again. "Do you want to come with us? I'm sorry I didn't think to ask earlier."

"No, but *danki*. I think I need to stay home and be with *Mamm* and *Dat*. Have a great time, and don't worry about me." He waved them off, and Ariana and Jesse continued toward Jesse's buggy.

"Tobias!"

He turned to see Mariella hurrying toward him, her purple dress fluttering around her legs. He stood up straight as a smile curved up the corners of his mouth. Why did she have such a strong effect on him? "Hi, Mari."

"I only have a minute," she said. "My parents are ready to go home." She pointed toward where her family was already climbing into their buggy. "I just wanted to tell you I'm grateful you confessed your sins and were reinstated today. I knew you could do it."

She smiled. Did she have any idea how that simple gesture affected him?

Stop! She's Ariana's best friend. She's off-limits.

"Mari!" Ammon hollered.

"I have to go." She began walking backward. "Have a *gut* afternoon."

"Mari, wait," he called, taking a step toward her. "*Danki* for being here today."

She laughed, the mirth lighting up her pretty face. "Why wouldn't I be? I'm a member of the congregation, and *mei dat* is the bishop."

"I just meant, well . . . *Danki* for being *mei freind*."

"I'll always be your *freind*." She waved, turned, and rushed off.

Tobias was surprised how much he wanted to see her again—and sooner rather than later.

CHAPTER FOUR

Tobias stepped from the mudroom and stopped in the doorway to the kitchen. Memories rolled over him when he saw his mother and sister starting to cook breakfast. The delicious aroma of eggs, bacon, home fries, and freshly baked bread transported him back to when he'd walked into the house every day after morning chores. It was as if time had stood still and he'd never left home.

But time hadn't stood still. He had left home, and now he had to rebuild his fragile relationship with his family—especially with his father, but even with *Mamm* and Ariana. As forgiving and kind as the women in his family were, he knew how badly he had hurt them. How could he have ever taken his precious loved ones for granted?

Ariana raised a dark eyebrow as she set dishes on the table. "Are you just going to stand in the doorway and stare at us?"

"No, I definitely want some breakfast if you and *Mamm* are making it. It already smells *appeditlich*." Tobias shoved away his worries and walked to the table. "May I help you serve it when it's done?"

Ariana chuckled. "Just wash up. *Mamm* and I can serve it."

Tobias washed his hands at the sink as *Dat* entered the kitchen through the doorway that led to the family room.

"*Gude mariye,*" Ariana and *Mamm* sang in unison.

"*Gude mariye,*" he responded before eyeing Tobias. "You're up early."

"I've been up for more than an hour now." Tobias leaned back against the sink as he dried his hands. "The animals are cared for. I'm going to start cleaning out the barn after breakfast."

Dat blinked. "I thought you'd sleep in today."

"There's no time to sleep in when chores have to be done. And since I've been gone, I thought I'd do them on my own this morning. You deserve a break, *Dat.*" Tobias tossed the wet paper towels into the trash can and then sat down at the table. When Ariana grinned at him, he winked at her in response.

He'd hoped to ask his father how the dairy farm was doing yesterday afternoon. But his father seemed relaxed, had even napped, and he didn't want to disturb him. Now seemed like the right time.

"*Dat,* I've been meaning to ask you. How's the dairy farm doing?"

His father raised his eyebrows, as if to question if his son was really interested, and Tobias nearly cringed. But they slipped into an easy conversation, and once again Tobias realized how grateful he was that Jesse had filled in on the farm while he was in Florida.

When breakfast was ready, *Mamm* took her spot at

the end of the table, opposite *Dat*'s, and Ariana sat down across from Tobias. They all bowed their head in silent prayer and then began to serve themselves. Tobias lifted the platter of eggs and scraped a pile onto his plate. Next he reached for the bacon and then the bread.

"Is Mariella still planning to come over today to work on the dresses for the wedding?" *Mamm* asked.

Tobias stopped chewing at the mention of Mariella's name. He turned toward Ariana and awaited her response.

"*Ya.*" Ariana forked some egg as she spoke. "She'll be here soon. We're going to work on the dresses and then start another quilt."

Tobias felt a little thrill. He'd have a chance to talk to Mariella again today. But why did he allow himself to be so excited? She'd never be interested in being more than his friend. She knew too much about his problems. He pushed away all thoughts about her and focused on his family.

"How are your wedding plans coming along?" he asked his sister.

"*Gut.* We're almost finished with the dresses, and we have some ideas for the table decorations." Ariana lifted her mug of coffee. "It's coming so quickly. I can't believe it's only a month away."

"I know." *Mamm* beamed. "I can't believe *mei boppli* is going to be a *fraa.*"

His mother and sister talked about the wedding plans the whole time they ate, and when all their plates were clean, he carried the empty platters to the counter. Then he turned to his father.

"Would you like to get started in the barn?" he offered.

"*Ya*," *Dat* said, agreeing and then heading toward the mudroom.

Mamm grabbed Tobias's arm before he could take a step. "*Danki* for helping your *dat* with the chores."

"It's my job to help him."

"I know that, but I also remember how frustrated you and your *dat* would get with each other." She released his arm. "I can tell you're trying to get his approval, but you already have it by coming back to us and making yourself right with the church. He may not say it or show it, but he's very, very *froh* you're back."

"He is?" He longed to temper the desperation in his voice.

"*Ya*, he is." *Mamm* touched his shoulder. "You're our *sohn*, and we'll always love you. Give your *dat* some time. He'll tell you how much he's missed you."

Tobias nodded before going to the back door. Maybe *Mamm* was right. Maybe *Dat* would open up to him someday.

. . .

Mariella sliced cooked chicken breast as she and Ariana worked at the kitchen counter later that morning.

"I like your idea for the table decorations." Ariana cut up celery beside her. "Plastic vases with flowers would be nice. They'd be just enough to dress up the tables, but simple enough to remain plain."

"That's what I was thinking. We can go to the store

later this week if you'd like," Mariella said, offering her assistance.

"Are you sure your *mamm* doesn't mind your being here so often?" Ariana asked as she scraped the celery pieces into a large bowl between them.

"No, she doesn't mind at all. *Mei schweschdere* help her around the *haus*, and *Mamm* is *froh* I'm helping to sew and sell quilts. She appreciates the extra money I bring home."

"Oh *gut*." Ariana smiled. "We can get back to sewing after lunch if you want to stay longer."

"I told *mei mamm* I might not be home until supper, so we have plenty of time."

Mariella cubed the remaining chicken and added it to the bowl. She was mixing in mayonnaise when the back door opened and then clicked shut. The voices of the Smucker men sounded from the mudroom, and her face heated. Although she'd been working in the sewing room with Ariana and Roseanne for a few hours, she hadn't seen Tobias since she'd arrived. She hoped to have a chance to talk to him alone before she went home.

Tobias stepped into the kitchen with his father in tow, and Mariella sucked in a deep breath. Tobias was so handsome clad in a deep-blue shirt and black work trousers. He pushed his hand through his thick, dark hair, causing it to stand up in a haphazard but adorable manner. He smiled at her, and she felt as though electricity zipped through her veins.

"Hi, Mari. Ariana mentioned you planned to come over today."

"*Ya*. We've been working on the dresses for the wedding. We're going to work on a quilt this afternoon."

"Hi, Mariella," Marvin said before looking at Ariana. "Where's your *mamm*?"

Ariana set a basket of rolls on the table. "She's in the sewing room. She'll be down in a minute. Mariella and I offered to start making lunch while *Mamm* finishes what she's working on."

"I'm going to go talk to her." Marvin walked through the kitchen, and then his footfalls sounded on the stairs.

Mariella returned to mixing her ingredients as Tobias crossed the kitchen and stood beside her at the sink.

"Chicken salad?" He peered into the bowl before turning on the faucet. He stood so close their arms nearly bumped.

"*Ya*. Do you like it?"

"I love chicken salad."

"I do too." She looked up at him and nearly lost herself in the depths of his dark eyes.

Stop it! He's Ariana's bruder!

"Oh, no!" Ariana announced, and Mariella jumped with a start. "We forgot the grapes!"

"We can't forget the grapes," Tobias said, mocking his sister with a smirk before scrubbing his hands.

Ariana took a bag of grapes from the refrigerator and moved to where she'd left the cutting board and knife she'd used to prepare the celery. "I'll slice them, and then you can mix them in."

"Okay."

"Would you like me to pour glasses of water?" Tobias offered.

"*Ya. Danki,*" Ariana told him over her shoulder.

When it was ready, Mariella split the chicken salad between two bowls and carried them to the table. Ariana put out bags of pretzels and potato chips and Tobias set out plates and utensils.

"Everything looks *appeditlich,*" Roseanne said as she and Marvin entered the kitchen. "*Danki* for making lunch."

"*Gern gschehne.*" Ariana gestured toward Mariella. "Mariella suggested chicken salad when I told her we had leftover chicken already cooked."

Mariella shrugged as everyone looked at her. "I was thinking about chicken salad the other day."

"It was a great suggestion," Tobias quipped as he moved to a chair.

As he tapped the chair beside him, his eyes looked as if they beckoned her. Did he want her to sit next him? If so, and if she did, would Ariana notice how happy Mariella was to be close to her brother?

Mariella hesitated, remaining by the sink.

"Let's eat." Marvin rubbed his hands together. "I can't wait to try your chicken salad."

"Mariella. Why don't you sit by Tobias?" Ariana suggested as she sank into a chair. "That way we can talk across the table."

"Oh." Mariella looked at Tobias, and he raised his eyebrows. "That sounds *gut.*" She slipped into the chair beside him.

When they closed their eyes for the silent prayer, Mariella's leg brushed against his, and she sucked in a startled breath. Did he notice how touching him affected her? Did he like being this close to her?

After the prayer, Ariana passed a bowl of chicken salad to each of her parents, and they scooped the salad onto rolls before passing the bowls along.

"This is fantastic," Marvin said after swallowing a bite of his sandwich.

Roseanne nodded in agreement, her mouth full.

"I nearly forgot the grapes," Ariana said, admitting her misstep with a laugh.

"Here." Tobias handed a bowl of chicken salad to Mariella. "Make your sandwich first."

She looked down at the empty roll sitting on his plate. "Don't you want to make yours?"

"I can wait." He reached for the bag of chips and set a handful of them on his plate. "Would you like some chips?"

"*Ya*, please." As she scooped the salad onto her roll, she smiled. Perhaps her dreams would come true some-day. Then they'd share many more meals together.

. . .

After he finished his late afternoon chores, Tobias moved through his father's biggest barn to the small shop at the back. Although it had a window, the November sunlight was dim outside. He crossed to the workbench and flipped on a Coleman lantern, surprised the battery still worked after five months.

In the warm yellow light, he ran his finger over the

tools. And then memories came back as he touched the half-finished birdhouse he'd started before leaving for Florida. For years he'd retreated to this shop to both escape his constant arguments with his father and defy him.

While *Dat* pushed Tobias to respect and appreciate the dairy farm, Tobias had pulled away from the farm, insisting he wanted to be a carpenter. He built the birdhouses and sold them in his uncle Titus's furniture store. The extra money he earned with his hobby had been nice, but he'd been more interested in irritating his father.

Tobias sank onto the stool in front of his workbench and hung his head as shame crawled onto his shoulders and dug its sharp talons into his muscles. He'd been thoughtless, immature, and cruel to his father, and he needed to find a way to prove to *Dat* that he was no longer that petulant person. The letter of apology he'd sent soon after he left hadn't been enough—he knew that. He was ready to be the son his father deserved. But was it too late to make up for his mistakes?

Trying to dismiss his worry, he began to clean and organize his tools. They looked as if they hadn't been touched since he left. He was about to hang a hammer on the pegboard above the workbench, when a voice sounded behind him.

"Tobias?"

Startled, he dropped the hammer with a clatter, and it bounced off the workbench before falling onto the floor beside his foot. He spun. Mariella was standing in the doorway.

Her cheeks flushed bright pink as she clapped one hand over her mouth. She was beautiful in her green dress, bright beneath her unbuttoned black coat.

"Hi." He chuckled as he sank back onto the stool, facing her. "I didn't hear you come in."

"I'm so sorry." She held up her hand. "I didn't mean to sneak up on you."

"It's okay. I was lost in thought."

"I shouldn't have intruded, but I wanted to say good-bye before I left." She started to back out of the doorway. "I'll see you—"

"Don't go." He popped up. "You're not intruding." He stood and pulled the extra stool out from beneath the workbench and set it next to his. "Please sit."

She wound one tie from her *kapp* around her finger as she stared at the stool, as if debating.

"Please," he pleaded, holding his hands as if to pray. "Just for a minute?"

"Okay." She crossed the shop and hopped up on the stool.

"*Danki.*" He turned toward her and leaned against the workbench. "Did you get a lot of sewing done?"

"*Ya*, we did." She smoothed her hands over the skirt of her dress and then hugged her coat against her body. "We're almost done with the dresses. And we started that new quilt."

"What pattern is the quilt?"

"It's a wedding ring with different shades of blue and purple. It's a custom order for one of your *mamm*'s customers."

"That's great."

She pointed toward the workbench. "What were you doing before I interrupted you?"

"Just cleaning up my mess."

"Are you going to make more birdhouses?"

"No. At least not now." He shook his head as he looked at the unfinished project sitting on the corner of the workspace, as if awaiting his attention. "I need to concentrate on the farm, not on my hobby."

"It's okay to have a hobby if doesn't interfere with your work."

He turned back to her and frowned. "This hobby always interfered with my work, and that caused problems with *mei dat.*"

Mariella studied him for a moment. "What's really on your mind?"

He lifted his eyebrows, surprised by the question.

Her eyes widened as she once again held up her hand. "I didn't mean to pry."

"You're not prying. I was just wondering how you knew I had something on my mind."

"You sort of wear your emotions." She pointed to his face. "Your brow is furrowed like you're trying to figure out a complicated puzzle."

He blew out a deep breath of air and rubbed his chin. "You're right. I am trying to figure out a complicated puzzle."

"Can I help?"

"I don't think so." He ran one finger along the edge of the workbench. "I'm trying to figure out how I fit into my family now that I'm back."

"That's easy." She leaned toward him. "You already

fit. Your *mamm* and Ariana talked about you almost nonstop today. They're so grateful God sent you home to them. You're their *sohn* and *bruder*, and that's what you need to be."

"*Danki*, but I don't think *mei dat* sees it that way."

Her golden-blonde eyebrows drew together. "I don't understand. Your *dat* seemed fine at lunch."

"I can't get him to really talk to me. He was silent while we worked out in the barn together today, except when we discussed what work we had to do." He picked at a loose piece of wood. "He won't really talk with me about anything meaningful."

"Hasn't he always been sort of reticent?"

He shrugged. "I suppose so. Except when I provoked him to anger or frustration the last few years."

"I imagine he'll open up to you when he's ready to talk. Don't you agree?"

"You're probably right. *Mamm* said the same thing." He smiled. "*Danki* for listening."

"Anytime. That's what *freinden* are for, right?"

"*Ya*, they are. I guess I should let you go before your parents worry about you."

"I was on my way out. I just wanted to check on you before I left."

She wanted to check on me? Before she said she just wanted to say good-bye. He paused, stunned by her thoughtfulness.

She held her hand out to him. "It was *gut* seeing you. *Gut nacht*."

He took her hand and, as he shook it, he enjoyed the softness of her skin. "Let me walk you to your buggy." He climbed off the stool, lifted the lantern, and kicked the hammer. "Ouch." As he leaned down to get it, his gaze focused on the wall behind the workbench. Something that resembled scratches caught his eye.

"What is that?" he whispered.

Mariella bent down beside him. "Is something wrong?"

He crawled under the bench and held the lantern next to the wall. "I've never seen this before." It was a carving. He ran his fingers over it as he took in what it said:

Tobias John Smucker 1971–1977

A chill slithered up his spine as he read his own name. But what did the dates mean? Who had carved this into the wall and why? Was this a relative? If so, why hadn't *Dat* told him about a Tobias John who lived in the seventies?

"Do you see a notepad and pencil on the workbench?" he called.

He heard rustling, and then Mariella's voice sounded above him. "*Ya*, I found them."

"Would you please write this down?"

"*Ya*." She bent down again.

He read the name and dates aloud and then climbed out from under the bench and stood.

"What does this mean?" she asked.

"I don't know, but I'm going to find out."

. . .

After saying good-bye to Mariella, Tobias headed into the house with the notepaper in this hand. His sister and mother had started supper preparations, and his father was at the kitchen table, looking over paperwork.

"*Dat*, was there another Tobias John Smucker?"

The kitchen fell silent for a beat as *Dat* looked up, gaping.

Ariana looked back and forth between their parents. "What is Tobias talking about?"

"How did you find out about him?" *Mamm* asked.

"His name is carved on the barn wall under my workbench." Tobias set the piece of paper on the table and pointed to it. "Why does it say 1971 to 1977? Did he die when he was only six?" He looked up at his father, whose face had now clouded with a frown. "Am I named after him?"

Dat shook his head—not to answer Tobias's question, but by the expression on his face, to signal he had no intention of answering it. He started for the mudroom. "I'll be in the barn. Don't wait supper on me."

Before Tobias could stop him, *Dat* was gone, the back door clicking shut. Tobias turned to his mother. "What isn't he telling me?"

Mamm sighed as she sank into a chair. "Sit."

Tobias and Ariana exchanged confused expressions before sitting down across from her.

"What is *Dat* keeping from us?" Ariana asked.

Mamm rested her hands on the table and divided a look between them. "He's not deliberately keeping anything from you. This is just too painful for him to discuss."

Tobias's stomach twisted as he waited for his mother's explanation.

"You already know your *dat* was only ten years old when his *dat* died in a farming accident. He was the oldest, which meant he had to become the man of the *haus*." She gestured toward the back door. "He had to be responsible for taking care of this very farm because his *mamm* had younger *kinner* to care for. That's what it was like for him until she remarried when he was sixteen."

"I know all that." Tobias pointed to the piece of paper. "Who was Tobias John?"

"He was your *dat's bruder*." *Mamm* placed one finger on the years. "Tobias died unexpectedly in 1977."

Ariana gasped. "That's so *bedauerlich*!"

"*Ya*." *Mamm* paused to dab her eyes with a tissue from her apron. "He was healthy and *froh* one day, and then the next day he had passed away from meningitis. There was no sign he was even ill. Your *mammi* found him in his bed."

She sniffed. "He died only a year after your *daadi* passed away, and it was crushing for the family. For a long time your *mammi* blamed herself for missing the symptoms of the illness, even though there were no symptoms. She always felt like she wasn't a *gut mamm* because of that, but she was. She did the best she could, and she had her hands full with her other *kinner*—your *onkel* Titus and *onkel* Danny."

Ariana blew out a loud puff of air and cupped her hand to her mouth as tears trailed down her face. Tobias swallowed against a swell in his throat.

"Your *dat* never forgot Tobias." *Mamm* wiped her eyes.

"And I'm named after him." Tobias nearly whispered.

"*Ya*, you are. When you were born, your *dat* wanted to name you in memory of his *bruder*."

"What else did *Dat* tell you about *Onkel* Tobias? I don't remember seeing a grave for him near *Mammi*'s," Ariana said.

"Well, he had just turned six when he died," *Mamm* began. "He was a sweet *bu*, and he loved to help out on the farm. He enjoyed taking care of the baby goats and the calves. And his grave is there, but the headstone is so small, I'm sure you *kinner* just never noticed it. And of course, we never pointed it out.

"In addition, the community understood how painful it was for the family to talk about him, so no one did. By this time, very few people remember him. Your *onkels* were too young to remember him, and they've never wanted to upset your *dat* by asking questions."

As *Mamm* finished, Tobias slumped in his chair. Guilt flooded his soul. For years he'd disrespected and argued with his father, not appreciating how much weight he'd carried on his shoulders. Why hadn't he acknowledged what a strong, intelligent man *Dat* had always been? He'd not only done all he could for *Mamm* and him and Ariana, but he kept his mother and brothers afloat, running the farm when he was only ten years old. How could he have even properly mourned his brother's death with so much responsibility and a grieving mother?

He probably couldn't. He was probably still trying.

And then a realization punched Tobias in the gut. This was why the farm meant so much to his father, why he had such a deep connection to it, and why it was so important that Tobias run it in the future. The farm had memories and a lineage *Dat* needed Tobias to protect and preserve. The farm was where his father had become a man and where his family had been born—and died.

And now it was Tobias's turn to ensure the Smucker family farm carried that history into the future.

But am I worthy of such a legacy?

CHAPTER FIVE

Mariella shivered as she tied her horse to the fence at the top of the Smuckers' driveway.

"Mari! *Gude mariye!*"

She turned to face the barn as Tobias walked toward her, smiling and waving. Her heart seemed to flip over in her chest as she took in his handsome face.

She hoped to have a chance to talk to him alone today. They'd spoken briefly at church, and she'd spent more time here helping Ariana with wedding tasks, but she hadn't had the opportunity to really talk to him since he found the carving on the wall. Nearly three weeks had gone by.

She swallowed a groan. Tobias would never be interested in her, and she needed to stop entertaining the idea of ever being more than his friend.

"Gude mariye." She fingered the hem of her short coat as he approached.

He jammed his thumb toward the house. "Are you looking for Ariana?"

"Ya. We're going to finish up the wedding decorations today."

"Oh. She and *mei mamm* went to the store, but they

should be back soon. Come inside. I'll make some *kaffi*, and we can talk while you wait for them." He started toward the house.

She hesitated, biting her lip. Why hadn't she called before she came over? She'd just assumed Ariana would be here since they discussed getting together today. On the other hand, here was the opportunity she'd been hoping for.

Tobias spun around, his eyebrows careening toward his straw hat. "Are you going to join me? I make the best *kaffi* in Lancaster County. At least, I think it's the best."

His smile was wide and genuine, but was he being this nice only because she was his sister's best friend? No, she realized he now thought of her as his friend too. But only a friend.

His expression clouded as his eyebrows pinched together. "Did I say something wrong? I wasn't trying to be prideful about my abilities with a percolator."

She laughed. "I didn't think you were prideful, but I don't want you to feel obligated to make me *kaffi*."

"It's just *kaffi*. I don't mind making it."

"I don't want to impose. I can sit in the kitchen and wait by myself."

He folded his arms over his chest. "Are we really arguing about *kaffi*?" He made a sweeping gesture toward the porch steps. "It's freezing out here. Let's have some *kaffi* and sweet rolls. *Mamm* made them this morning. I know I said *mei mamm* and *schweschder* will be back soon, but I'm not sure *how* soon."

"Okay." She followed him into the house. He got the

percolator going and then found the container with the rolls. She gathered plates, knives, and butter before they sat down at the table.

"I haven't had a chance to talk to you in a few weeks. How have you been?" he asked as he buttered a roll.

"*Gut.* We have the dresses ready for the wedding, and like I said, we're going to finish up the decorations today. I can't believe the wedding is next Thursday. That's only six days away. I'm thrilled for Ariana and Jesse. They're going to be so *froh* together."

He raised an eyebrow as he pushed the top back onto the butter container. "I didn't ask you about *mei schweschder*'s wedding. I asked how *you* are."

"Oh." She paused for a moment, absorbing the warmth in his dark eyes. "I'm fine. I've been busy working on a couple of quilts and helping *mei schweschdere* with a few sewing projects at home. We've decided to make a quilt for *mei dat* for Christmas, so we've been working on that for a couple of hours every morning after he leaves for work."

"That's nice. What does the quilt look like?" He lifted the roll and took a bite.

"It's going to be really *schee* with a large blue-and-gray star in the center." She gasped, realizing how prideful she sounded. "I'm sorry. I didn't mean to brag. I hope it will be *schee*."

He grinned and shook his head. "If you're making it, then it will be *schee*. I've seen a couple of the quilts you sold to the store in town."

"You have?"

"*Ya. Mei mamm* showed them to me. You're very

talented, and that's not prideful. It's the truth." He sipped his coffee as she digested his compliments.

"How have you been?" she asked before taking a sip from her mug.

"I'm doing all right." He broke the remainder of his roll in half as he looked down at his plate. "I've gotten into the swing of doing the chores on the farm again."

"How are things with your *dat*?"

He shrugged. "I guess they're fine."

She leaned forward and leveled her gaze with his. "What aren't you telling me?"

He scowled and leaned back in his chair. "We've been working side by side on the farm for three weeks now, but he still hasn't opened up to me."

"Has he talked to you about what you found in the barn?"

"No." He shook his head. "Did Ariana tell you the story about the *onkel* we didn't even know existed?"

"She did." Mariella frowned. "It's so *bedauerlich* that he died when he was only six years old."

"I know. *Dat* wouldn't tell us what the carving meant, but *mei mamm* did. She said it was too painful for him to discuss." Tobias shoved his hand through his hair. "I had no idea I was named after an *onkel*. Why did *Dat* never tell me?"

"I suppose it was because it was too painful, like your *mamm* said."

"I just want him to trust me and treat me like an adult now." He stared down at his mug as he gripped it. "But I guess I don't deserve that since I've been a terrible *sohn*. I was argumentative, disrespectful, and

difficult. I don't deserve his respect, but I'd do anything to earn it." He released the mug and pushed it
away, the liquid sloshing in protest.

"You will earn it. This is a new start for you and
for your relationship with your family and your community." Without considering the consequences, she
reached out and placed her hand on top of his. She felt
a spark like electricity jolting up her hand, sending heat
shooting up her arm to her neck. The feeling made her
swallow a gasp.

His intense eyes locked with hers, and a moment
passed as they stared at each other. Had he felt that
spark too? Was it possible he did care about her as
more than a friend? No, she had to be imagining this.
The years she'd spent longing for him to notice her had
clouded her judgment.

After a moment, she pulled her hand away and
cleared her throat, but neither of them broke eye contact.

"Your family loves you, Tobias," she began softly,
hoping to calm the tremor in her voice. "Your *dat* will
see how committed you are to the farm and the community now, but you may have to be the one to initiate
an open and honest conversation. Tell him how you feel
and see how he responds."

"I think you're right. I do need to try to talk to him
and see what he says." He dropped his eyes and then
took a long draw from his mug before getting to his
feet. "Would you like more *kaffi*?"

"No, but *danki*." She bit into her roll.

As he brought the percolator to the table, they heard
the back door open and close.

"Mariella!" Ariana exclaimed when she entered the kitchen. She dropped two large bags on the counter. "You have to see the ribbons I got for the table decorations. They're so *schee*! They're the same shade of purple as our dresses." She began pulling ribbon and tulle out of one of the bags as Roseanne set another bag on the table.

"I'll let you ladies talk about your womanly stuff." Tobias gave Mariella a wave and then a wink before he slipped out the back door.

• • •

"How long have you been out here?" *Dat* asked as he stepped into one of the barns the following Monday morning.

"For about an hour. I cared for the animals, and I'm going to start cleaning the stalls." Tobias adjusted his straw hat on his head. "You can go inside and eat breakfast. I'll be in there soon."

"No, no." *Dat* shook his head. "I'll wait for you." He studied Tobias for a moment. "You've been working hard this past month. *Danki*."

"*Gern gschehne.*" Tobias stood a little taller. It had been years since his father had complimented him, and although the words were simple, they lifted his soul. The desire to build a close relationship with his father again was overwhelming. He wanted *Dat* to really talk to him and share about his past. But how could he open the conversation?

Suddenly, Mariella's words from last week echoed in his mind:

Your dat *will see how committed you are to the farm and the community, but you may have to be the one to initiate an open and honest conversation. Tell him how you feel and see how he responds.*

Tobias remembered her pretty face as she placed her hand on his to console him. As soon as their skin made contact, he'd felt a zing of warmth and happiness deep inside.

"Tobias?" *Dat* raised a bushy eyebrow as a smile curved up the corners of his lips. "Why are you grinning like a Cheshire cat?"

"Am I grinning?" Tobias chuckled.

"*Ya*, you are. What's going through your mind right now?"

"I . . . uh . . . well, nothing really." Tobias started toward the corner where they kept pitchforks and shovels. "I'll start on the stalls."

"No, no." *Dat* reached out and touched his shoulder. "You're not leaving until you tell me what made you smile like that. Is it a *maedel*?"

Tobias stilled.

"Oh, so it is a *maedel*. Is she anyone I know?"

Ya, *you know her well.* "*Dat*, how did you know you were in love with *mamm*?"

Dat's smile widened. How long had it been since he'd seen his father smile with sincere happiness glowing on his tired face?

"I had known your *mamm* just about my entire life because we went to the same school and were in the same church district and youth group. One day we started talking at a youth gathering, and I guess we saw each other in a new light. It was as if we both suddenly realized we liked each other as more than *freinden*." He shrugged. "We started dating and we were married a year later."

"So it's possible to fall in love with someone you've known for most of your life." Tobias hadn't meant for the thought to escape his lips, but it was too late to retract it.

"So it *is* Mariella. I've had a feeling after seeing you two talking at church and at the *haus*." *Dat* tapped his shoulder. "She's a sweet *maedel*. She's a *gut* choice."

Tobias held up one hand. "Wait. I haven't told her how I feel. We've just been talking, and she seems to understand me better than, well, better than I think I understand myself."

"It's like that sometimes. Your *mamm* was always my strength when I needed it, more than I realized. I think it's *wunderbaar* that you've begun to think you can be more than just *freinden*."

Tobias leaned against the horse stall behind him. "I don't know if she would even want to date me. I mean, I'm sort of a mess. And I don't know if she feels the same way about me."

Dat gave him a knowing smile. "Oh, I think she does."

"How do I find out?"

"Just ask her. Be honest with her."

"What if she doesn't like me?"

"What if she does, and she's just waiting for you to ask her?" *Dat* asked. "How long do you think she'll wait?"

Tobias gnawed his lower lip as he contemplated his father's words. "You're right. She might be waiting for me to talk to her about where our relationship is headed. I'll try to do that soon."

"*Gut.*" *Dat* rubbed his beard and got a faraway look in his eyes. "I can't believe Ariana is going to be married on Thursday. It seems like only yesterday she was swinging on that old swing set by your *mamm*'s garden. You two have grown up so fast. I suppose your *mamm* and I will have *grandkinner* soon."

Tobias nodded. "*Ya*, the years have gone quickly. I think she and Jesse will be *froh* together."

"I think so too." *Dat* nodded toward the entrance to the dairy barn. "Let's go have breakfast. We can work on the chores together after we eat."

Tobias grinned. "*Danki* for talking to me, *Dat*. I hope we can talk more."

His father gave him a nod, and then they started toward the house, walking side by side.

. . .

"Knock, knock."

Tobias looked up from the devotional he'd been reading as he sat on his bed. Ariana was leaning against his door frame.

"Do you have a few minutes to talk?"

"*Ya*, of course." He pointed to the chair across from his bed.

His sister closed the door behind her and then sat down and hugged her arms over her pink bathrobe. "I can't believe I'm getting married tomorrow. How did that happen?" She gave a nervous laugh.

"Well, let's see." He closed his book and set it on the nightstand. "You started dating Jesse a few years ago, he built you a house, and then he asked you to marry him and you said yes."

She rolled her eyes. "I know that, but how did it all happen so fast?"

"I guess the years move by quickly, whether or not we want them to."

"Right."

"You must be excited. You've been planning this day for a long time."

"I am excited, but I'm also *naerfich*. I just hope I don't disappoint Jesse."

He chuckled. "You could never disappoint Jesse. He loves you."

"I know, but will I be a *gut fraa*? I hope I keep the *haus* the way he likes it, and I hope he likes the meals I cook."

"He will. You two make a great team." *I hope I can have that someday too.*

"*Danki.*" She paused. "How are you doing?"

"I'm great." He adjusted the pillow behind his back. "Everything is fine. I'm back into a routine with chores on the farm."

"Are you *froh* you came back?" Her expression clouded as her dark eyes seemed to search his.

"Of course I am. Why would you ask that?"

"I'm concerned I pressured you to come back when I begged you to be here for my wedding."

"You didn't pressure me. You helped me make the

decision, but it was my decision. And notice I came back well before the wedding."

"Are you sure?" Her eyes misted. "I don't want you to regret coming back."

"*Ya*, I'm sure." He scooted to the edge of the bed. "Listen to me. I came back because I missed my family and my community. I also wanted to make things right with *Dat*. And I did want to be sure to attend your wedding. I didn't want to miss seeing my baby *schweschder* get married."

"Okay." She sniffed. "You seem *froh*, but I wanted to make sure."

"I am fine," he insisted. "You just think about tomorrow and how *wunderbaar* your new life with Jesse is going to be."

"*Ya*, I will. I have everything packed. I can't believe I'm moving out. It doesn't seem possible." She pulled a tissue out of her pocket and wiped her eyes. "How are things with *Dat*?"

"They're *gut*. We've actually started talking this week. We're closer than we've been in years."

"That's fantastic. I'm so *froh*." She lifted and lowered her shoulders in a sigh. "I'm sorry. I guess I'm just emotional with my wedding day being tomorrow. I'm just so thankful God brought you home to us again. I wanted you to be here to see me get married, but I also wanted you to be a part of our lives again. You're important to our family."

"*Danki*." He swallowed hard as the weight of her words sank in. He hoped he could keep his emotions in check and not break down in front of his sister.

"Have you and *Dat* discussed the carving you found on the wall yet?"

"No, but I'm going to ask him about it soon. We've been talking about some other things, so I think he'll open up to me about it, at least eventually."

"That's *gut*. You're both so stubborn, but I'm sure you'll find a way to relate to each other without arguing. *Dat* seems happier lately, and I don't think it's only because he's *froh* for me and Jesse, or even just because you came home. I think it must be because you two are getting closer."

He was grateful Ariana could see the progress he and *Dat* were making, and he remembered the warm conversation he and his father had about Mariella. He opened his mouth to ask if she would approve of his dating her best friend, but then he changed his mind. He didn't want to take the chance of upsetting her the night before her wedding. He'd talk to Mariella first and then discuss it with Ariana—if Mariella agreed to date him.

Ariana stood. "I guess I should try to get some sleep. Tomorrow is going to be a long day."

"Everything will be perfect. Have faith."

"*Ya*, I will. You too." She smiled. "*Gut nacht.*"

"*Gut nacht.*" Tobias waved before she turned to go, and he watched as she closed the door behind her. Tomorrow his sister would become Ariana Zook, and, somehow, he'd find the courage to ask Mariella if she would consider being his girlfriend.

CHAPTER SIX

Tobias leaned against the pasture fence and gazed toward his house, where a group of wedding guests talked and laughed on the back porch. He looked out at the setting sun as it splashed the sky with vivid hues of purple, red, orange, and yellow, and smiled.

Ariana's wedding had gone well, and the weather had been perfect, with no rain clouds in sight. All in all, everything had been just the way Ariana hoped.

As his sister married his best friend, Tobias had sat with the rest of the unmarried men in the congregation. The long wedding ceremony resembled a Sunday service, including hymns, prayers, and sermons. When the first sermon was over, the bishop looked at Ariana and Jesse. "Now here are two in one faith—Ariana Kathryn Smucker and Jesse Elijah Zook." Ammon asked the congregation if they knew any scriptural reason for the couple not to marry. Hearing no response, he continued. "If it is your desire to be married, you may in the name of the Lord come forth."

Jesse took Ariana's hand in his, and they stood before the bishop to take their vows.

Tobias was where he could see Mariella, and while the couple responded to the bishop's questions, Tobias glanced at her. He nearly blushed when he found her looking at him too. She smiled, and he couldn't help but return the sweet gesture. Oh, how he wished he could read her thoughts!

His heart pounding, Tobias held her gaze until the bishop's traditional reading of "A Prayer for Those about to Be Married" from an Amish prayer book called the *Christenpflict* made him realize he was staring. He broke the trance and did his best to turn his attention back to the service. But it wasn't easy. Mariella had been staring at him too!

When the second sermon ended, the congregation knelt as the bishop again read from the *Christenpflict*. Then after he recited The Lord's Prayer, the congregation stood, and the three-hour service ended with another hymn.

Tobias helped the rest of the men rearrange furniture while the women set up the wedding dinner: chicken with stuffing, mashed potatoes with gravy, pepper cabbage, and cooked cream of celery, along with cookies, pie, fruit, and Jell-O salad for dessert.

After he'd eaten in the barn with family and guests, Tobias headed outside to get some fresh air and sort through his confusing thoughts. Ariana and Mariella were still inside at a table, sitting across from Jesse and his two brothers, Nathaniel and Caleb. The two women both looked beautiful in the purple dresses they'd made for the occasion, and he was sure Ariana thought her new husband and his siblings handsome, dressed in the same traditional black-and-white clothing all the men in attendance wore.

His younger sister was now married, and he was still trying to figure out his place in the community. He longed to ask Mariella to date him, and last night he'd decided to do it today. But he didn't even know how to be a boyfriend. Was it fair for him to ask her to give him a chance when he was still trying to figure out how to even be the son his parents needed?

"Tobias." *Dat* came and leaned against the fence beside him. "I was looking for you. Why are you hiding out here?"

"I'm not hiding. I just needed to get some fresh air. The barn was packed with people." He looked toward the porch and his eyes found Mariella talking and laughing with a few friends from the youth group. She must have slipped outside while he was admiring the sunset. She was stunning with her hair peeking out of her prayer covering. It was shining like spun gold in the light of the lanterns.

"The ceremony was nice," *Dat* said.

"*Ya*, it was." Tobias swiveled toward his father and gathered all the courage he could find inside. He might be debating about asking Mariella if she wanted to date him, but he had to take a chance with his father, to finally have an honest conversation with him. "Why didn't you ever tell me about your *bruder*, Tobias John?"

Tobias held his breath, hoping he hadn't chosen the wrong time.

But *Dat* only sighed and then ran his hand down his beard. "I guess your *mamm* told you the story?"

"*Ya*, she did. Right after I found the carving. I'm sorry for everything you endured when you were only a *kind*. I knew your *dat* passed away and you had to run the farm, but I didn't know about Tobias, and I didn't understand the weight of all the responsibility thrown at you at such a young age. Why did you never share that with Ariana and me?"

"I think I sort of suppressed those days. It was difficult for my entire family. I had to grow up quickly and deal with issues no *kind* should ever have to face. Losing *mei dat* was terrible, but losing *mei bruder* only a year later was even worse. *Mei mamm* blamed herself, and some days she was inconsolable." His voice sounded reedy and he paused to clear his throat. "I never wanted to forget about Tobias. That's why I made that carving in the barn soon after he died, even though no one knew about it but me. And that's why I named you after him as an adult. They were the only ways I had to keep his memory alive."

"I'm honored you gave me his name. *Danki*."

Dat's eyes widened for a fraction of a second, and then he looked toward the house.

"*Dat*, I know I said this in the letter I sent after I left home, but I need to say it to you in person. I'm sorry for all the pain I caused you, *Mamm*, and Ariana," Tobias said. "I was selfish. And before I left, I was disrespectful and cruel to you. You never deserved it. I don't know how to express how much I regret my actions, and I promise I'll never put you through that again. I understand now how much this farm means to you."

Dat's gaze snapped to his. "What do you mean?"

"For years you've been trying to tell me how important this farm is to our family, but I wanted to defy you.

So I said I wanted to be a carpenter, even though wood-working is only a hobby. I see now that the farm is part of our history, and I'm ready to help carry that legacy into the future." Tobias gestured around the farm as his voice faltered. "I'm ready to embrace what it means to be a Smucker, and I'll do my best to make you proud to call me Tobias in memory of your *bruder*."

Dat wiped a hand across his eyes. "You have no idea how *froh* I am to hear you say that, *sohn*."

"I mean it too."

"But I owe you an apology as well."

"No." Tobias shook his head. "No, you don't. I deserved the angry words you said to me. I didn't respect you the way a *sohn* should respect his *dat*."

"That's not entirely true." *Dat* held up his hands. "I was always hard on you, and I'm certain that was part of what drove you to drink and then drove you away from us."

"No, you can't blame yourself for my mistakes. I'm a man, and I chose to drink and leave. I'm grateful Jesse was here to help you, but I'm ready to do my part. You never have to worry about needing help from someone else. I will be here. I just have to ask you for one thing."

"What is it? Do you want to build a *haus*?" He pointed toward the pasture. "We can build a little *haus* for you to bring your *fraa* home to."

"Wait." It was Tobias's turn to hold up his hands. "Don't set a wedding date for me yet. I don't even know if Mariella is interested in dating me."

"I told you she is. I saw her watching you earlier. She's just as eager to date you as you are to date her."

Tobias chuckled. "I never thought you'd be a match-maker."

Dat smiled. "What did you want to ask me?"

"I want to stay close, like this." Tobias gestured between them. "Let's keep talking. I want to be close."

Dat nodded, his eyes bright. "I'd like that too."

And to Tobias's surprise, his father hugged him.

• • •

Mariella leaned forward on the porch railing as she peered toward the pasture fence where Tobias and his father stood close together. Warmth spread through her as she took in the exchange between father and son. It looked as if Tobias and Marvin were finally connecting, and Tobias's dream of working things out with his father was coming true.

Tobias had looked so handsome dressed in his black-and-white Sunday best as he sat in the congregation during the ceremony. Although she'd tried to keep her focus on her father and the service, her eyes defied her. It was as if Tobias had an invisible magnet that pulled her gaze toward him. And once, he was watching her with such intensity that heat seemed to course through her veins. She couldn't look away. Did he feel the same attraction that haunted her every time she saw him?

"What are you looking at?" Ariana came beside her and looked out toward the fence. "Oh, that's *wunderbaar*! *Mei dat* and *bruder* are finally talking." She turned toward Mariella. "Why are you blushing?"

"I'm not blushing. It must be the lantern light." Mariella turned her eyes to where Marvin was now embracing Tobias. "Look, your *bruder* and *dat* are hugging!"

Ariana followed Mariella's line of sight and sucked in a deep breath. "Oh, Tobias will be so *froh*."

Suddenly, she turned her attention back to Mariella.

"Wait a minute." Ariana touched her arm. "Do you like *mei bruder*?"

Mariella froze. She was caught! Was she going to lose her best friend now that the truth was about to be in the open? She couldn't lie. She turned to face her accuser.

"You *do* like Tobias!" Ariana grinned. "That's *wunderbaar*!"

"You think so?"

"Of course I do!"

"Now *you* wait a minute." Mariella held up her hand. "You're not angry with me?"

"Why would I be angry? You and Tobias are two of the most important people in my life. I would be thrilled to see you together. Besides, I think you're just what he needs. You're a *gut*, honest, hardworking, Christian *maedel*. I'm *froh* he has you in his life. I know he's had a difficult time, but he's a decent man. He has a kind heart, and I believe he wants to settle down and have a family."

"I think you're jumping ahead a bit too quickly." Mariella hugged her arms to her chest as if to protect her heart. "I don't think he's ready for that yet. I don't even know if he likes me. I don't know if he will ever see me as more than his little *schweschder*'s *freind*."

"I think he definitely likes you. He asks about you all the time. I don't know why I didn't realize that before."

"He does?" Mariella's stomach fluttered.

"*Ya*, he often asks if you're coming over, and he looks *froh* when I say you are. And now that I think about it, when did he start calling you 'Mari'?" Ariana nodded toward the fence. "You should go talk to him."

Mariella hesitated as she focused on where Tobias still stood. Marvin had started walking toward the barn. "Are you certain you'd feel comfortable if we dated?"

"*Ya*, I'm positive." Ariana touched her arm. "You have my blessing."

"*Danki*." Mariella took a deep breath and started down the steps.

. . .

Tobias couldn't stop smiling as *Dat* walked away. He'd just had the most emotional and honest conversation with his father he'd had in years. Not only did he feel closer to him, but it was also as if they had reached a new, more mature relationship. Everything was falling into place. Happiness flooded him. He finally, truly had his family back!

"It looked like you and your *dat* had a *gut* conversation," Mariella said as she approached him.

"*Ya*, we did! He finally opened up. *Danki* so much for encouraging me to initiate a talk about his *bruder*. It worked, and I owe it all to you!" He picked her up, and she gasped and then squealed as he spun her around.

When he set her feet back on the ground, they

stared at each other for a moment, and doubt crept into his mind. Had he crossed a line with her and blown his chance to ask her to be his girlfriend?

"I'm sorry." He shook his head. "That was much too forward of me."

"It's okay." Then she shook her head, as if to clear it. "You have to stop giving me all the credit. You're the one who had the courage to talk to your father. You did it all on your own."

"No, I couldn't have done it without you. I had the courage to talk to *mei dat* because you believed in me."

As he looked into Mariella's eyes, his heart swelled with admiration—and something else. What was the strange new feeling coursing through his veins? Was it love?

The question caught him off-guard.

"Tobias?" she asked. "Did you hear what I asked you?"

"What?" He shook away the startling thoughts. "I'm sorry. What did you say?"

"I asked what your *dat* said."

"Oh." He rubbed his chin as he considered their conversation. "He told me why he kept *mei onkel* Tobias's existence from us. That led to my apology for all the stress I caused him before I left. I was really surprised when he hugged me. I feel like we've come a long way toward repairing our relationship."

"I admire you for having the strength to take the first step."

"*Danki.* I feel so much better now that this burden is off my shoulders. I have *mei dat* back, and we promised to keep working on our relationship."

"What a blessing." She reached out and took his hand in hers. "I'm so *froh* for you. God brought you back to us, and he is healing your heart."

"*Ya*, God does give second chances, even when we don't deserve it." He squeezed her hand. "I'm so thankful he put you in my life."

Intensity sparked between them as he searched her eyes. "I admire you too, Mari. Your friendship means so much to me. I think about you all the time, and I care deeply about you."

. . .

Mariella held her breath as Tobias continued to hold her hand. Was she dreaming? Or had he just admitted he thinks about her all the time?

His expression darkened. "*Ach*, no. Did I say something wrong?"

"No, not at all." She wiped away her threatening tears with her free hand. "It's just that I've always dreamed of you telling me you cared about me."

"What do you mean?"

"I've liked you since I was ten years old."

"You have?"

"*Ya*. We were on the playground at school when one of the *buwe* pushed me off a swing. You defended me. You not only got my swing back, but you made the *bu* apologize. Don't you remember that?"

He laughed. "*Ya*, I do remember that. Wasn't it Josiah King?"

"*Ya*, that's exactly right, and he never bothered me

again after that." She squeezed his hand. "I never forgot that, but I also didn't think you'd ever see me as more than Ariana's best *freind*."

"You're so much more than that. You're my inspiration, my strength, and my rock. You've been the one person who has known what to say to keep me moving forward toward getting my family and my community back, and I'm so grateful for you."

Tears again pricked her eyes. "I'm grateful for you too."

"I've missed so much right in front me, and I'm sorry it took leaving and then coming back to realize how amazing you are." He released her hand and gripped her arms. "I've made a lot of mistakes, but I'm making amends. I still have a lot of issues to work out, but I'd be honored if you would give me the chance to show you how much I care about you. Would you consider being my girlfriend?"

She wasn't dreaming. "*Ya!* I would be so honored."

He ran his fingers down her cheeks, and she shivered. "Mari, I really want to kiss you. Would that be all right?"

She glanced around, and when she found everyone else distracted by conversations, she nodded. "I think a quick kiss would be okay."

Tobias grinned. Then he leaned down, and her breath hitched as she closed her eyes. He brushed her lips with his, and she savored the feeling of his mouth against hers. Her first kiss! And the man she'd loved from afar for years was kissing her!

When their lips parted, he leaned his forehead

against hers. "I'm not perfect, but I'll be the best boyfriend I can. You mean the world to me."

She smiled as a tear trickled down her cheek.

• • •

Mariella breathed in the warm June air as cicadas sang and the sinking sun began to color the sky. Tobias sat beside her with his arm resting on the back of her backporch glider.

The past six months had moved at lightning speed as she and Tobias had fallen into an easy relationship filled with long talks, laughter—and for her, a blossoming love. She had never been happier, and every night she prayed her relationship with Tobias would continue to grow.

"I've been thinking," Tobias began, breaking through her thoughts. "The months we've spent together have been the happiest I've had in my life."

She smiled. "I was just thinking the same thing."

"When I came home, I hoped everyone would accept me. Yet I never imagined I'd not only get my community back, but I'd fall in love with someone as special as you."

Tears instantly sprang to her eyes. *He loves me!*

"You've blessed me beyond measure, Mari, and I thank God for you every day." He took her hand in his and she turned toward him. "The night of Ariana's wedding, *mei dat* said I can build a *haus* on his farm. I saved most of the money I earned while I was living with *mei onkel*, so I have enough to start the construction. And *mei dat* said he would help me with whatever I need."

"That's *wunderbaar*."

"I'd like *mei haus* to be where I live with *mei fraa*—and our family if God chooses to bless us with *kinner*."

Her stomach tightened as he continued.

"They say home is where the heart is, and I guess that's why I can only imagine my home with you in it. My heart belongs to you, and I think your heart belongs to me."

He took a deep breath. "This may seem too soon, but I don't want to wait any longer. Mari, would you do me the honor of being *mei fraa*?" His dark eyes shimmered with what looked like hope, and his next words came in a rush even as aired stalled in her lungs.

"I want to start work on the *haus* within the next month so it can be ready by the fall. We can get married in December if you'd like. I'll do my best to take care of you and our *kinner*. I'll work hard and try to make you *froh*. I promise."

Her heart felt as though it could burst as happy tears poured down her cheeks. All her dreams were coming true! "I would be honored to be your *fraa*."

He leaned down, and when his lips brushed hers, the now-familiar electric pulses sizzled from her head to her toes. She closed her eyes, savoring the feel of his mouth against hers. When he drew back, she fought to calm her galloping heart.

"*Ich liebe dich*, Mari," he whispered in her ear, sending a shiver dancing up her spine.

"I love you too."

As he pulled her close, Mariella silently thanked God for sending Tobias back not just to his community and his family, but to a new life with her.

DISCUSSION QUESTIONS

1. Tobias is nervous when he returns to his community after five months. He's worried his family and community won't accept him back into their lives. Think of a time when you felt lost and alone. Where did you find strength? What Bible verses would help with this? Share this with the group.

2. Because alcoholism is considered a sin in the Amish faith, Tobias had to confess in front of his congregation to be welcomed back into the church. What surprises you about this tradition and the way it's conducted? What is your opinion of the Amish's practice of shunning/excommunication for sin?

3. What significance did the carving in the barn have in the story? What role did it play in healing Tobias's relationship with his father? Share this with the group.

4. Mariella is thankful God gave Tobias a second chance with his family, his community, and her when he came back to Pennsylvania. Have you ever experienced a second chance? What was it?

5. When Tobias left the community, he received treatment for alcoholism. Have you ever known anyone

who has struggled with that disease? What challenges did they face? Share this with the group.

6. While Tobias struggled to mend his relationship with his father, he turned to Mariella for advice. Does someone in your life help you through difficult times? How?

ACKNOWLEDGMENTS

As always, I'm grateful for my loving family, including my mother, Lola Goebelbecker; my husband, Joe; and my sons, Zac and Matt. I'm blessed to have such an awesome and amazing family that tolerates my moods when I'm stressed out on a book deadline.

Special thanks to my mother and my dear friend Becky Biddy, who graciously proofread the draft and corrected my hilarious typos. Becky—thank you also for your daily notes of encouragement. Your friendship is a blessing!

I'm also grateful for my special Amish friend who patiently answers my endless stream of questions. You're a blessing in my life.

Thank you to my wonderful church family at Morning Star Lutheran in Matthews, North Carolina, for your encouragement, prayers, love, and friendship. You all mean so much to my family and me.

Thank you to Zac Weikal and the fabulous members of my Bakery Bunch! I'm so grateful for your friendship and your excitement about my books. You all are amazing!

To my agent, Natasha Kern—I can't thank you enough for your guidance, advice, and friendship. You are a tremendous blessing in my life.

Thank you to my amazing editor, Becky Monds, for your friendship and guidance. I'm grateful to each and every person at HarperCollins Christian Publishing who helped make this book a reality.

I'm grateful to editor Jean Bloom, who helped me polish and refine the story. Jean, you are a master at connecting the dots and filling in the gaps. I'm so happy we can continue to work together!

Thank you most of all to God—for giving me the inspiration and the words to glorify You. I'm grateful and humbled You've chosen this path for me.

LOVE BIRDS

For my awesome sons, Zac and Matt, with love

GLOSSARY

ach—oh
appeditlich—delicious
bedauerlich—sad
bruder—brother
daadi—granddad
danki—thank you
dat—dad
Dummle!—Hurry!
freind/freinden—friend/friends
froh—happy
gern gschehne—you're welcome
gut—good
gut nacht—good night
haus—house
Hoi!—Get back here!
kaffi—coffee
kind/kinner—child/children
liewe—love, a term of endearment
maed/maedel—young women, girls/young woman
mamm—mom
mammi—grandma
mei—my
mutter—mother
onkel—uncle

schee—pretty
schmaert—smart
schweschder/schweschdere—sister/sisters
Was iss letz?—What's wrong?
Wie geht's—How do you do? *or* Good day!
wunderbaar—wonderful
ya—yes

AMISH HEIRLOOM FAMILY TREES

Martha "Mattie" m. Leroy Fisher

Veronica   Rachel   Emily

Annie m. Elam Huyard

Jason   Stephen

Tillie m. Henry (Hank) Ebersol

Margaret m. Abner *(Deceased)* **Lapp**

Seth (Deceased)   Ellie

Fannie Mae m. Titus Dienner *(Bishop)*

Lindann

Susannah m. Timothy Beiler

David   Irma Rose Beiler Smucker

Irma Rose m. Melvin Smucker

Sarah

CHAPTER ONE

Ellie Lapp hummed to herself as she hung her freshly washed laundry on the line that stretched from the back porch to the barn. The warm May afternoon air filled her lungs and the sun kissed her cheeks as she clipped her and her mother's dresses onto the line to dry.

It was still so strange not to see Seth's trousers and shirts among the clothes she had laundered in the wringer washer earlier. She had to remind herself that she no longer had to care for his laundry, not since he'd died a month ago in an accident at the shed company where he worked.

One month ago. She shivered despite the warm spring breeze. How could it have been that long already?

It seemed like only yesterday that her big brother was talking and chuckling at the dinner table, sharing a joke or funny stories from his day spent building sheds. As though it was only yesterday that he called her "Squirt" instead of Ellie. Only yesterday that she was working in her garden when he threatened to drench her with water from her watering can if she didn't laugh at one of his silly jokes.

But now Seth was gone, and since her father had died fourteen years ago when she was only five, Ellie and her mother were left alone in the too-big and too-quiet house on their small farm.

"Ellie!" Her mother, Margaret, sounded urgent as she appeared in the doorway behind her. "Daisy escaped the pasture fence again. *Dummle!*"

Ellie turned her head toward the gate leading to the small pasture and saw it was wide open. And Daisy the cow was trotting toward the road.

"*Ach*, no!" she muttered under her breath. Then she took off running after the cow, shouting, "*Hoi! Hoi!*" On several occasions she and Seth had retrieved wandering cows with the help of the neighbor's dog, Spike, and she longed for both Seth and Spike's help now. Corralling a cow was not easy when it was a one-person job.

Ellie dodged puddles from last night's rain as she closed in on Daisy.

"Daisy!" she shouted. "Daisy! *Hoi! Hoi!*"

She tried to mimic Seth's method of catching disobedient cows. She rushed closer, determined to get ahead of the animal and direct her back to the pasture.

As Ellie closed in on Daisy, her feet began to slide. She realized too late that she'd run right into a puddle. And, much to her dismay, her feet flew out from under her. She landed on her bottom in a puddle with a loud *splat*. When she looked down, she saw her purple dress, apron, stockings, and shoes were covered in dark brown mud.

"Ellie!" a male voice called behind her.

Ellie looked over her shoulder and saw Lloyd Blank, one of Seth's best friends from school, loping toward her.

Members of the community, along with Seth's friends, had been taking turns coming over to help Ellie and her mother with the animals since Seth's death. Seth's friends were pleasant to Ellie, but Lloyd was the only one who had always taken the time to acknowledge her. And Ellie had had a secret crush on him since she was a preteen. She'd never told anyone, not even her closest friends, especially not Lloyd's sister Rebecca, that she liked him. It was a far-fetched dream to believe Lloyd would ever consider her more than an acquaintance since she was the same age as Rebecca.

Now here she sat in a puddle as his lean, six-foot-two frame, brown hair, and powder-blue eyes that reminded her of the brilliant sky in springtime raced toward her. The sleeves on his blue button-down shirt were rolled up on his arms to just above his elbows, revealing the muscles he'd developed from working on the Blank farm.

Ellie fought the urge to cover her face with her hands as humiliation rained down on her. The boy she'd liked for years had managed to see her at her absolute worst. *Could this day get any worse?*

When he reached her, Lloyd's lip twitched as if he were holding back a smile. "Are you all right?"

"*Ya,* I'm okay." Ellie's cheeks heated with embarrassment. "I didn't see the puddle."

"Need help?" A smile spread across Lloyd's face as

he held out his hand. At least her hands were still free of mud.

"*Ya*," Ellie muttered, taking the outstretched hand. "*Danki.*"

He gently lifted her to her feet as if she weighed only a few pounds. She longed to find someplace to hide away from his sparkling eyes. But instead she glided her hands down her apron, making mud splatter to the ground, then craned her neck to peer past him. "Daisy is getting away!"

"I'll get her before she reaches the road," Lloyd said. "You stand ready at the gate." Lloyd followed the cow and Ellie ran to the fence. Her apron and dress felt heavier with the mud weighing them down, to say nothing of her shoes.

She turned to see Lloyd had caught up with Daisy and was waving his arms wildly, yelling "*Hoi! Hoi!*" as he herded her back toward the pasture. Ellie silently marveled at his skill as he commanded the cow. He was an expert, just as Seth had been.

Daisy trotted into the pasture, and Lloyd helped Ellie shut the heavy gate before turning to look at her.

"You have some mud on your cheek," he said with a grin. He looked like he was about to touch her face, but instead he pointed. "It's right there."

Ellie brushed her hand across her cheek. "Did I get it?"

Lloyd shook his head. "You smeared it."

Ellie swiped her hand over her cheek again, but knew she'd probably only made it worse.

"This lock needs to be repaired," Lloyd said, now studying the latch. "I'll work on that today."

"*Danki.*" Ellie gnawed her lower lip. She wanted to thank him for helping with Daisy, too, but she didn't want to gush. "I'm glad you came along when you did. I clearly wasn't going to be able to persuade her to come back. Seth was the expert when it came to herding cows."

Lloyd looked up from the latch. "You were doing fine until the mud got the best of you." His blue eyes sparkled with amusement. "I'm *froh* I could help."

"*Mamm* and I appreciate all you're doing for the farm," she said as she rested a hand on the fence. "You're a tremendous help."

"I haven't done much." Lloyd fiddled with the latch again. "I wish I could do more, but I'm busy with my chores at home too."

"I understand." Ellie searched for another subject to prolong the interaction. "I heard the youth gathering is at your parents' *haus* Sunday night."

"*Ya.*" Lloyd leaned against the fence. "Rebecca and Marie are excited. They've been cleaning like crazy."

"It will be fun." When he responded with an unenthusiastic shrug, she was alarmed. "You'll be there, right?" She wanted to kick herself as the words spilled from her lips. Why did she have to sound so immature and eager?

"I suppose I'll be around somewhere since I live there." He lifted his straw hat and raked his hand through his dark hair. "I don't know if I'll mingle since I'll be the oldest person there—other than my folks, of course. Twenty-four is too old for that."

"That's not true," she insisted. "You're not too old to

be a part of the youth group. You can still be an active member."

He smiled. "I'd make a better chaperone, but thanks for the encouragement."

"Seth used to go," Ellie continued, hoping to change his mind. "He and Veronica would stop by sometimes."

"That's true. He mentioned that a few times." He seemed to agree with her only to avoid further discussion. "So maybe I'll see you there."

"Okay." Ellie hoped he would.

"I guess I'd better work on this latch." Lloyd gestured toward the largest barn. "Are Seth's tools still in there?"

"*Ya*, they are."

"I'll fix this so Daisy doesn't try to escape again." His eyes moved to her dress. "You probably want to get cleaned up."

"Oh, right." She'd almost forgotten about the mud while they were talking, and she found herself feeling self-conscious once again.

"I'll see you later, Squirt." Lloyd grinned at her.

Ellie pursed her lips. Why did he have to ruin the moment?

"My name is Ellie. I'm too grown up to be called Squirt." She squared her shoulders and started toward the house as tears threatened her eyes. She was still just a child in his eyes. Why couldn't Lloyd see her as one of his peers? After washing some of the mud off at the outdoor pump, she rushed up the back steps and into the mudroom with renewed humiliation.

She blew out a deep sigh as she sat on a bench to take

off her shoes. She was being silly. After all, Squirt was the nickname Seth liked to call her. Lloyd knew that.

Mamm came into the mudroom. "Ellie! You're a mess! What happened?"

"I fell in a puddle," Ellie said, her voice quaking. "But Lloyd was able to stop Daisy. She's back in the pasture, and he's going to fix the latch on the gate."

"Oh, good." *Mamm* clicked her tongue. "I suppose we'll need to get the wringer washer going again for your clothes."

"*Ya*, you're right." Ellie pulled off her apron as her mother disappeared into the kitchen. She looked out the window to the pasture fence where Lloyd was already working on the gate. Disappointment stole over her. She'd managed to look immature in front of Lloyd, the only boy she'd ever cared about.

"Why aren't you going to get changed?" *Mamm* called from the kitchen.

"I am. I'll be right back."

Ellie walked to the stairs and climbed to the second floor. As she reached the landing, her glance fell on the closed door leading to Seth's room, and she stopped. She took a shaky breath as she stared at the door, her hands trembling.

The familiar sadness crept in. She hadn't seen the inside of her brother's room since the day of the accident, and the door called to her, inviting her to step inside and see the only tangible things he'd left behind.

She turned the knob and slowly opened the door. Both the stale air and her grief nearly overcame her as she stepped into the room. Her eyes filled with tears as she imagined Seth grinning at her as he stood near the window. His smile always lit up a room. Six years her senior, Seth had been tall and lean, towering over her by four inches. He'd become her protector and surrogate father after their father had died from a massive heart attack.

But now Seth, with the same seafoam-green eyes and sandy blond hair their mother had passed on to Ellie, was gone too. Her lower lip trembled and tears spilled onto her cheeks.

Ellie scanned the room, taking in all of Seth's things. Nothing had been disturbed since the accident. Her mother had avoided this room too. Seth's dresser stood in the corner with his favorite trinkets lined up on top of it, including the wooden sign that said *Love*. Veronica, his fiancée, had given it to him on Valentine's Day. The pegs on the wall held his jackets, and with the closet door cracked open, she spotted his trousers hanging there.

Her thoughts turned to Veronica, and a lump filled her throat as the events of the day of the accident assaulted her mind. Ellie had been baking when she'd heard a knock on the door and left the kitchen to see who it was. The bishop was on the front porch, telling her mother there had been a terrible accident. Her blood ran cold as he explained that Seth's boss had called him. Seth had fallen from the rafters of a shed. Ellie moved closer to her mother as the bishop explained that EMTs had come to the shop, but there was nothing they could do for Seth; he was already gone. They called the coroner, and Seth's body was going to be brought to their house. Her mother had dissolved into tears in Ellie's arms, and all Ellie could think about was how to tell Veronica.

Ellie called Veronica and managed to tell her to come to their house as soon as she could, but when Veronica and her father had arrived, and she asked Ellie what had happened, the reality of the situation flooded Ellie's soul. Her voice broke on a sob as she told Seth's fiancée he was dead.

In an instant, all their lives had been changed forever because their precious Seth was gone.

Ellie and her mother moved in a fog during the next couple of weeks. Before Ellie knew it, Seth was buried, and she and her mother were going through the motions of each day, doing their best to keep their little farm running without Seth to help with the animals. She was thankful for his friends and their family members who came by to assist with the chores, and for all the meals their community provided as they grieved. But how would they continue to pay for their household expenses without Seth's paycheck from the shed company? Her mother hadn't talked about that yet, but it wouldn't be long before they'd have to. Ellie knew her mother was downplaying their financial need when people asked if they needed help. Her mother didn't want to burden anyone, but Ellie suspected the time would come soon when they would have to face reality.

She stood and crossed the room to the window. After raising the green shade, she unlocked and lifted the window, sending a stream of warm, sweet air bursting into the stagnant room. She pushed away memories of her brother and then hurried to her own room to change clothes.

. . .

"Let's figure out what we want to have for supper." Ellie crossed the small kitchen to the propane-powered refrigerator later that afternoon. "What sounds *gut* to you, *Mamm*? I think we still have some—"

A knock sounded on the back door.

"I'll get that." Ellie hurried through the mudroom and found their neighbor, Sadie Esh, standing on the back porch, holding a covered dish. "Sadie," she said, opening the door wider to let Sadie step in. *"Wie geht's?"*

Sadie was a few inches taller than Ellie, so Ellie had to look up at the plump woman with graying brown hair and brown eyes.

"Hi, Ellie." Sadie followed Ellie into the kitchen. A delicious aroma filled the room.

"How are you, Margaret?"

"I'm doing all right." *Mamm* gave her a sad smile. "How have you been?"

"Fine, fine." Sadie placed the covered dish on the table. "I brought you supper."

"Oh, Sadie." *Mamm* lifted the lid and examined the chicken and dumplings. "It looks and smells *appeditlich*."

"Danki, Sadie." Ellie moved to the stove. "Would you like a cup of tea?"

"Oh, no, thank you." Sadie gestured toward the back door. "I can't stay. I have to help Katie pack."

"Pack?" Ellie asked. "Where is she going?"

"She decided to go to Ohio to spend time with my niece, Clara." Sadie rested her hand on the back of one of the wooden dinette chairs. "Just last week, Clara had her third baby in less than four years, so she's looking for some help. Katie is eager to get out there and spend some time with her cousins. I'm going to miss her, but she'll have fun."

"Oh my," Margaret said with a smile. "It sounds like Clara has her hands full, *ya*?"

"*Ya*, that's true." Sadie shook her head. "So now her boss, Gene Rider, is scrambling to find a replacement for Katie at his gift shop in town. Katie was working there part-time up until yesterday. If you know anyone who is looking for a part-time job, let me know. He asked me to check around."

"What shop is that?" Ellie asked as she leaned against the kitchen counter beside her.

"The Bird-in-Hand Gifts and Treasures shop up on Old Philadelphia Pike, across from the Farmers' Market," Sadie said.

"That's the shop that has the *schee* ornaments made out of metal, right?" Ellie asked.

"*Ya*, that's right." Sadie nodded.

"That's a busy place," *Mamm* chimed in. "Whenever I'm in town, I see lots of tourists going in and out of there."

"Katie really liked working there," Sadie continued. "She said Gene is very nice, and he has always been flexible with her schedule."

An idea ignited in Ellie's mind. She needed to find a

place to work as a way to contribute at least a fraction of what Seth used to earn. Maybe Bird-in-Hand Gifts and Treasures would give her the flexibility to work while still helping out at home.

"That sounds *wunderbaar*," Ellie said, contemplating the opportunity. Would *Mamm* permit her to take the job?

"Well, I have to get going," Sadie said, starting back through the mudroom. "I'll stop by to visit again soon."

Ellie and *Mamm* followed Sadie to the door and thanked her again as she left.

"Wasn't that nice of Sadie to bring us a meal? Our neighbors have been so kind." *Mamm* opened the cabinets and fetched two plates. "It smells fantastic."

"*Ya.*" Ellie lifted utensils from a drawer and brought them to the table. "I can't wait to try it."

They sat at the table and, after silent prayer, scooped the chicken and dumplings onto their plates.

"This is *wunderbaar*," *Mamm* said. "Sadie is a very *gut* cook."

"She is." But Ellie only moved a dumpling around on her plate as she considered asking *Mamm* about the job.

"Is something on your mind, *mei liewe*?" *Mamm* asked.

Ellie placed her fork on the corner of her plate and wished her expression wasn't so transparent. "I want to ask you something."

"What's that?" *Mamm* said, then dabbed her mouth with a paper napkin.

"I was thinking about Katie's former job at Bird-in-Hand Gifts and Treasures. I think I may want to look into it." When her mother's expression clouded with confusion, Ellie pressed on. "I need to find a part-time job, and it sounds like working there would be ideal."

"You want to get a job?" *Mamm*'s fork paused in midair as she studied Ellie.

"*Ya.*" Ellie fingered her own napkin. "I need to contribute more now that Seth is gone."

Mamm put her fork on the table and her expression warmed. "Ellie, you know my brothers have been paying the mortgage since your *dat* passed away."

"I know that, but Seth took care of everything else." Ellie's stomach tightened. "You don't have to protect me from the truth. I'm an adult, and I understand the situation we're in. I don't know what you've been thinking we'd do about our other expenses, *Mamm*, but my getting a job only makes sense."

Her mother's eyes misted, and a lump swelled in Ellie's throat. *Please don't cry,* Mamm. *Please don't cry.*

"I'll just work a couple of days each week," Ellie pressed on. "It will be enough to help with groceries, and probably anything else we need. We'll be frugal. But now that Seth is gone, I need to take care of you."

"But you've never worked in a store. And besides, it's not your responsibility to take care of me," *Mamm* said softly as she touched Ellie's shoulder. "We will be fine, and we'll take care of each other."

"How? What are we going to do when people stop bringing us meals?" Ellie asked. "We won't even have money to buy food without Seth's income—unless we have money I don't know about. Do we?"

Mamm shook her head. "No. At least not enough to

last. You're right. But I haven't wanted to burden you with it. I thought God would provide somehow."

"Please, *Mamm*." Ellie's voice quavered. "I really want to do this. I want to do this for *us*. Maybe this *is* how God is providing. If it doesn't work out, if some other option comes up, then I'll quit." She held her breath as she waited for her mother's approval.

Mamm sighed and then smiled. "All right. If it will make you *froh* to get this job, then I give you my blessing."

Ellie smiled, excited. "*Danki, Mamm*. I know this will be *gut* for us both."

CHAPTER TWO

Lloyd Blank closed the barn door later that evening and started toward the large white farmhouse where he'd lived since he was born. He yawned, and every muscle in his body ached from the work he'd accomplished since he'd risen at dawn. After completing his morning chores at his father's farm, he'd headed to the Lapp place. Although he was worn out from the extra work, he was thankful that his father allowed him the time to help Margaret Lapp.

When Seth died, Lloyd and several of Seth's friends promised Margaret they would all help with chores, and Lloyd had kept his promise. In honor of Seth, he longed to spend more than a couple of afternoons a week helping Margaret. But he had too much responsibility at home. Since he was the only son, Lloyd was expected to keep the dairy farm running alongside his father. He would also eventually inherit it.

Lloyd climbed the back porch steps and lowered himself onto his mother's favorite glider. As he moved the glider back and forth and looked at his father's line of four barns and vast pastures, his thoughts stayed on Seth. It still seemed surreal that Seth was gone. Lloyd had grown up with him, both in their church district and at school. They were instant friends beginning in first grade. Although they had taken different, busy paths after school—Lloyd becoming a dairy farmer and Seth going into construction—they still kept in touch, talking at church services and other gatherings.

But now Seth was gone. Lloyd sighed and rubbed his chin as grief hit him once again. He missed his friend. They had enjoyed long discussions about everything from farming to their personal lives. While Seth had been engaged to Veronica and was preparing for marriage, Lloyd still hadn't found the right *maedel*. But even though Seth talked nonstop about Veronica, Lloyd had been happy for them.

The sadness he saw in Veronica's eyes at church haunted him. His heart broke for both her and Seth's family.

As he continued to rock back and forth, his thoughts turned to Ellie. When he'd arrived at the Lapp farm today, he'd planned to muck out the stalls. Instead, he was surprised to find Ellie running after Daisy, their misbehaving cow. He'd heard Seth's hilarious stories about that rogue cow. She frequently found a way to open the latch on the pasture fence and take a leisurely walk around the farm or, like today, head for the road. Today was the first day he'd seen Daisy in action.

Lloyd was rushing after Ellie to help her catch the cow when she slipped and fell in the mud. His first reaction was to help her up. When Lloyd reached her, he had to fight back his amusement because she looked so adorable. He felt terrible that she had fallen, but she had the cutest expression on her face. Her clothes and shoes were all splattered with mud. She even had a smudge of mud on her face.

Lloyd had to swallow a bark of laughter when he lifted Ellie to her feet. He could tell she was embarrassed. He was certain that would have embarrassed his sisters too. He hoped someday they could look back on that and laugh together. He was just thankful he was there to help her corral Daisy and then fix that latch. He recalled that Seth said he repaired it more than once. Daisy was one smart cow.

He had spent the rest of the afternoon mucking the stalls and feeding the animals. When he spotted Ellie clad in a clean blue dress as she hung out the muddy clothes now washed, he hoped she wasn't still humiliated by her fall.

Lloyd crossed his arms over his chest as he contemplated Seth's little sister. He was old enough to remember when Ellie was a newborn. Ellie and his sister Rebecca were the same age, and he recalled their playing together at church services. The two girls became close friends at school and remained best friends after they'd finished eighth grade. Ellie was always a sweet girl, and she was attached to Seth, especially after they'd lost their father.

The back door opened and then clicked shut, interrupting Lloyd's thoughts. Lloyd sat up straight and nodded a greeting as his father took a seat in the rocker beside the glider. Lloyd's father was about thirty pounds heavier than him, and Lloyd heard the rocker creak a little as his dad settled in.

"The animals are set for the night," Lloyd said as he leaned back in the glider and crossed his long legs. "I was just enjoying the warm night."

"*Danki* for taking care of everything." *Dat* turned toward him. His father was a few inches shorter than Lloyd, but sitting they looked at each other eye to eye. Unlike Lloyd's blue eyes, however, his father's were brown, the same color as their hair.

"How was Margaret today?"

Lloyd folded his arms over his chest. "I guess she was okay. She got emotional when she thanked me for helping."

"I can't imagine losing a *kind*." *Dat*'s voice was wistful, causing Lloyd to feel a pang of emotion too. He rarely saw his father's emotional side. "I admire you for making time to help the Lapp family. You're generous with your time."

"Well, that's what we do, right?" Lloyd didn't want to make it a big deal, but he was glad his father felt that way. He not only enjoyed helping the Lapp family, but he was sure Seth would have done the same for him if he had been the one killed in an accident—especially if Lloyd's father wasn't around. The Lapp family had had only one son, just like Lloyd's family. If anything happened to his father, Lloyd knew he would be the one responsible for his mother and his sisters, Rebecca and Marie, who were only nineteen and sixteen. The burden of supporting family fell to the sons, and he wanted to do all he could for the Lapp family in place of his friend.

"I was surprised to see you out here," *Dat* said,

interrupting Lloyd's thoughts. "I expected to find you in your woodshop."

"Not tonight." Lloyd wiped his hands down his trouser legs, knocking dust and hay onto the porch. He wasn't in the mood for one of his father's lectures about his woodworking hobby, so he quickly changed the subject. "I'm pretty worn out from all the chores I did today."

"I imagine you are." After a few moments of silence, *Dat* stood. "Well, we'd better head inside. Work comes early in the morning."

"I'll be there in a minute." His thoughts were stuck on the Lapp family and their loss. He hoped his weekly visits were helpful. But for some inexplicable reason, he realized, he also couldn't wait to return to their farm and do more.

. . .

Ellie took a deep breath and ran her hand over her blue dress as she approached the Bird-in-Hand Gifts and Treasures shop the next morning. The glass in the large front window of the brick building was etched in script with the shop's name. A variety of detailed metal ornaments, keepsake boxes, photograph frames, decorative plates, mirrors, trays, dishes, and figurines adorned the window display that was garnished with potted plants and wooden furniture.

She had walked by the place dozens of times while shopping in town, but she had never ventured inside. Her hands trembled with a mixture of excitement and anxiety as she pulled the door open. A bell sounded above her, announcing her entry.

She passed shelves filled with more beautiful metal decorations on her way to the desk in the center of the store. A young woman there, clad in jeans and a gray blouse, smiled at her.

"Good morning. How may I help you?"

"Hi. I heard Gene Rider is looking for someone to help since Katie Esh no longer works here."

"Oh, wonderful!" The young lady motioned for Ellie to follow her toward the back of the store. "I'm Phoebe. My uncle Gene owns this shop. I can only work here part time due to my school schedule, so he needs someone else a couple of days a week."

"That would be perfect for me." Ellie hoped Gene would decide she was the best person for the job. She followed Phoebe into the back room, which was a large workshop cluttered with benches, tools, and machines.

A tall man with graying brown hair and a matching full beard looked up from a bench where he was working on a small metal ornament. He smiled as he stood.

Phoebe made a sweeping gesture toward Ellie. "Uncle Gene, this is Ellie Lapp. She's here about the job."

"Hi. Katie Esh's mother told me you're looking for someone to work part time. I'd like to apply." Ellie fingered her apron and her stomach tightened with apprehension. Was she ready to work in a busy store? She needed to be brave. She was counting on this job to keep her and her mother afloat. Despite her doubts, she forced herself to stand up straight.

"It's so nice to meet you." Gene shook her hand. "Have you worked in a shop before?"

"No, but I've helped out at my friend's vegetable stand." Ellie rattled off her experience working with a calculator and counting change. "I'm good with numbers, and I'm a fast learner. I know I'll do a good job for you."

Gene nodded and crossed his arms over his blue button-down shirt. "I'm looking for someone who can work Mondays and Fridays. Phoebe handles all the other days I'm open, which is every day but Sunday."

"That schedule would work well for me." Ellie grinned. *This will be perfect! I can still help* Mamm *at home!*

"Great. I'll need you to handle the front while I work back here to keep up inventory. That means helping customers, running the register, and keeping the showroom floor tidy. Let me show you around."

Gene gave her a tour of the shop and explained that each area was categorized by the type of item for sale, including home and accessories, jewelry, cities and sports memorabilia, and gifts for certain occasions.

"All these items are lovely," Ellie said as she examined an ornament featuring a horse and buggy in front of a farm scene. "You do incredible work."

"Thank you. That's one of our most popular items. The tourists love anything with a horse and buggy on it."

"That's the truth." Phoebe pointed toward the back of the showroom. "I'm trying to convince Uncle Gene to allow me to find some more Amish-made gifts to sell over in that corner. We have the typical quilts, cloth dolls, potholders, key chains, and homemade jellies made by the Amish, but I think it would bring in even more business if we had some unique Amish-made things to sell. The tourists will go crazy for that."

Gene looked skeptical. "I don't want to sell more quilts and potholders, even if they are unique patterns. Plenty of other shops sell those items."

"That's not what I meant." Phoebe sighed. "I'm talking about something completely different, unique." She turned to Ellie. "Can you think of something we could sell that would be different from what the other shops around here have?"

Ellie shrugged. "No, I really can't."

"I promise I'll find something, Uncle Gene." Phoebe smiled. "Just trust me."

Gene rubbed his beard. "Keep thinking about it. We've been losing sales since that new gift shop opened up the road in Gordonville. Maybe offering some unique Amish-made items is the way to go."

Phoebe leaned against the end of a set of shelves. "I'm sure we can figure something out."

"So, Ellie," Gene began, turning his eyes back to her, "what do you think? Do you want the job?"

"Absolutely," Ellie said, rubbing her hands together. "When would you like me to start?"

. . .

Ellie burst through the back door and into the kitchen. She was so excited she thought she might explode as she started walking through the downstairs in search of her mother.

"*Mamm?*" she called. "Where are you?"

"I'm in the sewing room," *Mamm* responded.

Ellie rushed there to find her mother pinning a new apron. "*Mamm*! I got the job!" She clapped her hands together, but then her smile faded as her mother frowned. "*Was iss letz?*"

"I didn't really want you to get the job." *Mamm* placed the apron on the table next to her treadle sewing machine.

Ellie sank into the chair beside the table. "*Mamm*, we talked about this. We need the money." She rested her hand on the surface of the table. "It won't be as much as Seth made, but I'll make enough money for groceries. We'll still need to cut back on other things."

"*Ach*, Ellie." *Mamm* shook her head, her green eyes full of concern. "You shouldn't worry about things like that."

"*Mamm*, you're wrong," Ellie said gently. "I should be worrying about things because it's just us now." She took her mother's hands in hers. "Like you said, we'll take care of each other. I'm only working Mondays and Fridays, so I'll still be here to help with the *haus* and the farm. I'm not leaving you to take care of everything. I'll help with the cooking and baking and gardening and laundry just like I do now."

Mamm gave a reluctant nod. "All right."

Ellie hugged her mother as her excitement swelled again. She couldn't wait to get started at her new job. This was the best way for her to take care of her mother, and she was certain Seth would be proud of her.

CHAPTER THREE

Lloyd sat on a stool in front of a long workbench in his woodshop at the back of the barn. The soft yellow glow of two Coleman lanterns lit the room, and the aroma of pine filled his senses as he whittled the small block of wood in his hand. While his fingers and tools shaped the wood, the stress from the day left his body and his mind cleared.

Woodworking was the only way he truly found peace after a long day of farm work. While his hands shaped a plain piece of wood, his mind found a perfect peace through relaxation and prayer.

The workbench was cluttered with woodworking tools and a table was covered with his creations—small, detailed birds whittled intricately by his hand. The hobby was a surprise even to Lloyd. When he was fifteen, he found whittling tools in the back of his grandfather's barn and asked what they were. His grandfather showed him how to turn a plain block of wood into something beautiful. Not only did Lloyd enjoy the time with his grandfather, but he found a new passion—whittling.

His grandfather passed away when Lloyd was eighteen, and his grandmother gave him the tools. Now

Lloyd whittled not only to keep his grandfather's memory alive, but also to enjoy the relaxation of the hobby.

The shop door opened with a *whoosh*, interrupting his thoughts. He glanced back over his shoulder and spotted his father in the doorway, an unreadable expression on his face.

"Hi, *Dat*." Lloyd spun on the stool to face him. "Is everything all right?"

"I was wondering where you were." *Dat* leaned against the doorway. "It's late, and I thought you would be heading to bed by now."

"I just wanted to get started on another bird." Lloyd nodded toward the block of wood in his hand. "You know I like to come in here and unwind at night."

"*Ya*, I know that, but you need your rest." *Dat*'s expression hardened. "This farm is your obligation, Lloyd. The farm will go to you since you're the only *bu*. It's your responsibility."

Lloyd's stomach tightened with resentment. "I know that." *Especially since you remind me all the time.* "All my chores are done. I love this farm, and I will take *gut* care of it when it's mine. I just needed some time to myself, and this is how I relax. You enjoy reading *The Budget* before you go to sleep, and I like to whittle. That's all it is, *Dat*. It's just a hobby."

His father crossed the shop and peered down at the wooden birds. "I hope you realize this hobby is prideful." He lifted a cardinal, regarded it as if it were pernicious, and placed it back on the table.

"It's prideful?" Lloyd crinkled his nose with confusion.

"How is this hobby prideful?" And why hadn't his father ever said this is what he thought?

Dat met his expression with a frown. "You're simply showing off your skill."

"I don't understand how I'm showing it off if the birds don't leave this shop." Lloyd pointed toward the table. "I create the birds and then leave them here. It's just something that makes me *froh*. *Daadi* did the same thing, and no one ever criticized him."

"You're more skilled than your *daadi* ever was." *Dat* started toward the door. "You need to get to bed, Lloyd. It's late." With a quick nod, he disappeared.

Lloyd examined the piece of wood in his hand as frustration surged through him. When would his father ever accept that his whittling was a hobby and nothing more? How could a hobby that made him happy be a sin? He wasn't hurting anyone and he wasn't bragging. After all, Lloyd wasn't a skilled woodworker. But he was a responsible adult who should be able to decide how to spend his free time.

He set the wood and the whittling knife on the workbench and switched off one of the lanterns. As he lifted the other lantern, he started toward the door, still chafing at his father's pronouncement. His father would never understand, but his grandfather had. Lloyd missed his grandfather more than ever on days like this.

• • •

Ellie stood at the cash register at Bird-in-Hand Gifts and Treasures on Friday morning and smiled as a

woman dressed in blue jeans and a white shirt deco-
rated with a sparkling butterfly design approached.

"Hi," the woman said. "I was wondering if you had
any other Amish gifts." The woman pointed toward
the back corner. "I see the quilts and dolls, but I'm
looking for something I can't find in every other store
in Lancaster County."

"Oh." Ellie pressed her finger to her chin while
contemplating the question. "Did you see the metal
ornament over there with the horse and buggy on it?
That's one of our popular sellers."

The woman frowned. "I was looking for something more . . . rare. I always take a gift home for my
sister-in-law when I visit here, and she doesn't like the
run-of-the-mill gifts. She's not interested in quilts or
straw hats."

"I'm sorry." Ellie forced a smile. "All we have are the
metal ornaments over there and also the Amish items
in the back corner."

"Oh well." The woman was still frowning. "Thanks
for your help." She walked toward the exit without buying anything.

Ellie was dusting shelves in the back corner of the
store later that afternoon when another woman came
up to her.

"Excuse me, miss." The woman with short, graying
hair and a round face gestured toward a display of cloth
dolls. "Do you have any other Amish-made crafts?"
She held up a doll. "These are cute, but I'm looking for
something my grandson would like."

"We have the straw hats," Ellie offered, but when

this woman frowned, too, Ellie glanced across the store. "We have metal trucks over by the sports items. Does he like trucks?"

The woman shrugged. "I suppose he might, but I was hoping to buy something Amish for him. I've been telling him about the Amish culture."

"Does he like quilts?"

The woman shook her head. "No, he doesn't." She smiled. "Well, I tried. Thank you for your help."

As Ellie watched the woman walk away, she thought about the conversation she'd had with Phoebe. Maybe she did need to help her and Gene find something special to sell.

. . .

After work, Ellie paid her driver and rushed up the rock driveway to the front door of her house.

"*Mamm!* Where are you?"

"I'm on the back porch," her mother responded through the open windows.

Ellie dropped her tote bag on a chair in the kitchen and hurried out to the back porch. Her mother was sitting on the glider and snapping string beans.

"How was your first day on the job?" *Mamm* asked.

"It was fantastic." Ellie sank onto the glider beside her and picked up a bean. "Gene trained me to use the electric cash register in the morning, and I quickly learned how to use it. I was ringing up customers before noon. He also gave me another tour of the showroom, this time more thorough to ensure I knew where the different types of gifts are located. He has the store set up by categories of gifts. For example, I had to know where to find treasure boxes if someone came in looking for one."

Mamm nodded. "That makes sense."

"*Ya*, it does." Ellie considered some of the customers. "A few people asked for more Amish-made crafts. Gene's niece thinks we need to add more unique items to the Amish section, and I think she's right. I just need to figure out what we can sell. Can you think of something unique that we don't see in many tourist shops?"

Mamm shook her head. "No, I can't. I'll have to think about that. So you liked the job?"

"Oh, *ya*. By the afternoon, I was running the showroom by myself, and I loved it." Ellie grinned as she snapped another bean and placed the snapped-off end and extra fibers into the discard bowl. She put the trimmed bean into the larger bowl with the others. "It's a lot of fun, and Gene said he'll pay me every other week. Do you need me to do anything now that you didn't get to finish today? Do I need to weed the garden again?"

"It's fine, Ellie." *Mamm* touched her shoulder. "I handled the garden today. You're helping me plenty now. I'm *froh* that you like the job."

Ellie glanced toward the pasture. "Have any animals tried to escape today?"

Mamm chuckled. "No, Daisy has been safely nestled in the pasture today. And Seth's friend Jason Huyard from work came by and took care of the animals earlier."

"Has Lloyd been by today?" Her stomach trembled a little when she said his name. She longed to keep her feelings for him tucked away, but her emotions always got the best of her. Why did she bother thinking about him? He'd never be more than a friend to her. The age difference would always come between them.

"Lloyd?" *Mamm* asked, shaking her head. "No, I haven't seen him, but I think he did a great job fixing the latch on the gate."

"That's *gut*." As Ellie snapped more beans, she wondered when she'd see Lloyd again. She hoped he'd decide to mingle during the youth gathering at his parents' farm Sunday night. In fact, hadn't he promised he would?

• • •

Ellie sat between Rebecca and Marie Blank at the youth gathering Sunday evening. Although the sisters were three years apart, they could nearly pass for twins since they were the same five-foot-five and had matching brown hair and eyes. Lloyd was the only child who had inherited their mother's blue eyes.

Three volleyball nets were assembled in the grassy lot adjacent to the Blank family's large white, two-story clapboard house. Teams of young people played at each homemade court, leaping, jumping, and laughing as the volleyballs sailed through the air. Small groups of young people sat nearby, some cheering on the teams and others oblivious of the games while they talked among themselves.

Ellie ripped out blades of grass while the sisters talked and the noisy games continued. Memories of playing volleyball with Seth and his friends took over Ellie's mind. She recalled the day Seth patiently taught her how to serve the ball. He showed her over and over again until she served it correctly, and his girlfriend, Veronica, returned it to her, bumping it gracefully over the net.

Why had Ellie thought coming to the youth gathering would be fun when the memories dampened her mood? She knew the answer to that question. She'd hoped to see Lloyd, but she hadn't caught a glimpse of him all afternoon.

"Ellie?" Rebecca's voice broke through Ellie's thoughts. "Are you all right?"

"*Ya.*" Ellie swiped her hands together to brush away the blades of grass and then leaned back on her palms.

Rebecca and Marie exchanged skeptical looks.

"Do you want to play volleyball?" Marie jammed her thumb toward the nets. "They're getting ready to change up the teams."

Rebecca's brown eyes brightened. "We could play together on the same team."

"*Ya!*" Marie agreed with excitement.

"No, but thank you." Ellie tried to force a smile, but she was sure it looked like a grimace instead.

"*Was iss letz?*" Rebecca's expression clouded with concern.

"You seem upset," Marie chimed in.

"I'm fine." Ellie feigned a yawn. "Just tired." She pointed toward the volleyball courts. "You can go play if you'd like. I'll be happy to root for you."

Another expression passed between the sisters, this time one of suspicion. Did they think Ellie wouldn't notice?

"Really, it's okay," Ellie insisted. "I know you both love to play. Don't let me hold you back."

Rebecca and Marie stood, wiped off their dresses, and headed toward the nets. Ellie watched them play for a few minutes, but she soon grew tired of sitting alone and decided to take a walk. She stood and started toward the house, nodding and greeting friends as she passed them.

As she ambled past one of the smaller barns, she noticed the door was open. She stepped inside and the scent of earth filled her nostrils. Her shoes crunched on hay as she moved past rows of shovels, saws, racks, and other tools toward a small room at the back, where another door was open to a smaller room.

Ellie hesitated in the doorway, but then stepped inside what looked like a small woodworking shop. She examined a workbench cluttered with whittling tools and then touched one of the knives, wondering whose shop she'd discovered. Seth had never mentioned that Lloyd liked to work with wood, so she doubted it was Lloyd's.

She moved to a table and found the most beautiful wooden birds she'd ever seen. She lifted one and nearly gasped as she examined the detailed work that had gone into this creation. The bird was small enough to fit into her hand, but it looked as if she were holding a real bird.

Ellie ran her fingers over the smooth wood, taking

in the wings, the beak, and the eyes. Whoever had created this bird clearly loved it.

She placed the bird back in its original spot on the table and then examined another bird. She scanned the table and surmised there had to be at least two dozen birds there representing different species. A few she recognized as seagulls, cardinals, and bluebirds. Others were familiar, but she didn't know the bird names.

Ellie gingerly picked up one of the birds whose name she didn't know and took in its intricacies. She suddenly remembered Phoebe Rider's comment about trying to find some unique, Amish-made item for the gift shop. What if Gene sold these beautiful birds? She hadn't seen anything like them in any of the shops in town.

This would be perfect! She excitedly held up another bird. Yes, it would be perfect. She just needed to find out who had made these birds and ask permission to show one to Gene and Phoebe.

"May I help you?"

Startled, Ellie spun around, nearly dropping the bird when she found Lloyd watching her from the doorway.

CHAPTER FOUR

Lloyd." Ellie righted herself as embarrassment burned the tips of her ears. She shouldn't have barged into this shop uninvited. Where were her manners? "I didn't hear you walk up behind me."

"Hi, Ellie." He stepped inside. "What are you doing in here?"

"Oh, well, I saw the barn door was open, and then I was curious to see what was back here." She spoke quickly, stumbling over her words. "I didn't mean to snoop."

"I didn't realize I had left the door open." He moved to the workbench and leaned his hip against it as he faced her.

"This is your shop?" Her eyes widened with surprise. Why hadn't Seth told her Lloyd did woodworking? Did Seth even know about this secret talent?

"*Ya.*" Lloyd shrugged. Ellie noticed the sunbeam coming through the window made his eyes seem a lighter shade of blue and gave his hair golden highlights.

"Where did you learn how to make these *schee* birds?" She held up the one in her hand and suddenly felt ashamed for touching his private things.

"*Mei daadi* taught me a long time ago. We used to make little projects together for fun." He looked down at the bench. "*Mei mammi* gave me his tools when he passed away, and *mei dat* let me set up a little shop back here. I just play around with the tools sometimes. It's a hobby really."

"Seth never told me about these birds. Did he know about them?"

"No." He shook his head, and he seemed self-conscious. "Only my family knows about them."

She took a step toward him and breathed in his scent, earth and wood mixed with soap. "This is the most *schee* carving I've ever seen in my life."

"*Danki.*" Lloyd shook his head. "But you're just being nice."

"No, I'm not. It's incredible." She turned the bird over in her hand. "What kind of bird is this?"

He took the bird from her hand, and she almost shivered when their fingers brushed together. He held the wooden creature up to the window and examined it in the sunlight. "It's a yellow warbler." He motioned for her to stand beside him. "See there?" He pointed to letters carved in the bottom of the bird. "I put the names of the species on the bottom."

Ellie shook her head with surprise. "How do you know so much about birds?"

Lloyd gave her an embarrassed smile. "I'm not really that smart." He pulled a thick book from one of the drawers in the workbench. "I use this to look up the birds. See?" He flipped to a page and pointed to a photo of a bird. "I model the carvings after the photos.

I'm really not some sort of genius. I just like working with wood."

"You have a real special talent." She smiled while imagining the birds in Bird-in-Hand Gifts and Treasures. "You need to sell these."

"No." He waved off the suggestion. "This is just something I do to relax after a long day."

"I'm serious, Lloyd." Ellie held up the carved bird again. "I just started working at Bird-in-Hand Gifts and Treasures in town. The owner is Gene Rider, and he makes beautiful metal items as gifts."

Lloyd folded his arms over his chest and nodded. "I've heard about that store, looked in the front window a time or two."

"Well, he's looking for something unique made by a local Amish person to sell there. He thinks it will help boost his sales because that's what customers have been requesting lately." She spoke quickly, hoping to use the right words to convince him. "Your birds are just what he's looking for. He could sell these birds for you, and you would make some extra money."

"No." Lloyd took the bird from her and placed it back on the table. "I already told you that it's just a hobby."

"You are so talented, Lloyd," she insisted.

"No one would want to buy them."

"You're wrong," she said, pleading with him. "I'm certain they will sell."

Lloyd's expression softened and he gestured toward the door. "Would you like to go for a walk?"

She blinked, stunned by his suggestion. Did he want to spend time with her or was he simply trying to distract her from talking about selling his carved birds? "*Ya*, I would."

"*Gut.*" Lloyd gestured toward the door, and they made their way out of the barn by the light still coming through the windows.

They started toward the pasture, but then Lloyd stopped and turned to her.

"Wait. Did you want to play volleyball?"

"No, not really." She gave him a shy smile.

"I thought you liked volleyball," he said, looking surprised. The volleyball games were still going strong on the other side of the house.

"I used to." Ellie ran her fingers along the pasture fence as they walked. "It's not the same anymore."

"It reminds you of Seth." His words were gentle.

Her eyes met his and she found sympathy there. "That's exactly right. Rebecca and Marie invited me to play with them, but I couldn't do it. I kept thinking about the day Seth and Veronica taught me how to serve and bump the ball. It was too painful."

Lloyd stopped walking. "I know what you mean. A lot of things remind me of Seth too."

"Some days are worse than others." She kept one hand on the fence. "I can't stand it when my *mamm* cries. It tears me apart inside."

"I imagine it does." Lloyd looked past her toward the youth group, and she wondered if she was holding him back from having fun.

"Am I stopping you from playing volleyball?" she asked.

"Who, me?" He smiled and shook his head. She

enjoyed seeing his handsome smile. "No, I don't belong out there with those young people."

"You're not old, Lloyd." She wagged a finger at him. "You were going to hide in your woodshop until I found you. You weren't going to keep your promise to mingle at the youth gathering."

He rubbed his chin. "I never promised you I would do that."

"*Ya*, you did."

"I said I would be around since I live here, but I never said I'd take part." He turned toward the house. "Are you thirsty? *Mamm* made her famous iced tea. Let's get a glass. We can sit on the porch and watch everyone play volleyball."

"That sounds perfect." A smile spread across her lips as Ellie followed Lloyd to the house. She'd never dreamt of spending so much time with Lloyd. She prayed he'd soon see her as more than a friend.

. . .

Lloyd stepped into the mudroom later that night and set his lantern down on the bench. He'd spent the entire evening with Ellie, and he was surprised that he'd had a good time with her. After they gathered glasses of iced tea and a plate of snacks, they sat on the porch together. They ate and talked until it was time for Ellie to head back home. They discussed everything from the weather to her brother and some of their mutual friends. She'd been sweet and funny, and for some inexplicable reason, he felt himself growing attached to her.

He mentally shook himself. But how could that be possible? Ellie was the same age as his sister Rebecca. Any feelings for her would be inappropriate. In fact, he'd be furious if one of his friends wanted to date Rebecca. He pushed the thoughts away as he sat on the bench and shucked his work boots. This was just craziness. Ellie was his friend, and that was all she'd ever be to him—a special friend.

"There you are, Lloyd." Rebecca appeared in the doorway. "I was wondering where you'd gone."

"I made sure the last of your friends got off safely and then checked on the animals." He set his boots under the bench and noticed she was lingering. "Do you need something?"

"No. I want to ask you something, though."

"What is it?" He leaned back on the bench, waiting for her response.

"I saw you talking to Ellie earlier. How was she?" Her expression was filled with concern.

Lloyd shrugged. "She seemed okay. Why are you asking about her?"

"She seemed really *bedauerlich* earlier." Rebecca rested one hand on the back of a chair as she talked. "Marie and I tried to convince her to play volleyball with us, but she didn't want to. I had a feeling it reminded her of Seth."

"Yeah, she told me that." Lloyd rested his ankle on his opposite knee. "We talked about Seth a little bit, but we also talked about other things. She was fine. I think it helped her to get away from the volleyball nets and think about something else."

"Oh." Rebecca grimaced and rubbed her forehead. "I'm such a bad friend. I didn't even think about that."

"It's not your fault." Lloyd shook his head. "Don't blame yourself. I think grief is unpredictable sometimes."

"*Ya.*" Rebecca's expression softened. "I suppose you're right. I'll try to be more attentive the next time I see her."

"She wasn't upset with you," Lloyd insisted. "You don't have anything to worry about."

"Oh good. I'm glad you could cheer her up. You two looked like you were enjoying each other's company." Rebecca tapped the back of the chair. "I'm going to head upstairs."

Lloyd nodded as she left. He stood, went into the kitchen, and crossed to the sink. As he filled a glass with water, his thoughts turned back to Ellie and their conversation in the woodshop. She'd seemed determined to convince him to sell his carved birds, and the excitement in her eyes surprised him. He'd never imagined anyone would show such an interest in his work.

For a split second, he had considered taking her up on her offer, but he couldn't allow himself to entertain the idea of selling his creations, especially after his father called his hobby prideful. He wouldn't dare disrespect his father, and besides, who would want his silly birds? Just because Ellie thought they would sell well at Bird-in-Hand Gifts and Treasures didn't mean anyone would actually buy them. It was a ridiculous notion, but he was still amused by her interest. Ellie was a sweet *maedel*.

He drank the water and set the glass in the sink before heading toward the stairs. He tried to push away thoughts of Ellie, but her pretty smile filled his mind. What was wrong with him? She was only nineteen.

Lloyd climbed the stairs to his bedroom and tried to shake off all his thoughts of Ellie. He'd enjoyed spending time with her tonight, but they were just two friends sharing conversation and pretzels and iced tea on the porch, and nothing more.

. . .

Ellie was still smiling when she arrived at Bird-in-Hand Gifts and Treasures Monday morning. She hadn't stopped smiling since she'd left the youth gathering last night. She had never in her wildest dreams imagined that she'd have the opportunity to spend an evening talking to Lloyd. It had been wonderful. She'd felt a strong connection with him while they talked. It was as if they really understood each other. Could he possibly like her as more than a friend? The possibility sent a shiver of excitement through her as she stepped into the showroom and set to work.

Ellie's thoughts lingered on Lloyd throughout the morning as she helped customers and kept the showroom tidy. When she wasn't busy with customers, her eyes frequently drifted to the back of the store where Phoebe suggested they add unique Amish-made goods. Maybe she'd been right when she'd told Lloyd the birds were an example of what those customers said they wanted in the Amish section of the store. Ellie found herself mentally designing a display for Lloyd's beautifully carved work. She would set up special shelves and arrange the birds by size, giving each one a good amount of space on the shelf so customers could appreciate the intricate detail.

She recalled the feel of the carved birds she'd held in her hands. She'd been overwhelmed by Lloyd's craftsmanship. How could he not appreciate his own talent? Why had he kept his creations a secret? Those birds deserved to be shared and loved by others. Why didn't he want to sell them? After all, God had blessed Lloyd with that talent, and they were called to share their talents with the world.

Ellie continued to contemplate the birds all morning. When it came time to break for lunch, she peeked into the workshop. Gene was sitting at his bench, polishing a metal treasure box.

"Gene?" she said, leaning into the room from the doorway.

"Hi, Ellie." Gene smiled over at her. "How are things going?"

"Everything is going fine. I thought I'd take lunch in the break room now." She pointed toward the small room next to his workshop.

"Sure thing." He stood and wiped his hands on a red shop rag. "I'll take care of the front while you're gone."

"Thank you." Ellie started toward the break room and then stopped. She felt compelled to tell Gene about Lloyd's carvings even though Lloyd had insisted he would never sell them. She lingered in the doorway and ran her finger over the woodwork while considering whether or not she should tell him about the birds.

"Is everything all right?" Gene asked as he tossed his shop rag onto the workbench.

"I think I found something unique," she said, now fingering the hem of her apron. "It's something I've never seen sold at the shops around here."

"Really?" Gene raised his eyebrows with interest. "What did you find?"

"Last night I was at my friend's house," Ellie began, "and I found out he whittles carved birds. They aren't just ordinary carvings. They're incredible." She cupped her hand. "I held a couple of them, and it was like holding real birds."

"Interesting." Gene rubbed his beard. "Do you think customers would buy them?"

"*Ya*, I do," Ellie said. "Last week a couple of customers asked for something more unique that was Amish-made. Another one asked me today. They all said they're tired of seeing the same gifts in every store, or at least they've already bought everything that appeals to them."

Gene frowned. "I can understand that. As I mentioned when Phoebe brought this up with both of us, I have to admit that sales have been down for a while. I'm concerned that I may have to cut back somehow if the sales drop much lower."

Worry seized Ellie's heart. She needed this job so she could help support herself and her mother. What if Gene meant he'd have to cut her hours—or her job altogether? "I think the birds might be perfect for the store. The detail is so real. He has all different birds, some I hadn't even heard of. He uses a bird manual as a guide and writes the species on the bottom of each carving. I think people would love to own them. As I said, they're different from anything I've ever seen at another shop."

"They sound great." Gene's expression brightened. "I'd love to see one of his carvings. Do you think you could get me one?"

"I can try." Hope swelled inside of Ellie. "I'll talk to him about it the next time I see him. Thank you so much for considering them."

"You're welcome." Gene nodded toward the door. "Enjoy your break."

Ellie spent the remainder of the day thinking about Gene's offer to look at one of Lloyd's carvings. Now she just had to find a way to convince Lloyd to let her show one of his precious birds to Gene. Maybe his carvings would be the key to keeping her job as it was.

. . .

Ellie scrubbed a pot later that evening as her mother wiped off the table. "Did you know Lloyd whittles beautiful carved birds as a hobby?"

"Lloyd Blank?" *Mamm* asked with surprise.

"*Ya.*" Ellie dried her hands and faced her, leaning back against the counter. "I found out last night at the youth gathering. I accidentally found his woodworking shop." She described the carvings in detail, and her mother's eyes widened. "He's never told anyone about his hidden talent."

"Oh my." *Mamm* shook her head. "Lydia never mentioned it to me either. That's really *wunderbaar* that he can make those."

"Apparently he never even told Seth. He's kept it a secret for years." Ellie shared the story of how Lloyd's grandfather taught him how to whittle and how he'd inherited the tools. "Remember when I told you Gene is looking for something unique that's Amish-made to sell at the store?"

"*Ya*, you said some customers were looking for something different to buy."

"Exactly," Ellie said. "I told Gene about the birds, and he wants to see one."

"That's great," *Mamm* said. "I'm sure Lloyd will be thankful that you shared the information about his birds with Gene. Maybe he can sell them and help his family."

Mamm returned to wiping the table and guilt nipped at Ellie. She had to tell her mother the whole truth.

"Actually, Lloyd already told me he doesn't want to sell the birds," Ellie admitted as she gripped her dish towel. "When I told him about the possibility of selling the birds at the store, he said it's just a hobby and refused to talk about it further."

Mamm tilted her head. "Are you saying Lloyd told you no, but you talked to Gene about the birds anyway, against Lloyd's wishes?"

Ellie sighed. "*Ya*, I did. Gene said sales are down and he may have to make some cutbacks. I was hoping maybe Lloyd's birds could help."

Mamm's expression was one of disapproval. "You

really need to respect his wishes. There may be some special reason why he doesn't want to sell them. If you push the issue, you could lose Lloyd's friendship."

The thought worried Ellie, but she held on to her belief that the birds needed to be shared with others, whether or not their sale made a difference in her job. "I don't think he realizes how special those carvings are, *Mamm*. He probably could make a lot of money for his family as well as make tourists *froh*."

Mamm's expression softened as she moved to stand beside Ellie. "Your intentions are pure, but it's Lloyd's decision. They're his carvings. The best thing you can do is respect his feelings about his work."

"*Ya, Mamm*." Ellie nodded as she returned to the dishes in the sink. But deep in her soul, she was certain she could convince Lloyd to sell the carvings. She just had to find the right words.

She also knew the fear of losing her job made her intentions a little less pure than her mother thought, but she was going to try to think only of Lloyd's best interests.

CHAPTER FIVE

Ellie pulled a weed from the garden and dropped it into the bucket at her feet. The afternoon sun warmed her neck and her back as she squatted down and tugged at a robust, green weed that seemed to have a root system as healthy as a hundred-year-old oak tree.

"Need some help?" a voice behind her asked.

As Ellie looked up, her sweaty hands slipped from the weed, and she fell backward, landing on her bottom at Lloyd's feet. Heat crept up her neck and into her cheeks. Why did she have to fall like a klutz in front of him again?

"I seem to keep finding you in the dirt." Lloyd held out his hand and chuckled. "Let me help you up."

Ellie reluctantly took his hand, and he again lifted her to her feet as if she were nearly weightless. "I'm really not a clumsy oaf." She wiped her hands down her apron.

"I know that." Lloyd continued to smile, and her heart thumped despite her humiliation. "It was that pesky weed. Let me help." He gave the weed a couple of yanks before it exploded from the ground in a tangled mess of roots and dirt. He dropped it into the bucket and then swiped his hands together.

"*Danki.*" She glanced down at her apron, thankful she wasn't covered in mud this time. "I didn't realize you were here. Have you been working in the barn?"

"No." He shook his head. "I just got here. I've been trying to get over here to help since Monday, but unexpected projects kept coming up at the farm. I guess Thursday is better than never, right? I wanted to say hello before I got started on the stalls."

A smile spread across her lips and she forgot her embarrassment. *He came to see me before he started on his work?*

"How's your week going?" he asked.

"Fine." She recalled her conversation with Gene on Monday, and despite her mother's warning, she decided it was the perfect opportunity to ask him again about his carved birds. She took a deep breath and plowed forward. "I told my boss Gene about your carvings on Monday. I explained how amazing they are."

Lloyd's smile faded. "Why did you do that?"

"I really believe they would be a great addition to the store," she continued. "Gene is interested in seeing one. I'm working all day tomorrow. You should stop by and bring that yellow warbler."

"Wait, Ellie. Slow down." Lloyd held his hands up to stop her from speaking. "Why did you tell him about the birds? I already said I don't want to sell them."

"I truly believe your birds will bring joy and happiness into the lives of the people who buy them, Lloyd." She folded her hands to plead with him. "Please reconsider."

He shook his head, and his frown deflated all her

hope like a punctured balloon. "No, I can't sell them." He gestured toward the barn. "I need to get to work. I'll see you later."

As he loped off toward the barn, Ellie wondered why he couldn't see the beauty in his own work.

· · ·

Lloyd moved the knife over the dove he'd been working on all evening. His thoughts had been stuck on his conversation with Ellie earlier that afternoon. He couldn't stop his laughter when she fell backward in the dirt. Even though it wasn't funny to see her fall, her expression was priceless. She looked both bewildered and embarrassed, and she was adorable.

Ellie never ceased to surprise him. He couldn't fathom why she had talked to Gene when Lloyd had asked her not to. Why was she so insistent on selling his birds? Seth wasn't as stubborn as his little sister. He had been even-tempered and patient.

Lloyd's fingers moved over the wooden dove in his hand, and he thought of Seth. He wanted to do something special in memory of him. This dove would be a humble memorial, but it seemed to be a fitting one. He would finish the dove in memory of Seth.

As Lloyd continued to work, he couldn't get the image of Ellie telling him about her conversation with Gene out of his mind. Although he was disappointed that Ellie had talked to her boss about the birds, he had enjoyed the sparkle in her light-green eyes as she gushed about his creations. He couldn't explain this sudden awareness of Ellie. What was wrong with him? He'd seen her grow up. It wasn't right for him to think of her as anything other than a friend.

A tap on the doorframe interrupted his thoughts.

He looked over his shoulder and found Rebecca standing in the doorway. "Hi, Becca."

"It's late," she said, crossing her arms over her blue dress. "*Mamm* asked me to come and get you."

"I was just finishing up." He placed the knife on the table.

"What are you making now?" Rebecca closed the distance between them and took the bird from his hand. "This is *schee*, Lloyd."

"*Danki*," he said as she turned it over in her hand. "It's going to be a dove."

"This is fantastic, Lloyd." Her eyes were wide as they met his. "You are so talented."

"Do you really think so?" The question leapt from his lips before he could stop it. He couldn't stand sounding so vulnerable. Why did it matter that someone liked his work? It was just something he did for relaxation.

"*Ya*, of course I do." She sank onto the stool beside him.

"Ellie thinks I should sell the carvings at Bird-in-Hand Gifts and Treasures in town. I don't think I can, though. *Dat* would never permit it."

A knowing smile spread across Rebecca's lips. "Do you like Ellie?"

He was speechless for a moment. "Why would I like Ellie?"

"You hesitated." Rebecca's smile transformed into a sly grin. "You do like Ellie. I had a feeling you two liked each other when I saw you talking at the youth gathering, but I didn't want to say anything."

"We don't like each other," Lloyd said quickly. "I couldn't possibly like her."

"Why not?" As she set the bird on the table beside her, she looked bewildered. "Ellie is *schee*, smart, and funny. What don't you like about her?"

"It's not that." Lloyd shoved his hand through his hair. "It wouldn't be right for me to like her that way. She's Seth's little *schweschder*."

Rebecca chuckled. "Lloyd, in this community, we're all someone's *bruder* or *schweschder*."

He blinked, speechless. He hadn't expected that response.

She stood. "Let's go before *Dat* comes looking for you."

Lloyd flipped off one lantern, then lifted the other one and used it to guide their way back to the house. As they walked in silence, his thoughts were consumed with Ellie. Was Rebecca right when she said Ellie liked him? These feelings were brand-new and confusing. He tried to push the thoughts away, but they lingered in the back of his mind.

. . .

Lloyd sat between two of his friends during the church service the following Sunday. Rebecca's words from Thursday evening echoed again through his mind as the hour-long main sermon played like background noise to his deep thoughts.

His sister had simply stated that everyone in the community was someone's sibling, but he understood the deeper meaning. Rebecca had given him permission to like Ellie as more than a friend. The idea still didn't sit right with him, though. He still felt as if he would break an unwritten code between Seth and him. He could never imagine one of his friends dating Marie or even Rebecca, so how could he entertain the notion of asking Ellie to be his girlfriend?

Still, Rebecca's words lingered in his mind, overshadowing his other thoughts.

As the minister continued to talk, Lloyd's eyes moved to the unmarried women sitting on a section of benches across from the unmarried men. Ellie was sitting between Rebecca and another friend. She was dressed in a light-green dress that complemented her eyes, and her golden hair peeked out from under her white prayer covering. She was beautiful, and he watched her as she leaned over to Rebecca and whispered something. Both of the young women grinned and then looked down toward the barn floor as if trying to hide their amusement at whatever Ellie had whispered.

Lloyd glanced down at the hymnal in his hand and tried to make sense of the confusing feelings swirling inside of him. Ellie was sweet and beautiful, but no, she was too young.

After the service was over, Lloyd helped the other men convert the benches into tables for the noon meal, then sat with his friends while they waited for lunch.

They were all discussing the rising price of diesel needed to run milking machines when he felt a gentle bump on his shoulder. He turned and found Ellie smiling at him.

"*Kaffi?*" She lifted her coffeepot.

"Oh, *ya. Danki.*" Lloyd handed her his cup. "How are you?"

"I'm fine. You?" Ellie smiled. Oh, how he loved that beautiful smile.

The thought caught him off guard for a moment. "I'm fine too," he said quickly.

"*Gut.* I'll see you later." She moved on to the next person at the table, and he realized he didn't want her to go.

Lloyd tried to think of a reason to see her again and an idea struck him when she reached the end of the table. As she exited the barn to return to the kitchen, he stood and followed her outside.

"Ellie," he called. "Wait a minute."

She spun to face him and raised an eyebrow with concern. "Is something wrong?"

"No, no." He closed the distance between them. "I want to ask you a question."

"Oh?" She held the coffeepot close to her chest. "What did you want to ask me?"

"Are you going to the youth gathering tonight?" Suddenly self-conscious, Lloyd stuffed his hands in the pockets of his trousers.

"*Ya*, I am." Ellie nodded.

"I am too," he said. "Would it be all right if I picked you up?" he asked.

Her eyes widened with shock. "That would be fine."

"Great," Lloyd said. "Rebecca, Marie, and I will get you on our way out there." He turned to head back to the barn.

"Lloyd," she called after him, and he whirled around. "I thought you said you were too old for the youth gathering." Amusement twinkled in her eyes.

He shrugged with a grin. "I guess one of my *freinden* changed my mind. She said people of all ages go to the gatherings."

Ellie grinned. "You have a very *schmaert* friend." With that she turned to go.

Lloyd chuckled as she walked toward the house. He couldn't wait to see her later.

• • •

As her pulse pounded with excitement, Ellie rushed from her room and down the stairs. She was still flying high with anticipation after Lloyd had offered to pick her up for the youth gathering this evening. Did the invitation mean he planned to ask her to be his girlfriend? The notion caused her insides to warm. She'd dreamt of being his girlfriend since she was twelve, and now she was almost certain it could actually happen.

She walked into the family room, where her mother was reading a Christian novel. "I'm ready to go." She crossed to her mother's chair and kissed her on the cheek.

With suspicious eyes, *Mamm* peered at her over her half glasses. "Why are you so eager, Ellie?"

"I'm just looking forward to seeing my *freinden*."

Ellie grinned. "Lloyd, Rebecca, and Marie are picking me up in a few minutes." She started for the door. "See you later."

"Be safe," *Mamm* called.

As Ellie stepped outside, she heard the *clip-clop* of Lloyd's horse making its way up the rock driveway to her house. Her stomach fluttered as the buggy drew near. She found his sisters were in the back, so she climbed into the front. She greeted Rebecca and Marie as she settled into the seat beside Lloyd.

"*Danki* for picking me up," Ellie said.

"We're glad you could join us," Lloyd said. When he smiled at her, her pulse quickened again.

Lloyd guided the horse back down the driveway toward the main road. During the ride, Marie and Rebecca discussed the boys they hoped to see at the youth gathering. Ellie chimed in now and again, giving her thoughts on the boys they liked while Lloyd mostly shot Ellie sideways glances with rolled eyes.

When they arrived at the farm hosting the event, Ellie climbed down from the buggy and Rebecca and Marie jumped out after her. The sisters immediately started toward the volleyball courts, where the majority of the youth were already gathered.

Ellie lingered behind while Lloyd took care of the horse. She'd hoped to get some time to talk to him alone.

Rebecca stopped walking and looked back at Ellie. "Aren't you coming with us?"

Ellie hesitated, and Rebecca gave her a knowing smile. She winked, then ambled on.

Ellie swallowed a gasp. How did Rebecca know she

liked Lloyd? Had she been too obvious with her feelings even though she'd tried to keep them to herself? Panic surged through her. Did all their friends know she liked Lloyd?

"Ellie," Lloyd said, interrupting her thoughts as he appeared behind her.

She spun toward him and hoped her cheeks weren't as red as they felt. "*Ya?*"

He gestured toward the volleyball courts. "Do you want to play volleyball this time?" His easy smile relieved her worry.

Ellie shrugged. "I don't know. Do you?"

Lloyd shook his head. "Not really, but we could sit near the volleyball courts and talk."

"I'd like that." Ellie was glad he wanted to spend time with her, and a smile teased the corner of her mouth as she followed him toward the makeshift courts.

When they reached a flat patch of lush green grass, he pointed down.

"Would you like to sit here?" he asked.

"*Ya.*" She sat on the ground and smoothed the skirt of her green dress over her legs. "It's a *schee* night, *ya?*"

Lloyd sank down beside her. "It sure is." He stared off toward the volleyball games, where the young men and women bounced the ball over the nets as they laughed and shouted.

Ellie searched his expression. She hoped she wasn't holding him back from enjoying the games with other friends and he'd been too polite to go off without her. "You can go if you want. You don't have to sit here with me."

He glanced at her. "No, I really don't want to play. I was just thinking back to when I used to play with *mei freinden* when I was younger."

Ellie shook her head and grinned. "You talk like you're forty."

He gave a bark of laughter. "You're funny, Ellie."

"*Ya?*" Her smile widened. "I will take that as a compliment."

"I meant it as a compliment." He studied her for a moment. "Do you remember any of the jokes your *bruder* used to tell?"

"Of course I do." She picked a blade of grass from her dress. "I remember the last one he told me. It was the morning of the accident."

"What was it?" Lloyd rested his elbow on his bent knee.

"Seth came into the kitchen that morning and said, 'Hey, Squirt! What nails do carpenters hate to hit?' I played along and said, 'I don't know, Seth. What nails do carpenters hate to hit?'" She paused. "Do you know what the answer is?"

Lloyd shrugged. "No, I can't say that I do."

"Fingernails!" she announced, then laughed.

He groaned and then laughed too. "That sounds like Seth, all right." He rocked back on his hands.

"He was still chuckling about that when he left for work." Her eyes misted as she recalled the details of the morning. "That was the last time I saw him alive. I still remember the warm sound of his laugh. I dream about him some nights. A couple of times I've woken up in the middle of the night and thought I heard him laughing."

She turned toward Lloyd and found him studying her. "You're the only person I've ever told that to."

"Really?" He looked surprised.

She nodded. "I hadn't told anyone the last joke he shared with me. And I hadn't told anyone about the dreams." She knew now that she longed to share all her secrets with Lloyd.

"I'm honored that you told me." His expression was full of empathy. "I miss Seth's jokes."

"I remember another one," she blurted out. "What did the green grape say to the purple grape?"

Lloyd grinned. "I don't know."

"Breathe, stupid!" A belly laugh bubbled up from her toes, and some of the pent-up sadness evaporated from deep in her soul.

Lloyd laughed, too, and for a moment she wondered if he was laughing at the joke or at her ridiculous reaction to such a corny joke. But somehow she knew Lloyd was laughing with her, not at her.

"I miss those jokes," Ellie admitted with a sigh. "I miss our talks too. Seth and I used to talk about everything. I never had to worry about what he might say or think if I shared my feelings with him."

"He was a *gut* listener." He leaned back on his hands again and was quiet for a moment. "Tell me about your new job."

"I really like it. The shop is so *schee*. Have you ever been in it?" she asked as she pulled at a dandelion.

He shook his head. "I don't think I've ever been in it, but I have checked out the window display. Gene does great work."

"He does. It's beautiful. It stays busy there too."

"How many days are you working?"

"Two." She tossed the dandelion. "I work Mondays and Fridays. You'll have to stop by."

He nodded. "Maybe I will sometime. You can give me a tour."

Ellie's stomach quivered with the possibility. "That would be nice." She hoped he would.

When Lloyd smiled over at her, she knew she was falling in love with him. She also hoped he wouldn't break her heart continuing to think of her only as Seth's little sister.

CHAPTER SIX

Lloyd stepped out of the hardware store and glanced down at the bag he gripped in his hand. Although he had bought everything listed on the crumpled paper he'd jammed into his trouser pocket, he was certain he'd forgotten something. He was distracted, and the trip to the hardware store wasn't in the forefront of his mind. Instead, he was thinking of Ellie's radiant smile. She'd been on his mind ever since he'd dropped her off at her house last night.

He'd spent the entire time at the youth gathering talking to her, and he hadn't regretted a single moment. In fact, it was the most fun he'd had at a youth gathering in years. He'd hung on every word of their conversation. They'd talked about Seth and shared some of their favorite memories of him. Then they talked about friends, her new job, and his work on the farm. The hours had flown by, and too soon it was time for him to take her home.

This morning Lloyd had awoken thinking about her, and he couldn't wait to see her again. He made a quick list for the hardware store during breakfast, called for a driver, and after his morning chores were complete, headed to town.

Now standing in front of the hardware store, Lloyd glanced down the block and spotted the sign for Bird-in-Hand Gifts and Treasures. If he were honest with himself, he would admit why he'd truly come to town. The reason lay only half a block away. Ellie had told him she worked on Mondays, and he was eager to see her again.

Lloyd walked up the block and went inside the shop. He stood by the door and watched Ellie while she helped a customer at the cash register. She was beautiful clad in a dusty-rose-colored dress. She smiled, and her face seemed to glow as she spoke with the woman. After wrapping up the items and placing them into a bag, she took the customer's money and thanked her for coming in. Then she looked toward the front of the store and gasped when she saw him.

"Lloyd!" She rushed over to him. "I'm so surprised to see you here."

He lifted the bag from the hardware store. "I was in the neighborhood, so I thought I'd stop by to see you. You said I should see the shop sometime."

"I'm so glad you came by today." She motioned for him to follow her toward the front window display. "Since no customers are here, I can give you a quick tour."

Lloyd followed her around the store as she explained the theme of each display. He stood close to her and breathed in the scent of her shampoo, some kind of flower mixed with cinnamon. She explained Gene's process for creating the elaborate metal ornaments, pointing out which items were the most popular with the tourists.

When they reached the back of the shop, Ellie gestured toward the Amish items. "This is where we keep the Amish gifts. Gene's niece, Phoebe, would like to add more unique, locally made items to the collection."

Lloyd's shoulders stiffened. He didn't want to discuss selling his birds again, and he hoped she wouldn't pressure him. He didn't want that subject to ruin the mood. She paused for a quick moment, and he was thankful when she didn't mention the birds.

"Would you like to meet Gene?" she offered.

"Sure," he said.

"He's in the workshop, which is in the back." She led him to a doorway.

"Hi, Gene," she said as they stepped into the large shop cluttered with tools. "This is my friend Lloyd Blank."

"Hi, Lloyd." Gene stood and shook Lloyd's hand. "How are you?"

"I'm fine." Lloyd gestured back toward the showroom. "You have a really nice store and your metal work is just amazing."

"Thank you." Gene glanced at his watch.

Lloyd looked at the clock on the wall and an idea sprang into his head. "It's almost noon. Could I possibly take Ellie out for lunch?"

Ellie looked surprised, and she gave him a questioning look.

"I promise I won't have her out too long," Lloyd continued. "We'll just go across the street to the Bird-in-Hand Restaurant and get something quick."

Gene smiled at Ellie. "That sounds like a great idea.

I'll run the front until you get back. You can take your time too."

"Thank you," Ellie said. "I just need to grab my purse from the break room."

Lloyd said good-bye to Gene and headed to the front door. He examined a few decorative metal dishes until Ellie emerged with a black purse dangling from her shoulder. They walked together to the Bird-in-Hand Restaurant, where they were seated at a booth.

"Gene is nice, isn't he?" Ellie asked after the waitress had taken their orders.

"*Ya*, he is." Lloyd ran his fingers down the condensation on his glass of water. "The shop is really *schee*, just like you said it was."

She tilted her head and her light-green eyes twinkled with anticipation. "You know, you could talk to him about your birds if you want to. I've already told him about them, and I know he'd love to find out more."

Lloyd shook his head, but instead of being frustrated with her as he expected to be, he was flattered. She was determined for him to sell his birds, but it felt like a compliment instead of harassment. "I'm really not interested in selling them, but *danki* for offering to help. They're sort of a stress reliever for me. Designing and making the birds helps me clear my head after a long day of farm work. While I'm whittling, I sometimes pray or just think about my day and what I have to do the following day. It helps me unwind."

Her expression became bemused. "I just don't understand why you don't want to sell them. You have so many of them, and they just stay in your shop where no one can enjoy them. God gave you that talent, and he wants us to share our talents with others to celebrate his glory. Why do you want to hide that talent when there are so many people who could cherish those birds?"

He contemplated her words as he continued to run his fingers over the glass. Although he understood her point, his father's admonition echoed loud and clear in his mind. "Selling them would be prideful. If I charged money for them, then I would be bragging about my talent."

Ellie shook her head. "I disagree."

He had to change the subject. "I can see why you like working for Gene. It really is a nice store. It didn't seem like it was too busy this morning, though."

"No, it really hasn't been busy today." Ellie smiled, and he was certain it lit up the room. "I'm glad you stopped by on a day when it wasn't. I'm not certain I could've left to have lunch with you if there had been a store full of customers."

The waitress appeared with their lunch orders. She placed a turkey sandwich in front of Ellie and an Angus burger in front of Lloyd. After a silent prayer, Lloyd lifted a fry.

"Ellie, I've been wondering something," he began.

"What's that?" She took a bite of the sandwich and then blotted her mouth with her napkin.

"I was a little surprised when you told me you took this job. You hadn't worked outside of the home much, except for helping out at Lizzie Ann King's vegetable stand, right?" He bit into the juicy burger.

"*Ya*, that's right." She examined her plate as if avoiding his stare. "I felt it was time for me to do something to help out."

"Is everything all right at home?" he asked as worry filled him. "Are you and your *mamm* financially okay without Seth?"

"We're doing okay." Ellie's smile faded. "My uncles have taken care of the mortgage since *mei dat* passed away, but Seth managed everything else." She met his gaze, and he saw a hint of sadness in her beautiful eyes. "I feel a responsibility to do my part since I'm the only one left to take care of *Mamm*. It's not like *mei onkels* can do any more than they are."

Lloyd placed the burger on his plate. "I understand. Since I'm the only *bu*, I'll inherit the dairy farm. I feel a lot of pressure to make sure the farm is run well and the family is financially stable. If *mei schweschdere* don't marry, I'll have to take care of them too."

"I never realized how much pressure Seth was under until he was gone." Ellie's eyes shimmered with tears, and he hoped she wouldn't cry. "Now that he's gone, I need to try to take care of *Mamm* just as well as he did."

She wiped away a stray tear, and he started to reach for her hand. He stopped with his hand in the air, not wanting to be too forward. He quickly pulled his hand back and lifted the burger.

"I'm certain you're a wonderful support to your *mamm*, Ellie. Don't be so hard on yourself."

Ellie nodded and her smile returned. "*Danki*." She lifted her sandwich. "This is *appeditlich*. Thank you so much for lunch."

"*Gern gschehne*," he said, grateful to see her smile again. "Thank you for the company."

They spent the rest of lunch discussing their plans for the week. After they were finished eating, Lloyd paid the check and they walked back to the store. When they reached the door, Lloyd held out his hand.

"*Danki* for joining me at lunch," he said as she shook it. "I'm sure I'll see you at your farm this week."

"*Wunderbaar.* I look forward to it." She smiled as she said good-bye and stepped inside.

Lloyd knew there was a spring in his step as he walked down the sidewalk to meet his driver. He felt a strong connection growing between Ellie and him, and once more, he couldn't wait to see her again.

. . .

Ellie hummed softly as she swept the front porch and thought about Lloyd. During the last three weeks, they had fallen into a comfortable pattern. Lloyd came to the Lapp farm twice every week to help with chores. They spent time together while he was there sharing a snack or a meal. They visited at church on Sundays after the service and at youth gatherings. Lloyd even stopped by to see her at the shop again a couple of times, including the Saturday she subbed for Phoebe when she was sick.

Ellie felt their friendship growing as they learned more about each other. She couldn't squelch the notion that his feelings for her were growing, but she was afraid to truly believe that he might like her as more than a friend. She hoped someday he would see that she cared for him. Until then, she allowed herself to enjoy his company and looked forward to the days when he visited the farm.

Now on this Tuesday afternoon she swiped her hand across her forehead as the mid-July sun beat down. She heard the *clip-clop* of a horse approaching on the rock driveway, and her heart felt like it turned over in her chest when she saw it was Lloyd. She'd hoped he would come to help with chores today, and she was thankful that God answered her unspoken prayer.

She waved as he climbed down from the buggy.

"Ellie," he called as he walked to the porch. *"Wie geht's?"*

"I'm doing great." She leaned against the broom. "Are you here to help with chores?"

"That's one of the reasons I came over." He climbed the porch steps. His dark blue shirt complemented his bright eyes. "I also have something for you."

"You do?" Ellie propped the broom against the railing as curiosity consumed her.

Lloyd reached into his trouser pocket and pulled out something hidden in his hand. "I made this in memory of Seth, and I want you to have it." He opened his hand and held it out.

Ellie opened her own hand, and Lloyd placed a carved bird in it. His fingers brushed hers, lingering for a long moment. She enjoyed the warmth of his skin against hers. She examined the carving, a beautiful, delicate dove.

"Lloyd," she whispered, her voice strangled with emotion. "It's the most *schee* bird I've ever seen."

"It's a dove." His voice was equally soft and sentimental.

"It's perfect. *Danki* so much." She nodded, and her eyes stung with threatening tears. "I'll treasure it."

"I know you will."

She looked up into his eyes and something between them sparked. They studied each other, and her breath caught in her throat. Did he feel the same overwhelming force pulling them to each other? Did he care for her the same way she cared for him?

"I better get to work." Lloyd took two steps back. "I'll see you later."

Ellie held the dove close to her chest. It was the most meaningful and beautiful gift she'd ever received. She would cherish it forever.

. . .

Lloyd hurried toward the barn, aware of an unexpected warmth inside. He'd never experienced such a strong, overwhelming emotion for anyone. He didn't know how to handle it, and the urge to flee overtook him. What did these feelings mean? Where had they come from?

Lloyd grabbed a shovel and began mucking out the first stall he came to. As he labored, he remembered how it had felt to touch Ellie's hand. He couldn't stop thinking about the tenderness in her eyes as she contemplated the bird. The carving had obviously meant so much to her, and the expression on her beautiful face had touched something deep in his soul.

When he had finished the dove last night, he decided

to bring it over and give it to Ellie today. He had created the dove in memory of Seth, but as the bird took shape, he realized he wanted to share it with Ellie. He had never before given away one of his birds because he'd never felt they were good enough to share as gifts. Yet Ellie was the first person who had ever shown a real interest in the birds, and he was determined to share one with her. She had become his champion, his dear friend.

No, Ellie was more than a friend. She had become something much more precious than only a friend.

He stopped shoveling when he realized what those deep emotions meant.

He *loved* Ellie.

Yes, he loved Ellie with his whole heart.

Rebecca was right when she'd said they were all someone's sibling in this community. Ellie may be Seth's little sister, but she was also a beautiful young woman in her own right. And Lloyd wanted to be more than her friend. After all these years he had finally figured out whom he loved, and she had been a part of his life since they were children.

Lloyd's heart pounded with a mixture of worry and excitement. Now he had to find a way to tell her how he felt, and he prayed she felt the same way.

• • •

Later that evening, Ellie knocked on her mother's bedroom door. She cradled the beautiful carved dove in one hand.

"Come in," *Mamm* called.

Ellie stepped inside and found *Mamm* propped up in bed with two pillows behind her back, reading another Christian novel. "I want to show you something." She held out the carved dove. "Lloyd gave me this today. He made it in memory of Seth."

Mamm closed her book and placed it on the nightstand. She took the dove and turned it over in her hands. "Ellie," she said with a gasp, "this is amazing. Look at the detail."

"I know." Ellie sank onto the edge of the bed beside her. "I told you he's talented."

Mamm continued to examine the bird. "I can't get over how beautifully crafted this is. Lydia never told me Lloyd is so talented."

"Lloyd has kept his talent a secret for a long time." Ellie traced her fingers over her mother's blue quilt.

Mamm handed her the bird. "You need to put this in a special place and cherish it. That was made out of love."

Ellie smiled when she heard the word, and her cheeks heated.

"Ellie?" *Mamm* gave her a knowing smile. "Is there something you want to tell me about you and Lloyd?"

Ellie's eyes widened with surprise. "What do you mean?"

"Do you have feelings for Lloyd?" *Mamm* patted the quilt next to her. "Come here and talk to me."

Ellie scooted up next to her and leaned back against the pillow. "There really isn't anything to tell."

"I've seen you and Lloyd talking and sometimes eating together when he's here. You seem to enjoy each other's company."

Ellie nodded. "We talk when he's here, and even at church and youth gatherings, but I'm not sure if he likes me the same way I like him."

"Your *dat* and I started off as friends," *Mamm* said with a smile.

"I know." Ellie fingered the stitching on the quilt. "I just don't know if he could ever consider me as more than a friend since he's older than I am. He said he was too old for youth gatherings."

"He may have said that, but he's been attending them, hasn't he?"

"*Ya*, he has." Ellie looked down at the dove again. Lloyd hadn't missed a youth gathering since he'd picked her up to attend one together weeks ago. "He seemed different today when he gave me the dove. I think this meant a lot to him, and he seemed almost nervous when he gave it to me."

"It was a gift from his heart," *Mamm* said.

Ellie turned the bird over in her hand, studying the detail. Her thoughts turned to that corner in the shop that she'd love to design for Lloyd's beautiful creations. "I know Gene would love this. He'd love to sell these in his store."

"Ellie." *Mamm*'s voice held a hint of a warning. "Lloyd told you he doesn't want to sell them. You have to respect his wishes."

Ellie nodded. *Mamm* was right, but if Gene saw the bird and loved it, maybe she could persuade Lloyd to change his mind. And maybe these beautiful carvings could boost Gene's sales and keep him from possibly taking away her job.

CHAPTER SEVEN

Ellie touched the wooden bird hidden in her dress pocket on Friday afternoon. Although her mother had warned her not to go against Lloyd's wishes, she'd carried the bird to work today with the intention of showing it to Gene. Every time she'd planned to show it to him, however, a customer had interrupted her. She hoped the perfect opportunity would present itself before she left for the day.

At five, she rang up the last customer and then flipped the sign from Open to Closed before starting to shut down the register.

"How were sales today?" Gene appeared from his workshop and approached the counter where she had been counting out money.

"It was fairly busy," Ellie said. "At least, I think it was a little busier than this time last week." She placed the cash in the moneybag and zipped it up.

Gene sighed and shook his head. "I haven't wanted to tell you this, but sales have continued to go down these last few weeks. I was hoping they would pick up during the summer, but they haven't. I think I may have to start cutting back your hours." He leaned against the counter as his frown deepened. "I'm really sorry to do

this to you, Ellie. You're a great worker, but I'm not selling enough stock to keep you here two full days. I'm
going to have to cover the showroom myself on one of
your days."

Ellie nodded as alarm gripped her. How was she
going to buy groceries for herself and her mother only
working one day a week? Friends and neighbors had
stopped bringing meals over to their house weeks ago,
and the cupboards would be bare without her pay-
checks. Where could she quickly find another job?

She suddenly remembered the carved dove in her
pocket and considered showing it to Gene. Doubt filled
her. Was she making a mistake by going against Lloyd's
wishes? Would Lloyd understand why she did it, because
she had her and her mother's livelihood in mind?

"Do you want me to drive you home tonight?" Gene
offered, interrupting her thoughts. "I need to run a few
errands on my way home, and I could save you the cost
of a driver."

"Oh." Ellie was surprised by the offer. "That would
be nice."

"Why don't you call your driver, and I'll finish closing out the register."

"Thank you." Ellie dialed her driver's cell phone
number and canceled the ride. Then she slipped her
hand into her pocket and trailed her fingers over the
dove. She was absolutely sure God would want Lloyd to
share his talent, and . . .

"Gene," she said as she pulled the bird from her
pocket, "do you remember when I told you about my
friend who makes the carved birds as a hobby?"

"Yes, I do. I thought you were going to bring one for me to see." Gene placed the moneybag on the counter and turned to her as she held out the bird.

"This is a dove he made in memory of my brother." She placed the bird in his hands.

"Ellie." Gene gaped. "This is gorgeous."

"Do you remember Lloyd?" Ellie asked. "He took me out to lunch a few weeks ago. He's the one who made this."

"Really." Gene turned the bird over in his hand. "He didn't sign his name, though."

"He's very humble," Ellie said. "It's our way. He only puts the species of bird on the bottom. He models them after pictures in a book he has."

"This is breathtaking." Gene looked at her. "Ellie, this could be the key to getting our sales back up to where they used to be. Tourists would go crazy for this. This would be perfect. This is exactly what Phoebe had in mind when she said she wanted to sell something unique that was Amish-made. I don't think we could keep these on the shelves."

He turned the bird over in his hands again, taking in every inch of it. "I'd love to discuss price. Of course, I'll pay him what he's worth. I'm certain he's poured plenty of time, along with his heart and soul, into creating this. Do you know how long it took him to make this?"

"I have no idea."

"Does he live near you?" Gene pulled his keys from his jeans pocket.

"*Ya*, he does." Was Gene suggesting . . .

"Could I meet him again? Do you think it would be all right if we stop there on our way to your house?"

"*Ya*," Ellie lied. "Amish are used to people just stopping in." It was true that Amish were used to people stopping in, but Lloyd wouldn't be happy when he found out why they were visiting. Ellie shook her head as her mouth dried. What had she done? She certainly hadn't thought this through. Lloyd would be furious when she showed up with Gene asking about the birds. But she had to think of her mother.

The worry transformed to dread and pooled in her stomach. She wasn't prepared for this.

After they finished closing the store for the night, Ellie followed Gene to his vehicle and gave him directions. She wrung her hands as Gene steered his burgundy SUV through town and toward Lloyd's place. She was certain she would lose Lloyd's friendship forever when she arrived unannounced with Gene. She should've left the dove on her dresser this morning.

As the SUV's tires crunched on the rocks leading to the Blank family farm, Ellie's stomach twisted with apprehension. Not only was she about to lose Lloyd's trust, she may also lose her job when Gene found out she hadn't had Lloyd's permission to show him the carved bird. The SUV came to a stop and they climbed out. Thankfully no one else in the family opened the front door to greet them.

"He's probably doing his evening chores," Ellie said as she led Gene back to the large barn. Just as they got there, Lloyd stepped out. He met Ellie's eyes and lifted his eyebrow in question.

"Hi, Lloyd," Gene said. "Could I talk to you for a moment?"

Lloyd nodded as confusion twisted his handsome face. His father, Wilmer, stepped out of the barn behind him, and Ellie felt sick with apprehension. This would be far worse than she'd ever imagined. She should've heeded her mother's warning last night.

"Hi," Gene said to Wilmer. "I'm Gene Rider. I own Bird-in-Hand Gifts and Treasures up on Old Philadelphia Pike."

Wilmer shook his hand, his expression mirroring Lloyd's. "I'm Wilmer Blank, and this is my son, Lloyd. How may we help you?"

"Ellie has been telling me about Lloyd's talent with carving birds." Gene pulled the dove from his pocket. "She showed me this one today, and I can't get over the precision and detail."

To Ellie's horror, Lloyd's expression transformed from confusion to pure anguish. Ellie tried to tell him she was sorry with her eyes, but he just stared at her, his expression becoming more and more pained as the moments passed. Her soul filled with regret, and she longed to apologize to him. Instead, she stood cemented in place, feeling helpless as their friendship dissolved right before her eyes.

"I'd love to talk to you about selling these at my store," Gene continued, oblivious to the silent conversation passing between Ellie and Lloyd. "I've been looking for something unique to sell from the Amish community, and these birds would be perfect."

Lloyd shook his head and turned to his father, whose mouth had formed a thin line.

"I'd love to see what else you have if you have a

moment," Gene continued. "I know I've shown up here unannounced, but I couldn't wait to talk to you."

"We appreciate your offer, Gene," Wilmer began. His voice was polite but had a cold edge. "Unfortunately, this isn't the best time."

"Oh, I understand," Gene said. "I can come back another time, and we can look at what you have and then discuss a fair price. Since I'm also an artist, I understand how much time and emotion you've invested in your carvings."

Lloyd's cold blue eyes locked on Ellie, sending a chill through her. She crossed her arms over her chest as if to guard her heart. How could she hurt him like this? She wanted to take it all back. If only she could start the day over again and put the bird in a safe place, locked away from the world.

Holding up the dove, Gene went on. "I'm certain tourists will be glad to pay a good amount for something this beautiful that is also Amish-made. They go crazy for anything Amish, especially if it's authentic and unique."

Wilmer gave him a curt nod. "I'll need to discuss this with Lloyd before we give you an answer."

"I understand completely. You don't want to rush into this." Gene pulled a business card from his pocket. "You and Lloyd can discuss it and then give me a call."

Wilmer took the card and regarded it with a scowl. "We will be in touch."

"Wonderful." Gene handed the carved bird to Ellie. "I'm so glad you shared this with me today. I'm certain this is going to work out well for the store and also for Lloyd and his family." He turned his attention back to Lloyd and Wilmer. "I look forward to talking with you soon. Have a nice evening." He nodded at them and started back toward the SUV, his western boots crunching on the rock pathway.

Ellie held the dove close to her chest and watched Lloyd. His frown was now a grimace. The hurt and disappointment in his sad eyes cut her to the bone. Her heart pounded so hard that she was certain he could hear it.

"Lloyd, I'm so, so sorry. I only thought that—"

"Ellie?" Gene called, interrupting her. "Are you ready to go?"

"Just a minute," she said, still staring at Lloyd.

"Just go, Ellie." Lloyd spat the words at her through gritted teeth. "You've done enough."

She hesitated, hoping he'd tell her everything would be all right.

"You should go, Ellie," Wilmer chimed in, his words full of warning.

Ellie tried to clear her throat as a lump formed. She nodded and then hurried to Gene's car, praying that somehow she could salvage her precious friendship with Lloyd.

• • •

Lloyd was certain he was going to be sick. He could taste the betrayal like bile rising in his throat as Ellie walked to Gene's fancy SUV. He had given her that precious dove out of love and respect for both her and for Seth. Yet she had given it to Gene just to prove how much money Lloyd could make by selling his special creations.

He had never imagined that she would use him and then double-cross him this way. He had believed Ellie Lapp was genuine. She was the first girl he'd ever loved, and she had smashed his trust into a million pieces.

"What do you have to say for yourself, Lloyd?" His father's voice boomed over the SUV's engine as it motored toward the road. "I told you your carvings were a prideful hobby, and you went behind my back and tried to sell them."

Lloyd swiped his hand down his face and took a deep breath in an attempt to curb his flaring temper.

"Lloyd?" *Dat*'s voice grew louder. "I'm talking to you."

"I hear you, *Dat*." Lloyd turned toward him. "I didn't give the carving to Gene. I gave it to Ellie as a gift, and she works for Gene."

"You need to concentrate on your responsibilities *here*." *Dat* pointed to the ground for emphasis. "You don't have time for trivial hobbies like carving. I will not permit you to sell them, either."

"I had no intentions of selling them." Lloyd's voice rose as fury gripped him. "I just told you. I didn't give the carving to Gene. Ellie has been trying to persuade me to sell them ever since she wandered into my shop the night we hosted the youth gathering. I've told her more than once that I don't want to sell them, but she won't take no for an answer. I gave her that carving as a gift yesterday, and I guess she took it to work and showed it to Gene."

He kicked a stone with his muddy work boot. "Ellie went behind my back and tried to sell it. I never asked her to do it. I know how you feel about the carvings."

"Well, I'm going to call Gene and tell him the answer is no. We're not going to sell the carvings, no matter the price." *Dat* stuffed the business card into his pocket. "I'll call him tomorrow. It's time for supper."

Dat started toward the house, but Lloyd remained by the barn. He was frozen in place, staring off toward the driveway as he contemplated Ellie and his shattered trust.

"Are you coming inside?" *Dat* called.

"I'll be there in a minute." Lloyd pointed toward the barn. "I forgot to do something."

"Oh." *Dat* studied him and his expression softened slightly. "Fine. Don't be long." He headed up the path to the house.

Lloyd leaned back against the barn door and took deep breaths in an attempt to calm his temper. He never expected Ellie to betray him, but she had. Confusion washed over him. Why would she hurt him that way? He had believed the connection he felt with her was real. Had he been blind? Was he wrong when he assumed she loved him too?

None of this made sense, but now Lloyd had to find a way to recover quickly. He couldn't allow Ellie to hurt him again. No, he couldn't let her know how much pain she'd caused him. Instead, he would treat her like an acquaintance and never let her see how much she had meant to him.

From now on, Lloyd would regard Ellie as someone

he hardly knew and never let her know how her betrayal had cut him to the core. He stood up straight and walked toward the house, hoping he could conceal his splintered soul.

. . .

"I made your favorite," *Mamm* said as she sat across from Ellie at the kitchen table. "It's the last of our chop meat. We'll have to go shopping after you get paid."

Ellie stared at her plate as the aroma of barbecued meat loaf, mashed potatoes, and string beans caused her stomach to sour. She couldn't get the image of Lloyd's anguished eyes out of her mind.

"Ellie?" *Mamm*'s voice broke through her mental tirade. "What's wrong, *mei liewe*?"

"I did something terrible." Ellie's voice hitched on the last word. "I think I've lost Lloyd's friendship forever."

"What happened?" *Mamm* asked, putting her fork on her plate.

Ellie explained how she showed the carved bird to Gene after he gave her the news about her hours, and then she described the scene at the Blank farm. *Mamm*'s eyes filled with empathy when Ellie told her how upset Lloyd looked.

"You were right, *Mamm*, and I should've taken your advice." Ellie's voice quavered. "I've made a mess of things, and now Lloyd will never trust me again. When Gene finds out I didn't get permission to show him the carved bird, he won't trust me either. I was too impulsive, but when Gene said he was going to cut my hours, I panicked." Tears sprinkled her cheeks as her emotions poured from her broken heart. "I was afraid we wouldn't be able to buy groceries if he cut my hours, and I thought selling the birds might help the store and save my job."

"Just calm down, Ellie." *Mamm* handed her a napkin. "I imagine Lloyd is upset, but you can always apologize. We all make mistakes sometimes. Explain to him that you didn't mean for this to get so blown out of proportion, but you will make things right. You'll tell Gene you didn't have permission to show him the carving and you realized it was a mistake. Both Lloyd and Gene will understand, and it will all be forgiven and forgotten."

Ellie wanted her mother to be right, but she knew it was more complicated than that. "I went against Lloyd's wishes. He won't ever trust me again."

Mamm reached across the small table and touched her hand. "Lloyd is a *gut* man. He will forgive you." Her expression brightened. "I think he cares about you. I can see it in his eyes when he looks at you. When you talk to him, speak from your heart, and he will listen."

Ellie wiped her eyes and nodded. "I hope you're right."

"I know I am. And, Ellie, I think both of us need to trust that God will care for our needs. We don't have to worry so." *Mamm* pointed her fork toward Ellie's plate. "Now, eat your supper."

Ellie forked a piece of meat loaf, and even though it normally was her favorite, it tasted like sawdust. Deep in her soul she was certain she'd lost Lloyd forever, but she prayed her instinct was wrong—and for forgiveness in letting her worry get the best of her.

CHAPTER EIGHT

Ellie scrubbed a breakfast dish in hot, frothy water the following morning. She glanced out the window as she worked and yawned. She'd spent most of last night tossing and turning as she recalled the hurt expression on Lloyd's handsome face. She turned her mother's advice over in her mind and wondered if she could somehow find the right words to apologize to Lloyd.

A knock on the back door startled her. She dried her hands on a dish towel as she made her way to the mudroom. When she saw Lloyd scowling at her from the porch, she gasped. She tossed the dish towel onto a bench and opened the screen door.

"Lloyd?" Ellie searched his face and found hurt and anger brewing in his eyes. "How are you?"

"Can we talk?" he asked.

"*Ya*, of course." Ellie smoothed her hands over her black apron and stepped out onto the porch. She sank onto the glider as Lloyd leaned against the railing across from her. His posture was rigid and his expression was frosty as he crossed his arms over his chest. She missed his warm smile and wondered if she'd ever see it again.

"I was awake most of last night," he began. "I kept trying to figure out why you went against my wishes and tried to sell my carvings behind my back after I told you more than once that I wasn't interested in selling them."

"Lloyd, I—"

"Wait, please." He held up his hand to shush her. "Let me finish. I gave you that carving as a gift, a special gift in memory of Seth, and you used it to go behind my back and show it to Gene. You betrayed me, Ellie." His frown seemed more sad than angry, and it bore a hole in her soul.

"I didn't mean to hurt you," she began, her voice thick. "I was wrong, Lloyd. Please forgive me. I made a mistake."

Lloyd ran his hand down his face and gritted his teeth. "I just don't understand it. That dove was meant for you and only you."

"I know that." A single tear trickled down her hot cheek. "I will explain everything to Gene and tell him that I didn't have permission to show him the dove. I'll tell him you had made it clear that you didn't want to sell the carvings. Let me explain it all to him, and I'll make it right."

He shook his head. "I just don't understand what you were thinking."

"I wasn't thinking clearly." She stood and took a step toward him. "Please forgive me. I can't stand the thought of losing your trust and your friendship. Let me fix it, Lloyd. Please."

Lloyd regarded her with disappointment. "I don't think you can fix this. My father is angry with me now. He thinks I went behind his back to try to sell the carvings, and he had already made it clear that it is a wasteful and prideful hobby."

Ellie gasped. "I'm so sorry. I never meant to make things difficult between you and your *dat*." She swiped another tear. "Let me talk to him."

"No, you've done enough." His words stung, and for a moment neither of them spoke. Then as he walked toward the steps, his boots were heavy and loud, cutting through their painful silence.

"Lloyd." She started after him. "How can I make this right? There must be a way."

He shot her a glare over his shoulder. "I told you I don't think you can fix this, Ellie."

"But I have to. I don't want to lose your friendship." She folded her hands, pleading with him.

"Unfortunately, you've already lost it." He descended the steps as tears flowed from her eyes. "Tell your *mamm* I'm working in the barn."

As Lloyd walked away, Ellie sank down on the porch steps and dissolved into sobs.

. . .

Ellie sat alone at the youth gathering a week later. She had wanted to stay home, but *Mamm* insisted she get out of the house and see her friends after sulking for so long. She'd tried to talk to Lloyd when he came to the farm to help with chores, but he avoided her, saying he was too busy to talk or insisting there was nothing left to say. She had explained to Gene that she'd made a mistake when she shared the carving, and Gene told her it wasn't a problem. He and Phoebe would try to find something else to sell. Ellie was thankful that she still had her job, though it was now only one day a week and she and her mother were making every dollar stretch until God provided another solution. But she wanted to win Lloyd's friendship back. She missed him so much that her heart ached for him.

"Ellie?" Rebecca sat down beside her in the grass parallel to the volleyball games. "Are you all right?"

"*Ya*, I'm fine." Ellie tried to force a smile, but it was weak.

"What's wrong? You've been acting strange all evening."

"I made a mess of things with your *bruder*." Ellie's voice quavered, but she fought against her threatening tears. She explained what happened when she shared the wooden dove with Gene and then the subsequent fallout between Lloyd and her. "When Gene said he was going to cut my hours, I panicked. *Mei mamm* and I need my paycheck to buy groceries. Seth used to cover all our household expenses with his salary from the shed company. Now that he's gone, we're struggling to stay afloat." A single tear splattered on her cheek and she pushed it away.

"*Ach*, Ellie." Rebecca squeezed her hand. "I had no idea. Why didn't you tell me you and your *mamm* needed help?"

"I didn't want to burden anyone." Ellie sniffed. "I never meant to hurt Lloyd. I've tried to apologize to him, but he won't talk to me. I've lost his friendship, and it's eating away at me. I miss him, and I want to make things right. I want to fix this."

Rebecca frowned. "So that's why he's been in such a rotten mood."

"What do you mean?" Ellie brushed away another stray tear.

"He's been moping and snapping at everyone at the *haus*." Rebecca crossed her legs under her purple dress. "I had a feeling something was bugging him, but he wouldn't talk to me. I imagine he misses you as much as you miss him. I tried to convince him to come tonight, but he refused. He said he had something to do, but I didn't believe him."

Ellie sighed. "I have been trying to figure out what I could say or do to make things right between us, but nothing seems to work. I've tried talking to him when he came to work on our farm, but he refuses to listen. Do you have any advice?"

Rebecca pulled at a blade of grass while she thought for a moment. "Why don't you let me talk to him?"

Ellie nodded with emphasis at the glimmer of hope. "That would be *wunderbaar*. Please tell him I'm sorry, and I'll do anything to make things right between us. Tell him I miss him, and I want another chance to be his friend."

"I'll do my best." Rebecca patted her arm. "Lloyd sometimes listens to me, so I'll give it a try when I get home tonight."

Ellie smiled her first genuine smile since she and Lloyd stopped speaking. *"Danki."* She silently prayed Rebecca could make Lloyd realize how much she missed him and wanted his forgiveness.

. . .

Lloyd sat on the back porch and looked up at the stars glimmering in the clear sky as cicadas sang in the distance. For over a week he'd tried to put Ellie and her beautiful smile out of his mind, but no matter what he did, his thoughts always turned to her.

This evening he found himself wondering if she had gone to the youth gathering. Had she been disappointed that he hadn't gone, or had she found another young man to spend time with in his place? The thought of Ellie liking someone else sent jealousy coursing through him, even though he was still angry with her. How could he be angry with her but not want her to like someone else? The paradox made no sense at all.

The *clip-clop* of a horse coming up the rock driveway signaled that his sisters were home from the gathering. He met them at the barn, and after Rebecca and Marie climbed down from the buggy, he began to unhitch the horse.

"I'll help you," Rebecca offered.

"I've got it," Lloyd insisted. "You can go in the *haus*."

"No, I want to talk to you." Rebecca's voice was full of determination. "I'll help."

They unhitched the horse, and he led it into the barn. After stowing the animal in the stall, they walked together toward the house.

"I spoke with Ellie tonight," Rebecca began, and Lloyd stopped in his tracks. "She was really upset."

Lloyd stared at Rebecca, holding his breath as he waited for her to continue.

"She misses you, and she's heartbroken." Rebecca rested her hands on her hips. "She never meant to hurt you, and she can't figure out how to make things right between you. I can tell she loves you, Lloyd. You need to forgive her."

"Ellie hurt me." Lloyd finally admitted the words aloud, and a weight lifted from his shoulders. "She betrayed my trust, and I don't know how to forgive her. She went against my wishes by trying to sell my carvings."

"I know that." Rebecca's brown eyes were full of understanding. "And Ellie knows that too. Do you know why she tried to convince Gene to consider selling your carvings?"

Lloyd shrugged. "She just wanted to see them at the store."

"That's not it at all." Rebecca shook her head. "Seth's paycheck used to cover all their household expenses. Now that Seth's gone, Ellie and Margaret don't even have enough money for food. It's true that she was still considering showing him the dove because she believes so much in your talent, which is why she took it to work with her. But she was still reluctant to go against your wishes until Gene said he had to cut her hours because sales are down. When she heard that, she panicked and showed Gene the carving."

"What?" Lloyd felt as if he'd been punched in the stomach.

"Ellie had hoped that by selling your carvings she could not only help you have confidence in your work, but help Gene also, and save her job. She had no idea *Dat* told you your hobby was prideful. You didn't share that with her."

"Why didn't she tell me things were that bad for

her and her *mamm*?" Lloyd asked, his voice thick with emotion. "I even asked her once if they were all right."

Rebecca shook her head. "I don't know why she didn't tell you, but she didn't even tell me until now, and I've been one of her best friends since we were *kinner*. She feels terrible for going behind your back. She regrets it, and she wants to make it up to you. You have to give her a chance."

Lloyd studied his hands as her words soaked in. Why hadn't Ellie felt she could tell him she needed help? Hadn't they become close enough over the past weeks? Guilt and shame coursed through him. Why wasn't he a better friend to her?

"You're both miserable, Lloyd," Rebecca continued. "You need to talk to her. We all make mistakes, but it's also our way to forgive. So stop being so stubborn and forgive her. She loves you, and you love her too."

He nodded. "You're right."

She smiled. "I know I am. Now, tomorrow you can tell her you forgive her." She pointed toward the house. "Let's go in. It's getting late."

Lloyd followed her up the steps, and his thoughts turned to Seth. He remembered how Seth told him he would always take care of his mother since his father had passed away. When they reached the porch, he stopped at a new thought. His carvings were an opportunity to help Seth take care of Margaret and Ellie and also keep Seth's memory alive.

"Becca," he said, making her turn around. "I just had the best idea. Do you think *Mamm* and *Dat* are still awake?"

"They might be." She gave him a befuddled expression.

Lloyd hurried through the kitchen and family room to his parents' bedroom. He spotted faint light flickering under the door, and he knocked softly.

"Come in," his father's voice called.

"Dat?" Lloyd asked, pushing the door open. "I need to discuss something with you."

Both his parents were propped up in bed reading. They lowered their books to their laps and studied him.

"What's going on?" *Dat* asked.

"I have an idea, and I want you to hear me out." He stepped into the room and Rebecca followed him. "You have already agreed with me that we need to do what we can to help Margaret Lapp. Well, I believe that my carvings could help her."

His father shook his head. "I don't understand."

"Ellie told me she took the job at Gene's store to help support her mother. I only found out tonight how much she needs the job. Although her *onkels* make the mortgage payments on their farm, Seth used to take care of all the household expenses, including buying groceries. Now that he's gone, they have no money for food," Lloyd continued as he stood at the foot of the bed. "Gene has cut back the number of hours Ellie can work because sales have been down at his shop. Ellie thinks my birds can help boost their sales.

"I want Gene to sell my carvings at his place, and I'll give all the money I earn to Margaret and Ellie. My carvings will help support them since Seth isn't here to take care of them anymore."

"That's a great idea," Rebecca said as she sidled up to Lloyd.

His father scowled. "I don't know. It's still prideful to sell those birds."

"How is that prideful?" *Mamm* asked, placing her book on her bedside table. "Seth used to make sheds to support his family. Lloyd will be doing the same thing, except that he's making birds."

"I agree," Rebecca chimed in, grinning at Lloyd. "I think Seth would love that, and Ellie will too."

"*Dat*, please," Lloyd continued. "I really want your permission for this. God has put this in my heart. I believe my birds are supposed to help someone, and I want to use them to help Margaret and Ellie. Please give me your blessing on this."

"I think it's a *wunderbaar* idea, Wilmer." *Mamm* touched *Dat*'s hand. "Other people are helping Margaret, and this is another way for us to help, giving Lloyd our blessing and supporting his efforts."

His father nodded and his expression softened. "You're right, Lydia. We need to do our part by approving this plan. You have my blessing, Lloyd."

"*Danki.*" Lloyd smiled as hope flourished in his soul. "*Gut nacht.*"

Lloyd followed Rebecca out to the kitchen. "I can't believe I didn't think of this earlier."

"Ellie will love it." Rebecca touched his arm. "This is a wonderful way to help her and her mother."

"I can't wait to tell her." He started for the back door.

"Where are you going?" Rebecca asked.

"I'm going to see Ellie," he said.

"But it's late," Rebecca called after him.

"I can't wait until morning." Lloyd sprinted out the back door and down the porch steps. As he hurried to the barn to retrieve his horse and buggy, he hoped Ellie was still awake.

. . .

Ellie was drifting off to sleep when she thought she heard the sound of horse hooves crunching up her driveway. She leapt out of bed and peeked out the window. She gasped when she saw a horse and buggy making its way to the back porch.

She pulled on her robe and rushed down the steps to the back door, pushing it open just as Lloyd climbed the steps.

"Lloyd?" she asked, clutching her robe tight to her body and hoping *Mamm* was still asleep. "What are you doing here?"

"I had to talk to you." He gestured toward the glider. "Would you please sit with me? I promise I won't take too much of your time." His expression was anxious, and his warm eyes pleaded with her to say yes.

"All right." Her pulse leapt as she sank onto the glider beside him.

"I owe you an apology," he began. "I'm so sorry for losing my temper with you. I realize now that you never meant to hurt me, and you believe my carvings should be shared."

"I was wrong." She shook her head.

"No. Actually, you were right." Lloyd smiled, and her insides swelled with hope. "I should sell them, and I want to sell them."

"You do?" Ellie regarded him with suspicion. "I don't understand."

"I decided tonight that I want to sell them at Gene's store, and my father gave me permission." Lloyd took her hands in his, and she enjoyed the security of his warm skin against hers. "I want to sell them in memory of Seth and give all the money to you and your *mamm*."

"Why would you give the money to us?"

"Rebecca told me you need to work to even be able to buy groceries." His expression clouded with concern. "Why didn't you tell me you needed help?"

A lump swelled in Ellie's throat. "I don't know." She shrugged. "I guess I didn't want to ask for help. I thought I could take care of *mei mamm* myself."

"I want to help you take care of your *mamm*. I know that's what Seth would want me to do. If the sales help Gene increase your hours again, and you want to keep your job, too, that's your decision. You aren't a *kind*. But I want to help."

Ellie sniffed as tears filled her eyes. "Lloyd, that is too generous."

"It's not nearly enough to show you how much I care for you," he said. "Ellie, I love you. I've loved you since you fell in the mud while you were chasing Daisy. I'm so sorry I was upset with you for showing the dove to Gene. You're the sweetest, most thoughtful *maedel* I've ever met, and I know you would never betray me. I can't stand the thought of losing you." He touched her cheek and wiped away a tear. "I would be honored if you would be my girlfriend."

Ellie was speechless as she searched his eyes. Was she dreaming? Had Lloyd truly said he loved her? This couldn't possibly be real.

"Will you be my girlfriend?" he asked, worry filling his expression.

"*Ya*, of course I will." Her heart raced with happiness. "I love you too. I've loved you since I was twelve years old."

"You have?" His eyes widened with shock.

"*Ya*." She smiled. "I was hoping that someday you'd figure out how I felt about you and then decide to love me too."

"*Danki* for waiting for me." Lloyd leaned down and brushed his lips over hers, sending her stomach into a wild swirl. "I'm so sorry it took me this long to figure out how strongly I feel about you. I promise I will never let you go."

As he kissed her again, Ellie closed her eyes and silently thanked God for her precious friendship with Lloyd and his wonderful carved birds. Then she chuckled at her next thought.

"You know what I think Seth would say, Lloyd? I think he'd call us the love birds."

Lloyd chuckled too. "And I think he'd be right."

Discussion Questions

1. Ellie is determined to convince Lloyd to sell his special carvings despite his clear objections. While Ellie's intentions are good, she is not taking into consideration what Lloyd truly wants. Think of a time when you may have had misguided intentions for a loved one. Share this with the group.

2. At the beginning of the story, Lloyd sees Ellie only as Seth's little sister. His feelings for her change throughout the story. What do you think causes this transformation?

3. Lloyd feels Ellie betrayed him when she showed the carved dove to Gene Rider. Were you ever betrayed by a close friend or loved one? How did you come to grips with that betrayal? Were you able to forgive that person and move on? If so, where did you find the strength to forgive? Share this with the group.

4. Ellie truly regrets going behind Lloyd's back and showing the carving to Gene Rider. Did you ever lie to someone or do something behind their back and then have to ask for forgiveness? Did that person forgive you? Why or why not? What Bible verses would help with this?

5. Which character can you identify with the most? Which character seemed to carry the most emotional stake in the story? Was it Ellie, Lloyd, Margaret, or someone else?

6. Rebecca is determined to help Lloyd and Ellie work out their differences. Have you ever found yourself as the peacemaker due to a family, social, or work situation? If so, how did you handle the conflict? Did it turn out the way you'd hoped? Share this with the group.

7. Lloyd's father calls the carvings prideful at the beginning of the story. He changes his opinion, however, near the end of the story and agrees to allow Lloyd to sell the birds after Lloyd explains that God has called him to use the carvings to help the Lapp family. Think about a time in your life when you were certain of God's will. Share this with the group.

8. What did you know about the Amish before reading this book? What did you learn?

Linda Byler

Kelly Irvin

Acknowledgments

As always, I'm thankful for my loving family. Special thanks to my special Amish friends who patiently answer my endless stream of questions. You're a blessing in my life.

To my agent, Natasha Kern—You are my own personal superhero! I can't thank you enough for your guidance, advice, and friendship. I'm thankful that our paths have crossed and our partnership will continue long into the future. You are a tremendous blessing in my life.

Thank you to my amazing editor, Becky Monds, for your friendship and guidance. Thank you also to editor Jean Bloom, who always helps polish my stories and connect the dots between my books. You're a blessing! I'm grateful to each and every person at HarperCollins Christian Publishing who helped make this book a reality.

Thank you most of all to God—for giving me the inspiration and the words to glorify you. I'm grateful and humbled you've chosen this path for me.

DON'T MISS THIS NEW AMISH COLLECTION BY AMY CLIPSTON!

Available in print and e-book

The *Kauffman*

Amish Bakery Series

A GIFT of GRACE

AMY CLIPSTON

A SEASON of LOVE

AMY CLIPSTON

A PLACE of PEACE

AMY CLIPSTON

A PROMISE of HOPE

AMY CLIPSTON

A LIFE of JOY

AMY CLIPSTON

Kauffman
AMISH CHRISTMAS COLLECTION

Amy Clipston

Enjoy Amy Clipston's Hearts of the Lancaster Grand Hotel series!

Available in print and e-book

ABOUT THE AUTHOR

Amy Clipston is the award-winning and bestselling author of the Amish Heirloom series and the Kauffman Amish Bakery series. She has sold more than one million books. Her novels have hit multiple bestseller lists including CBD, CBA, and ECPA. Amy holds a degree in communications from Virginia Wesleyan University and works full-time for the City of Charlotte, NC. Amy lives in North Carolina with her husband, mom, two sons, and three spoiled rotten cats.

. . .

Visit her online at amyclipston.com
Facebook: AmyClipstonBooks
Twitter: @AmyClipston
Instagram: amy_clipston